# Praise for the novels of Sarah Morgan

"The ultimate road-trippin' beach read and just what we all need after the long lockdown."
—*Booklist*, starred review, on *The Summer Seekers*

"Warm, funny and often insightful, *The Summer Seekers* is a satisfying dose of escapism with plenty of heart."
—*Shelf Awareness*, on *The Summer Seekers*

"Morgan expertly avoids cliché and easy fixes, resulting in a deeply believable portrait of a family relearning how to love each other. Readers will be delighted."
—*Publishers Weekly*, starred review, on *One More for Christmas*

"Sarah Morgan's writing always hits me right in the feels."
—*Harlequin Junkie* on *Family for Beginners*

"Morgan's gently humorous aesthetic will leave readers feeling optimistic and satisfied."
—*Publishers Weekly* on *A Wedding in December*

"Packed full of love, loss, heartbreak, and hope, this may just be Morgan's best book yet."
—*Booklist* on *One Summer in Paris*

"The perfect gift for readers who relish heartwarming tales of sisters and love."
—*Booklist* on *The Christmas Sisters*

"Her lovingly created characters come to life, the dialog rings true, and readers will fly through the pages and then wish for more."
—*Library Journal*, starred review, on *How to Keep a Secret*

## Also by Sarah Morgan

*The Christmas Escape*
*The Summer Seekers*
*One More for Christmas*
*Family for Beginners*
*A Wedding in December*
*One Summer in Paris*
*The Christmas Sisters*
*How to Keep a Secret*

### *From Manhattan with Love*

*Moonlight Over Manhattan*
*Holiday in the Hamptons*
*New York, Actually*
*Miracle on 5th Avenue*
*Sunset in Central Park*
*Sleepless in Manhattan*

### *Puffin Island*

*One Enchanted Moment*
*Some Kind of Wonderful*
*First Time in Forever*

### *The O'Neil Brothers*

*Maybe This Christmas*
*Suddenly Last Summer*
*Sleigh Bells in the Snow*

Look for Sarah Morgan's next novel
***Beach House Summer***
available soon from HQN.

For additional books by Sarah Morgan,
visit her website, www.sarahmorgan.com.

# SARAH MORGAN

# Family for Beginners

HQN

ISBN-13: 978-1-335-93598-4

Family for Beginners

First published in 2020. This edition published in 2022.

Copyright © 2020 by Sarah Morgan

Recycling programs
for this product may
not exist in your area.

This edition published by arrangement with Harlequin Books S.A.

For questions and comments about the quality of this book,
please contact us at CustomerService@Harlequin.com.

HQN
22 Adelaide St. West, 41st Floor
Toronto, Ontario M5H 4E3, Canada
www.Harlequin.com

**Printed and bound in Barcelona, Spain by CPI Black Print**

To RaeAnne Thayne,
who is as warm and wonderful as her books

# Family
## for
# Beginners

# prologue

*Clare*

$W$as destroying evidence always a crime?

Clare scrunched the letter into her pocket and walked across the damp grass to the lake. It had been raining all week and the ground was soft under her boots. The wind blew her hair across her face and she swept it back, needing to see clearly.

She wasn't built for moral dilemmas, and yet here she was, required to choose between the two things she valued most. Loyalty and honesty.

Where the grass met the narrow shingle beach, she stopped. Across the water, nestling among the tall reeds on the western shore of the lake, was the boathouse. Behind it was dense woodland, offering an enviable degree of privacy. As a child, she had played there with her best friend, Becca, dodging uneven planks and cobwebs as they'd transformed themselves into pirates. They'd launched canoes, and splashed around in the freezing water, shrieking in delicious terror as their limbs were roped by tangled weeds.

Her own child had played there, too, although she'd been less relaxed than her parents. Perhaps because she understood what degree of adventure was possible here, she'd insisted on life belts and supervision at all times.

She'd lived in London and Paris for a while, but this little corner of England with its lakes and mountains was the only place that had ever felt like home.

After her father died, she and Todd had moved here to be close to her mother. It had been Todd's idea to convert the boathouse into a luxury property. An architect, he saw potential in the most dilapidated buildings, but in this case his vision had been inspired. Splintered planks and broken windows had been replaced by stone, cedar and acres of glass. The upturned crates that had provided rough seating were long gone. Now, when Clare had time to sit down, she relaxed into deep sofas, cocooned by linen and luxury. But the true luxury was the position. The peaceful waterfront location attracted the most discerning of travelers, people seeking to escape the stress of the modern world and sink instead into the sybaritic pleasures of life on the lake, where their nearest neighbors were ducks and dragonflies. There were plenty of people willing to pay good money for that degree of seclusion. Clare and Todd rented out the boathouse for enough weeks of the year to guarantee themselves a healthy income.

The boathouse was visible from only one corner of her garden and occasionally Clare would glance across and see guests seated on the deck, sipping their champagne while watching the coots and cormorants sheltering in the reed beds. At night the only sounds were the whisper of the wind, the hoot of an owl and the occasional splash as a bird skimmed the surface of the water in search of sustenance.

Privacy was assured because this section of the lake was only accessible from Lake Lodge, and the entrance to the main house was easily missed from the road unless you knew where to turn. Hidden from view and mostly concealed by an overgrowth of azaleas and rhododendrons were large iron gates, and immediately behind those gates was the Gatehouse where her mother now lived. From there a long, graveled driveway wound its way to the house.

Clare's mother had moved into the Gatehouse after Clare's father had died, insisting that Clare and Todd move into the bigger property. Almost on impulse, they'd sold their small London apartment and moved back to a place where the pace of life moved slowly. Like others, they came to breathe the air, walk the mountains and sail on the many lakes.

Her friendship with Becca had grown and matured here. Maybe it would have ended here, but now she'd never know because Becca was gone.

The boathouse held no evidence of their final conversation, and she was glad of that.

But now she had written evidence, sent the day before Becca had died.

*I wish I'd never told you.*

Clare wished that, too.

Her eyes stung. Grief. Frustration. She wished they hadn't had that last talk, because now it was the only one she could remember. Their decades of friendship had somehow shrunk down to that last stressful hour. She'd been so angry with her friend, her loyalties stretched to snapping point.

She hadn't known that summer would be their last together. If she had, would she have tried harder to bridge the gulf that had opened up between them? Maybe not. She'd been angry, but now that anger was shaded with guilt, because death often brought guilt along as baggage.

Did loyalty still matter when the person was dead? Did honesty matter when all it would produce was pain?

"Clare!" Her mother's voice drifted across the garden. "What are you doing out here in the rain? Come indoors."

Clare raised a hand, but she didn't turn.

She had a decision to make, and she'd always done her best thinking by the water. She considered herself an ethical and moral person. At school she'd been teased for always doing the "right thing," which had made it all the more extraordinary that her best friend had been a girl who made a point of always doing the wrong thing.

And now Becca had left her with this.

She was so lost in thought she wasn't aware of her mother until she felt her hand on her shoulder.

"You don't have to go, you know."

Clare stared at the lake. Its surface was dark and stippled by rain. In the summer it was idyllic, but with angry clouds crowding the sky and small waves snapping at the shore, the sense of menace matched her mood.

"She was my best friend."

"People grow apart. It's a fact of life. You're not the person at forty that you were at fourteen. Sometimes one has to accept that."

Had her mother sensed the tension between the two friends on that last visit? She'd walked down from the Gatehouse to see if she could help on that last day when Becca and Jack were busily packing the car and herding kids and luggage.

Clare had hoped the chaos would conceal the fragile atmosphere, but her mother had always been emotionally intuitive. Fortunately, Jack and Todd had been too busy talking cars and engines to notice anything. When they'd left, Becca had brought her cheek close to Clare's. Clare thought she'd murmured *"sorry"*, but she wasn't sure and as Becca never apologized for anything it seemed unlikely.

"I can't remember a time when she wasn't in my life." She felt her mother's hand on her arm.

"And yet the two of you were always so different."

"I know. Becca was bright, and I was dull."

"No!" Her mother spoke sharply. "That wasn't it at all."

Perhaps *dull* was the wrong word. Steady? Reliable? *Boring?* "It's all right. I know who I am. I'm comfortable with who I am." Until recently, she'd been able to sleep at night, satisfied with her choices. Until Becca had presented her with an impossible one.

"You steadied her and she brought out your more adventurous side. She pushed you out of your comfort zone."

Why was that always considered a good thing?

In this case it hadn't been good.

Clare was so far out of her comfort zone she couldn't have found her way back with a compass or SatNav. She wanted to cling to something familiar, which is why she stared at the boathouse. But instead of all the happy times, all she saw was Becca, her beautiful face smeared with tears as she unburdened herself.

"I know something happened between you. If you want to talk about it, I'm a good listener." Her mother produced an umbrella and slid her arm into Clare's, sheltering both of them.

Should she tell her mother? No, that wouldn't be fair. She hated being in this position. The last thing she was going to do was put someone else where she was standing now.

She was an adult, and way past the age where she needed

her mother to untangle her problems and make decisions for her.

"I'm going to the funeral. My flight is booked."

Her mother adjusted her grip on the umbrella. "I knew you would, because you're you, and you always do the right thing. But I wish you wouldn't."

"What if you don't know what the right thing is?"

"You always do."

But she didn't, that was the problem. Not this time. "I've already told them I'm coming."

Her mother sighed. "It's not as if Becca will know or care if you're there."

The rain thudded steadily onto the umbrella, the sky sobbing in sympathy, sending lazy drips down the back of Clare's coat.

"I'm not going for Becca. I'm Izzy's godmother. I want to be there for her."

"Those poor children. I can't bear to think about it. And Jack. Poor Jack."

*Poor Jack.*

Clare stared straight ahead. "What do I say?" She knew her mother wouldn't give her the answer she needed, because Clare hadn't asked the question she really wanted to ask.

"They'll find a way." Her mother was brisk. "Life never sends us more than we can cope with."

Clare turned to look at her, seeing lines and signs of age that hadn't been there before her father had died. "Do you honestly believe that?"

"No, but I always think it sounds good when people say it to me. It's reassuring."

Clare smiled for the first time in days. On impulse she hugged her mother, ignoring the damp coat and the relentless drip from the umbrella. "I love you, Mum."

"I love you, too." Her mother squeezed her shoulder, the same way she had when Clare was a child and facing something difficult. *You've got this.* "Is Todd going with you?"

"I don't want him to. He's still working on that big project." In fact Todd had insisted that he'd drop everything to go with her but she'd refused. This was something that would actually be easier alone. "I'll only be gone four days."

"Will you stay at the house?"

Clare shook her head. Jack had suggested that she stay with them in Brooklyn, but she'd refused. She'd told him she didn't want to make extra work, but the truth was she wasn't ready to see him yet. Jack, with his warm nature and quick smile. She remembered the first time Becca had mentioned him. *I've met a man.*

Becca had met plenty of men, so to begin with Clare had barely paid attention. She'd expected this relationship to be as short-lived as the others.

"He's a good man," Becca had said and they'd laughed because up until that point Becca had never been interested in good men. She liked them bad to the bone. She blamed her upbringing. Said that she wouldn't know what to do with a man who treated her well, but apparently with Jack she'd known.

Clare remembered the first time Becca had shown her round the house in Brooklyn. *Look at me, all grown up— four bedrooms, three bathrooms and a closet for my shoes. I'm almost domesticated.*

Almost.

There had been a twinkle in her eyes, that same twinkle that had helped her laugh her way out of trouble so many times at school.

Clare gripped the letter.

Attending the funeral wasn't going to be the hardest

part. The hardest part would be pretending that nothing had changed between her and Becca. Kissing Jack on the cheek, keeping that unwanted nugget of knowledge tucked away inside her.

Her mother brushed raindrops from her coat. "Will the family come here next summer, do you think?"

"I don't know. Probably not." For the past twenty years their two families had spent three weeks together at Lake Lodge. Marriage, kids, life in general—none of it had interfered with that time. It was theirs. A sacred part of their friendship. A time to catch up on their lives.

And then there had been that conversation. One conversation that had changed everything.

And the letter, of course. Why a letter? Who even wrote letters in these days of email and instant messaging?

She'd found it in the mailbox, tucked in between a letter from the bank and an advert for a local pizza delivery service. She'd recognized the bold, loopy writing immediately. At school Becca had frustrated the teachers with her inability to conform. Her handwriting was like everything else she did—individual. Becca did things the way she wanted to do them.

Clare had carried that letter back to the house and set it down on the kitchen table. An hour had passed before she'd finally opened it, and now she wished she hadn't. Letters got lost in the mail, didn't they? But not this one. She already knew what it was going to say, but somehow having it in writing made it worse.

She'd almost sworn when she'd read it, but she tried never to swear aloud.

As she held the letter in her hand she could hear Becca's voice: *Say fuck, Clare! Go on! If ever there was a time for you to vent, it's now.*

"You're getting wet." She kissed her mother on the cheek, sure now of what she was going to do. "Let's go indoors. Hot tea and toasted muffins."

Her mother looped her arm into hers. "It's all horribly sad. You were a good friend to her, Clare, remember that."

Was that true? Did a good friend tell the truth no matter what the cost? Or did a good friend offer support even when she considered the action to be heinously wrong?

They reached the house and scrambled indoors out of the rain.

Her mother left the dripping umbrella on the stone floor and walked toward the kitchen. "I'll put the kettle on."

"I'll be there in a minute. There's something I need to do." Clare hung up her coat, retrieved the letter from the pocket and walked into the living room where a fire was blazing. In the evenings the whole family gathered here to talk, play games or watch TV. *Charmingly old-fashioned*, Becca had called it in that same ambiguous tone she used for compliments and mockery.

Clare paused for a moment, thinking about her friend and the times they'd sat in this very room and laughed together.

Then she took a deep breath and dropped the letter into the fire, watching as the edges turned black and curled under the heated lick of the flames.

Becca was dead, and the letter and its contents should die with her.

That was her decision, and she'd learn to live with it.

# 1

## *Flora*

The first time she saw him, he was standing outside the store staring at the flowers in the window. His hands were thrust into the pockets of his coat, the collar turned up against the savage bite of a New York winter. It was the type of raw, freezing day that turned each breath into a white puffy cloud, the sky moody and heavy with menace. People scurried past, heads down, going about their business with grim determination.

Not this man. He didn't push open the door and seek refuge from the cold as so many had done before him that morning. Instead he lingered, a blank expression on his face as he scanned the array of blooms that splashed color over the monochrome of winter.

"Guilt flowers." Julia plucked twelve long-stemmed roses from the bucket and placed them on the workstation. "He's going to buy guilt flowers. I bet you ten dollars he's had an affair, and he's looking at those flowers trying to figure out which of them says sorry in a way that isn't going to get him kicked out of the house."

Flora didn't take the bet, and not only because she knew Julia didn't have ten dollars to throw away. Maybe the man hadn't had an affair, but he certainly wasn't celebrating anything. His features were strained, and the fixed line of his mouth suggested he'd forgotten how to smile.

"Why does it have to be an affair? Maybe he's in love, and she doesn't return his feelings. Maybe he's going to buy love flowers. He's going to put them in every room."

It was an exchange they had all the time, a to-and-fro about the motivation of the buyer.

When it came to explanations Julia veered toward the dark, which Flora never understood because her colleague and friend was happily married to a firefighter and was the mother of three loving, if demanding, teenagers.

Flora was more hopeful in her approach. If it rained in the morning, it didn't mean it was going to rain in the afternoon.

"Does he look like a man in love to you?" Julia sliced through the stems at an angle, the way Flora had taught her. "It's minus digits out there. People are only outdoors if they have to be. If they're buying things essential to life. Like chocolate."

"Flowers are essential to life."

"I'd risk frostbite for chocolate. Not flowers. Flowers are not essential."

"They're essential to *my* life. Strip off those leaves. If you leave them under the water they'll rot, then the bacteria clogs the stems and the flowers die."

"Who knew it was so complicated." Julia removed them carefully and then glanced at the window again. "He's messed up, don't you think? Made a major mistake, and he's figuring out how big the bouquet has to be to make it up to her."

"Or him."

"Or him." Julia inclined her head. "He looks tired. Stressed. He'd rather be at home in the warm, but instead he's freezing to death outside our window, which tells me it's something big. Maybe his partner found out about his affair and he's wondering whether it's throwing good money after bad to try to change their mind."

"Maybe he's been married for thirty years and he's marking the moment."

"Or maybe," Julia said, "he's buying flowers to try to fix a day he's ruined for someone. What?" She paused to breathe. "You're the one who taught me that flowers tell a story."

"But you always see a horror story." Flora rescued a rose that was about to fall and breathed in a wave of scent. She tried not to touch the buds, but she could imagine the velvety softness under her fingers. Where other people used meditation apps to promote relaxation, she used flowers. "There are other types of stories. Happier types."

Celia, the store owner, tottered past in ridiculously high heels, her arms full of calla lilies. She had a florid complexion and a slightly flattened face that made Flora think of dahlias. Her personality was more thorny than a rose, but her brisk, no-nonsense attitude made her particularly good at dealing with dithering brides.

"You need to hurry up with those roses if we're going to get them delivered in time for Mrs. Martin's dinner party tonight. You know how particular she is."

"We'll be done in time, Celia, don't worry." Flora smiled and soothed. It came naturally to her. She'd calmed more storms in teacups than she'd drunk cups of tea.

"Our mission is to provide the very best customer service and the most beautiful flowers."

"And we will." Flora could almost feel Julia grinding her teeth next to her. She willed their boss to move on before her friend exploded.

Celia paused, her demeanor shifting from irritable to ingratiating. "Can you work Saturday, Flora? I know you worked last Saturday but—"

"—but I don't have family commitments." Flora still hadn't got used to the fact that she no longer had to visit her aunt on weekends. Even though her aunt hadn't even been aware of her presence for the last year of her life, visiting had still been part of Flora's routine. She'd been surprised by how strange it felt not to go. Equally surprised by the grief she'd felt. She and her aunt hadn't been close, although Flora had *tried* to be close. "It's fine, Celia. I'm happy to work." She knew Celia was taking advantage. She probably should have said no, but then Celia would have been in a mood and Flora couldn't handle it. It was less stressful to work. And she didn't mind that much. Weekends were always the hardest time for her, and she didn't fully understand why.

Moving into an apartment of her own had been the culmination of a dream. It was what she'd wanted, and she'd been shocked to discover that getting what you wanted didn't always make you happy. Her life didn't look, or feel, the way she'd thought it would. It was like arriving in Rome, only to discover that your guide was for Paris. She wasn't sure whether it was the apartment itself that was at fault, or her expectations.

Her mother had always emphasized that life was what you made of it, but Flora couldn't help thinking that what you made depended on the raw ingredients you were given. Even the best chef couldn't do much with moldy vegetables.

Having ticked that problem off her list, Celia strode off and Julia snipped the ends off a few more roses with more violence than before.

"I thought you were going to stop people-pleasing?"

"I am. Obviously it's a gradual thing."

"I don't see gradual. I see you letting her bully you into working the weekend. Again."

Julia was the first person to comment on that particular trait, and the first person to challenge her to tackle the issue.

"I don't mind. I'm saving being assertive for something big and important."

"You need to start small and build up. Why are you so afraid to stand up to her?"

Her heart thumped harder at the mere thought. "Because then she'll fire me. I'm not good with conflict." Or rejection. That was her big one.

"She is not going to fire you, Flora. You're her biggest asset. Half the customers only come here because of you, so you don't have to please her the whole time."

"I think it's a hangover from constantly trying to please my aunt. My world was a better place when she was happy." Although her aunt had never been *happy* as such. It was more that her disapproval levels had fluctuated.

And dealing with her had given Flora useful experience. She was good at handling difficult people. She'd even, on rare occasions, made her aunt smile—the biggest test any people pleaser would face in a lifetime. Causing an upward lift of Gillian's lips represented the pinnacle of achievement. The people-pleaser's equivalent of the summit of Everest, the four-minute mile or rowing the Atlantic. Given that the world was full of difficult people, Flora had decided she might yet have reason to be grateful to her aunt for providing her with so much practice.

Julia didn't agree. "I teach my kids to stand up for what they want and believe in. Also that they're responsible for their own happiness."

"Exactly. And I'm at my happiest when the people around me are happy."

"Saying yes doesn't make you happy. It just makes the other person happy and removes you from conflict. And you feel bad about yourself for not having enough courage to say no."

"Thanks Ju. I didn't feel bad about myself, but now I do."

"I'm being honest. If I'd ever met your aunt I would have told her what I thought of her."

Flora winced as she imagined that particular confrontation. "My aunt wasn't exactly warm and affectionate, that's true, but she was my only family. She took me in when I had no one. She felt that I owed her, and she was right."

"I'm not sure there should be 'debt' between family members, but if there is then you paid that debt a thousand times over. Okay, I get it, she gave you a home, but she gained a live-in carer. And Celia is not your aunt."

"If I'd said no she would have asked you, and you have Freddie's indoor track event this Sunday, and Geoff isn't working so you'll be having his mother over and doing Sunday lunch, and you promised Kaitlin you'd take her to buy a dress for that family thing you have at Easter."

Julia gasped as a thorn pierced her finger. "How come you know my schedule better than I do? Hearing you say it aloud makes me realize how crazy my life is."

Flora said nothing. She'd do anything, just about anything, for a slice of what Julia had. Not the craziness—she could reproduce that easily enough—but the closeness. The interwoven threads of a functioning, healthy family created something bigger than the individual. Something strong and enduring. To her aunt, Flora had been a loose thread. Something to be brushed off.

"You have a beautiful family."

"Are you kidding? My family is a pain in the neck. Freddie has a girlfriend so now they're sprawled on the sofa every night holding hands and gazing at each other, and Eric keeps teasing him so you can imagine how *that* pans out, and Kaitlin—well, I could go on. Let's just say I envy you not having to share your space with anyone. You go home, and it's just you."

"Yes." Flora watched as Julia placed the roses carefully, shaping the bouquet. "Just me." This was the life she'd dreamed of living when she'd been sharing a house with her aunt. She had an apartment of her own. Small, lacking in charm, but all hers. She had friends. Her diary was filled with activities and invitations. She should be grateful and happy. She was lucky, lucky, lucky.

"When you go home at night everything in your apartment is exactly the way you left it. No one has moved stuff around, or buried it under piles of their own crap. You don't have a dozen pairs of sneakers tripping you up when you walk through the door, no one banging on the door yelling *'Mom!'* when you're trying to use the bathroom, no one sprawled over every inch of the sofa."

"No one bangs on my door, that's true, and it's just me on the sofa." Flora removed a couple of stray leaves that Julia had missed. "Brilliant really, because I can stretch my legs out and flop like an octopus and no one complains."

"I'm surrounded by chaos. You have blissful silence."

"Blissful."

"When you choose flowers for yourself, they're always beautiful. If I'm lucky, Geoff sometimes buys me a bunch from the convenience store."

But at least he'd bought her the flowers.

No one had ever bought Flora flowers. She spent her days producing stunning arrangements for other people, but was never the recipient.

"I read the other day that single women with no children are the happiest of anyone."

"Mmm." Who had they asked?

"You have the perfect life. Although I still want to fix you up with someone. You need a man."

Flora was less convinced. All the men she'd dated had only been interested in one type of intimacy. And that was fine. More than fine on occasion, but it was like gorging on ice cream when your body was craving something nutritious and truly nourishing. Satisfying in the short term but offering no long-term sustenance.

No, what she really wanted was to matter to someone, the way she'd mattered to her mother. She wanted to be important to someone. Connected, the way Julia was. She wanted to have someone's back, and know they had hers. She wanted someone to know her and she wanted to be needed. What was the point of being here if no one needed you? If you didn't make a difference to someone's life?

She had so much to give, and no one to give it to.

She was lonely, but she'd never tell anyone that. If you admitted you were lonely, people assumed there was something wrong with you. The media talked about an epidemic of loneliness, and yet admitting that you felt that way was a statement of failure. She was thirty, unattached and living in the most exciting city in the world. People assumed her life was like a day on the set of an upbeat sitcom and from the outside it probably looked that way, apart from her apartment, which was more like the set of a murder mystery. On the inside? On the inside, deep in her heart, she was crushingly lonely but if she told people they'd judge her and tell her all the things she was doing wrong. Or they'd invite her out, and she knew that wasn't her problem. It wasn't the number of connections she made in her social life that mattered, it was their depth.

When people asked, she told them what they wanted to hear because anything else would make them uncomfortable.

*Yes, I stayed in last night and it was great. I had a chilled evening and caught up on phone calls.*

*My social life is so crazy it's good to have a night in doing nothing.*

Weekdays were easier than weekends when time seemed to move at half pace, and whatever she did she was aware she was doing it alone. Running in the park meant witnessing the intimacy of other people. Dodging mothers with children, couples holding hands, groups of friends laughing and drinking coffee on a bench. Shopping meant rubbing shoulders with women choosing outfits for an exciting night out.

Flora did everything she could to avoid confronting that silence that Julia seemed to prize above everything else. She went running with friends, called friends, had meals with friends, joined a pottery class, an art class, listened to music and podcasts, streamed movies. In the bathroom she sometimes turned on her electric toothbrush just for the noise, but eventually she had to lie down and close her eyes and then the silence enveloped her like a smothering cloud. Not that her apartment was quiet. Far from it. Above her was a big Italian family who thundered their way from one room to another and argued in voices designed to break the sound barrier, and next door was a couple who indulged in noisy sex sessions into the early hours. She was surrounded by the sounds of other people living full and happy lives.

"I'll be fine. My weekend plans are relaxed. Yoga. Brunch with a friend. It's not a problem. You know I love working here."

"You love Celia?"

"I love the flowers."

"Phew. For a moment there I was going to suggest you got professional help. And you're right that if you'd refused to work this weekend I would have ended up doing it, and thanks for that, but one day I want to hear you say a big loud 'no' to her."

"I will." She was well aware of the downsides of people-pleasing. In the few relationships she'd had, she invariably spent so much time pleasing the other person she forgot to please herself. That was usually the point where she ended it, in a charming *it's not you it's me* kind of way that left no hard feelings.

Julia watched Celia haranguing another member of staff. "What is her problem?"

Flora took advantage of her lapse in concentration to make a few swift adjustments to the arrangement. "She's anxious. She owns the business and these are challenging times. We worry enough about our own jobs. Imagine if we were responsible for everyone else's, too."

"I don't think it's concern for us that's keeping her awake at night. No wonder she lives alone. She probably ate her first husband. Or maybe he dissolved when she dripped acid on him. If she was a flower, she'd be hemlock." Julia had a flare for the dramatic. She'd had dreams of being an actress, but then she'd met her husband. Three children had followed in quick succession. She'd done various jobs in her time, and Flora was forever grateful for the day she'd walked through the doors looking for work.

Julia admired the roses. "I'm getting better, don't you think?"

Flora added a couple more stems of foliage and trimmed one of the stems a little shorter. "You have an eye for it." In fact Julia didn't have much of an eye for it, but there was no way Flora would hurt her feelings by telling her that and she knew how badly her friend needed the job.

"I'll never be as good as you, but I'm still learning and you've been doing this since you could walk." Julia eyed the guy outside. "Do you think he hit her and he's here to buy 'sorry I bruised you' flowers?"

"I hope not."

"You should come over the next Sunday you're free. Have lunch. My way of saying thank you."

"I'd like that." Flora loved having lunch at Julia's even though the banter between her friend and her husband gave her the odd pang. No one knew her well enough to tease her.

"I'd invite you to stay over and have a night away from that apartment of yours, but you know we're in very tight quarters. And trust me you do *not* want to share a bed with Kaitlin. Is your landlord still raising your rent?"

"Yes." Flora felt a twinge of anxiety. She'd made a half-hearted attempt to look for somewhere else, but there was a depressing gap between what she'd like and what she could afford.

"And has he sorted out your cockroach?"

"Not yet. And I have more than one cockroach."

Julia shuddered. "How can you be so relaxed?"

"I'm just pleased they have friends."

"See that's the difference between us. I think extermination, and you think cockroach dating service. Roach.com. Have you talked to him about it?"

"I sent him a strongly worded email."

"And what did he say?"

"Nothing. He hasn't replied."

"And how long ago did you send it?"

"A month?"

"A *month*? Knowing you it said 'Darling landlord, if it's at all possible for you to sort out my damp apartment and the cockroach I'd be hugely grateful but don't worry if it's an inconvenience.'"

"I was firmer than that." But not much firmer, and her words hadn't had an impact.

"What about the damp? Has he found the cause?"

"He hasn't looked. I'm worried because that suspicious damp stain on my ceiling is spreading."

"Maybe your neighbor has died and his rotting corpse is slowly decomposing and leaking through into your apartment."

"If he's decomposing, he's making a lot of noise about it. He was singing opera last night." She glanced up and saw the man still standing there. He had to be freezing cold. Should she open the door? Offer him shelter? A hot drink? "Maybe it's his mother's birthday and he hasn't had time to buy her a gift." She saw it all the time, people who rushed in and grabbed one of their ready-made bouquets without expending thought or time on the selection process.

Flora didn't judge. Instead she took pride in the fact that her hand-tied bouquets were a talking point in this little corner of Manhattan's Flower District. Like her mother before her, she loved creating a bouquet to a specific brief, but was equally happy creating something that took the pain out of decision-making. Some people were nervous when buying flowers, dazed by choice, afraid of making a mistake.

Flowers, in Flora's opinion, were never a mistake. Her mother had always insisted on fresh flowers. It wasn't enough to be surrounded by them in the store where she worked, she'd insisted on filling her home with them. There would be a large arrangement in the entryway, welcoming guests with scent, another bunch in the living room and small posies in each of the bedrooms. Violet Donovan had considered flowers to be art, but essential art. If economy became necessary, then it would be made in other areas, like clothing or dining out. When reflecting on early childhood, most people remembered events. Flora's earliest memories were all of fragrance and color.

That had lasted until she was eight years old and she'd gone to live with her aunt who didn't share her sister's obsession with flowers.

*Why waste money on something that dies?*

Flora, raw in her grief, had pointed out that everything dies and surely the important thing was to make the most of it while it was alive? Up until that point she'd skipped through life, but she'd soon learned to tiptoe, picking her way carefully through every situation. She'd learned quickly what made her aunt angry, and what simply made her scowl.

At that moment the man lifted his gaze from the flowers and stared straight at Flora. He couldn't have known they'd been talking about him, but still she felt her face bloom peony pink with guilt.

Her smile was part welcome, part apology. It didn't occur to her to pretend she hadn't seen him.

"Whoa," Julia muttered. "Do you see the way he's looking at you? Geoff looked at me that way and a month later I was pregnant. You're either going to be the love of his life, or his next victim depending on whether you're the romance or thriller type. Maybe he's going to use rose petals to bury your body. Or the body of his wife."

"Stop it!"

"Maybe he's staring at your dress. I wish I could get away with wearing that. You manage to look edgy and arty. I'd look a mess. I mean—red dress and purple tights. No one but you would think to put those colors together. Kaitlin would refuse to be seen with me, whereas she thinks you're the coolest person on the planet. And where did you find those earrings?"

"In the market."

"Whatever. You're rocking that look. Although I wouldn't want to look at you if I had a hangover."

"I like clothes to be—"

"—happy. I know. You're all about spreading a smile. Everyone else I know is moan, moan, moan, me included, but you're like an oasis of sunshine in an otherwise dark and stormy life."

"Your life will be stormier if you don't finish that bouquet fast."

Julia snipped the rest of the stems and then glanced up again. "Still there. The man is going to get frostbite soon. Look at his eyes. Full of secrets."

Flora didn't answer. She had secrets, too. Secrets she'd never shared. That wasn't the saddest part. The saddest part was that no one had ever been remotely interested in digging deep enough to find them. No one had wanted to know her that well.

"Maybe he simply doesn't know which flowers to choose."

"Well if anyone is going to find out the truth about him, it's you." Julia added foliage, and tied the stems so that that recipient would have to do nothing but put them in a vase. "People tell you everything, probably because you're too polite to tell them to shut up." She blew her hair out of her eyes. "You care."

Flora did care. Like flowers, people came in all colors, shapes and sizes and she appreciated them all. Her mother had been the same. People would walk into the store for flowers, and stay for coffee and a chat. As a child, Flora had sat quietly among the blooms, bathed in the warmth and the scent and the soothing hum of adult conversation.

Finally, the door opened and he stepped into the shop, bringing with him a flurry of cold air and a sense of antici-pation. Heads turned. There was a lull in the conversation as people studied him, and then returned to whatever they'd been doing before he'd made his entrance.

"Okay I have to admit he's hot. I bet whatever it is he does, he's the best," Julia said. "I can almost understand why someone would have an affair with him. He's all yours, but if he asks you out, don't invite him back to your place. Unless he works for pest control." She disappeared into the back of the shop where they stored more flowers.

Flora felt a rush of exasperation.

He wasn't hers, and he wasn't going to ask her out. He was ordering flowers, that was all.

"How may I help you?" She pushed her conversation with Julia to the back of her mind. If he was having an affair, it wasn't her business. Human beings were flawed, she knew that. Life was messy. Flowers brightened life's mess.

"I need to buy a gift. For a young woman." His eyes were ice blue and a startling contrast to the jet-black of his hair. "A special woman."

Maybe Julia was right. Maybe it was an affair.

You saw the whole spectrum of life working in a flower

shop, from celebration to commiseration. It shouldn't have bothered her, but still she was disappointed.

"Is there an occasion? Anniversary? Apology?"

His brows knitted together. "Apology?"

Had she said that aloud? Silently she cursed Julia for infecting her with cynicism. "If you tell me the occasion, I can recommend the perfect flower to convey your message."

"I doubt that."

"Try me. I love a challenge. What is it you want the flowers to say?"

He studied her. "I want them to say sorry for all the times I've screwed up over the last few months. All the times I've said the wrong thing, or done the wrong thing; stepped into her room when she wanted privacy, or left her alone when she wanted company. I want them to say that I love her, and I will always love her, even though maybe I don't show it in the right way. I want them to say that I'm sorry she lost her mother, and that I wish I could bring her back, or make the pain go away. I especially wish her mother were here now, because she would have known what to buy our daughter for her seventeenth birthday and I don't." He paused, conscious that he'd perhaps said too much. There was a faint flush of color across his cheekbones. "And if you can find a way to say that in flowers, then you're smarter than I am."

Flora felt pressure in her chest and a thickening in her throat. His pain had spilled over and covered her, too. The silence from the back of the store told her that Julia was listening.

Dead wife.

"It's your daughter's seventeenth birthday." And he was marking the day without the love of his life. His daughter's mother. His partner. Flora wanted to gather him up and hug him. And she wanted to gather up his daughter, too. She knew loss, and understood the great tearing hole it left in a life. You were left to try to stick together pieces that no longer fit. Your life became a patchwork, with a few holes.

"Becca—my wife—would have known exactly what to buy her. She always chose the perfect gift no matter what the occasion. She probably would have thrown a party of some sort, with all the right people—but I'm not my wife and sadly she didn't leave notes. Her death was sudden. I'm winging this."

Flora breathed slowly. He didn't need her crying for him. He needed her to solve his problem. And gifts were always difficult. She tried hard to buy the right gift for people, but she knew she wasn't perfect. Becca, apparently, had been perfect. She imagined a cool blonde who carried a notebook and scribbled ideas for gifts the moment someone mentioned something in passing.

*Buy Tasha a silk scarf in a peach shade for Christmas.*

On Christmas Day Tasha would open her gift and gasp, unable to believe that someone had chosen so well.

No one would ever return a gift bought by Becca.

No one would ever look at it and think *I already have three of those.*

No wonder he missed his wife. And he did miss his wife, she could see that.

He had a powerful physical presence, and yet he seemed a little lost and dazed. Flora hadn't known it was possible for someone to look so strong, and solid and yet totally vulnerable.

"Flowers are a perfect idea." She felt a sudden urge to lighten his load. People-pleasing wasn't always about being cowardly. Sometimes it was just about wanting to help someone. "Great choice."

He glanced at the bouquet Julia had just finished. "Roses?"

"There are better choices for a seventeenth birthday. Tell me a little about her. What does she like?"

"At the moment? I'm not even sure. She doesn't open up to me." He rubbed his forehead with his fingers and then waved his hand apologetically. "You probably think I'm a terrible father."

"You're here, trying to find the perfect gift for your daughter, that makes you a thoughtful father. Grief is always difficult."

"You speak from experience?"

She did. She was sure she knew everything he was feeling, and everything his daughter was feeling although Flora had been younger, of course. Was there a good age to lose a loved one? Flora didn't think so. Even now, so many years later, she would catch the scent of a flower and miss her mother. "What does your daughter like to do in her spare time?"

"When she's not at school, she helps take care of her sister. Molly is seven. When I get home and once Molly is in bed, she mostly shuts herself in her room and stares at her phone. Do you have flowers that say 'maybe you should spend less time on social media'? It's a thorny subject, so maybe those roses would be more appropriate than you think. Or perhaps a cactus."

So there was a sense of humor there. Buried, possibly mostly forgotten, but definitely there.

"We can do better than a cactus." Flora stepped out from behind the counter and walked toward the buckets that held an array of blooms. She'd been at the Flower District on West Twenty-Eighth Street before the sun was up, powered by caffeine as she foraged for nuggets of perfection and dodged trucks that were unloading crates. Only flowers could tempt her to leave her bed at that hour of the morning. So many growers focused on shelf life at the expense of color and scent, but Celia relied on her to choose quality and Flora would never contemplate anything less. Her mother had taught her the importance of seasons and now, at the tail end of winter she'd selected alstroemeria and amaryllis, carnation and chrysanthemum. She'd scooped up great bundles of foliage, tallow berries and seeded eucalyptus and stashed them on the metal shelves provided for that purpose. She could never walk past narcissus without adding them to her growing pile. Everywhere she went, she touched and smelled, burying her face deep into flowers and inhaling scent and freshness. She treated flowers as someone else might treat wine, as something to be sampled and savored and for Flora the early morning trip was a sociable event, not only because she knew so many people, but also because so many people had known her mother. It was familiar, a connection to the past that she treasured.

Finally, when she'd finished, she helped Carlos load up the van they used for deliveries and together they transported their precious cargo to the store. Once there her selection was sorted, trimmed of leaves and thorns, and the stems cut. Then her day shifted to customers and she handled walk-ins, internet orders and regulars. Her legs ached but she was so used to it that these days she barely noticed.

Her gaze drifted past the hydrangeas and lilacs, and lingered on the alstroemeria before moving on.

She thought back to her own teenage years, and then stooped and hand-selected a bunch of gerberas in sunshine yellow and deep orange. "These should be the main focus."

He inclined his head. "Pretty."

"The Celts believed that gerberas relieved sorrow."

"Let's hope they were right."

She could feel him watching her as she selected tulips and roses and then assembled the bouquet. She took her time, trimming the stems and adding foliage. She stripped leaves, removed thorns from the roses, angled the stems and checked the balance and position of the flowers, aware the whole time that he was watching her.

"You're good at that."

She identified the binding point and tied the bouquet. "It's my job. I'm sure you're good at yours."

"I am. And I enjoy it. I should probably feel guilty about that."

"Why?" She wrapped the flowers carefully, added water to the pouch and tied them. "It's not wrong to enjoy what you spend your day doing. I'd say it's obligatory." She wondered what he did.

Despite the fact that he was floundering with his daughter, there was a quiet confidence about him that suggested he didn't doubt himself in other areas of life. Underneath the black coat his clothing was casual, so probably not a lawyer or a banker.

Advertising? Possibly, but she didn't think so. Something in tech, maybe?

No doubt Julia would be full of ideas and wouldn't hold back from expressing them.

*Serial killer.*

*Bank robber.*

"I feel guilty because sometimes when I'm at work, I forget."

"That's something to feel grateful for, not guilty. Work can often be a distraction, and that's good. Not every pain can be fixed. Sometimes it's about finding a way to make each moment better. These flowers should stay fresh for more than a week. Add flower food. Change the water every day. Strip off any leaves that are under the water. It will help to keep the flowers looking good." She handed them over. "Oh, and remove the guard petals from the roses."

"Guard petals?"

"This," she pointed with her finger to the curled, wrinkled edge of a petal. "They look damaged, but they're there to protect the rose. Once you get them home, peel them away and the flower will be perfect. I hope she loves them."

"Me, too." He produced his credit card. "Given that you may be saving my life, I should probably know your name."

"Flora." She ran the card through the machine. "Flora Donovan." She glanced at the name as she handed it back.

Jack Parker. It suited him.

"Flora. Appropriate name. You have a gift for what you do and I'm the grateful recipient."

Flora wondered if Becca had been good at arranging flowers.

"Are you having a party for your daughter?"

"She said she didn't want one. That it wouldn't be the same without her mother there. I took her at her word." He slid the card back into his pocket. "Was that a mistake?"

It must be so hard for him trying to get under the skin of a teenage girl.

"Maybe a party wouldn't be right. You could do something different. Something she wouldn't have done with her mother."

"Like what?"

"I don't know—" Flora thought about it. "Is she athletic? Go to an indoor climbing wall. Or spend the day making pottery. Take her and her friends to a salsa class. Or do something together. If she's feeling lost, what she really wants is probably to spend quality time with you."

"I wouldn't be so sure. Dads are an embarrassment when you're a teenage girl."

Flora wished she had the experience to know. She would have given a lot to be embarrassed by her dad, but her dad had wanted nothing to do with her.

*You're my world*, her mother had always said but after she'd died Flora had wondered whether life might have been easier if their world had included a few more people.

She wanted to ask him more about his daughter, but there was a queue of customers building and Celia was frowning at her across the store.

But he seemed in no hurry to leave. "How long have you worked here?"

"I don't remember a time when I didn't work here." She glanced up at the high ceilings and the large windows. "My mother worked here, too, before she died. I helped her from the moment I could walk. Many of our customers were my mother's customers. We deliver flowers right across Manhattan." And she was proud to be continuing what her mother had started. It brought the past into the present and gave her comfort.

"How old were you when you lost your mother?"

"Eight." Barely older than his younger daughter was now.

"And your father?" His tone was softer now, and she was grateful for his sensitivity.

"My mother raised me alone."

"How did you handle it—losing her?" He sucked in a breath. "I apologize. That was an unforgivably intrusive question, but right now I'm at that stage of looking for answers everywhere. Something I can do, something I can say—I'll try anything."

"I'm not sure I handled it. I got through it, the best I could." Her life had gone from warm sunshine to bitter cold.

She'd moved from a warm, safe place to one where she felt vulnerable and exposed. "I'm not sure what helped me, would help others."

"What did help you?"

"Things that made her seem closer. Flowers. Flowers were like having my mother with me."

He studied her and she could have sworn for a moment that he saw her. Really saw her. Not the rose-colored dress or the hyacinth tights, or the hair that tumbled and turned and refused to behave in a predictable manner much to the annoyance of her aunt, but the gaps inside her. The pieces that were missing.

He smiled, and she felt warmth spread through her and spill into those gaps. Her heart beat faster and stronger.

There was so much charm in his smile. She was pretty sure that he'd be single for as long as he chose to be and not a moment longer.

"You seem to have turned out all right." He was in no hurry to leave. "I've been worrying my girls won't be okay. That their lives are ruined. But here you are. You give me hope that we might get through this."

There was a strength to him, a seam of steel, that made her sure he would get through anything.

"You'll find a way." She was instantly embarrassed. "Sorry. That sounded trite. Like one of those self-help quotes that pop up on the internet. *Live your best life.*" The fact that he smiled felt like an achievement.

"I hate those quotes. Especially the ones that tell you to dance in the rain."

"I love dancing in the rain." Better than dancing in her apartment, where her elbows knocked against the walls and her neighbors complained about the noise.

His gaze held hers and again there was that feeling of

warmth. "Do you get a lunch break? Would you join me for something to eat? Or a coffee?"

Her heart woke up. Was he asking her on a date?

"Well—"

"You're wondering if I'm a crazed serial killer. I'm not. But you're the first person I've talked to in a long time who seems to understand."

She saw that his eyes were green, not blue. And she saw that he looked tired. Maybe he was aware of that, because he gave a faint smile and she found herself smiling back. The brief moment of connection shocked her. It was the closest she'd been to experiencing intimacy with another person in a long time. Ironic, she thought, that it was with a stranger.

"I don't think you're crazed, and I don't think you're a serial killer."

"I asked you for coffee because you're easy to talk to." The focus of his gaze shifted somewhere behind her. "I'm assuming that scary-looking woman glaring at me is your boss?"

Flora didn't even need to look. "Yes."

"In which case I'm going to get you fired if I stand here talking any longer. I don't want that on my conscience. Thank you for listening, Flora. And thank you for the advice."

He was handling two traumatized girls by himself. Wounded. Hurting.

Who looked after him? Did he have no one supporting him?

He'd lost his wife, who'd clearly been perfect in every way. *Becca.* It seemed deeply unfair that people who had managed to find each other in this busy, complex world, should then lose each other. Maybe that was worse than never finding someone in the first place.

She shouldn't get involved. Coffee and conversation wasn't going to fix anything.

But who could say no to a single father who was desperately trying to do the right thing by his daughters?

Not her.

"I could do coffee," she said. "I get a break in an hour."

# 2

## Izzy

"You're bringing someone to dinner? You're *dating*? You have to be kidding me. It's not even been a year since Mom died, and you've already forgotten her." Izzy stopped folding laundry and clamped her mouth shut. Had she really said that aloud? Guilt washed over her. She'd done so well holding it all together, but now her dad had opened a door she'd kept closed. His words had released all the rubbish she'd been hiding inside, like the cupboard holding all of Molly's toys. Izzy could barely close the door. And now her hands were shaking and misery covered her like a film of sweat. Her body had felt weird, as if she was inhabiting someone else's skin that didn't quite fit. She had dizzy spells, moments when she felt oddly detached, panicky flashes when she thought she might totally flip out in public and humiliate herself. At the beginning people were constantly checking she was okay. *How are you doing, Izzy?* And she'd always answer that she was fine. Apparently they'd believed her, and their comments had shifted to *You're totally amazing. Your mom would be so proud of how you're handling this.* If grief was a test, then apparently she'd got a good grade. She'd even felt proud of herself on occasion, an emotion that was way too complicated for her brain. Was surviving something to be proud of?

Gradually people had stopped tiptoeing around her and gone back to their normal selves and their normal lives. People rarely mentioned it now. She'd thought that might be easier, but it turned out it wasn't. They'd moved on, but she hadn't. Her life had been shredded and she was still trying to stitch the fragments together alone with fingers that were raw and bleeding. Whatever she did there was no patching over the fact that there was a big mother-shaped hole in her life. She was trying hard to fill it for her dad's sake, but mostly for Molly's sake.

Had her father given any thought to the impact dating would have on Molly?

How could he *do* this? She didn't understand love. What exactly was its worth if it didn't even leave a mark? If you could move so easily from one person to another?

She knew she should probably be pleased for him, but she couldn't summon that emotion. If he moved on, where did that leave them as a family? Where did it leave *her*?

The sound around her faded and she could hear the blood pulsing through her ears.

She felt lost and panicky.

Maybe this relationship wasn't serious. She wanted to whip out her phone and type "grief and rebound relationships" into the search engine. Even though he hid it well, she knew he was hurting and vulnerable. She wasn't going to let some opportunistic woman take advantage of that. The last thing little Molly needed was a parade of strange women marching through the house.

Her father put his arm round her but she ducked away, even though she needed a hug more than anything.

He looked stunned. "What's wrong? You're not normally like this."

"Sorry. Long day." Clamping her jaws together, Izzy shook another towel out and folded it.

"Do you really think I've forgotten her?"

"I don't know. Seems that way, that's all."

It freaked her out that he could be so calm. She tried to be the same, but he set a high bar. Did he cry? Did he ever howl in the shower like she did? Her tears poured down the drain along with the water. She wanted to know she was normal, that she wasn't the only one who felt this bad, even though deep down she knew it would scare her to see his tears.

It was a totally crap situation, but if he could be brave and stoic then so could she.

If he could hold it together then so could she. She'd managed well, hadn't she? Until today.

She folded another towel, and then another, until she had a neat pile. It amazed her how soothing it felt to have completed that one small task.

Mrs. Cameron came in every morning to clean the house and do the laundry, but it was Izzy who removed it from the dryer and folded it all. She didn't mind. It was a bit like meditation.

"I made homemade veggie burgers for supper."

"Again? Didn't we have them two nights ago?"

"They're Molly's favorite." But maybe she should have been making her dad's favorite, not her sister's. *Pressure, pressure, pressure.*

"You made a good decision, Izz. You're my superstar. Your mom would have been so proud." He picked up the stack of towels she'd folded. "Molly didn't eat the lunch I made her this morning."

"Did you give her ham? She hates ham."

"She does?" He looked surprised. "I'll try to remember that. What would I do without you? You're a good cook, and you're so great with Molly."

"She's my sister. Family." She was struggling to hold the family together, and now he was planning on inviting a stranger into their home. Although the woman obviously wasn't a stranger to him. Had he had sex with her? Izzy felt her face turn hot and her chest tighten. A girl at school had panic attacks all the time. Izzy had never had one, not a proper one, but she suspected they were lurking round the corner. What if she had one when she was watching Molly? She forced herself to breathe slowly, and tried not to picture her dad naked with another woman.

The problem with being a family was that every member was affected by the actions of an individual. This should be her dad's business, except it wasn't.

"I haven't forgotten your mom, Izzy." His quiet tone poked at the small, miserable part of herself that wasn't bursting with anger.

Maybe he hadn't forgotten her, but he'd moved on. Her head was full of questions, most of them beginning with *"why."*

Why had this happened to her mom? And why didn't her dad feel guilty, when she felt guilty *all the time*? Guilty for all the times she hadn't hugged her mother or told her that she loved her, guilty for never making her bed and for leaving empty milk cartons in the fridge. Most of all she felt guilty about that last fight they'd had before her mother had left the house that night. The one she couldn't talk about. The one she hadn't mentioned to anyone, not her friends and certainly not her dad. She didn't dare say anything to her dad. If she did—well, she couldn't. No way. It would change everything. The family she'd been working so hard to protect would be blown apart.

Thinking about it stung like squeezing lemon onto a cut.

"When is she coming? I'll take Molly to the park or something."

"I don't want you to do that. I invited her here so she can meet you both."

Were all men so clueless? She was used to people doing and saying the wrong thing around her, it happened all the time, but the fact that her own dad couldn't see the bigger picture was particularly hurtful. "You don't think that's confusing for Molly?"

"She's a friend, that's all. You and Molly have friends over."

Izzy dragged the rest of the laundry out of the dryer. "So are you telling me this is a sleepover situation?" She saw color streak across her father's cheeks.

"It's dinner, that's all."

She was tempted to tell him to take the woman out for dinner somewhere else, well away from the family home, but part of her thought it might be better to keep it close. At least then she'd be able to see what was going on. What did this woman want exactly?

She reached for a sheet she'd washed earlier and saw her dad frown.

"Why are you washing Molly's bedding? Mrs. Cameron should be doing that."

"Molly spilled her drink." The lie emerged with an ease that probably should have worried her, but didn't. She'd promised her sister that she wouldn't tell anyone she'd wet the bed for the fourth night in a row. The only way to keep that promise was to launder the sheets herself.

Did her dad even know that Molly crawled into Izzy's bed in the middle of the night when she'd wet her own, bringing with her a zoo of soft toys? It had started in those early weeks and then become a habit. Every night Izzy, drunk from lack of sleep, helped wash her sister and change her pajamas, then tucked her up in her own bed along with Dizzy the Giraffe. Molly would immediately fall asleep, but Izzy would lie there awake for hours, often drifting off only as the sun started to rise. She was tired at school and her grades were slipping. Twice she'd fallen asleep at her desk, and sometimes she walked into furniture.

Some of her friends had taken to calling her *Dizzy Izzy*. It didn't do anything for her mood to be given the same name as her sister's soft toy.

They had no idea what her life was like, and neither had her dad, and she had no intention of talking about it. She'd learned more about people since her mother died than in her entire life before that. She'd learned that people focused mostly on their own lives, not other people's. And when they did think about other people, it was mostly in relation to themselves. Her friends didn't think about her life, except when watching Molly meant that she had to say no to something they'd arranged. It wasn't intentional or malicious. It was carelessness. Thoughtlessness. Those two human characteristics that caused more pain than the words suggested they should.

Was bringing a woman home thoughtlessness, too?

Izzy didn't know much about anything, but she knew it wouldn't be good for Molly to see another woman in the house. She didn't feel great about it, either.

In that moment she missed her mother so badly she couldn't breathe. She wanted to turn the clock back. There was so much she wished she'd said and done. No one had ever told her it was possible to feel angry and sad at the same time.

She remembered the night before her mother had died. After their terrible fight, her mother had swept into the room to let her know they were going out.

Her dark hair had been swept up in an elegant knot, and her black dress had flowed in a silken sweep to the floor. Izzy had badly wanted to continue their conversation, only this time without the shouting, but before she could speak her father had stepped into the room and the moment had passed.

Izzy had felt frustration and anxiety, but had promised herself she'd make her mother talk about it the next day. But there had been no next day. Her mother had collapsed suddenly from an undetected aneurysm in her brain. She'd died before she reached the hospital.

Their world had collapsed that night. For Izzy it had remained in ruins, but apparently her father had been busy rebuilding his.

"It's dinner, Izzy. That's all. She isn't sharing my bed. She's not moving in. But I like her." He hesitated. "I like her a lot and I think you and Molly will, too."

Izzy knew for sure she wouldn't like her. There was no way, *no way*, she was ready to see her father with anyone else. Where would that leave her? Where would she fit in that scenario? Right now her dad needed her. Would that change if he had another woman in his life?

"How long have you been dating?" She tried to mimic his calm. "How did you meet her?"

"Remember the flowers I bought for your birthday? She's a florist. She made that bouquet you loved so much."

Izzy *had* loved the bouquet. It had made her feel ridiculously grown-up. She'd considered it thoughtful, but now she discovered that the choice had been driven by someone else's thought. The gift shrank in her head.

"You've been seeing her since my birthday?"

"We went for a coffee that day. She's been through tough times, too. She was about the same age as Molly when she lost her mother."

That wasn't good news. She'd think she understood them, and she most certainly didn't. Families, Izzy decided, were the most complex things on the planet. "But you've seen her more than that one time."

"She works near my office. I've seen her for lunch a few times."

A few times. Enough times to want to bring her home to meet the family.

"You never mentioned it."

"There was nothing to mention."

"But now there is."

Her father put the towels down. "I know this is difficult, and sensitive, but I'm asking you to keep an open mind."

Molly had only just stopped crying herself to sleep. Would it all start again if her dad brought someone home? "So what? You want me to run round the house taking down all the pictures of Mom?"

He rubbed his fingers over his forehead. "No, I don't want that. Your mother will always be part of our lives." He let his hand drop. "You've turned the same color as those white sheets you're holding. Are you doing okay, Izzy? Really?"

"I'm great." The words flowed automatically. She'd said them so many times she almost believed them, even though a part of her was wondering why this was happening to her. What had she done to deserve it? She wasn't perfect, but she wasn't awful. She recycled. She'd given money to save endangered whales. She hadn't yelled when Molly had spilled blackcurrant juice on her favorite sweater.

"If you ever want to talk—" He paused. "It doesn't have to be to me. The hospital gave me the name of someone. A psychologist. I mentioned it a while back and you didn't want to, but if you change your mind—"

"I haven't changed my mind." She couldn't think of anything more awkward. No way could she tell anyone what was going on in her head. It was just too *big.* And there was no one she trusted. She couldn't even write about this on her blog, and she spilled everything there. She called it *The Real Teen*, and talked about everything from periods to her views on global warming. It was anonymous, and that was so freeing. She wrote things she would never say aloud. Things she could never say to her dad, and things she could never say even to her friends. She'd done it for herself, and had been surprised to quickly gain a following. It had grown at a ridiculous rate, and now people left comments. Sometimes just an *OMG I feel the same way*, but occasionally a longer reply detailing the issues in her own life and telling Izzy how much her post had helped. It gave her a buzz to know she was helping people. She liked saying things that others were afraid to say. While her friends were posting selfies and talking about clothes and makeup, she talked about the serious stuff. Words had so much power. She didn't understand how so few people seemed to get that.

She'd already decided she wanted to be a journalist. Not the sort that interviewed celebrities on red carpets about subjects that mattered to no one, but the sort who shone a light into dark corners. She wanted to tell truths and expose lies. She wanted to change the world.

Her father was watching her. "I'm worried about you."

"Don't." She didn't want him worrying about her. She didn't want to be a burden.

"We should be talking about college. Maybe we should do a few campus visits."

She tensed. "There's plenty of time." She didn't tell him she was thinking of not going. She didn't want to leave the family. "Can we talk about it another time?"

"Sure." He hesitated. "It's what your mom would have wanted."

People didn't always get what they wanted, did they? Except that, ironically, her mother usually had. Except for dying, of course. That hadn't been part of her plan.

Her dad picked up the towels again. Izzy had a feeling he was looking for things to do.

"I'll take these upstairs. Are you sure you want to cook for Flora?"

That was her name?

"I want to cook." She'd show this woman that they were a close family. That there was no room for anyone else.

There was no way she was going to college. She was going to stay home and get a job so that she could keep an eye on things. Maybe she could monetize her blog or something. Other people did it. People got paid for waving stupid handbags in front of the camera. Why couldn't she be paid for saying important stuff? People commenting on her blog admitted to things they never said in public. They were talking about things that were *real*. If she could get her traffic up, that would help. And employers liked people with real life experience.

"Thanks, Izzy." Her dad reached out one more time to hug her and Izzy moved away. She didn't trust herself not to crumble.

She saw the pain cross his face and felt her breath catch.

Was she a horrible person?

"Sorry. I need to get on, that's all. I have to check Molly's school bag for tomorrow, read to her and then I have an essay to do."

"I'll try to persuade her to let me read to her so you can have a break. I know I'm second best, but I'll give it a go."

"It's okay." She liked to feel needed and Molly's love was like a balm.

"I'm worried you're working too hard."

"I like doing it." She liked the fact that she was keeping things as normal as possible, even though it was far from the life they'd had. She liked being useful. Needed. Indispensable.

"I appreciate what you're doing, and I'm pleased you're going to meet Flora. And I'm not trying to replace Becca. I'm trying to keep living, one day at a time, which is all any of us can do." He sounded tired. "Fortunately love isn't finite. You don't use it all up on one person. It's like a river that keeps flowing."

Some rivers dried up. And that was how she felt. She'd cried so much she felt permanently dehydrated. And her dad didn't know half of what was going on in her head. He didn't know all the stuff that had happened, and she couldn't tell him.

"I'm not trying to erase your mother, Izzy. Far from it." He put his hand on her shoulder. "You don't think we deserve happiness? You don't think your mom would have wanted us to be happy?"

Izzy didn't know the answer to that. Her mother had always been the center of attention, always the star, whether it had been at a party or a school event. Becca Parker lit up every room she entered. People around her were dazzled by her brightness. Izzy had heard her parents described as a "beautiful couple," and it was true they attracted attention wherever they went, and not just because her mother had always insisted on arriving late and last for everything. It had driven Izzy crazy, but she no longer remembered that. All she remembered was that everyone had paid attention to her mother.

"Everything is cool, but you should be careful." She said it casually. "She's probably after your money."

"You think that's the only reason a woman would want to be with me?" For the first time since he'd walked into the room, he smiled. "I'm not that bad a judge of character. Relax, Izzy. You'll like her, and I know she's going to like you. It's all going to be fine."

Seriously? He thought it was going to be fine?

This family was already a total mess, and he was planning on making the mess worse. Izzy wasn't going to let that happen. She needed to keep this family together, no matter what. For herself, sure, but also for Molly. Molly relied on her, and Izzy wasn't going to let her sister down.

Her objective wasn't to make sure Flora liked her, it was to make sure the woman never wanted to set foot in the house again.

# 3

## *Flora*

It was a relaxed dinner, that was all.

True, she'd changed her outfit three times, but that was because this evening was important. It was important, *essential*, that his daughters liked her, and she was confident she could make that happen. It helped that she had a pretty good idea of what they were going through. She hoped that, in time, she might even be able to help a little. She'd make it clear that she had no intention of disrupting their family or causing the slightest ripple in their safe, familiar world. Not for one moment did she think she could replace their mother, and she didn't intend to try. She'd encourage them to think of her more as an older friend.

She imagined Molly, the younger, crawling onto her lap for a hug and Izzy being relieved to finally have someone to share those thoughts and feelings you could only share

with another woman. Flora hadn't had that. Her aunt hadn't
been the hugging type and their conversations had been focused on the practical. Even now Flora found it hard to talk
about her feelings and she assumed it was because she'd had
no practice. She'd been left to comfort herself, and figure
things out for herself. She didn't want that for Jack's girls.

Was she jumping ahead of herself? Possibly, but where
was the harm in dreaming a little?

*Jack.*

She thought, maybe, that she was falling in love and the
idea terrified and excited her in equal amounts. Was he in
love with her? She wasn't sure, but she knew that if their
relationship was going to move to the next level, then his
daughters would have to love her, too.

Jack had made it clear they needed to take this slowly and
be discreet. She was fine with that, and not just because of
the girls. These feelings were new to her, too.

She'd dated occasionally over the past few years. Most
notable had been Mr. Hedge Fund Manager who she'd met
when she'd made the mistake of enrolling at an early morning yoga class. He'd been told by his doctor to reduce his
stress levels and so had decided on yoga, but hadn't seemed
to realize that Downward Dog wasn't designed to allow you
to take a closer look at your phone. The phone joined them
for every date, sitting on the table during dinner like a chap-
erone. The only hedge she knew anything about was green
and needed pruning, and despite her efforts she'd been unable to learn anything that equipped her to have an even
vaguely knowledgeable conversation with the man. The relationship had gone downhill faster than the markets. Next
had been Ray. Ray was a schoolteacher, passionate about
basketball. Flora had endured eight games before he'd complained that she wasn't "engaged." She'd been affronted. She

was the master at faking interest in something, and in this case she'd done her homework. She'd learned about the chest pass, the bounce pass and the outlet pass. She'd yelled and punched the air when he'd yelled and punched the air. She'd thought she'd mirrored his reactions, but he'd sensed something lacking under her carefully choreographed enthusiasm.

She knew now that what had been lacking was motivation. She hadn't been motivated to make the relationship work. He'd been right. She hadn't been engaged. Not with him, not with Mr. Hedge Fund. She'd tried to show interest in what they enjoyed, without revealing her own interests.

But now there was Jack. Smart, handsome, caring Jack. That first coffee had turned into lunch, and they'd started to meet regularly. Their friendship had deepened, warmer feelings creeping up on them stealthily and unannounced. She couldn't quite remember when she'd first noticed the shift. Was it that day at the Brooklyn Botanic Garden when he'd taken her hand in his? Or their first kiss by the fountain in Central Park?

Flora had never had a relationship that she hadn't had to work hard at, not with her aunt and not with boyfriends, so it was a revelation to discover that she could be herself with him. Not her *whole* self of course. There was still plenty he didn't know about her, feelings she kept tightly packed away in storage inaccessible to all but her. No doubt there was also plenty she didn't know about him but what she knew, she liked.

He seemed to know something about almost everything, so instead of typing her questions into a search engine she just asked Jack. They visited the Frick Collection and she didn't bother with an audio guide because she had Jack telling her a little about everything in a way that brought the art to life. Her mother had possessed the same gift and that small connection seemed to pull them closer together like tiny invisible threads. They headed to the Bronx and visited the New York Botanical Garden, a place Flora had often visited with her mother. Here in this lush oasis, among the buds and blooms, she knew more than he did and he questioned her constantly. What was that flower? What climate did that particular tree like? What would she plant in a garden if she had one? He was the first man she'd dated to show an interest in who she was and what she enjoyed. And the interest was mutual. So far, she hadn't had to take a crash course in any of his interests in order to keep the relationship alive. Jack worked in a senior tech role for a company that specialized in artificial intelligence, and his few attempts to describe what he did had made her eyes cross. Fortunately he didn't seem to need to talk about his work when they were together and gradually she'd stopped her internet searches on "tech for beginners."

It wasn't as if they were short of conversation topics. The only subject off-limits for him was his wife. He talked about her in relation to the children, and how they were coping, but didn't talk about his own emotions. She'd been sensitive, approaching the topic with the care of someone peeling the bandage from an open wound, but he'd shut her down gently and eventually she'd stopped asking. She respected the fact that there were things he didn't want to talk about. She was the same.

But now she was about to meet his daughters and they, of course, were his biggest interest.

They'd talked about it just the day before, sitting close together on their favorite bench in the park. She never would have thought she could have experienced heart-racing, dizzy, romantic feelings in a park, but it turned out that it wasn't where you were that mattered, it was who you were with.

Whenever she was with Jack, the rest of the world vanished for her.

Physically it was all very low-key of course. Interlocked fingers, the hard pressure of his thigh against hers. It wasn't much, but it seemed to be more than enough to send her brain and body into meltdown. She was so *aware* of him, her response vastly out of proportion to the limited, restrained contact they'd had. It made her feel better to know she had the same effect on him. She felt his tension, and saw the occasional flash of heat in his gaze. It wasn't coincidence that they always met in public places. It was an unspoken acknowledgment that the only way to take this slowly was to impose certain restrictions on themselves.

"Are you nervous of meeting them?" He'd asked the question as they'd sat there, close together.

"The girls? A little." She hadn't wanted to lie to him. "I'm also excited. From what you've told me, they're smart, interesting, special people." And she loved the way he talked about them with such pride. It said a lot about his character that he was such an engaged father. She hoped his children knew how lucky they were.

What scared her most, if she was honest, wasn't his girls, it was how much she wanted this relationship to work.

"You're incredible, do you know that?" He'd taken her hand and pressed it to his thigh, making it hard for her to focus on the conversation.

"Me?"

"It would be too much for most people. Dating a man with two kids. Most people would run away from a ready-made family, but you're so open and optimistic about everything."

She wouldn't have described herself as open. She was careful. Cautious. Protective of herself. But with Jack it was different.

Because she badly didn't want this to end, she'd already quizzed him in-depth. She knew that Izzy wanted to be a journalist, and that Molly had loved to draw and dance, although she'd stopped both after Becca had died. Flora loved to draw and paint, too, so she was hoping that maybe, if she was careful, she might be able to persuade Molly to draw with her. Still, she knew she had to be careful not to push things. The pressure from her aunt to "get over it and move on" had stressed her enormously.

Shaking off the past, Flora paused at the end of the street clutching flowers and a bottle of homemade lemonade. Jack had said his daughter was making dinner, and Flora figured lemonade went with pretty much everything.

Not that she knew much about teenagers but she was impressed that Izzy was doing the cooking.

Had his wife been a good cook? Had she taught her daughter? Flora imagined her carefully selecting menus, and spending hours providing her children with balanced, healthy meals.

She braced herself against the ripple of insecurity that threatened to shake her optimism.

Jack wasn't going to be measuring her against his wife, and neither were his children.

It had been less than a fifteen-minute subway ride from her apartment, but it felt like a million miles. This was Brooklyn's most historic neighborhood, with wide, leafy streets and mesmerizing views of the Manhattan skyline across the East River. Now, in spring, blossom filled the sky with fragrant clouds, showering the cobbled streets with soft petals.

Checking the directions on her phone, she moved to one side to avoid a young girl on a scooter and smiled at the young mother who was running behind her, trying to keep up. It seemed like a family neighborhood, and considerably more upmarket than the area where she lived. On her way here, she'd walked past a couple of bistros and a boutique. She imagined living somewhere like this, picking up a bag of peaches on her way home, exchanging a laugh and a joke with a street vendor.

Even the names of the streets were charming. She'd passed Cranberry Street, Pineapple Street and Orange Street. People who lived here got their five a day just by walking around, she thought. Even the air felt fresher than it did in the center of Manhattan. The streets outside her apartment mostly smelled of garbage.

She was ten minutes early. Did that matter?

Nerves were jumping around in the pit of her belly, but she always felt that way before seeing Jack.

A man striding past gave her a wide berth and she realized it was because she was smiling at nothing in particular.

Feeling positive, she walked up the steps and rang the bell.

One day, she promised herself, she was going to have a proper front door of her own. Maybe flanked by olive trees, or pots filled with trailing plants.

Jack opened the door. He was wearing jeans, and his shirt was open at the neck. His feet were bare and there was a hint of shadow on his jaw. Here in his own domain, he seemed younger and more relaxed.

"You found us okay?" His gaze connected with hers and she felt a searing flash of chemistry that almost knocked her off her feet. Feeling a little disorientated, she stepped into the house. His fingers brushed lightly against hers, sending a shimmer of heat coursing through her. For a wild moment she thought he was going to simply kick the door shut and drag her against him, but instead he closed the door with deliberate care, his arm braced against it as he took a steadying breath, steeling himself.

It was a moment before he turned to face her. The atmosphere was charged with tension. It had all the intensity of sex, without the actual sex.

She gave him a sympathetic smile and unfastened her coat. "How's it going?"

"Nothing that a long, icy shower won't cure. You look great in that dress." He spoke in a low voice. "And I love your hair when it curls like that."

"It's a style I like to call 'the indecisive.'" She handed him her coat. "I pulled my dress over my head so many times while trying to decide what to wear I produced enough electricity to power the whole borough."

His laughter broke the tension. "I'm pleased you came. And the girls are excited to meet you."

"I can't wait to meet them."

As he hung up her coat, she glanced around curiously.

She'd imagined a slightly messy, cozy family home. Maybe some signs of a man who was struggling to cope. It was nothing like that.

The walls of the entryway were decorated in a soft palette of whites and creams that reflected the light and added to the feeling of space. She'd never been in such ordered surroundings. It reminded her of a spa. She half expected a woman in a white coat to swipe her credit card and escort her to a treatment room for a facial.

A large vase full of calla lilies sat proudly on a console table. Her hands itched to rearrange them, but nothing here cried out to be touched. There was no mess. No unopened mail that needed sorting, no house keys, no casual detritus waiting to be stowed away. Everything was already in its place.

"Are you selling your home?" She spoke without thinking and saw his eyebrows lift.

"No. Why would you think that?"

Because her mouth was bigger than her brain. "It's so tidy. The only time I've ever seen living space this tidy is when people are selling. Sometimes we're asked to do the flowers to help showcase a property."

"Mommy liked it tidy. We try to keep it the way she liked it." The shy voice came from the stairs and Flora turned and saw a young girl standing there. Her hair was dark and caught up in an uneven ponytail. Her blue dress hung around her skinny frame and she was carrying a limp giraffe that probably hadn't seen the inside of a washing machine at any point during its life. She stared at Flora, unsure whether she was looking at friend or foe.

"Hi there." Flora gave her a warm smile. "You must be Molly." She stepped forward but the little girl shrank back, clutching the giraffe to her chest.

"Come here, Molly." Jack held out his hand. "Come and say hi."

Molly didn't say "hi." Instead she ran to him as if he were a lifeboat and Flora the storm.

Jack scooped child and toy into his arms. "What's the matter, honey?"

"She's wearing shoes." Her voice was barely audible. "Mommy doesn't let us wear shoes in the house."

Jack's gaze met Flora's over the top of Molly's head and she bent to pull off her running shoes. She could feel her face burning.

"I was so excited to see you, I forgot to take them off." Her fingers slipped and slid on the laces. She was eight years old again and fumbling with her coat under the glare of her aunt's disapproving frown.

*I chose not to marry and have children so we'll have to find a way to tolerate each other.*

Nothing stressed Flora more than knowing she was being tolerated. She wanted to be accepted. Welcomed. Loved.

Protected by her father's arms, Molly gained confidence. "Do you wear shoes in your house?"

"I don't have a house, I have an apartment. And I don't own it, I rent it. It belongs to someone else, and he doesn't care too much about things like leaks and damp." And cockroaches. "It's not as special as your home." The thought of all the people and activity that had probably taken place on her floor made her want to walk around in thigh-length boots and a hazmat suit, not bare feet.

Still, when she'd dreamed of a family home it hadn't looked like this.

Flora placed her shoes neatly to the side of the entryway.

"We have a shoe cupboard." Molly pointed, and Flora followed directions and opened a door. Behind it was a large concealed cupboard complete with shoe racks.

"Well look at that!" Flora tucked her shoes inside. "I bet that's a perfect place to play hide-and-seek."

Molly gave her an odd look. "It's a cupboard. You'd get dirty."

"But sometimes getting dirty is fun, and—" Flora stopped "—and, you're right, you would get dirty and that is such a pretty dress. It would be a shame to get it dusty." It had driven her aunt mad that Flora could never stay clean for five minutes.

"Your dress is very bright and dazzly."

"Thank you." Flora glanced down at herself. "I made it myself."

Molly frowned. "Why? You couldn't afford to buy one?"

Jack cleared his throat. "Flora made it herself because

she's talented. And I think it's time to move this conversation on, young lady. Let's go through to the kitchen and see how your sister is doing with dinner and what we can do to help." He put Molly down and sent Flora a look of apology.

She smiled, signaling that it wasn't a problem although of course it was a problem.

Telling herself that this was bound to take time, Flora followed them through to the back of the house. If this was a test, she'd failed dismally.

As she followed him toward the kitchen she glanced through an open door into the living room, and noticed the elegant white sofas. White sofas? How did they not get filthy? Flora hoped she wasn't going to be invited into that room. She'd be terrified to sit down in case she marked the fabric. A selection of art books were stacked on a low table and a large cream rug covered the oak floor.

It looked like a room straight out of a design magazine. If she hadn't known a family lived here, she would have guessed the occupants were a professional couple who spent most of their time in the office or entertaining friends who wouldn't spill a drop of red wine.

The house had a cool, elegant feel with art and large photographs crowding the walls. She looked more closely and saw that all the photographs were of the same person, a dancer. She was almost impossibly graceful and ethereal, the camera capturing the height of a gazelle-like leap into the air, the elegant stretch of her arms, the curve of her instep as she balanced *en pointe*. It all looked effortless.

She turned her head and saw Molly watching her.

"That's my mommy. She was a famous dancer."

Dancer.

And now, of course, it all fell into place. Becca. Jack's wife was Becca Parker. *The* Becca Parker, darling of the media and ballet-loving audiences across the globe, a dancer who displayed the perfect combination of athleticism and grace, power and poise. Those photographs portrayed the triumph and nothing of the struggle. And they only told the early part of Becca's story.

As her star was rising, Becca Parker had damaged her knee and been unable to perform again. Another person might have sunk into depression. Not Becca. She'd turned her recovery into a triumph and invented a fitness regime she called "Becca's Body." She'd invested in first one studio and then another until her company was running classes across the major cities of the US.

Flora had never taken a Becca's Body class. She had neither the budget nor the motivation. And she definitely didn't have the right body.

Staring at those photographs, she felt like a small, ungainly elephant. She had a feeling Becca wouldn't have been impressed by her.

Flora knew she was good at many things, but she was the first to admit they weren't particularly *impressive* things. She could restore a flagging plant to health, create a stunning bouquet, dance the tango, perform a perfect cartwheel, paint in watercolor and pastels, and turn random pieces of fabric into clothes. What she couldn't do was keep her living space neat and tidy, throw away a book, or stomach an oyster. And not in a million years would she want to run a business.

She straightened her shoulders and sucked her tummy in. "Your mommy was very beautiful."

"She was perfect in every way." The cool voice came from the doorway to the kitchen and Flora turned and saw a girl studying her. She wore skinny jeans, ripped at the knees, and a top that left most of her smooth, flat stomach exposed.

Her eyes were green like her father's, her skin a perfect ivory with hardly a blemish. She was older than Molly, a teenager, so presumably this had to be Izzy.

Flora had imagined some wounded, bruised, uncertain creature. She'd pictured a fractured family that she could somehow help to heal. This girl didn't look broken. She was frighteningly cool and the fierceness in her eyes suggested that help was not only unnecessary, it was unwelcome.

She stood in a relaxed dancer's pose, one foot resting against the other. Her hair, the same dark shade as her father's, fell straight and shiny over one shoulder, smooth and well behaved. Instinctively Flora brushed away one of the curls that bounced happily out of whichever style she'd attempted that morning. Never, in a million years, would she look as cool as this girl.

"Izzy." Jack reached out his hand. "Come and meet Flora. Flora, this is my Izzy." There was no missing the pride in his voice or the love in his eyes. His daughter flashed him a brief smile, before turning back to Flora.

"Isabella." She extended a hand, the formality reminding Flora of a job interview.

Molly chewed her finger. "You hate being called Isabella."

"By the people close to me, yes, but I prefer people I don't know to use my full name." Izzy played affectionately with her sister's hair and then pulled her close. "Don't bite your fingers. Did you get your reading book ready?"

"It's on the bed."

"Good girl. We'll read it together later."

It was clear to Flora that Izzy was sending a message.

We're a unit. A team. No outsiders allowed.

Her nerves multiplied, increasing from a few butterflies to an entire flock. She'd expected two children who were lost and a little bereft. She'd imagined being able to help. How could she have been so naive? They didn't want her here. She stood for a moment, frozen, suppressing the instinct to run.

She thought about Izzy's description of her mother.

*Perfect in every way.*

They might as well have said *there is no way you can ever match her, so don't even try.*

Flora took a breath. She wasn't trying to replace. She wasn't trying to match. And she wasn't going to pretend to be something she wasn't. Not this time. Not with Jack.

She decided to focus on the younger sister, who was probably the less scary of the two. "Do you dance, Molly?"

Molly shrank against her sister.

"Molly is a beautiful dancer," Jack said. "But she hasn't danced in a while."

Flora hadn't danced after her mother died, either. "I'd love to see you dance sometime."

Molly buried her face in Izzy's chest.

"Hey." Izzy gently shifted her away. "You don't have to do anything you don't want to do. But there's no need to hide. We face the things that scare us, right? Come and help me while I finish fixing dinner."

Flora felt uncomfortable. Was she the thing that scared them?

Molly took her sister's hand and scuffled with her into the kitchen.

Flora followed them into the room. "What a beautiful kitchen."

The room was filled with late evening sunlight. The windows faced over a garden shaded by tall trees, a lush oasis in this stark, urban desert. Close to the house was a bluestone patio, surrounded by Japanese maples and cherry trees. There were pots waiting to be planted, and Flora imagined the place in the height of summer, with color cascading from those pots.

Unlike the rest of the downstairs, this room was light and welcoming.

Molly watched her. "Mommy loved the garden."

Flora felt a rush of hope. At least the child was still speaking to her, even if she was clinging to her sister while she did it. "I love gardens, too. I work with flowers. I could plant those pots for you, if you like?"

"You're a guest. Guests don't work in the yard. Please do sit down, Flora." Izzy's smile was bright and brittle.

"Yes, sit down, Flora. You're not planting any pots. This is your night off. When it's the three of us we eat at the breakfast bar, but we've laid the table in your honor." Jack gestured to the table that was laid neatly with mats and napkins. He didn't seem to have noticed anything strange about Izzy's behavior. Flora wondered if she was being oversensitive. No one was entirely themselves the first time they met someone, as she knew only too well.

She sat down at the table and glanced at Jack, desperate for a hint of warmth or connection, but he wasn't looking at her.

"What would you like to drink?" He was friendly, but that was all.

She admired his self-control and understood it, but still she missed the intimacy that had become part of the time they spent together. It felt strange not to touch him, not to slip her hand into his and feel the warmth of his grip. There was a different kind of tension in the air. She wasn't sure if it was expectation or threat. The house seemed to be holding its breath.

Maybe Jack had accepted that tension was inevitable. She was the one at fault for assuming this would be easy. Families weren't something an outsider could easily join. She, of all people, should know that.

Still, she was determined to try. Blending in and pleasing people was something she was good at. She could do this. She *knew* how to do this.

"I made homemade lemonade." She produced the bottle from her oversize bag.

"Delicious. Thank you." Jack reached into a glass-fronted cabinet and pulled out tall glasses. "Girls? Lemonade?"

"Not for me, thank you." Izzy's smile was polite as she busied herself preparing food. "I'm avoiding sugar."

It was the sweetest cut. She'd had worse injuries handling roses, but for some reason this barb hurt more. It reminded her so much of her aunt. *Why did you waste time and money making that?*

Jack seemed more amused than annoyed. "I didn't see you holding back on the chocolate yesterday."

"Which is why I'm not eating or drinking sugar today. I'll have water." She strolled to the fridge, glass in hand, and filled it with ice and then water. Virtue shone from her and Jack pushed Molly's glass toward Flora.

"Lemonade is Molly's favorite. You're going to love this, honey."

Molly didn't mirror his enthusiasm, but she didn't reject the idea either so Flora poured the lemonade and held her breath. Was there a scarier audience than a seven-year-old?

Molly sipped cautiously.

Flora didn't breathe until she saw the child take a second sip.

Molly gave a tentative smile. "It's yummy."

It was like being given a promotion and a pay rise at the same time. She wanted to fall on Molly and sob with gratitude, but she managed to restrain herself.

"I'm glad you like it."

Izzy turned her back and smacked a pan down on the stove. "We're having veggie burgers. I hope that's all right."

"I hate veggie burgers," Molly said and Flora smiled.

She could sense the personality peeping through the layers of shyness. It gave her hope.

Izzy threw her sister an exasperated glance. "Since when? Last week they were your favorite. And it's Saturday. We always have veggie burgers on a Saturday."

"Because Mom liked them. But I hate them."

"How can you hate something so tasty? Izzy is a genius in the kitchen, Flora." Jack smiled at his daughter. "You should try her pancakes. When a day starts with those, it's impossible for it to be a bad one."

Izzy's smile vanished in a blink. "I only make those for breakfast." And it was clear from the rigid lines of her body that if she had her way Flora was never going to be invited for breakfast.

Flora moved the subject along. "Veggie burgers sound great. You made them yourself? I'm impressed. You'll have to give me the recipe. I love to cook."

"It was my mother's secret recipe."

The remark nudged Flora a little further out of the circle.

Izzy waited until the burgers were sizzling on the griddle, and then flipped them neatly.

Daunted by her cool competence, Flora focused on Molly. "Is your school close to here, Molly?"

Jack gently prized Molly's hand from her mouth. "Are you going to answer Flora?"

Flora thought the answer to that was going to be a quick shake of the head, but then Molly spoke.

"I can walk. Izzy takes me, because it's close to her school."

"That's kind of her."

"She's my sister," Izzy said. "It's what sisters do."

It seemed to Flora that Izzy was fulfilling more of a maternal role than a sisterly one, but she didn't have the experience to judge.

"She does it because Daddy has gone when I wake up," Molly said. "He goes to work early, but sometimes he comes home early to see me before bedtime." This volley of information earned her another frustrated glance from her sister.

"Have you washed your hands, Moll?"

"Yes. Clean." Molly waved her hands in the air. "Can I have more lemonade?"

"*May* I have," Izzy said, "and also I didn't hear a 'please.'"

"May I, please?" Molly pushed her glass forward and Flora topped it up.

Thank goodness for Molly. "My favorite subject at school was art. What's yours?"

"I used to like drawing." Molly sipped her drink. "But I don't anymore."

"I love to draw." Encouraged, Flora reached into her bag and pulled out the art pad and pencil she carried everywhere. "What's your favorite animal?"

Molly stared at her. "A fox."

Izzy frowned. "It's a giraffe."

"It's a fox." Molly was firm and Flora quickly sketched a fox, including a few trees in the background.

"There. You can keep it and color it if you like." She pushed the sketch across the table, hoping to tempt the little girl, but before Molly could grab it, Izzy snatched it up.

"Molly doesn't like coloring." Izzy walked the picture across the kitchen. For a moment Flora thought she was going to dump it in the recycling but then at the last minute she seemed to change her mind and put it down on the countertop. "Fetch the salad, Molly. It's ready in the fridge. And grab the ketchup. These are nearly ready."

What had she done wrong? Why wouldn't Izzy want Molly to color the picture?

Izzy toasted burger buns and put them on a plate in the center of the table, along with bowls of salad and the burgers themselves. "I didn't put them together—that way everyone can take what they want."

Flora decided that the best thing she could do with Izzy was make a fuss of the food.

She was about to reach for a bun when Izzy spoke.

"I wasn't sure if you'd want one, Flora. My mother never ate the bun. She avoided carbs."

Flora redirected her hand to the burger and salad and served herself. "I don't eat the bun, either." Her stomach argued loudly with her decision. Her brain argued, too, although a little more quietly. Was she really going to do this? Was she going to change her habits to please this girl? Yes, she was. She could hear Julia's voice in her head, telling her to be more assertive, but there was no point in being assertive if it destroyed all chances of developing a relationship. It was just one burger bun, that was all, and it wouldn't hurt her to skip the carbs.

Molly took a bite of burger, complete with toasted bun. "Are we having ice cream after?"

"We were, but you drank all that sugary lemonade so now we're having fruit." Izzy served herself, leaving Flora to deal with the full force of Molly's disappointment.

She was the killer of ice cream moments. The death of comfort.

Meanwhile, Izzy was cool and composed.

Flora studied her, trying to work out which emotions were bubbling beneath the composure. Resentment? Misery? Nothing was on show. And then she saw Izzy's hand tremble as she put a plate in front of her and realized she was nervous.

Instantly Flora's own nerves fell away. She wanted to say something to indicate that she was a friend, not a foe. She wanted to say that she probably understood at least some of what Izzy was feeling.

She glanced at Jack to see if he'd picked up the tension in his daughter, but if he had there was no sign of it. He was tucking into his burger and was focused on Molly, listening as she talked a little about her day.

"Marcy is having a sleepover for her birthday, but I don't want to go."

Jack helped himself to more salad. "You don't think it would be fun? You love Marcy."

Molly picked at her burger. "I want to stay home."

Flora felt a rush of sympathy. She remembered all too well those feelings of insecurity that had tied her to the house.

Jack frowned. "But—"

"—she doesn't have to go if she doesn't want to." Izzy ate daintily. "She can have Marcy over here the day after or something. We'll make cakes. Don't pick the lettuce out of your burger, Moll."

Molly poked the lettuce back inside her burger and took a martyred bite. "It tastes like grass."

"You've never eaten grass." Izzy's eyes crinkled at the corners as she smiled at her sister. Then she turned her attention back to Flora and the smile vanished as abruptly as lights in a power cut. "So, Flora, my dad says you're a florist." She was almost ridiculously formal, ticking off suitable conversational topics from a mental list.

Flora persevered. "Yes. I think my love of flowers came from my mother. She was a florist, too, and very talented.

There was no plant or flower she couldn't recognize." She hesitated. "I lost my mother when I was about the same age as Molly."

Molly reached for the ketchup. "Where did you lose her?"

"I mean—she died."

Izzy froze for a microsecond and Molly squirted ketchup on the table.

*Mistake*, Flora thought in a panic. Big, *big* mistake.

Molly's eyes were huge and shiny with tears. "Our mom died."

Izzy threw her napkin over the ketchup, sent Flora a furious look and put her arm around her sister. "It's okay, bunny. I'm here."

Flora felt sick. What had she done? It had all been going so well and now she'd blown it. "I'm so sorry that happened to you." Why, oh why, hadn't she stayed silent? She didn't even like talking about her own experiences. Instead of reassuring them, she'd left them feeling sad, threatened and anxious. And now they were bonded together against her.

Jack's gaze was fixed on Molly, and Flora could feel his helplessness, and his fierce determination to protect his daughters.

She hadn't made things better, she'd made them a thousand times worse.

"Come here." He scooped his younger daughter onto his lap and pulled her plate closer to his. Molly leaned into him, her head on his shoulder, strands of her hair clinging to his shirt.

"I miss Mommy." She crawled onto him, clinging with arms and legs, weighed down by sadness.

"I know. We all do, and that's okay." He held her with one arm and stroked her leg with the other. "But we have each other and we are going to stick together like all the ingredients in this yummy burger your sister just made."

"Can I stay on your lap?"

"Sure, although I might eat your burger by accident as well as my own. As long as you're okay with that." He was rewarded with a small laugh from his younger daughter.

Izzy was frantically rubbing the table even though the ketchup was long gone. Her cheeks were flushed and she kept blinking. Flora wanted to reach out and take that tense hand in hers, but she didn't dare. Instead she glanced at Jack to see if he'd noticed the reaction of his elder daughter, but his focus was on the younger.

Flora wanted to disappear. This was all her fault.

"I'm sorry I said that. I didn't—it was thoughtless."

Molly spoke from the safety of Jack's arms. "When your mommy died did you live with your daddy, like we do?"

Flora's breathing was shallow. She just wanted the conversation to stop, but she was the one who had started it.

"I moved in with my aunt. She was my only family. I lived with her until I moved into a place of my own. She died last year."

Izzy put her burger down. "You have no family? No one at all?"

Jack frowned. "Izzy—"

"I have lots of good friends," Flora said, "and friends can be like family." Except they weren't. None of them seemed to fill that big, empty gap inside her. Her aunt hadn't filled it, either. In some ways her aunt was the one who had made Flora aware of the big, empty gap. She'd done her duty and taken in a child, even though she'd never wanted children. Flora was constantly aware of her sacrifice. Guilt had shadowed her until the day she'd finally moved out.

"*Like* family," Izzy said. "But not *actually* family."

"Actual family have the same blood," Molly said helpfully. "They're related."

Flora managed a smile of assent and met Izzy's sharp gaze.

The girl said nothing more, but the message was clear.

Maybe Flora didn't have a family of her own, but there was no way she was moving in on this one.

# 4

## Izzy

Izzy was sprawled on Charlie's bed eating popcorn while her friends dressed for the party. Her dad was at home with Molly and this was supposedly her night to do her own thing and be a teenager. How? She felt about a hundred years old.

She joined in conversation about clothes and boys, but she wasn't thinking of the party. She was thinking about her dad and Flora.

Flora.

Had they seen each other again? How serious was it? She'd spent so long studying the two of them she'd almost burned the burgers. She'd imagined them sneaking away from work to be together. What did they do when they met at lunchtime? Were they sleeping together? Where? She was pretty sure they hadn't used the house, but there was always Flora's apartment.

She imagined them curled up naked on a large bed, surrounded by fresh flowers.

Were they in love? What happened if they *were* in love?

Suddenly it was hard to breathe. There was no air in the room.

"Izz? Are you even listening—" Avery thrust a bottle of nail polish under her nose. "This color?"

"Looks great." What if they decided to get married? Would her dad discuss it, or just announce it, like he'd announced that she was coming to dinner? She hadn't been given a choice. She hadn't been given a choice in any of the things that had happened to her lately.

Her life had been shattered. She still hadn't stuck together the pieces, and now it seemed the shape might change again.

Her friends collapsed with laughter over something Izzy had missed and she forced a smile, trying to join in. Did she used to find hair and nails and what she wore important? She couldn't even remember.

Drenched in panic, she tried to focus on her friends.

Music thumped out of the speakers and Izzy knew that any moment now Charlie's mother would holler upstairs to turn it down because she couldn't hear herself think. The predictability of it scratched at her skin.

It was Saturday night. In her previous life, Saturday nights were always reserved for friends, for hanging out, for doing teenage things. Being here should have felt good. Home made her think of her mom, and it was emotionally exhausting. Spending time with her friends should have been a distraction, but it wasn't. She felt displaced.

"Charlie!!" The voice came up the stairs, decibels louder than the music. "Turn that noise down, now!"

Charlie rolled her eyes and cranked up the volume. "I'm drowning her out. She's annoying the hell out of me. First it's my grades, then it's what I'm wearing, the way I'm talking…"

Avery blew on her nails. "I had a fight with my mom, too. She wanted me home by eleven. How embarrassing is that? Also, the car. They wanted me to learn to drive, and now there's like a fight every time I want to borrow it. I can't wait to go to college, and I'll be applying on the other side of the country to get away from the nagging."

There was a humming in Izzy's ears.

They moaned the whole time. About trivia. Stuff that just didn't matter. The contrast between what they thought was important and what she thought was important was so vast they might as well have been living on different continents. If she'd crawled past them bloodied and injured, would they even have noticed? That was how she felt on the inside.

Was she a terrible friend? If it mattered to them then it should matter to her, too, shouldn't it? Or were *they* terrible friends, not understanding how she felt?

She reminded herself that probably qualified as "all or nothing thinking." No one was terrible. Everyone was doing the best they could, but there were days when she felt their best wasn't enough for her.

There had been a time when the trivial stuff had mattered to her, too. What would she give now for her biggest worry to be whether she wore the blue top or the red top?

"The first thing I'm going to do when I'm in college is buy a new wardrobe and new makeup." Charlie swiped orange nail polish onto her nails. "Mom won't see how I'm spending my money, and if she does find out she won't be able to do anything. It's going to be so great to get away."

It didn't seem to occur to them that moaning about their mothers might be tactless. They were supposed to be her best friends, but these days she felt isolated and alone.

Freaked out by her own thoughts, she grabbed the can and knocked back her drink. The sudden rush of sugar gave her energy. Maybe the sugar was the reason she decided to speak up. Or maybe it was because she was sick of being silent and pretending she thought what they thought. Felt what they felt. Maybe part of her wanted to shock them. She wanted to shake them and tell them to wake up to what they had.

She'd had a fight with her mother, too, and she hadn't been given the chance to put it right. And now she had to handle those feelings all alone. She wouldn't want the same thing to happen to them.

If she could turn the clock back, her motto would be *a hug before bed, and nothing left unsaid.*

But how could she not have talked about that phone call she'd overheard? There was no way she could have ignored it, although maybe she should have found a way to have the conversation without shrieking.

"Your mom cares, that's all."

Charlie admired her nails, spreading her fingers until her hand looked like a starfish. "Yeah, that's what I'm telling you. She cares about herself. Everything has to be the way she wants it. I might add a glitter strip to this. What do you think?"

"She cares about *you*, you dumbass." Izzy scrunched the empty can in her hands, her knuckles turning white with the force of it. "She says all that stuff because she cares."

Charlie rolled her eyes. "You have no idea. You don't have any of this shit to deal with—" Her voice tailed off as she realized, too late, what she'd said.

"Yeah, I'm so lucky to have lost my mom. Makes life so much easier." Izzy didn't recognize her own voice. It was as high-pitched and shrill as the school fire alarm. If her friends had any sense they'd evacuate, but they didn't. They sat there gaping at her. "I bet you envy me. No one to tell me what to do. No one to tell me to turn my music down or wear my skirt longer. I mean it's great, really. I can't tell you how cool it is."

Charlie glanced at Avery. Avery turned pink and gave a tiny shake of her head, embarrassed and defensive at the same time.

Izzy was furious with herself. This was the second time in as many days that she'd lost it. What was happening to her?

Panicking because now she was going to have to have a conversation she didn't want, she slid off the bed and walked to the window.

"Ignore me. I'm tired, that's all."

"Sorry, Izz." Avery spoke in a small voice. "We weren't thinking. You know we didn't mean it that way. We were just being normal around you, that's all. You said you got sick of people tiptoeing. Treating you weirdly, like a freak, you know?"

She knew.

Izzy stared out the window, watching as Charlie's mother climbed into the car. Her mother had hated driving. She'd taken cabs everywhere. Everyone teased her because when she reversed out of the drive she often went across the corner of the grass, leaving deep gouges, stripes of brown across green. Izzy missed seeing those tire marks. Just one of those small details you didn't even notice until a person had gone.

She felt a sudden urge to tell Avery and Charlie what was going on, or at least part of it. They were supposed to be her friends. She should treat them the way you were supposed to treat friends. Maybe, if she did that, she'd feel normal for a few seconds.

"My dad is seeing someone."

There was a moment of shocked silence.

Avery dropped the nail polish back into her bag. "You mean, a woman?"

"Of course, a woman. Grief doesn't make you change your sexual orientation." She wrapped her arms round herself. Why did she feel so angry and moody all the time? Maybe she should join a gym. Take up kickboxing or something, instead of snapping the heads off those closest to her.

Avery sat down on the bed next to her, a gesture that reflected the impact of this news. "How do you know?"

"He brought her home."

"OMG you met her?" Charlie abandoned the makeup and flopped down on the bed, too. "What's she like?"

*Smiley,* Izzy thought. Smiley, pretty and absolutely nothing like Izzy's mother. Her mom would never have worn bright colors, or let her hair tumble wild over her shoulders the way Flora did. Flora was arty, a little bohemian and—

*Cool.*

Izzy sat, drenched in panic. Where had that thought come from? Flora wasn't cool, she was a homewrecker.

"Izz?" Charlie prompted her. "What's she like?"

What did it matter what she was like? They were asking all the wrong questions.

She wished now that she hadn't told them about Flora, but it was too late to take the words back.

"I met her for a couple of hours, that's all." But Flora had made her dad smile. Several times.

Izzy hadn't seen her dad smile properly in a long time. He delivered forced smiles of course. The ones that said he was doing okay. She knew all about those smiles. They originated from the outside and took so much effort your face ached. But spontaneous smiles? Smiles that came from inside, and were genuine? She hadn't seen one of those from her father before Flora came to dinner.

"Does she have kids of her own?"

"I don't think so." But she didn't know. She didn't know anything about Flora and she'd been so panicked and threatened to see another woman in the house she hadn't asked many questions.

"Probably doesn't have kids, or she would have talked about them. But let's hope she at least *likes* kids. Was she kind to Molly?" Charlie caught Avery's eye. "What? We've all read the stories about wicked stepmothers. And Cam's stepmother really is a witch. She brews all these herbs. It's seriously creepy. I never drink anything that hasn't come out of a sealed can when I'm over at his place."

Izzy's chest felt tight. "She's not going to be my stepmother." But they'd voiced her deepest fear. That this relationship wasn't casual. That it wasn't going to go away, it was simply going to get worse.

She imagined sleepwalking to the bathroom one morning and bumping into Flora. Worse, Molly bumping into Flora. Izzy would have to talk to her about sex. The thought made her sweat.

"I guess it might be nice to have an adult around," Avery said tentatively. "They could look after Molly and we'd see more of you. I mean, you're always busy doing stuff in the house."

"I don't mind. I like it."

She didn't want anyone interfering around the house, and she didn't want anyone else taking care of Molly. How could they? They wouldn't know how to handle her the way Izzy did. Having a stranger around would simply add to Molly's stress, and her little sister was already stressed enough. The night after Flora had come for dinner, Molly had taken ages to settle. When she'd eventually fallen asleep, she'd had the worst nightmare of her life. She'd woken up sobbing and it had taken Izzy over an hour to settle her down again. She'd almost fetched her dad, but she knew he had to be up early in the morning and although she'd never admit it to anyone, she liked the way it felt when Molly crawled into her bed. It gave her something to focus on other than herself. It kept her head in the moment, rather than allowing her brain free rein to explore the past and the future.

Her job was to keep everything as normal as possible in the home. To be indispensable. So she'd cuddled Molly, flicked on the low light her sister found comforting and read to her until she'd fallen asleep again. With Molly clinging to her, Izzy could pretend everything was going to be all right. Molly loved her. Molly needed her. Somehow, this whole mess would work out.

Izzy had wondered about the nightmare, though. Was Flora responsible? She felt angry with her dad for making a bad situation worse. Still, at least her dad and Flora hadn't been hugging and kissing at the table, so there was that. She'd been watching for it, ready to intervene if she witnessed any behavior unsuitable for Molly. But there was nothing. Izzy might have thought that her father and Flora were no more than friends if it hadn't been for that one glance. That one single, longing glance Flora had sent her father and that Izzy had seen.

He hadn't noticed because he'd been focused on Molly at the time, but Izzy had noticed.

"So, I mean—" Avery paused, like someone about to step onto ice and wondering if it would give way and drown her in frozen waters "—presumably he likes her or he wouldn't have brought her home to meet you. Meeting the kids is kind of a big deal."

How could a few words crush you?

She'd been trying to minimize it in her head. "Maybe."

"I guess it's not so surprising. Your dad is kinda hot."

Charlie made a choking sound. "That's gross."

"I mean for an older man. And don't pretend you haven't noticed."

Izzy longed for an ejector seat. She wanted to shoot herself out of the house, preferably to another planet. "This conversation is getting weird."

"Will she be going with you to England for your summer vacation?"

"What? No, of course not." She hadn't even thought of that, but she was thinking of it now and it made her dizzy. Flora at Lake Lodge? No way. Every year since Izzy was born they'd spent three weeks of the summer in the beautiful English Lake District with her mother's best friend and her family. Aunt Clare was her godmother. Their lakeside vacation was one of the highlights of Izzy's life. Exercise and excitement. Freedom and fresh air. Aiden.

*I love you, Izzy. Always have.*

Thinking about him calmed her a little. She hadn't shared the detail of last summer with anyone. Would she have done so if her mother hadn't died? She wasn't sure. At the time it had seemed too special and precious to share as a morsel of gossip. Her friends talked about boys the way they talked about mascara, comparing and contrasting qualities. Izzy didn't see Aiden that way. He wasn't one of those boys who was waiting for the right moment to shove his hand up your dress. When her bike had broken down, he'd fixed it. She could have fixed it herself the way her dad had taught her, but she'd liked the fact that he was prepared to get oil on his skin and sweat on his clothes to help her. She'd been convinced what they had was special, but time had eroded that conviction along with many others. Special last summer didn't mean special now, did it? Feelings changed. She wanted to turn the clock back to the time when her mother was alive, to the summer Aiden had told her he loved her and she'd believed him. To a time when life seemed simple and her thoughts were full of Aiden, and college, and possibilities.

If she'd known how much her life was about to change, she would have savored each second. The thought of not going to Lake Lodge and seeing Aiden again made her feel something close to desperation.

"But your aunt Clare was your mom's closest friend—" Although Charlie's voice tailed off, the implication of her words still hung in the air. Why would they spend the summer with their mother's closest friend when their mother was no longer with them?

"Not just my mom's. She's a family friend. Dad adores her, too. We all do." She didn't mention Aiden. She had to stop thinking about Aiden. He hadn't said those words since. The messages they'd exchanged had been factual. *Made the football team. Went sailing with Dad.* Love could die. People could die. "Molly would be gutted if we didn't go. We've been trying to keep everything the same."

Surely if there was a question of them not going, her father would have mentioned it?

An image of the lake floated into her mind. It was so peaceful there, the air fresh and clean. There was something about the awe-inspiring scenery that made problems shrink. Right now she badly needed hers to shrink. She was tired of being trapped in a place filled with memories of her mother. True, Lake Lodge was also somewhere she associated with her mother, but not in the same way as home. The house belonged to Aunt Clare and her family, and was filled with their family treasures and personal items. Izzy wouldn't be confronted by a large photograph of her mother when she came down to breakfast. Even the memories would be different. She remembered her mother lying on a sunlounger, a book open next to her, one knee bent as she talked to Clare. Her mother, curled up in the library while rain thundered against the windows and turned the waters of the lake choppy. Her mother had been a different person on those vacations, at least in the first few days. After that she'd become restless, longing to return to the fast lane.

Once, she'd taken Izzy's hand and pulled her toward the lawn that stretched all the way to the lakeside. "Listen," she'd said. "What do you hear? Nothing, right?"

Izzy had dutifully listened. "I hear birds? And the water." Faint splashes. The ripple of tiny waves as they hit the shoreline. They were the most relaxing sounds she'd ever heard. Izzy would have lived there if she could, but apparently her mother didn't agree.

"Exactly. Birds and water. Don't you miss the sounds of the city?"

Izzy didn't, but she felt pressure to give the answer her mother expected. Life was always simpler when things were the way her mother expected, so she'd nodded, and hadn't admitted that she loved the place with a passion. Not just the lake, but the Lodge. She loved the large windows and her turret bedroom with its views over the lake. She loved the fact that the house was lived in. The deep sofas were slightly worn, the furniture scuffed. Aunt Clare never expected you to take your shoes off or eat and drink only in the kitchen. It was a house that welcomed dogs and muddy boots, laughter and life in all its messy glory. Izzy was able to relax in a way she was never able to relax in her own home. In Brooklyn they basically lived in the kitchen and the bedrooms. The elegant living space was reserved for her parents and entertaining. In the Lakes there wasn't a single room that was out-of-bounds.

And then there was the enormous garden, with its deep, dark corners and tangle of ancient trees. The star of the show was the giant horse chestnut with its sturdy branches perfect for climbing. Izzy loved the lake with its glassy surface and deep sense of mystery. Most of all she loved the boathouse. She'd often wondered what it would be like to live somewhere like that. Maybe she wasn't a city person.

And it wasn't only the place she loved, it was the people.

When they were little, Izzy and Aiden would sneak out of bed and sit at the top of the stairs, listening to the clink of glasses and the musical sound of adult laughter. It had sounded so grown-up to Izzy, who had longed to be old enough to join them. Aiden had said it would probably be boring, but she didn't think so. Her mother and Clare had been at school together and were still best friends. Izzy envied their closeness. Every other sentence seemed to start with *Do you remember that time...*

Izzy wondered about that as she sat feeling isolated with her supposedly best friends. She tried to project herself forward ten years and imagine herself saying *Do you remember that time...* but her brain wouldn't play the game. She didn't want to remember this time.

She found it hard to talk to anyone, but she was sure she'd be able to talk to Aiden. He'd understand what she was going through. He always understood. They'd always been able to talk about anything and everything, maybe because they weren't bogged down in the day-to-day detail of each other's lives. There was something about rigging a boat on the lake and scrambling up craggy slopes that made talking natural and easy. She wished they lived closer. At the end of every summer they made the same promises to stay in touch but then life came in like the tide and washed away their good intentions. They were sucked into their own lives and the only news she had of him was what she saw popping up on social media, and everyone knew that was mostly fake. Aunt Clare had flown over for the funeral of course, and hugged Izzy so tightly she'd thought her bones would crack. She'd read a poem and talked about the importance of friendship. She'd looked terrible; pale and exhausted, her voice faltering as she'd spoken the words but Izzy knew she'd looked terrible, too. She'd been using every last ounce of energy to hold it together and hadn't said much to Clare.

Now, she wished she had. She wished she'd ask if their summer would be the same as it always had been. She'd just assumed, and the promise of a summer at Lake Lodge had been like a blanket warming her on a cold night. She wanted to feel the grass under her bare feet as she ran down toward the water's edge. She wanted to feel the breeze on her face early in the morning, and dip her limbs in the cool, clear water. Lake Lodge was the perfect summer retreat, a place she associated with happy times. Would it be weird without her mother there? Probably, but she loved it so much she thought it would probably be okay. Maybe she should email Aunt Clare, just to be sure.

Her friends were looking at her, waiting for cues.

Charlie gave an awkward shrug. "It must be weird, but I guess it's great, really, that he's happy."

Because she'd been thinking about Aiden it took a minute for her to realize they were talking about her dad.

They were basically saying she was selfish. That her feelings were all about her, when they should be about him.

Izzy felt more alone than she ever had in her life before.

She wanted her dad to be happy, of course she did, but what if his happiness meant hell for the rest of them? She didn't want him to be with Flora. She didn't want him to be with any woman. So what did that make her?

A bad person. She was a bad daughter. A bad friend. Bad.

She wished they'd talk about something else, but Avery didn't seem inclined to do that.

"So what next?"

"I don't know." And it was bothering her. She didn't like not knowing. She'd invested everything in doing what she could to keep life the same, and now her father had rocked the boat so hard it was taking on water.

She'd expected him to ask what she'd thought of Flora, but he hadn't. Did that mean he didn't care what she and Molly thought? Did they have no say in their future? Or did it mean he wasn't seeing her again?

Her spirits lifted a little as she focused on that possibility. If it was still on he'd be talking about her, wouldn't he? Inviting her round again. He hadn't mentioned her, and Izzy hadn't seen him leave the room to take a call.

The most likely explanation was that the relationship was over.

She felt a rush of optimism. If that was the case, then at least some of her problems were over, too.

# 5

## *Flora*

"So how was the date?" Julia tugged Flora into the cold store at the back of the shop. "The kids fell in love with you, right? You're their new mommy, and you're all going to live happily ever after."

*Hardly.*

The relationship was over. She'd blown it.

"It was…interesting." The evening had brought back memories of sitting at the table with her aunt. Flora had invariably picked at her food and wondered how it was possible to feel lonely when you were sitting across from another human being. She'd had the same feeling in Jack's house. "Little Molly was very shy, which is natural I'm sure. The older one was a little wary."

Wary? She was pretty sure Izzy had hated her on sight, and Flora had plunged in with her well-meaning conversation and people-pleasing techniques and made things worse. She didn't even blame them for rejecting her, but now the past churned around inside her like a deep, dark sludge.

It was pathetic that she should care so much about belonging and being accepted.

"Teenagers are always wary," Julia said. "Mine look at me suspiciously when I walk into the room. They're worried I'm going to ask them to do something. Welcome to family life."

She hadn't felt welcomed. Not by those who were alive, and not by those who were dead. Throughout the whole uncomfortable evening, Becca had been gazing down at her with those watchful sloe eyes. She'd smoldered down from the walls like a security system.

*Stay away from my family.*

Was it selfish to wish Becca hadn't had such a large visible presence in the home?

Yes, it was. Becca's pictures probably brought comfort to the children. And to Jack. She remembered how much it had hurt her when her aunt had packed away all the photographs of her mother. *Looking at them will make you unhappy. Remind you she's gone. Photographs simply kept the past alive.*

Flora had sneaked a photograph under her mattress. She'd looked at it every night and it had comforted her. Knowing that, how could she blame the children for wanting pictures of Becca on the walls?

She thought about Izzy.

"Do your teenagers cook and do a lot around the house?"

Julia gave a shout of laughter. "Are you kidding? I can't even get them to put a plate in the dishwasher without a fight."

"Izzy ran the house. She didn't seem like a typical teenager."

"A teenager is a unique and unpredictable animal. They

adapt to their surroundings." Julia frowned. "Which, now that I think about it, is probably the definition of a virus, too. Go figure. Even after they leave home you feel the aftereffects."

Her friend always managed to make her smile.

"She cooked. From scratch. Homemade burgers. Veggie. She even toasted the buns."

"And she's seventeen?" Julia's eyes widened. "Color me impressed. Lucky you."

She didn't feel lucky. She'd been so positive that she could make this work, that she could help, but she'd blown any chance of that by mentioning her mother.

Should she tell Julia about that? No, because then questions would follow. Questions Flora didn't want to answer. And she didn't want to admit to her stupid fantasy of showing up like Mary Poppins and transforming their lives.

She forced her mind back to work. "We need to scrub out these buckets and change the water."

"This job is all glamor. I'll scrub the buckets, you deal with the flowers and cut the stems. You're so good at that part. I mangle everything I touch." Julia picked up a bucket. "It seems to me that it went really well. I'm no psychologist, but it could have been a disaster. Those kids have had massive change forced upon them. They're trying to adjust, and then their dad brings home another woman. That could have gone badly."

It had gone badly.

"Mmm."

"You could have felt the need to compete with the dead wife."

"Trust me, there is no competing. Becca has already won hands down." That, at least, she could be honest about. "She's *the* Becca, of Becca's Body."

"Oh wow, I took one of her classes once. I needed a month of physio to recover."

"According to Izzy, everything she did, she did brilliantly."

Julia emptied out the old water and cleaned the bucket. "She loved her mother. We see those we love through rose-tinted glasses."

Or Izzy could have been exaggerating to make her feel small and insecure.

"Becca didn't have a single vice. She didn't eat carbs, she did a ton of stuff for charity. Even her hair did everything it was supposed to do." Thinking about it made Flora gloomy. "Just looking at her photo made me feel like a sloth. Her body was so hard and honed you would have bruised yourself if you'd bumped into her. I'm more of a soft landing."

"Flora—"

"You should have seen the pictures." She trimmed stems and put the flowers back into fresh water. "She was so thin and perfect."

"—and also no longer here," Julia said gently. "You don't need to compete, Flora. Be yourself. Be *you*. That's the woman Jack can't stay away from."

Being herself had never really worked for her in the past. She'd spent so many years trying to please her aunt that at some point she'd lost track of who she was.

Julia finished cleaning the last of the buckets. "So what happens next?"

"Nothing. He hasn't called."

"Is that unusual? How often does he usually call?"

"Every evening, before we go to sleep."

Julia stared at her. "What do you talk about?"

"I don't know. What we've done during the day, that kind of thing." They mostly focused on the present. She didn't talk about her past, and he didn't talk about his wife. And there was something intimate about those late-night conversations when they were both in bed. Not that they were in bed *together*, of course, but it was the next best thing and the closest they were going to get right now.

"If you're talking that often, you should definitely call him."

And force him to admit the kids didn't like her? The fact that he hadn't called told her everything she needed to know. She was braced for the most seismic, monumental rejection of all time. "I'll leave it for now."

"Coward." Julia helped put the flowers back in the buckets. "Maybe it's time you stopped talking and moved on to the action part of the relationship."

"That isn't an option." They were past that, and even if they weren't she wouldn't have been surprised if Izzy had installed cameras and alarms.

"Well you definitely can't take him back to yours. Your apartment isn't designed for passion." Julia frowned. "I'm not sure what it *is* designed for."

"It doesn't even matter." She cleaned the knife carefully. "It's over."

And she felt battered and bruised even though it hadn't actually happened yet.

Julia was frowning. "Flora, this is the first guy you have liked in a *long* time. Message him."

"If he wanted to get in touch, he would."

Julia thumped the bucket down. "I can't believe he hasn't at least called you. Men are spineless."

"He's not spineless. He is putting his kids first, which makes him a good dad." Both the kids were probably now in therapy, thanks to her tactless intervention.

Her phone beeped. She fumbled in her and her heart performed acrobatics as she read the message. "It's Jack. He wants us to meet in the park at lunchtime."

"There you go. Great news."

It wasn't great news. It meant face-to-face rejection, rather than being dumped by phone or text.

The mere *thought* of what was to come made her hyperventilate.

How should she handle it?

The answer came to her in a flash. She'd end it with him, sparing them both the pain of meeting face-to-face and pretending everything was fine.

She'd call him right now, and she wouldn't think about little Molly, with her pale face and faltering smile. Jack would never know that she was possibly in love with him, or that she'd had silly dreams about becoming part of his family.

She called his number, but he didn't pick up. He was probably already on his way to meet her, determined to do the right thing.

Left with no choice, she headed to the park.

Braced for this to be their final conversation, she was startled when he swept her up and kissed her under the falling blossom. His mouth, his breath, his words all mingled with hers as he guided her back into the sheltered shade of the cherry tree with strong hands and an unmistakable sense of purpose. She felt the roughness of the bark against her back and the hardness of his body pressing against hers. She closed her eyes and there was nothing but scent and sensation, an almost agonizing thrill that she'd never felt before. She melted under the skilled stroke of his tongue, and the knowing brush of his fingers. Her tummy clenched and her blood raced and she felt a thudding disappointment that their intimacy had never extended beyond erotic kisses. He kissed her with such ravenous hunger and frantic desperation, she assumed it had to be a prelude to goodbye.

She was going to be the one to say it first. But not right now. In a moment. It would be criminal to cut short a kiss this good.

"I missed you." He kissed his way from her mouth to her jaw, and from there to the delicate point where her neck met her shoulder. "And I owe you an apology."

She was struggling to think let alone talk. "Mmm?"

"For not getting in touch. I had a crisis at work, and then I had a parent teacher conference at school because Molly isn't doing so well, and between one thing and another time vanished." He dragged his gaze from her mouth to her eyes. "Single parent issues. I'm trying to be Mom and Dad."

"I understand. And I think you're doing an incredible job." And she had to end it right now before she fell any deeper.

"I'm not so sure. I forgot to take Dizzy the giraffe when we went the store yesterday. I underestimated the role he plays in each shopping expedition. I bought a brand of yogurt that apparently everyone but me knows is 'yucky,' and I left Molly's drink at home so I grabbed something from the shelf that I was later told had so much sugar in it her teeth will probably fall out by Friday." He kept his arms round her. "And then there was the conversation. I wasn't expecting to have to answer a question about where babies come from in the baked goods aisle."

"She asked? Oh that's adorable." *End it, Flora! Just end it.*

"In a very loud voice. She saw a baby in a stroller. I tried telling her that the baby had come from the car just outside, but she didn't buy it. She wanted to know its entire life history from conception to birth."

Flora could picture Molly, wide-eyed, and Jack, stumbling and fumbling. Even in her current state of stress, the thought of it amused her.

"I assume you do know where babies come from?" They were breaking up and she was flirting? She was treating this like a final fun date. Was she a masochist?

"I have a vague clue, although I confess that the sexual frustration I've suffered lately may have caused a degree of brain damage. In the end I gave her a very brief and basic explanation, based on advice given by a bunch of articles I found on the internet when I was searching on my phone while loading the cart with bagels. Again, the wrong ones because apparently we don't eat whole wheat. In case you didn't already know, there are a lot of 'yucky' foods on sale out there. I had no idea she was so fussy, but I didn't used to do the shopping. And she's having such a rough time I don't want to take a stand over things like food."

"You said she was having problems at school. Has something specific happened?" She promised herself that she'd end it just as soon as she'd had an update on his daughter.

He hesitated. "Nothing. Don't worry. It's not your problem."

He was right. It wasn't her problem.

*End it, Flora, end it.*

"We're friends, Jack. Friends share the things that worry them." It wasn't strictly true. She rarely shared what worried her, but this wasn't about her. Right now there was a little girl hurting the way she had once hurt. "Tell me about Molly." She tugged him across the grass to the nearest empty bench.

He stretched out his legs. "Molly's always been a talker. Confident. Outgoing. The problem was getting her to listen, not getting her to speak, but now she rarely speaks in class. Since Becca died, she's been withdrawn and quiet. The night you visited, I barely recognized her. The old Molly would have been chatting about everything, showing you her toys, demanding that you watch her dance. She loved to dance."

Flora's heart ached for her. "Her world has changed, and she hasn't yet changed with it. But she'll dance again one day, I'm sure of it."

"Were you the same?"

"Changed? Of course. Nothing in my life stayed the same." She didn't usually talk about it, but if her experience could help Molly in some small way then she was willing to do so. And they were about to break up anyway so there didn't seem much point in guarding her words or trying to protect herself. "I didn't only lose my mother, I lost my home and the world I knew. It will take time for Molly to adjust to her new normal. I expect her emotions are all over the place." And she'd probably made it worse.

"I've noticed that occasionally she'll laugh at something and then she immediately stops and looks horrified. It's as if she thinks she's not allowed to have fun anymore."

Flora understood that. "You feel guilty. Disloyal. And you're afraid that if you laugh, it might appear that you loved the person less."

"Can you remember when you started to feel like your old self?"

This conversation was becoming more personal than she'd intended.

"No one stays the same throughout their life. We're all changed and formed by the things that happen to us and to the people we love. And people carry on, even when they're wounded." As, no doubt, she was about to prove yet again.

"Did it get easier?" He shifted on the seat so he could see her face properly. "And don't sugarcoat it. I genuinely want to know. It's been a year. I need to figure out what I can do to help Molly."

Molly. She'd finish the conversation about Molly and then she'd end it.

"If anything the second year was harder than the first for me. Everyone else had moved on. People forgot. But I didn't. The reminders were constant. Every time there was a parent teacher evening, every time my friends moaned about their parents." Thinking about it ripped her open. Why was she doing this to herself?

Molly. She was doing it for Molly.

"Did anything help?"

"A teacher at my school suggested I write down everything I could remember about my mother. That turned out to be comforting."

"That's a good idea. I'll try that." He stood up and held out his hand. "Let's walk. What sort of person were you back then? How did you change?"

"I became anxious." She strolled with him along the path, trying not to think that this might be the last time. "I was wrenched away from everything I knew, and I found it hard to find any comfort or sense of safety in my new life. All I wanted was my mom. I felt very insecure."

"Makes sense. You'd seen everything disappear. You couldn't trust in the permanence of anything."

"Exactly."

"And your aunt made you feel like an outsider." His hand tightened on hers. "And yet you handled it, and you've grown into this great person—" he stopped walking and pulled her toward him "—and that makes me a little less worried for my girls."

Flora wasn't sure she should be a source of inspiration to anyone. She often thought her life was a total mess.

On the other hand she *had* handled it. And it was true that she had major insecurities, but she was handling those, too.

Normally she was guarded, but she'd just told him things she hadn't told anyone before and was still in one piece.

"How is Izzy doing?"

"She's really stepped up. I'm proud of her. I worry about her, of course, but I'm assuming a few ups and downs are natural and on the whole she's coping remarkably well. You saw her the other night—she has it all sorted."

Flora didn't think she had anything sorted. "Was she always helpful around the home?"

"No. Typical teenager I suppose. Mostly focused on herself. Becca had a thing about mess. She liked everything to be neat and tidy, and Izzy was never tidy so there were a few explosions about that. But now she's my superstar. I couldn't manage without her. And she has so much patience with her sister." He tugged her out of the path of a mother jogging with a stroller. "Izzy was especially close to her mother, so it's hard for her, but you'd never know it."

She'd known.

Flora thought about the tension in those hands as they'd cleaned up ketchup.

She wanted to ask if she'd made things harder by visiting, but she already knew the answer to that one. "It must be hard for all of you, but your girls will be okay because they have each other and they have you. Molly is probably feeling insecure, but you are so good with her, so present and so is Izzy, that the feeling will fade in time. And she still has her home, her school and her friends. She's going to be okay, I'm sure she is. So is Izzy. It helps that you're so willing to talk about it."

"Does it help you to talk about it?"

"I don't know. I've never talked about it before." She saw the shock in his face.

"Never?"

"No." These were intimate, private details and she'd never been close enough to anyone to contemplate sharing.

"You can talk to me." He pulled her against him. "Anytime."

How was she going to do that when they were about to break up?

She stayed with her head resting against his chest for a moment, just a moment. Finally, when she was confident she wasn't going to bawl like a baby with a bad attack of colic, she eased away from him. "What about you, Jack? How are you doing?" He'd listened to her, so it was only fair she did the same for him.

"Me? I'm fine."

"You can't be fine, Jack."

He took a deep breath. "I'm handling it. It's the girls I worry about."

Maybe he just didn't want to talk about himself.

She tried not to feel hurt that he wouldn't share his feelings with her.

"Jack—"

"And now I'm feeling guilty." He tightened his grip on her hand. "I haven't seen you in days and all I've done is talk about the children."

It felt to Flora as if all they'd done was talk about her, and the combination of truth and trust had created a new intimacy between them. An unwanted intimacy, given the circumstances.

And she couldn't stand the waiting any longer. "Look, Jack, I appreciate you meeting me. It's brave of you to do this in person."

"Do what in person?" His fingers were in her hair. His mouth brushed the corner of hers, his lips teasing and lingering.

She closed her eyes.

Maybe she could allow herself one more kiss. Just one.

"End it. Face-to-face."

He lifted his head abruptly. "End it? Why would you think I'm going to end it?"

She reeled slightly. Opened her eyes. "Aren't you?"

"No!"

"Jack, we both know the evening didn't go that well. And I'm not taking it personally. Introducing another woman to your children is a really big deal. I don't blame you for thinking it's all too much." Her own feelings rose inside her and she pushed them down. "I guess the timing was all wrong."

"I have no idea what you're talking about." He lifted her chin with his fingers. "The kids loved you. You were a hit. The evening went well."

It had been one of the most uncomfortable evenings of her life.

"I—I thought Izzy was a little—" How should she put it tactfully? "It was a big deal having me in the house."

"It was a big deal, yes. It came as a shock to her when I mentioned that you were coming, but that's not surprising in the circumstances. I was a bit concerned about how she'd handle it, but she seemed fine about it." He frowned, searching his memory. "Did Izzy say something to you? Something I missed?"

"No."

"Then why would you think she had a problem with you? She was polite."

"Yes."

Flora thought about the looks, and the questions. The subtle comments. Had he really not noticed? "She seemed a little tense."

"Teenagers are almost always tense about something.

Work. Friends. The planet. Life in general. They are a seething mass of hormones on a good day. And then she's dealing with this, too. She misses her mother. That's all you were seeing. Kids are always wary when they meet someone new, and this was never going to be easy. But I understand why you'd be wary. You felt unwelcome at your aunt's, and you're assuming you're unwelcome now."

The fact that he knew that much about her was scary but also refreshing and a little thrilling.

It seemed he wasn't suggesting they break up.

So now what?

Should she go through with her plan and end it now? What if they carried on and broke up in a few months when she'd fallen even harder for him? For the first time in her life, she felt a true connection with someone and presumably that connection would only grow deeper.

On the other hand, there was still the children.

"Oh I forgot—" Jack reached into his pocket and pulled out a sheet of paper. "This is for you."

"Me?" She unfolded it and swallowed. "It's the picture I drew for Molly."

"She colored it. Spent ages on it, trying to make it as good as possible. It felt like progress actually. She hasn't picked up a coloring pencil since her mom died. Anyway, she wanted you to have it."

"She—me?"

"Yes. I don't know how I could have forgotten. I've been carrying it around for days. She wanted you to have it and put it on your wall."

Molly had thought about her. Molly had given her a picture. Molly wanted her to put it on her wall.

Her throat felt thick. Emotion filled her chest. She felt light-headed and realized she was breathing too fast.

"I love it." It was the most beautiful thing she'd ever seen. Yes, the coloring was outside the lines, but who cared? *Molly.* "I'm definitely going to put it on my wall. I'm going to frame it."

He smiled. "You don't need to frame it, Flora."

"I do. Knowing that she colored it for me means so much." It was a little freaky to admit just how much but perhaps he guessed because he pulled her close.

"The other night was an ordeal for you, wasn't it? You're the one who probably wants to end it because this situation is so complicated and messy."

"End it?" She was croaky. "What makes you think I want to end it?" She held the picture away from him so he didn't crumple it more than he had already. She'd iron it before she framed it.

"Ours will never be a simple relationship. And maybe I should let you go, but I'm not that selfless."

"Good." Her insides flipped over as she thought what might have happened if she'd spoken up sooner. "I wouldn't know what to do with a simple relationship. Give me an emotional mess any day."

He made a sound that was half laugh, half groan. "I don't want this to stop, Flora." He cupped her face in his hands. "Being with you makes me smile, and I didn't think I'd ever want to smile again. You make me happy. I like to think I make you happy, too."

"You do." It was the happiest she'd ever been in her life. Her thoughts floated to a place she'd never allowed them to go before. Surely, feeling this way, there was no problem that together they couldn't overcome?

Molly had colored in the picture. Molly wanted her to hang it on her wall.

And now the only thought in her head was *We'll make this work. Somehow, we'll make this work.*

True, there was still Izzy to worry about but a teenager was bound to be more complex than a younger child and no one built a relationship in one meeting. It was going to take time, and Flora was willing to put in whatever time was necessary.

Jack didn't seem to think there was a problem, and he knew his own child better than she did. Didn't he?

# 6

## *Izzy*

"She's late." Izzy checked the soufflé. It had been her mother's dinner party showpiece and it was Molly's favorite, but it wasn't a dish that forgave late arrivals. Why had she picked something so complicated? Because hopefully soufflé was something the saintly Flora couldn't cook. *Intimidation by soufflé.* "What time did you tell her?"

"Midday. And she has today off, so I'm sure she'll be here any minute. Smells delicious, Izz. What can I do to help?"

*Break up with her and focus on the family.*

She glanced at her father. "You could call her. Check what time she'll be here? Maybe she's one of those people who is relaxed about timing." And she knew her father liked people to be where they said they were going to be, when they said they'd be there.

"Call her, Dad." *Make her feel bad.*

"Good idea." He pulled out his phone and dialed, and Izzy tried not to mind that he didn't even have to search for the number.

She turned away and pulled oil and vinegar out of the cupboard to mix a dressing for the salad.

"Flora? Is everything okay?" Her dad's voice had an edge of sharpness. "We were expecting you at twelve."

*And you're late*, Izzy thought happily. *You are so, so late and my dad is going to hate that.*

*You are probably already in his rearview mirror.*

*Goodbye, Flora.*

She wore her best martyred expression as she pulled the soufflé out of the oven. Maybe she'd mention that she would never have chosen to make that if she'd known Flora wouldn't be on time. Her dad would feel guilty and annoyed. Flora would be flustered and embarrassed, and Izzy would be forgiving and generous.

Her plan was blown apart by her father's next words.

"You're kidding! When? How?" His tone hardened. "Did you call your landlord?"

Izzy rarely saw her dad angry. He was always even tempered and calm and he never reacted with emotion. But he was showing emotion now.

"Dad?"

His knuckles were white on the phone. "Give me his number—" There was a pause while he listened. "Yes, I know you can handle it yourself, but—" Another pause and Izzy saw her dad pull in a deep breath. "Okay, okay. I won't interfere, but—" He pressed his fingers to the bridge of his nose the way he only ever did when he was stressed. "I know I'm being overprotective."

Since when had her dad been overprotective? He was a

great believer in equality. He claimed to be a feminist, although Izzy wasn't convinced.

But something about Flora's current predicament seemed to have triggered his most basic instincts.

Izzy wondered what excuse Flora had come up with. Whatever it was, it was a good one, and clearly lunch wasn't going to be consumed anytime soon.

Accepting the imminent death of her soufflé, she poured vinegar into the oil. They didn't mix. It made her think of her family. They were the oil, and Flora was the vinegar. Right now she was sitting in the middle of them, turning everything acid.

"That's terrible. You should stay here," her father was saying. "We have plenty of room."

Oil and vinegar forgotten, Izzy felt a lurch of panic. "Dad?"

He threw her a reassuring smile, but Izzy wasn't reassured. She didn't like the tone of her father's voice. Gentle. Caring. It was a voice you used with someone you loved, not a casual friend in trouble. "What's happening?"

Her father lifted his hand to stop her talking, and turned back to his conversation. "Flora, I insist. You need somewhere to live until it's fixed."

Live? Live?

*What the—*

This sounded like so much more than a lunch invitation.

Inside her head, where she lived most of her life now, Izzy used a word that she knew would get her grounded for weeks if she said it aloud.

"Grab a cab," her father was saying, "I'll pay when you arrive."

Why would he pay? Couldn't Flora afford a cab?

Flora worked in a flower shop. It wasn't a job Izzy had ever thought about. What did a florist even do?

Maybe money *was* a factor in the relationship.

Her father ended the call and Izzy held her breath. Please let it be something simple. Please don't let it be as bad as it sounded.

"Dad?"

He turned, distracted. "Sorry. Poor Flora. What a morning."

"What happened?"

"Her home has flooded. A pipe burst in the apartment above her or something. The ceiling came down. There's plaster all over her bed. Everything is underwater and most of her things are ruined. Such bad luck. Can you believe that?"

She could believe the bad luck part. Since her mother had died life had poured nothing but crap on her. What she was less inclined to believe was Flora's sob story.

Was her apartment really flooded, or was it a ploy?

Her father was being taken for a ride.

Izzy's brain switched into journalist mode. The first step was to verify the story. She wasn't going to be one of those journalists who were casual with the truth. Her readers were going to be able to trust every word she wrote and spoke. And she was starting right now. She was going to take a look at the "flood."

"Poor Flora. How could you even think of asking her to grab a cab? She must be in such a state. We should go get her, Dad."

"Get her?"

"If her stuff is underwater, how is she going to rescue it all by herself? We can all help." And they could all witness the fact that the "flood" was nothing more than a figment of Flora's imagination.

Izzy had a brief daydream where she became an undercover reporter, rooting out lies and dishonesty. Corrupt CEOs would hear her name and tremble. They'd be afraid to take her calls or give an interview because they'd know she was coming for them.

"What about your soufflé?"

Did a journalist following the scent of a story pause to worry about food? They did not.

She shrugged. "What does food matter when a person is in trouble?"

Her father reached out and hugged her. "You're a thoughtful girl, Izzy."

She wasn't thoughtful. She was fighting for her place in this family, although he didn't know that of course. "Let's go. I'll rescue the soufflé and you call a cab and get Molly ready."

"I should probably tell Flora we're coming."

"Let's surprise her." She didn't put it past Flora to throw a bucket of water over the floor of her apartment if she needed to. "It will be spontaneous and supportive if we just show up."

"Great idea. How did I end up with someone as special as you?"

"You got lucky, I guess." Izzy made the joke and pushed aside the guilt. It was all in a good cause. He'd thank her later. Maybe he'd even admit it had been a massive mistake.

*From now on it's just the three of us. I don't need anyone but you and Molly.*

They wrangled Molly into the cab and headed into Manhattan. As usual the traffic was grim, which meant plenty of thinking time. As views of the skyline flashed past the windows, Izzy pondered the likely scenario awaiting them and Flora's speechless embarrassment at being caught out.

In the end, she was the one who was speechless.

As they stood in the doorway of Flora's apartment, Molly stared in wonder from the safety of her father's arms. "Why is your home underwater?"

"A pipe burst in the apartment upstairs and it brought my ceiling down and flooded everywhere. I've had an exciting morning." Flora was bright and cheerful, but Izzy could tell she was close to tears. Her voice was high-pitched and her smile was a little too wide.

*Brave*, Izzy thought grudgingly. If it had been her apartment—and please God don't ever let her live anywhere this bad—she would have fallen face-first into the flood and tried to drown herself.

Now Izzy was wishing they hadn't come and seen it in person. It was truly awful. She was pretty sure the apartment Flora lived in didn't look that great when it was dry, but with water sloshing around the ankles it was dank and depressing. Izzy couldn't believe anyone lived here.

The uncomfortable images she'd had of her father and Flora using her apartment for secret sex vanished. There was nothing romantic about this place. She'd seen her father's bank account online and there had been no hotel bills, so unless Flora was paying, which seemed unlikely given the fact that she couldn't afford a cab over to Brooklyn, they still hadn't had sex.

That gave Izzy hope. Sex wasn't always serious, she knew that. Half her friends had done it just because they felt it was time, not because they were "in love." But she had a feeling that for her father sex would make a relationship serious.

Her mother had always said that she'd married Jack because he was a forever type of guy.

Izzy wished she hadn't had that thought because now she was thinking of her mother and with the thoughts came utter misery followed by anger. Why? *Why?*

Her parents should have been together forever. They should have lived side by side until they were both old and boring and had no teeth, and instead—

Izzy gulped.

Right now she badly needed her dad *not* to be a forever type. She needed him to be a one-night-stand type. The type who moved on.

She tensed as he shifted Molly onto his hip and reached out his free arm to Flora.

"Come here."

The fact that he was willing to comfort her in front of Molly alarmed Izzy more than the water sloshing round her ankles.

"Probably best not to give me sympathy. I don't want to raise the water level farther by crying." Flora stepped away from him and squelched her way across what had presumably once been a carpet, toward a bed. "I managed to rescue some of my books, and my laptop is fine. My clothes are mostly ruined but it's all replaceable. It's people that matter, not things."

Did she seriously mean that?

Molly pointed. "You saved my picture!"

Izzy followed the direction of her sister's finger and there, sure enough, was the fox Flora had drawn. *Seriously? All your worldly goods were under threat and you saved a stupid piece of coloring?*

Flora was smiling. "Of course I saved your picture. It's my favorite thing. I didn't want it to be damaged."

Molly preened and Izzy gnashed her teeth.

It was just a fox, not a van Gogh. "Were you in the bed when the ceiling came down?"

"No. Fortunately I felt water dripping on me and got out of bed to investigate about two minutes before it collapsed." Flora rubbed her hands over her arms and stared at the mess. "It's my fault."

"What?" Even Izzy, who was desperately looking to blame Flora for everything and anything, couldn't see how one person could have caused this. "How?"

"There was a weird stain on the ceiling. I've watched it slowly growing. I mentioned it to the landlord, but he didn't bother investigating. Now it seems it was probably a slow leak from the pipe in the upstairs bathroom. I should have been a little more forceful."

Izzy stared at the mess. "You should."

Flora straightened her back. "The landlord has called a plumber. And the insurance people are coming to take a look. He'll fix it, I'm sure."

She didn't look sure and Izzy, who knew nothing about home maintenance, was even less sure. Could this place be fixed? It seemed to her that it should be knocked down.

She felt a sinking feeling in her gut as her father reached out and pulled Flora against him in a protective gesture that Izzy wished she hadn't witnessed. He *cared*.

And this time Flora didn't resist. She clung to him as if he was a lifeboat. There was so much water in the place that had there been an actual real lifeboat Izzy might have jumped in, too.

The tightening of her father's mouth was a blow to the gut. When her father wore that look he always won whatever fight he and her mother were having. Her mother would shriek hysterically and wave her arms like the original drama queen and her father would stand strong and steady and wait until she'd finished to make his point.

"You're staying with us. No arguments."

*I have arguments*, Izzy thought. *I have a ton of arguments.*

Flora shook her head. "That would be too much of an imposition."

*Yes. It would.*

A few hours ago she'd been alarmed at the thought of Flora coming over for lunch, and now she was moving in. And Izzy couldn't even accuse her of engineering it. Even she didn't believe Flora had somehow sneaked into the apartment upstairs and flooded it.

"But where will you go? You can't stay with your family," Molly said, round-eyed, "because you don't have family."

Izzy made a mental note to talk to her sister about tact and diplomacy at some point, but right now she had other priorities.

"Don't you have friends?" The words burst from her mouth before she could stop them. "Can't they help you?" Her friends had been pretty crap, but it didn't stop her from hoping that there were better versions out there somewhere.

Flora gave another one of her brave smiles. "My closest friend is Julia."

Izzy breathed a sigh of relief. Flora had a friend called Julia. She was going to stay with Julia. She didn't have to live with them. "You should call her right away. We can help you move there."

"I can't stay with her, even for a few nights." Flora extracted herself from the circle of Jack's arm and seemed to pull herself together. "She has three kids and their apartment is tiny."

Izzy was about to say that if they were used to feeling cramped then one more wouldn't make a difference, but her dad was shaking his head.

"And we're not talking about a couple of nights, honey. This is going to take a while to fix."

Honey? *Honey?* He called *her* honey.

"I know. And I've already decided to find a new apartment. I should have done it a while ago." Flora looked a little stunned as she looked around her. "The place was supposed to be my dream, but—" She broke off and Izzy waited for the end of the sentence.

But what?

She opened her mouth to say *If this was your dream, what do your nightmares look like*, and then realized that would simply emphasize the fact that Flora needed alternate accommodation.

Her dad was clearly thinking the way she was. "If you're looking for a new apartment, all the more reason to have somewhere else to stay for a while. You don't want to rush a big decision like that. What do you think, girls?" He shifted Molly onto his other hip. "We have plenty of room for Flora, don't we?"

Molly nodded. "You can live with us. You won't fit into my clothes, but I can lend you toys."

Flora's eyes misted. "You're far too kind."

She wasn't wrong about that.

Izzy wanted to put her hand over her sister's mouth. Molly had been virtually mute when Flora had come over to dinner. Izzy wished the trend had continued. "Flora isn't going to live with us, Molly. She's going to *stay* with us."

Molly twisted her hair round her finger. "I said that."

"When you live with someone it's forever, and this won't be forever. It's temporary."

Both her father and Flora turned to look at her.

Flora spoke first. "This is an imposition. Are you all sure about this?"

Izzy tensed.

Her father and Molly were both nodding. They looked at her, waiting for her to join in welcoming Flora to their home.

The horror of it choked her. Flora was moving in. She'd be there for breakfast, lunch and dinner. She'd be part of the family. She'd probably try to help out as much as possible around the house, and that was Izzy's job. Her father said she was his superstar, but how could she carry on being his superstar if Flora took over? What would her role be? She wouldn't be needed, and if she wasn't needed—

"Izzy?"

Her dad was looking at her. She licked her lips. "Yeah, I'm sure." Sure it was going to be a disaster for her. She wanted to run to her dad and hug him. She wanted to tell him everything, all the awful stuff she was hiding, but she knew she couldn't. She'd never felt so alone in her life.

All she could do was hope Flora didn't get too comfortable. And she could probably help with that part.

"The guest room is already made up," she said politely, "because I changed the sheets after we last had guests."

Maybe, while Flora was eating lunch, she'd put a few additional touches to the room to remind her this wasn't home. More photos of her mother wouldn't hurt, just so that no one forgot what was really going on here.

Flora's eyes turned shiny. "You're all so generous."

"You're welcome," Molly said kindly. "And now can we have lunch? I'm very hungry."

Izzy thought about the soufflé, collapsed and sad on the

kitchen table. She felt exactly like that soufflé. To think she'd been worried about today. This was so much worse.

Flora wasn't just joining them for lunch. She was moving in.

# 7

## *Flora*

"This is where you'll be staying." Izzy flung open a door and Flora hovered on the threshold of the room, feeling a little sick and shaky. In the time it had taken to load Flora's things into bags and battle the traffic back to Brooklyn, the afternoon had slowly drained away. On the drive Izzy had assured her that a ruined lunch didn't matter one bit, in a tone so cheerful that it was clear it mattered a great deal. Judging from the glint in Izzy's eye, she didn't just think Flora had ruined her lunch—she thought she'd ruined her life.

If Jack hadn't been so caring and Molly completely adorable, she would have decided right away that this was a bad idea. Molly's offer to lend her toys had almost made her bawl.

Aware that Izzy was watching her, she stepped into the room.

Light flooded through the windows. After a stressful

and emotional day, a feeling of calm swept over her. The kaleidoscope of anxiety stopped turning in her head. The room was decorated in neutral shades of gray and cream. Flora had an urge to add a few touches of color; cushions in vibrant jewel colors to the bed, wild meadow flowers in a vase. But she wasn't complaining.

She was used to dark and damp, and this was sunny and spacious with glorious views over the pretty garden. Cherry trees clustered together with bridal beauty, and the explosion of creamy pink blossom brought back such vivid memories of her mother that she almost doubled over. Most of her memories had faded, blurred by the passage of time, but one remained in her head with startling clarity. They'd visited the Botanic Garden in Brooklyn, near Prospect Park. Her mother had made a picnic and they'd sat on the grass in the sunshine, admiring the pastel perfection of the blossom. Later, her mother had painted the scene and Flora had hung it on her wall. It was the first thing she'd rescued when the water had started pouring into her apartment.

The view from this room would be beautiful all year round, but she guessed it would never be more beautiful than it was right now. She wanted to collapse onto that wide comfortable bed, wrap herself in the soft cream throw and just admire the colors through the window. She wanted to switch off the part of her brain that was worrying she was never going to persuade Izzy to trust her. A large rug covered the wide oak planks. There was an armchair by one of the windows, and next to it a small table stacked with books. At the end of the room was a fireplace, which gave the room a cozy feel even though it wasn't lit.

If she could have chosen her perfect house it probably would have been this one, although she would have decorated it differently of course. It nestled comfortably among the neighboring buildings, sure of its place. Belonging.

She glanced at Izzy, and encountered a frozen look of despair in the few seconds before she masked it.

She should have gone to Julia's and shared a bed with Kaitlin.

"It's kind of you to do this for me," she said, and Izzy's smile was stiff and frozen.

"You're welcome."

Flora almost wished Izzy would yell and cry and tell her she didn't want her here. At least then she'd know what she was dealing with.

They'd arrived with Flora's bag of damp belongings and Izzy had insisted on being the one to take Flora upstairs while Jack and Molly unloaded the pathetic dregs of Flora's life from the car to the house. *I'll show Flora round and help her feel at home.*

Flora had a feeling she was being tested. "It's a beautiful room, Izzy." It was beautiful, if a little clinical for her tastes. She preferred a room to feel lived in, and to be filled with individual touches. This room was like staying in a very upmarket hotel.

"My mother designed it. She was very stylish."

"I can see that." The implication was that Flora wasn't stylish, but she didn't blame Izzy for thinking that given the state of her apartment.

She imagined Becca standing in this room, her dancer's body perfectly poised and balanced as she made decisions. *We'll keep the color scheme neutral and add touches of luxury with drapes and cushions.*

She would have stood in front of that full-length mirror and flung open windows to let in blossom-scented air. She would have stroked her well-behaved dark hair over her shoulder and laughed a throaty laugh, utterly at home in these sumptuous surroundings and sure of Jack's love.

Flora had never been sure of anyone's love except her mother's, and she could barely even remember how that felt now. The yearning was so powerful her insides felt hollowed out. It wasn't only that she missed her mother, she missed the possibilities and the promise of the life they might have shared, the laughs, the trips, the confidences. She'd missed out on so many special moments.

Half a dozen photos were clustered on the nightstand and without thinking Flora picked one of them up.

"That's my mother on top of Mount Kilimanjaro," Izzy said. "She climbed it to raise money for charity."

Of course she did. "That's—impressive."

"She loved a challenge. There was nothing she couldn't do." Izzy snatched up another photo, gripping it until her fingers whitened. "This is her crossing the finishing line of the New York Marathon. And here—" she grabbed another one "—this was taken after she'd rowed the Atlantic with five other women. One of the TV stations filmed a documentary on it. It was an insane adventure and a huge achievement. She believed very strongly that it was important to live a meaningful life." She laid out her mother's qualities like tiny stones, presumably hoping they'd become stuck in Flora's feet.

"So impressive." Flora was out of adjectives. Her vocabulary wasn't expansive enough to acknowledge Becca's many qualities with any degree of originality. She was starting to wonder why Jack was with her. She couldn't row her way out of a bath.

"Do you run, Flora?"

Flora wanted to run now, down the stairs, through the door and back to her underwater apartment. Instead she put the photo back carefully, placing it a safe distance from the edge. It wouldn't do to drop Becca. "I've never run a marathon, but I've always wanted to." She had no idea what made her say it. Pride? The desire to connect with Izzy? An insecure need to demonstrate that there was at least one thing that Becca had done that she could do, too?

Izzy's eyes narrowed an instant before she gave a sweet smile. "That's great. We can run together while you're staying here. I'd love the company."

*Stupid, stupid.* How had she allowed herself to be trapped? She wasn't sure she was capable of running to the end of the street, let alone a decent distance. She'd probably drop dead, which would be a win for Izzy. It might be the only chance Flora had of winning her approval.

"I'd love that, too. Great."

"It will be fun."

It would be torture. "I agree."

"Early mornings are better for me because then Dad is still in the house to watch Molly." Izzy put the photographs back carefully. "If we leave at 5:00 a.m. we should be back by 6:30."

"Did you say 5:00 a.m.?"

"Yes. Is that too late? You'd rather make it 4:15? Mom did that occasionally when she had a lot going on."

Flora didn't know why Becca had died, but she was starting to wonder if it could have been exhaustion.

"Five sounds like a good time." She told herself it would be like doing the run to the flower market, only her reward would be blisters instead of blooms.

"Great. We'll be back before Dad leaves for work. Does that sound like a good idea?"

It sounded like the worst idea Flora had heard in a long

time, but that was what you got for allowing yourself to be intimidated by a tricky teenager and a dead woman.

Izzy flipped her smooth hair back over her shoulder. "We'll start tomorrow. I'll wake you at 4:45. Do you like tea in the morning?"

At that time the only thing that was likely to get her out of bed was a bucket of iced water over her head, but Flora didn't say that. If she was doing this, then she was doing this. "I prefer to run on an empty stomach. I'll have breakfast when we get back."

"Yeah?" Izzy looked surprised. "My mother didn't eat breakfast. She fasted all day and ate a small dinner in the evening. Usually just protein and vegetables."

"Your mother was an impressive woman." *Oh for goodness sake, Flora, use a different word. Any word!* "Special."

"She was. Dad said she was the most special person he'd ever met."

There really wasn't an answer to that.

Flora glanced at the photos again. Apart from the one taken on Mount Kilimanjaro, they were all of Becca and her family. There was one of Becca sailing, her hair flying in the wind as she laughed up at Jack. Flora was sure that in the same situation half her hair would be in her mouth and the other half in her eyes.

Behind that there were two black-and-white photographs of Becca hugging the two girls. She was barefoot, dressed in jeans, and all Flora could think was that this was a woman who seemed to have had it all. Until she didn't.

Life, she thought, had a sick sense of humor.

"I can move the photographs if they bother you," Izzy said, and Flora stirred.

"They don't bother me."

"I hope you'll be comfortable. My mother wanted it to be

the perfect guest room." Did she emphasize the word *guest* or was that Flora's imagination?

Flora thought about all the times she'd tried to talk about her mother, and the times her aunt had cut her off. Flora had found it indescribably difficult. In time she'd forgotten *how* to talk about her mother and she didn't want that for Izzy. If Izzy wanted to talk about Becca, then she'd listen.

"You must miss your mother very much."

Izzy's fingers sank into the throw. "We're fine. We have each other. We have to stick together, that's all."

And now here was Flora, intruding. "I'm sorry that you suddenly have a guest, disrupting your family routine."

"It's not a problem. I know it won't be for long." Izzy stood up abruptly, and gestured to an open door. "I've put fresh towels in the bathroom, and there are toiletries, too. They were my mother's favorites. I hope you'll like them, but of course if you'd prefer something different—"

"I don't need anything different. I don't want to change a thing." She wanted to blend seamlessly into this family, not disrupt it, although there was little chance of that.

Izzy had declared war.

"Dinner is at six. It's family time." Izzy paused. "I could put yours on a tray and bring it up here? You've had a stressful day. You'd probably appreciate the chance to settle in quietly."

The message was clear.

And although Flora felt desperately uncomfortable for herself, she felt even worse for Izzy. Without the photographs to hold she paced the room, driven by a restless energy.

Flora had never seen so much emotion contained in such a small package. How did it all fit? She wondered how the girl kept it inside and then remembered she'd done exactly the same thing herself. Their situation was different, but she suspected the feelings were pretty much the same, all of them driven by insecurity and a knowledge that so many things in life were beyond your control.

But this small thing wasn't.

Flora smiled. "If you're sure it's all right with you, I'd like to eat here, thank you."

Izzy stopped pacing. Her shoulders and hands relaxed. Flora caught a glimpse of what she might have been like before life piled weight on her tensions.

She walked to the door. "I'll bring you something. And if you need anything else, let me know."

Alone, Flora sat on the edge of the bed for a moment, in the place where Izzy had sat only a few moments before.

She wasn't a psychologist, but she suspected that her appearance on the scene had pushed the older girl right to the edge.

Should she talk to Jack about Izzy? Tell him what she'd observed?

Feeling out of her depth, she stood up and opened her two suitcases.

Trying to ignore the six photos of Becca—did she dare put them in the drawer?—she unpacked her things, hung them up and pulled out the small framed photograph of her mother that she always kept by her bed.

She placed it in front of the photos of Becca. It was good to have a friendly face in the room, and seeing her mother reminded her that you didn't have to run a marathon or row the Atlantic to live a worthwhile life. Small deeds counted, too. And right now her one small deed was not to make things worse for Izzy.

On impulse she added Molly's picture, leaning it against two photos of Becca. Every time she looked at that fox she felt more cheerful.

Molly had wanted her to have it. Molly had wanted her to frame it. And that was what she'd done.

Her attempt to personalize the room lifted her spirits. Feeling better, she walked into the bathroom. There was a freestanding tub and what seemed like acres of marble.

Flora picked up one of the bottles and read the label. All she knew about the brand was that it was expensive. She imagined Becca ordering it for her guests. *Nothing but the best*, she might have said to Jack, and he would have gone along with it because no one would dispute Becca's taste.

Her guests had probably never wanted to leave.

On impulse she locked the door and filled the tub. She felt grubby after clearing her apartment. Maybe a soak in Becca's scented oils would put her in a better mood. It would certainly make her look better. She was pretty sure Becca had never eaten her dinner smelling of damp.

She soaked for a while, then washed and dried her hair and changed into a dry pair of jeans and a pretty top she'd dyed herself at home.

When she opened the door there was a tray on the table by the window. On it was a bowl of soup and a warm bread roll.

Flora was just settling down to eat her lonely dinner when the door burst open and Jack strode into the room.

"Are you okay?"

"Yes. Of course." Her breathing wasn't something she usually noticed, but each time she saw Jack she became aware of the unsteady, uneven in and out. Looking at him sometimes made her feel dizzy. She found herself studying every part of him, from the angle of his jaw to the slope of his cheekbones to try to work out what it was that made him special.

He pulled her to her feet. "Are you really upset? Why didn't you tell me instead of hiding up here on your own?"

"I'm not hiding—and I'm not upset. I mean, it hasn't been the best day of my life, but I'm fine. I'll find somewhere else, or maybe the landlord will fix it—"

"You are not going back to that place." His arms tightened round her, providing the security she'd just lost. "You're staying here until we find a better option. A much better option."

"It isn't fair on your kids for me to move in like this. It's unsettling."

"You're a friend. I want my kids to grow up knowing we should help our friends." He eased her away from him. "You've been alone for most of your life, Flora. But that's not the case anymore. You have us now."

She felt warm inside. Cocooned. Supported. His arms felt like a sanctuary.

"How is Molly?"

"Sorting through her things to find something that will help you feel at home. Don't be surprised if you find your bed full of soft toys next time you open the door. I assumed you were going to unpack your things and come and join us."

"I had a soak in the tub."

"Good. But that doesn't explain why you insisted on eating in your room."

Was that how Izzy had presented it?

This conversation was like walking barefoot over broken glass.

"I don't want to intrude on your time with your girls."

"We're really happy to have you here. I know you've had a tough day. I can understand why you'd want to hide away, but I don't think it's a good idea. You need to get to know the girls. I want that." He stroked her curls away from her face.

"I thought, maybe—" How could she put this? "I know you eat together every day at six. It's family time, and I respect that."

"What are you talking about?" He let his hand drop. "I'm rarely home by six. Izzy and Molly usually eat together and I join them when I can. Mealtimes are rarely fluid or routine in this house."

"Oh."

"Also—" He rubbed his fingers over his forehead. "This is a little awkward, but we have a rule that no one eats in their rooms. If we're eating, we eat at the table. We talk. And I understand that today is an exception and that you're upset, but is there any way you could eat downstairs with us? I can't have one rule for the girls and another for you. I hope you understand."

"I understand." She understood all of it, including the fact that Izzy seemed determined to drive a wedge between her and Jack.

She couldn't tell him, of course. That was out of the question.

Jack scooped up the tray and walked to the door.

"Let's go. The girls are waiting. And tonight, when the girls are in bed, you and I are sharing a bottle of wine on the terrace."

Flora had visions of taking a sip and collapsing on the terrace, poisoned.

Trying to calm her imagination, Flora followed him down the stairs and into the kitchen where the girls were already seated.

As soon as Flora walked into the room, Izzy put her spoon down. "Is there something wrong with your food?"

"Flora is eating at the table with us." Jack unloaded the tray that Izzy had carefully laid.

"We're not allowed to eat in our rooms," Molly said and Flora gave her an apologetic look.

"I know."

"Why did you want to eat in your room? Don't you like us?"

Flora felt Izzy's tension and knew she had to find a way to protect Izzy, while at the same time not offending Molly and not flagging to Jack that there was an issue. She had no idea how to handle the situation. When it came to the intricacies of family life, she was a beginner. "I was feeling a little tired, but I'm better now."

Izzy fiddled with her bread. "Flora has been through a trauma. If she wants the privacy and comfort of her own space, then she should have it. Eating at the table is a family rule, and Flora isn't family."

Flora took the punch without flinching, but Jack cast a thoughtful look at his daughter.

"She's a friend. We help our friends."

Flora picked up her spoon. Her appetite had gone, but she didn't want to draw more attention to herself by not eating.

Jack changed the subject. "I had an email from Aunt Clare this morning." He reached across and pulled Molly's bowl closer to her. "She wanted to know if we're going to stay with her in Lake Lodge this summer. Funny that she should reach out now, because I've been thinking about it myself and wondering what we should do."

Izzy sat up a little straighter. There was a spark of excitement in her eyes. "What did you tell her?" Her tone suggested mild interest, but Flora could tell that his answer was important.

"I told her we'd talk about it and get back to her. A vacation would be good for us. We haven't been away since—" he paused "—since last summer."

There was silence round the table.

Izzy put her spoon down. "It was the week before Mom died."

"Yes." Jack took a mouthful of his own soup and then glanced at his other daughter. "Molly? What do you think? Do you want to go to Lake Lodge this summer like we usually do?"

"But we usually do it with Mommy. We always do it with Mommy."

"We do, that's true." Jack put his spoon down, too. "And we'll miss her, but that doesn't mean we can't go if you'd like to. Aunt Clare is inviting us."

There was a pause. Molly fiddled with her spoon.

"It would be weird without Mommy. Different."

"It will be different. Sometimes in life we have to do things that are different."

"Like when I started my school?"

"Exactly. Nothing stays the same, even when we want it to very much."

"Do you think it would upset Mommy if we went without her?"

Flora felt tears scald her eyes and a hard lump block her throat.

"No, honey." Jack's voice was rough. "Mommy would want you to be having a good time and living a full life. She'd want you to be happy."

How did he always know exactly the right thing to say? Everything he did came from a place of kindness. Rescuing her. Comforting his daughter. Every word, every gesture, reeled her in a little further.

"I'd like to go to Lake Lodge," Izzy said. "I'd like to see Aunt Clare and Uncle Todd. It would be good to get away." Her gaze slid briefly to Flora who was left with the distinct impression she was the one Izzy wanted to get away from.

"And Aiden," Molly said. "You forgot Aiden."

Seeing the flush spread from Izzy's neck to her face, Flora had a feeling that Izzy hadn't forgotten Aiden at all.

"Becca and Clare were at school together in the early days. Then Becca won a scholarship to a prestigious ballet school, and when she graduated she joined a ballet company in the US." Jack included Flora in the conversation. "Clare's parents are British. They live in a fabulous property in the Lake District."

"There are mountains," Molly said. "And we go sailing and climb trees."

"We do." Jack smiled at her. "We've been meeting up there every summer since before the children were born."

"If we go, you'd be able to play with Chase," Izzy said. "You love Chase."

Jack nudged the bread closer to Flora. "Chase is the dog."

"Because he chases everything." Molly gripped her spoon. "Maybe we should stay here this summer."

Because different was sometimes terrifying, Flora thought. Because sometimes the safe and familiar felt better. She remembered how terrified she'd been by the enormous changes in her life. "What are your favorite things to do when you stay with your aunt Clare?"

Molly nibbled at her bread. "Playing with Chase. And I like swimming in the lake. Mommy was a champion swimmer at school. She won everything."

It seemed to Flora that Becca had been champion at pretty much everything. She wanted to know if there had been anything she'd done badly, and then hated herself for being so shallow and insecure. "Did she teach you?"

"Aunt Clare taught me."

Flora imagined Becca poised at the edge of the lake, impatient to power her way to the other side.

Izzy finished her soup. "Do you like to swim, Flora?"

"No." That was one thing she would never lie about. Water terrified her. No way was she pretending to love it. She should probably tell them the reason, but it wasn't something she talked about. Not with anyone. "What else do you do when you're there?"

"We play in boats. Aunt Clare taught us to sail."

Water. Everything to do with water.

"That sounds like fun." For someone who enjoyed water. That someone wasn't her. "Did Mommy love doing that, too?"

Molly nodded. "Mommy was a brilliant sailor."

Of course she was.

Flora was aware of Becca gazing down at her from her position on the kitchen wall. The photographer had caught her in the split second before she'd laughed and the result was an image full of mischief.

It seemed to Flora that she was laughing now.

*You think you're going to make my family fall in love with you? Think again.*

She shifted her position in her seat so she could no longer see the photograph. "Is the lake deep?"

"You can't see the bottom. We wear life jackets. Aunt Clare makes us."

"And you love it," Izzy says, "which is why we should go this summer. You'll have me, and you'll have Dad. It will be like being here, only better."

Flora decided she couldn't force any more soup down.

Jack was looking at his daughter. "You'd really like to go, Izz?"

"Yes." Izzy pushed her bowl away. "It would be good to get away. I love Lake Lodge. I love seeing Aunt Clare. And I love fell running."

"Mountains are called fells where Aunt Clare lives,"

Molly said helpfully, seeing Flora's blank look. "And it isn't because people fell off them. I know because I asked."

"The word *fell* comes from Old Norse word *fjell*," Izzy said. "It means hill."

Molly poked at her food. "I'd like to see Aunt Clare and Chase. But what if it feels funny without Mommy?"

"You could try some new things," Flora said. "Things you didn't used to do with your mommy. New adventures." The suggestion won her an approving smile from Jack.

"Great idea. You could go rock climbing. You've never done that."

A glob of soup dripped from Molly's spoon onto the table. "Rock climbing might be fun. What else?"

"Horseback riding," Flora said. "That's always fun."

Molly considered. "I'd like that."

"So—" Izzy leaned across and mopped it up. "Is that a yes? We're going to Lake Lodge this summer?"

"Let's live with the idea for a few days and see how we feel. We'll talk about it again before I reply to Aunt Clare. Family decision, right?" Jack finished his soup. "I have to go into the office for a few hours tomorrow. Will you guys be all right here?"

"I'm not working tomorrow," Flora said. "I can help."

"I have it covered." Izzy stood up and cleared the plates. She shook her head when Flora stood up to help her. "You're a guest, Flora. Guests don't clear up."

"Flora's going to be living here for a while," Jack said easily, "so you should let her help you, Izzy. You do so much around the place, it would be good to share the load. Maybe now Flora is here you'll be able to see more of your friends. You deserve some time off."

Maybe that was the answer. Lighten Izzy's load. Pick up

some of the household chores so that Izzy had more time to see friends.

Flora was filled with renewed optimism. "I'm happy to help in any way I can. I'd love to spend more time with Molly." She smiled at the little girl. "We'll have so much fun."

"I don't need time off." Izzy stacked the dishwasher noisily, plates clashing against each other.

Flora flinched. Now what? Surely Izzy should be pleased about that. Julia's children couldn't wait to be excused from chores.

"You won't be leaving before six thirty will you, Dad?" Izzy dropped cutlery into the basket. "Flora and I are running at five."

Jack raised an eyebrow in Flora's direction. "You're a runner? You never mentioned it."

And there was a good reason for that.

"It's something I do now and then." When she was late for work. When she felt threatened by some guy walking behind her.

Jack looked at her oddly. "Really? That's…great."

She had a feeling he didn't think it was great at all, but she didn't understand why. It made her realize that despite their growing closeness, there was still plenty he didn't know about her and plenty she didn't know about him. Most of what she'd learned about Becca she'd learned from Izzy, not him. It seemed Jack couldn't bear to talk about her, and she didn't want to make his pain worse by asking.

"I saw that there is a park near here." She grabbed a napkin and wiped Molly's fingers. "We could take our paints, sit on a bench and paint what we see."

Molly brightened. "Now?"

Izzy frowned. "We don't go to the park after we've eaten. Molly reads her book and then goes to bed."

"I'd like to go to the park." Molly bounced slightly in her chair and glanced at her father for permission. "Can we?"

"Why not?" He smiled. "Sounds like a plan to me."

Izzy was tense as a bow. "But we never—"

"Sometimes it's good to do different things, Izz." Jack was as patient with her as he was with Molly. "We'll go to the park for half an hour, that's all. The fresh air will be good for all of us."

"The park, yes," Molly said. "But I don't want to paint. I don't like to paint anymore."

"No problem." Flora stood up. "I might paint, and if you decide to help me, that's fine. Or I might just do some more drawing and you can help me color it in."

Izzy slammed the dishwasher closed and Molly looked at her.

"Will you come, too?"

"Of course! You don't think I'd leave you, do you?" Izzy ruffled her sister's hair and bent to give her a kiss. "Fetch your coat in case it rains. The sky is looking dark."

Flora had been hoping that Izzy would choose to stay at home, but it was clear the teenager didn't intend to leave Molly's side.

Flora grabbed the bag containing all her art equipment, and was halfway out of the door before she realized she'd left her coat on the back of the door in her apartment.

Jack frowned at the sky. "You don't have a coat?"

"Not with me. If it rains, I'll get wet. Don't worry." Flora hooked the bag over her shoulder. Molly was looking excited, and there was no way she was going to cancel this trip given that it had been her suggestion. "It will probably be drier outside than it was in my apartment." Her joke didn't have the impact she'd hoped it would.

"We must have a coat you can borrow." Jack strode back into the house and tugged open a door. Reaching inside he grabbed a cream trench coat and thrust it at her.

"That's Mom's coat." Izzy's hand locked on his arm like a vice. Jack lowered his head and spoke quietly.

Flora couldn't hear what he said, but Izzy let her hand drop. Bone-white with misery, fists clenched by her sides, she took a step back and allowed him to pass.

Both girls watched in silence as he handed the coat to Flora.

Becca's coat.

She hesitated, and not only because she doubted it would fit. "I don't think—"

"Wear it." His voice was steady. "It's no use having a coat that no one wears."

Flora glanced at Izzy. Her mouth was pressed together, as if she was trying to hold back a thousand words she wasn't allowed to speak.

Her pain was so tangible that Flora felt she could reach out and touch it.

While she was figuring out how to handle this latest situation, Jack took the coat back from her and held it in an old-fashioned gesture, giving her no choice but to slide her arms into it.

The sleeves were a little tight and there was no way she'd be able to do the buttons over her chest, but it would protect her from the worst of the rain if the dark clouds above them did as they were threatening to do. The storm she was most afraid of was the one building around her.

She looked doubtfully at the children, checking their reaction, and then Molly gave her a wobbly smile.

"It's okay," she said, and her bravery increased Flora's growing affection for her. If she ever was lucky enough to have a little girl of her own, she hoped she'd be just like Molly.

She crouched down so that she was on the same level.

"This was your mommy's coat, and it must feel very strange seeing someone else wearing it. If you'd rather I didn't wear it, that's okay."

Molly shook her head. "I don't mind. I thought I might, but you don't look like Mommy." She reached out and touched one of Flora's curls. "Your hair is more tangled."

For once, Flora was grateful for her misbehaving hair. She took Molly's fingers and gave them a squeeze. "My hair," she said, "is the most independent part of me." She straightened and looked at Izzy, but the teenager avoided her gaze.

"Let's do this," she said, and slammed the front door shut so hard it shook the house and Flora's brief moment of euphoria.

Despite that, the trip to the park was less awkward than she'd anticipated. Izzy bumped into a group of friends, and while they were chatting Flora and Jack took Molly on the swings and the slide.

Despite the earlier threat of bad weather, the sun peeped from behind the clouds and Flora left Jack with his daughter, settled herself on a bench and pulled her sketchbook out of her bag.

Ten minutes later, curiosity got the better of Molly and she joined her.

Sitting down on the bench, she peered at the sketchbook. "It's a girl on a swing." She bent closer. "She has a ponytail, like me."

"It is you." Flora tilted it toward her. "What do you think?"

"You drew me? Daddy! Come and see." She shifted on

the bench, her legs swinging, too short to reach the ground. She looked so young, and yet her view of the world had been changed forever. All the assumptions she'd made about family, love and security had been shattered.

Flora ached for her.

Jack sat down on the other side of her and leaned across. "That's brilliant. Hey, Molly, it even looks like you."

"Can I keep it?"

Flora carried on shading with her pencil, adding definition. "Of course." When she was satisfied, she flipped over the page and started again, this time capturing the shape of the tree and the flowers.

Molly was watching so closely her nose almost touched the pencil. "Where did you learn to draw?"

"My mother taught me. When I was little she wanted to make sure that I paid attention to small things. Plants. Flowers. Trees. People." She moved her pencil across the page. "She believed in really enjoying every moment and not wasting it worrying about yesterday or tomorrow."

"Does it make you sad when you talk about her?"

"A little, but mostly I like it. It's a way of keeping her alive and remembering her." Flora kept sketching even though all her attention was on Molly. "Does it make you sad?"

"I'm already sad so it doesn't change much."

Flora resisted the temptation to hug the little girl. "What used to make you smile?"

"Dancing, but I don't like to do that anymore."

Flora nodded. "Anything else?"

"Painting." Molly studied every pencil stroke Flora made. "You're good at drawing."

"Well that makes us a good team, because I can draw something and then you can color it. Would you like to do a sketch?" she asked casually, and was pleased when Molly nodded.

Flora set her up with paper and a pencil and the two of them sat quietly, Molly copying what Flora was doing. She worked carefully, her tongue caught between her teeth as she concentrated.

Flora felt Jack's fingers lightly brush her neck and turned her head. His gaze was fixed on his younger daughter. She had a feeling he was holding his breath.

"That's great, Molly." His voice was rough. "I'll put it on my wall at work."

Flora watched as Molly concentrated. "You're good. You pay attention. What do you enjoy drawing most?"

"Animals. I liked your fox."

Flora flipped the page again and did a quick sketch of a horse. Molly giggled.

"I like it. Can you teach me to do one the same?"

Flora demonstrated stroke by stroke, while Molly copied her. They argued cheerfully about whether Molly's drawing looked more like a cow than a horse.

"Definitely a horse." Jack smiled at Flora across the top of Molly's head. "You're brilliant."

In that moment, the complexities of their relationship were forgotten. It was just the two of them.

"She *is* brilliant," Molly said. "My horse doesn't look like her horse."

"A painting doesn't have to look exactly like the thing you're copying. Sometimes it's just an impression."

"Like Monet." Molly switched her green pencil for a red one. "I know about Monet. Aunt Clare went to Paris and sent us a postcard. Mommy said she'd take us to Paris one day."

"I promise we'll go to Paris." Jack stretched his legs out. "If you'd like to."

"Would Flora come?"

"Would you like her to come?"

Flora held her breath, knowing this could go either way. But Molly nodded.

"Yes. She can tell us about the paintings."

Jack winked at her. "It's not that we like you or anything. Just that we need a tour guide."

Flora was laughing, but Molly frowned.

"We *do* like her. You're silly, Daddy."

"I am. I'm very silly." He seemed lighter, younger, when he was with Molly. It made Flora feel lighter, too. Hopeful.

Warmth spread through her as she acknowledged that Molly seemed to be accepting her, at least on some level.

"Why are you all smiling?" Izzy appeared in front of them like a dark cloud on a sunny day.

Molly thrust her picture out. "My drawing is like Monet, and we're all going to Paris. Flora is coming, too."

Izzy's expression froze. "When? We agreed to stay with Aunt Clare this summer."

Molly's jaw jutted out. "I want to go to Paris."

"We're going to spend the summer at Lake Lodge, like we always do."

"Can Flora come with us there?"

"No!" Izzy spoke quickly. "Flora has a job. And this is a family holiday. Flora isn't family. It would be awful for her to be with a bunch of people who have known each other forever."

And just like that the door slammed shut on the family group with Flora on the wrong side.

It hurt more than she would have expected it to, given that being on the outside was something she was used to.

All the lightness and laughter had been sucked from the air. The warm, hopeful feeling vanished.

"We still haven't decided what we're doing this summer." Jack stood up. "Time to go back to the house."

Flora and Molly packed up their drawings, and Jack walked ahead with Izzy. His arm was looped round her shoulder and they appeared to be deep in conversation.

Molly slipped her hand into Flora's. "You look sad. Don't worry, your apartment will dry out soon. When I spill my drink, it dries quickly."

Flora tightened her grip on Molly and then felt guilty for using a small child as an emotional comfort blanket. "I hope you're right."

It was later, much later, when she and Jack were finally alone in the kitchen.

Flora took the wine Jack handed her. "Thank you. Is Molly asleep?"

"Yes. Crashed out after the third chapter. All the excitement of having a new houseguest, I think. I can't thank you enough."

"For what?"

"For persuading her to draw. I know she colored in your fox the other night, but this was on a whole different level. She was like the old Molly."

"I didn't say anything."

"No, you were cleverer than that. You made sure she was so intrigued by what you were doing that she wanted to do it herself. It's the first time she's drawn anything since Becca died. I haven't seen her this chatty in a while and she smiled more today than she has in a long time. That's down to you." He opened the door to the garden and they both stepped onto the terrace. "Watching her with you this evening was the first time I've thought she might actually be okay."

"I love her. She's smart and thoughtful and she makes me laugh."

"It's been so tough on her. She hasn't handled it as well as Izzy, but she's younger so I suppose that's to be expected."

"Izzy was upset about the coat."

"Yes." He rubbed his fingers across his forehead. "That was my fault. Probably a mistake, but it looked like rain, you didn't have a coat and the coat was there—it's impossible to get it right all the time. We have the odd moment like that when Izzy is visibly stressed, but generally she's handling it well."

Flora was no expert, but she didn't think Izzy was handling it well at all.

"She's great with her sister."

"Yes, right from the moment Molly was born the two of them have been inseparable." He put his glass on the table and sat down on the seat, tugging her down next to him. "I'm not sure how I would have coped this last year without Izzy."

"Where is she now?"

"Officially? In her room doing homework, although I suspect she's messaging her friends."

They were alone, and yet not alone.

If she glanced up, would she find Izzy watching them?

"Thank you for coming to the rescue today, Jack. I couldn't believe it when you arrived at my apartment. That must have been inconvenient and annoying for the girls. I'll start making phone calls first thing on Monday and find somewhere else to live."

"Why would you do that?"

"Because I'm sure the last thing the girls want, or need, is me staying here. You probably already pushed your luck by coming to get me."

"Coming to get you was Izzy's idea."

"Really?" She couldn't have been more surprised by that news. "Izzy suggested coming into Manhattan to get me?"

"Yes. She heard me on the phone and was worried."

"That was thoughtful and incredibly kind." She was touched, relieved and a little bemused.

She'd been so sure that Izzy resented her, but what evidence was there for that?

She'd talked about Becca. But what was wrong with that? It was good that she felt comfortable enough to talk about her mother. Flora was being oversensitive.

Having rationalized it, she raised her glass. "You have wonderful daughters."

"I think so, but I'm willing to admit to bias."

She was conscious of how close he was. She had to physically stop herself from lifting her mouth to his. "You should be biased. You're their dad. It's part of the role. They're lucky to have you."

"What happened to your dad?"

"My mother spent a summer painting in Europe. Tuscany. Corfu. Paris. She met a guy and they traveled and painted together for a while. When the summer ended, she came home and discovered she was pregnant." It was something she'd never discussed with anyone. Not Julia. Not even her aunt.

"She never tried to contact him?"

"Yes. He didn't want a family. He blamed her for getting pregnant." It was easy to talk in the sheltered, leafy cocoon of his garden. The warm evening air was sweetened by the scent of honeysuckle and jasmine, and distant city noises blended with the call of birds and the hum of insects.

"You've never thought of trying to trace him?"

"No." The last thing she needed was to meet someone else who wasn't interested in her, but she didn't share that.

He took her wineglass and set it down next to his on the table.

"I'm sorry you lost your home."

"I'm not. It's not as if it was the dream. I mean, for a while it was—I couldn't wait to have my own place." She'd never told anyone this before. Dreams were perhaps the most intimate thing you could share with a person, fragile and easily damaged. "When I was living with my aunt I used to *literally* dream about it. I felt so lonely, I cheered myself up by imagining a home that was all mine. And it didn't have to be huge or fancy. I was just excited about having my own place. Filling it with books. Deciding what to put on the walls."

"And?"

She stared into the darkness. "It never felt the way I imagined it would feel. Having my own place didn't feel fun or freeing, it felt lonely. I've been as lonely in that apartment as I was with my aunt. You probably think that's pathetic."

"No. I love your honesty. I love that you don't feel you have to put on a show for me. You're a special person, have I told you that lately?" His head was close to hers, his smile so compelling she couldn't help but smile back.

She could have resisted the broad shoulders and the sexy eyes. She might have been able to ignore his sharp mind and the way he listened and paid attention to small details. But his smile? His smile was lethal, and that was her downfall.

Their heads moved closer together, although she wasn't sure if she was the one moving or him.

"You're special, too." *That mouth*, she thought. Smiling or serious, he had the most expressive mouth.

He leaned closer. Any closer and they would have been touching. "Do you feel lonely now?"

"No. Not lonely." A little confused. A lot desperate. But definitely not lonely.

"Taking this slowly is killing me, by the way." His gaze dropped to her mouth. "I'm trying to assess the chances of Molly wandering in if you sleep in my room."

"Too risky. Not a good idea."

He sighed. "Sadly, I know you're right. It would be a great idea for us, but not so good for my kids." He brushed away a curl from her cheek. "This can't be easy for you."

"It's fine." She knew it wasn't easy for him, either. She wondered if the hardest part was forming a relationship with another woman. She wanted to ask, but knew better than to mention Becca.

Without warning, he captured her face in his hands and kissed her. It was brief and restrained, but no less intense for that. His tension flowed into her and his palms held her firmly as he deepened the kiss.

When he finally broke away she was glad she was sitting down. As it was, she thought it might take her heart and hopes a while to return to earth.

She picked up her glass and took a large swallow.

With a wry smile, he tapped his wineglass against hers. "To us."

*Us.*

The word added to the new feeling of intimacy. She wasn't sure she'd ever really been an "us" before.

No, right now she definitely didn't feel lonely.

She nursed her glass. "So you'll go to the lake with your friends this summer?"

"Honestly? I don't know." He finished his wine. "The kids always loved it. They enjoy the fresh air and spending time outdoors. There's a freedom there that they don't have here. And Clare and Todd—well, they're a nice family. I'm sure we'd have a good time, but I don't want to be away from you for three weeks. Maybe you could come, too."

"To England?" Was he joking? He had to be joking, surely. "I don't think so."

Spend three weeks with Becca's closest friend?

*Awkward* didn't begin to describe it.

On the other hand she didn't relish the thought of three weeks away from him, either.

"I think it would be great." He leaned forward, resting his arms on his thighs. "Will you think about it?"

"I'm thinking about it. Even if I could persuade Celia it was a good idea—which I doubt I could—I don't think it would work."

"It's one of the most beautiful places I've ever visited. Lake Lodge is set right on the edge of the water in acres of private land. Wait—" He dug his hand in his pocket and pulled out his phone. "I have a photo." He scrolled and then showed her the screen.

She saw a lake framed by mountains and dense forest. It seemed that a whole world, compact and quite breathtakingly beautiful, was contained in that one shot.

Apart from the water, it did look idyllic.

"It's not the place that worries me, Jack." True, the lake itself wasn't appealing but presumably water-based activities were optional.

"So it's the people? The Dickinsons are always welcoming. They're a very laid-back family."

Maybe, but how laid-back would they be if Jack were to show up with a new woman a year after Becca's death?

She handed his phone back. "You assume that everyone is going to be fine that we're together."

"Why wouldn't they be?"

"These people were friends of Becca's. They might resent you bringing another woman to stay."

"Or they might not. They're my friends, too. I hope they'd be relieved and pleased. I would, if the situation was reversed."

Men were different, she thought. It wasn't Clare's husband

she was worried about. It was Clare herself. Her friendship with Becca hadn't been a casual thing. Apparently they'd been as close as two friends could be since they were in kindergarten.

"What about the girls?"

"What about them? Molly invited you—you heard her."

"That was an impulsive, spontaneous child thing. I don't for one moment think she meant it."

"What if she did mean it?" He swept aside protests like dust.

"There's still Izzy—"

"What about Izzy? Things are going great. You're running with her tomorrow. Which is both surprising and adorable by the way."

"Adorable?"

He gave a faint smile. "Because you're doing it to get closer to my daughter. It's the most thoughtful, crazy thing anyone has done for me in a long time."

It was the craziest thing she'd done for anyone in a long time.

"Maybe I'm doing it for me, because I think physical fitness is important."

"Do you?"

"Yes. So many diseases are linked with lack of exercise, but everyone knows that working out on your own is boring so I'm superexcited to have Izzy to run with." She could tell he didn't believe her.

"Is there anything you need?"

"What are you offering? Ambulance? First responder at the ready?"

He laughed. "I was thinking more of a good pair of running shoes."

"Oh." She smoothed her hair back from her face and tried to recapture dignity. "I have running shoes."

"They wear out over time."

Hers had never been given a chance to wear out. "Mine are fine. I suppose if you have a spare oxygen tank that might be useful."

He leaned across and kissed her. "You," he said, "are so damn cute."

"When I cross the finish line of the New York Marathon, you're going to apologize for patronizing me."

"I'm not patronizing you. I think you're incredible. But no one goes from couch to marathon in one session, Flora."

"Who said anything about a marathon? We'll start gently."

"Izzy is fast and fit. Don't let her push you. But it's great that you're doing this. First you get Molly drawing again, and now this. Izzy used to run all the time, but she stopped after Becca died." He frowned. "I don't know why. Maybe because running without her mother felt wrong. But now she's asked you to go with her. That's really positive."

"I hope so."

Flora had a sneaking suspicion that Izzy's invitation to run had been motivated by darker forces, like a desire to see her father's new girlfriend die of natural causes.

Either way, the following morning promised to be interesting.

# 8

*Izzy*

People said running was good for your mental health, but right now it wasn't doing anything for hers.

Izzy increased her speed in the hope that moving faster might help her escape her feelings.

She hadn't run since her mother had died and not only was she out of condition, but it also brought back memories. No matter how fit she'd been, her mother had always been able to outpace her. At the time it had frustrated Izzy, that she could never be as good as her mother at anything she did.

Now, she just wished she had a chance to run with her again. She could picture her mother ahead of her, pulling into the distance. Izzy might have called after her to wait, but her mother never waited for anyone. She followed her own agenda. If you couldn't keep up you were left behind.

Now it was Izzy in the lead, and Flora was the one lagging in her wake. Izzy didn't want her to catch up in case Flora saw the tears drying on her cheeks.

She pounded along the street, longing to stop and drag air into her heaving lungs but she could hear the rhythmic sounds of Flora's feet close behind her.

Why had she suggested running together? *Because she had thought Flora would say no.*

Far from dragging her feet, Flora had been up before Izzy and had been waiting by the front door when Izzy had appeared downstairs. And although Izzy would have drowned herself in the East River before admitting it, Flora looked good. She was wearing the coolest pair of leggings Izzy had ever seen, a silvery gray leopard print that caught the light and sculpted her lower body. She'd actually apologized for them, telling Izzy they were her yoga pants and the only pair she owned, and Izzy had shrugged dismissively and hoped Flora couldn't see envy seeping through her eye sockets and out of her pores. She was glad her dad wasn't awake to see Flora dressed for running. She was pretty sure he would have tripped over his tongue, fallen down the stairs and then she and Molly would have been orphans.

With her bubbly long hair tied in a ponytail, Flora looked energetic and enthusiastic.

Izzy felt tired and testy and she hadn't even run two steps.

And now, here they were, feet pounding in rhythm, synchronized.

Feeling irritable, Izzy increased her pace.

At this rate the last laugh was going to be Flora's. That's if either of them had the breath to laugh.

They reached the Brooklyn Bridge as the sun rose. In the distance she could see the Statue of Liberty and New York Harbor, and beneath them the sparkling expanse of the East River.

It had been her mother's favorite run, and Becca had always insisted on going early before the route was crowded with pedestrians and cyclists.

The only place she'd ever stopped was on the bridge and then she would throw back her head, take a sip of water and smile a self-satisfied smile, allowing herself less than a minute of contemplation. *We live in the greatest city in the world, Izzy. City of dreams.*

Shaking off the image, Izzy glanced over her shoulder and saw Flora had stopped at the edge of the bridge. Her eyes were closed, her face was red and she was panting for breath.

Izzy stopped, too. Respect bloomed inside her. Grudging, but there.

"Are you okay?" She had a feeling that if she killed Flora, her father wouldn't be pleased. She liked to think she wouldn't be pleased either, but lately she didn't recognize herself. She didn't examine her responses too closely, because she wasn't sure she was going to like what she saw.

Flora dragged in a great gulp of air. "I'm so unfit." But she was laughing in between the pants and Izzy found herself almost smiling, too.

It unsettled her, so she turned away and stared at the Manhattan skyline as her mother had always done.

"It's the greatest city in the world. City of dreams." She parroted her mother's words and then felt foolish. They sounded wrong coming out of her mouth, and not only because she hadn't visited that many cities. The irony was that her mother didn't believe in dreams. She believed in action. Goal setting. She was constantly moving forward.

"I've lived here all my life and this is the first time I've seen the sunrise from here."

"Do you want to run onto the bridge?"

"No. I'm good here." Flora leaned on the rail. "It's spectacular."

Was it?

Izzy stared at the sky and realized it actually was pretty cool. Streaked red and orange, the colors reflected off the water and the buildings.

Flora took a slug of water. "So what's your dream, Izzy?"

"What?"

"Your dream. What is it?"

Izzy stared at her. How was she supposed to answer that? *For you to leave my dad alone. For my mom to come back to life. For me to unknow what I know.*

Flora didn't want to hear any of that any more than Izzy wanted to say those thoughts aloud.

"Dreaming is a waste of time."

"Oh no." Flora sounded distressed. "Dreaming is never a waste of time. Dreaming is creative. It allows you to imagine a life unlike the one you're living."

Izzy took another mouthful of water. "Better to have goals than dreams. Better to know where you're going and plan how to get there." Maybe she shouldn't have said that. What if Flora took that as a prompt to form a strategic plan to nail Izzy's dad? "We should get going because my dad needs to get to the office this morning." Without giving Flora the opportunity to answer, she turned and jogged back the way they'd come.

Back at the house, Izzy went straight to the shower and when she came downstairs she found Flora in the laundry room.

Her hair was damp and curled madly so she'd obviously just come from the shower, too. Her cheeks were plump and pink and her smile when she saw Izzy was a friendly, welcoming curve. Everything about Flora shrieked comfort and warmth. She was like a bowl of hot soup on a freezing day.

Izzy felt her irritation mount.

"What are you doing?" She watched as Flora loaded towels into the machine.

"These were waiting to be done, so I thought I'd help."

Panic swarmed down on her. "I don't need help."

She reminded herself that no matter what Flora did, Molly still needed her.

No one understood Molly the way she did.

Flora paused, towels clutched to her chest, a question in her eyes. Izzy had an uncomfortable feeling that the other woman could read everything in her head. She hoped that wasn't the case.

"You're a guest." She grabbed the towels from Flora. "You don't have to do laundry." Guest, get it? *Guest.*

"I'd be doing it at home. You've been good enough to let me stay here so it seems only right that I help. Please let me." There was a kindness to Flora that for some reason made Izzy feel worse.

And now she'd look rude if she didn't let her help. It made her wonder if Flora had been put on this planet simply to make Izzy feel bad about herself.

"Whatever. In that case I'll go and make Molly's breakfast."

There were footsteps on the stairs and her dad appeared, Molly in his arms.

"Look who I found upstairs." He kissed Molly on the cheek and put her down. "How was the run?"

"It was great," Flora said, and the words sounded genuine. "Honestly, it really woke me up. And I've never seen the river and the skyline at that time of the morning before."

Aware that her dad was looking at her, Izzy tried to smile, too, even though she knew it was a poor effort.

"It was great," she echoed, trying to sound convincing. She was exhausted with saying one thing, while meaning another. Was she thoughtful or a hypocrite? Tactful or manipulative?

"I'll be back in time for lunch." He glanced at his watch. "What are you going to do while I'm gone?"

Izzy turned her attention to her sister, knowing exactly how she'd love to spend the morning. "Shall we do some baking? Make cupcakes?" It was Molly's favorite thing, particularly when they reached the decorating part.

She expected squeals of excitement and a hug, but Molly shook her head.

"I want to finish my painting with Flora."

It was a kick in the guts. There had never been a time when Molly hadn't wanted to bake with her. It was her favorite thing, although apparently not since Flora arrived.

"Maybe we could do both," Flora said and Izzy felt a rush of humiliation that Flora might have guessed how hurt she felt. She didn't want Flora to have access to her feelings. She didn't want, or need, Flora for anything.

This situation was horrible, *horrible*.

She couldn't be the first person to have gone through this, surely, although of course her case came with its particular complications.

"Don't worry." She worked at sounding cheerful. "I have a ton of things to do this morning."

She'd write her blog. Maybe she'd even talk about the fact that her dad was dating. See if any of her commentators had anything useful to say on the subject. *Why*, she wondered, *would anyone dive back into a relationship when they'd had their heart broken?*

Why wasn't her dad wounded or wary? Or if he *was* wounded and wary, why wasn't that holding him back?

She wanted to think it was something inside her dad, an intrinsic optimism, rather than anything special about Flora. Did "the one" even exist? It was something she'd been thinking about a lot lately. Presumably not, or people wouldn't get divorced. Unless the reason they were divorced was because they hadn't married "the one." In which case humans were obviously seriously bad at identifying the right relationship.

How *could* "the one" exist? It was illogical. There had to be any number of people you could be happy with, which basically made love a gamble. Izzy was well aware of the dangers of gambling.

Leaving Molly with Flora, she vanished to the sanctuary of her bedroom and tried to focus on her writing. Every now and then she closed her eyes and tried to block out the delicious gurgles of laughter coming from Molly in the kitchen.

Feeling sick, Izzy stared at the screen without seeing any of the words she'd written.

Her dad often said she was his hero. He was proud of the way she'd held the family together. Izzy hadn't realized how fragile her position was or how quickly a hero could be replaced. Everything was going smoothly and then one day you turned around and you were no longer doing the laundry and your little sister no longer wanted to make cakes with you.

If things carried on like this, Izzy would no longer be needed.

Where would that leave her?

# 9

## *Flora*

"You've moved in?" Julia stared at her. "All this happened at the weekend and you didn't call?"

"I knew you were busy." Flora rubbed her hand over her ribs. It hurt when she breathed in. Everything hurt. "Also, there was nothing you could have done. You don't have room for overnight guests."

"Going from dinner to moving in is a big step. Why are you hugging your ribs?"

"I went for a run yesterday and my bra is designed for yoga. I'm having trouble moving my arms. If I need anything from a high shelf, you're going to have to get it."

"You ran somewhere?" Julia broke off the conversation to ring up a bunch of freesias for a woman in a sharp suit. "Have a wonderful, blossoming, perfectly scented day!" She beamed at the woman, waited until she'd reached the door of the store and then turned back to Flora. "You? Ran?"

"I did. At five in the morning. It was beautiful, although I had to prize my eyelids open to see it. I watched the sunrise." And tried desperately to keep up with Izzy without having a heart attack. She knew she couldn't rely on Izzy to give her mouth-to-mouth resuscitation.

"I guess that's romantic if you're awake enough to see it. Did he kiss you? Propose?"

"I didn't run with Jack. I ran with Izzy."

"The teenager?" Julia leaned against the counter. "So now you're best buddies?"

"Not exactly." She couldn't fathom Izzy at all. She'd spent all of the day before trying to make her life easier. She'd thought Izzy would appreciate having more time to herself, but it hadn't turned out that way. When Molly had chosen painting over baking, Izzy had been hurt and Flora had been unsure how to handle it.

"I can't believe you've moved in with him, when only last week you thought you were breaking up."

"I haven't 'moved in' exactly. And I have my own bedroom."

Julia grinned. "Shame about that."

"I wouldn't want to upset little Molly. She's adorable, Ju. I love her so much." She thought about the uncomfortable moment with the coat. "And she's so brave. You know she's upset, but then she sticks her chin out and gets on with it. And she is so good at art. She doesn't think she is, but the way she focuses and checks the perspective—"

"Yeah, yeah, I get it. You love Molly. But what about Jack? Are you in love with him?"

Flora thought about the moment they'd shared in the garden. Not the chemistry, although that was exciting, but the connection. He was interested in her. He cared about her. He understood her. It was a little terrifying. "It hasn't been that long."

"Long enough for you to fall in love with his daughter. And now you're living with him."

"I'm not living with him in the sense you mean. I'm living with him because of life, that thing that gets in the way of everyone's best plans. My apartment is mostly underwater thanks to the leak, and I have nowhere else to go. He has a massive brownstone with five bedrooms. It seemed crazy to say no. Can I help you?" She smiled at two teenagers who were hovering by the flowers. Having talked to them and ascertained that they wanted something special for their mother's birthday, she sent them away with large bunches of cheerful blue cornflowers. "Where were we?"

"You were telling me the guy basically owns a castle. Just remember the castle comes with a dragon."

"If you're talking about Izzy, she isn't a dragon. She's a wounded, grieving girl." And hard to reach. Impossible to reach.

"Last week you were convinced she didn't like you."

"I don't think it's personal. I'm not sure she'd like anyone who tried to muscle in on the family. And I think I was probably being oversensitive. She invited me running."

Julia made a sympathetic sound. "I hate to be the one to break this to you, but she was trying to kill you. Still, at least now I understand why you're walking around like a robot with joint issues. Admit it—you can hardly move."

Flora shrugged. "I admit it. Hugging, or anything that involves moving my limbs, is off-limits for a few days."

Julia gave a wicked grin. "Let's hope that today isn't the day Jack decides to have athletic sex with you."

Flora rubbed her thighs. "It's not funny. I was trying to do some of the things her mother used to do."

She forced herself to stop thinking about her aching limbs and made up a bouquet for one of her regular customers.

"The roses will last a week, Mrs. Mason, if you care for them properly." She handed them over. "Trim the ends, then pop them into a vase with flower food and about a liter of water."

"You've made them look so pretty, Flora. I'm going to put them right in water the way they are. They never need arranging when you've done them."

Julia nudged her. "You've got company."

Flora glanced up as Jack pushed open the door and strolled into the store. A few heads turned. Mrs. Mason's eyes widened.

"Well now isn't he a hottie?"

"Mrs. Mason!" Julia gave a shocked and delighted laugh.

"What? My grandchildren like to expand my vocabulary. And even without their help, I know an attractive man when I see one, and he is very handsome. Is he yours, Flora?"

"Oh! I—not exactly—I mean—"

"He's hers." Julia leaned forward, sharing a woman-to-woman moment with one of their favorite customers. "What do you think?"

They were both staring at Jack and Flora wondered whether it was too late to escape through the back window.

"I approve," Mrs. Mason said. "He has strong shoulders. Good arms. I like a man with good arms. What about you?"

Julia pondered. "I like a man with—"

"Will there be anything else, Mrs. Mason?" Flora dived in before Julia could say something that might lose her a precious customer.

"No, dear. Don't worry about me." Mrs. Mason waved

her away in the most indiscreet way possible and then Jack approached and smiled at her.

Flora thought Mrs. Mason might be about to collapse at his feet.

"I'm Serena Mason. I've been coming here for years. I wouldn't allow anyone else to do my flowers. Flora is so talented, as well as being one of my favorite people."

Jack laughed. "She's one of my favorite people, too." He turned to Flora. "Are you free for lunch?"

"I am if she isn't," Julia said cheerfully and Flora ignored her.

She checked the time. "Ten minutes?"

"Ten minutes works for me. I'll be in the coffee shop next door. Join me when you're ready." He walked away and Mrs. Mason sighed.

"What a dreamy man. Who will do the flowers at your wedding? You can't possibly do your own flowers."

"I'm not getting married so that's not a problem that needs solving." Flora bundled Mrs. Mason out of the door with her bouquet of flowers and hoped Jack hadn't overheard.

"She's not wrong. That man is dreamy." Julia cleared up her mess. "It's a shame he has baggage."

"A child is never baggage!" Flora gripped the edge of the counter. Her heart was racing and she felt a little breathless. How could that one word produce such an intense response? "His girls are adorable, and an important part of his life." She wouldn't, couldn't, think of them as baggage.

"Sorry." Julia put her hand on Flora's arm. "I hit a nerve."

Flora opened her mouth to change the subject, but in the end all that left her mouth was the truth.

"I was baggage. I heard my aunt say it once. 'My sister left me her baggage.'"

"Oh Flora—" Julia's eyes were warm with sympathy.

"You weren't baggage. You were a gift, but your aunt was too blind to see it."

"An unwanted gift. Believe me, there is no worse feeling for a child than knowing you're unwanted." And it was different, of course, because Molly and Izzy had Jack, but Flora didn't want to cause them a moment of insecurity. That was more important to her even than her feelings for Jack.

And what *were* her feelings for Jack?

Was it love? Maybe. Or maybe she was simply enjoying the novelty of being with someone who seemed to be genuinely interested in her.

Flora walked, or rather limped, the twenty paces to the coffee shop. Every step was agony, her muscles screaming in protest as she moved.

If Izzy suggested running again tomorrow, she'd be in trouble.

Jack was sitting at a table by the window, and there was a coffee and her favorite chicken salad waiting.

"Do you want something stronger than coffee and water?"

"This is great, thank you." She sat down and took a sip. "So why the surprise visit?"

"I wanted to spend time with you."

"I'm living in your house."

"I'm not sure if that makes our relationship more, or less, frustrating. We haven't exactly had much alone time." He moved his chair closer to hers and leaned forward. "I've been thinking about the summer. You can't stay on your own in the house."

Her heart plunged like an express elevator. "I understand." She was going to have to find somewhere new to rent, and she'd have to do it quickly. "I've already started looking for somewhere to live."

"You're looking for apartments? Why?"

"Because I can't face going back to the old one even if he manages to fix it. Even without the water disaster, there wasn't much to be excited about." It was unsettling to realize how much she was enjoying living as part of his family. Even the situation with Izzy couldn't tarnish the shiny feeling she had when she woke up in the mornings. "But I understand that I can't stay in the house, so don't worry. I'm already working on a solution."

"You're misunderstanding me. You can stay with us for as long as you like, but I don't want to leave you when we're away in the summer."

"You're worried I'm going to have a massive party and trash the place?"

He laughed. "No, I'm worried about missing you. And whatever happens, you are not moving into another crappy apartment, Flora." He reached across and took her hand. "We can do better."

She probably should have been nervous about how much she liked the "we" in that sentence.

"I'll try to make sure the next one isn't so crappy."

"I wish I could move you from the spare room to my room. It's starting to drive me crazy." His thumb made a slow circle of her palm and her heart beat as fast as it had when she'd been running.

"Me, too, but we have to take things slowly, I understand that."

"If this feels bad, I can't even imagine how it will feel to be on different continents for three weeks during the summer." He tightened his grip on her hand. "Come with us to the Lake District. I mean it."

Excitement and euphoria mingled with trepidation.

He wanted her to join them on vacation. She was flattered. Excited. On the other hand, *lakes*? He was asking her to spend time in a place with lakes? She hated large bodies of water. The thought made her hyperventilate. She was a dry land person. She could tell him, but then he'd want to know the reason and she wasn't ready to talk about that. Not even with Jack. She never talked about that.

But staying here meant three weeks with no Jack—and also no Molly—

Why couldn't it have been the Caribbean? But then she would have had the sea to contend with. A nice city break? Paris? London? Anywhere but a place called the Lake District.

She shuddered.

"Do you think the girls would be okay with me coming?" She pushed her uneaten food to the side of her plate. "It's the first time you've been on this holiday without Becca."

"All the more reason to take you with us."

"All the more reason to keep things as normal and familiar as possible."

"It won't be familiar." He rubbed his fingers across his forehead. "Normal doesn't look the same as it did. Whether you come or not, it's going to be different. So come. Unless you don't want this to be more than it already is."

So far their relationship had drifted along. This was the first time either of them had made an attempt to define it.

"I...do want more."

"Good. Because I do, too. So spend the summer with us."

She thought about what it would mean. The Lake District. Lakes. On the other hand, there would also be Molly. Spending time with her would be so much fun. And Jack. And it would give her a chance to get to know Izzy a little better in a more informal atmosphere. Maybe it would be easier away from her own territory.

She'd just make sure to stay clear of all water activities.

"All right." Decision made, she felt a rush of excitement. "I'll talk to Celia."

"Your boss didn't strike me as the most sympathetic of people. Will she say yes?"

Flora thought about all the weekends she'd worked, all the holidays, and the number of times she'd slogged to the flower market when her colleagues were too hungover or too generally lazy to show up. "I think she'll say yes."

Surely Celia would be reasonable when Flora pointed out how flexible she'd been? The more she thought about it, the more she wanted to go with Jack and his girls. By the time she arrived back at work she was fired up and determined.

"Celia, could I please have a word?"

"Not now," her boss said. "I have four—"

"Now," Flora said, surprising both of them with the force of her tone.

She almost apologized for sounding so assertive but then realized that you couldn't be firm one minute and wobbly the next. If she was doing this, she was doing this.

"I wondered if it might be possible to—" *pathetic, pathetic.* She stopped in midsentence and lifted her chin. "I need to take three weeks off from the middle of July."

Celia frowned. "Is this some sort of joke?"

Flora's heart beat faster. Celia wasn't happy, and Flora preferred people to be happy. But Celia wasn't her aunt. Flora didn't owe her anything except her dedication as an employee. And she'd gone way beyond that.

It was time she grabbed a little happiness for herself. "It's no joke."

"Staff are allowed a maximum of a week at a time."

"I know, but I took no vacation time at all last year, and I have worked most weekends and every holiday for—" she searched her brain "—actually since I started working here."

"You're seriously asking me for three weeks off?" Celia's expression was so threatening that Flora had an almost overwhelming urge to apologize and back down. *Three weeks? You're right, it's a ridiculous request. Ignore me.*

But then she imagined Jack and the girls on vacation by themselves. Taking long walks in the forest, and enjoying lazy evenings under the stars. And she knew that if she backed down now, not only would she not get to go on vacation with Jack, but Celia would never stop giving her the armpit work slots.

She clenched her fists and dug her nails into her palms. "Actually, Celia, I'm not asking. I'm telling you. As a courtesy." Panic engulfed her. Her legs weakened as she imagined Celia showing her the door.

Celia was obviously imagining that too because she straightened her shoulders in an aggressive stance. "And what if I tell you your job won't be here when you come back?"

Flora felt a wave of dizziness. What if Celia was serious? What if she lost her job? "I hope that won't be the case because I enjoy working here—" that wasn't exactly true, but there was a limit to how assertive Flora was prepared to be in one session "—and I think there are many of your regular clients who would miss me if I wasn't here."

Celia's eyes narrowed and her mouth tightened. "Fine," she said finally. "But not a day longer than three weeks."

Flora almost died of shock. Part of her wanted to check that she'd understood correctly. *Are you sure? Do you mean it?* Fortunately her instinct told her to quit while she was ahead. And she smothered the impulse to hug Celia, because her boss was about as huggable as a cactus.

"Thank you." Flora turned and guided her shaking legs

across the store to where Julia was wrestling with a huge hand-tied bouquet.

"What are you looking so pleased about?" Julia cursed as she trapped her finger under the knot she was tying. "And how do you make this look so easy? I'm the only person who can lose a finger making a bouquet."

"I stood up to Celia."

"Well good for you. And not before time." Julia finally managed to tie the bouquet. "Does this look okay?"

Flora tweaked it a little. "It's great."

"So what did you say no to? Another weekend? Another early morning? That woman really pushes her luck."

"I'm taking three weeks off in the summer." She gave Julia a summary of her encounter with Celia but instead of punching the air and congratulating her, her friend looked appalled.

"You're going on a three-week vacation? I can't believe you asked Celia for that."

"You're the one who told me to stand up to her."

"I know, but I was talking about not letting her force you to work every weekend. Not this. Three weeks with the dead wife's best friend? Doing all the things the wife used to do? Are you sure about this?"

Flora's stomach lurched. She was sure. She *was*. "Yes. I'm excited. I want to be with Jack. Being with Jack means being with his girls and fitting into his life. Fitting in with whatever they usually do as a family."

"What about the friend? She might not be thrilled to see her best friend's husband with another woman. She might stab you between the shoulder blades the moment you arrive. Before you know it, your body will be decaying in that forest."

Why was it that Julia always managed to articulate the fears Flora had been trying to ignore?

"I promise not to turn my back on her."

"What are the sleeping arrangements? Have you even had sex yet?"

Mortified, Flora glanced across the store. "Could you keep your voice down? I don't think they heard you in Florida."

"You haven't answered my question."

"Not *actual* sex, although we have had some very erotic moments."

"Where?"

Flora wished her friend wasn't quite so insistent on details. "Everywhere. I think about sex a lot when I'm with him. He's very—"

"Yes, I noticed—" Julia waggled her eyebrows "—but, Flora, at some point you have to do more than *think* about sex."

"We've done more than think. We've kissed."

"You kissed." Julia stared at her. "And?"

"There is no 'and.' We've kissed. And it is always amazing, and stop looking at me like that because frankly kissing him was better than any sex I ever had."

"You must have had terrible sex."

"I wouldn't say I've been particularly lucky in my past relationships, but that's mostly my fault. I'm usually so intent on pleasing other people, I find it hard to please myself. But that's ending. I'm working on it."

"Well you need to work on it faster. Call this an intervention if you like. Right now you're in a celibate relationship where your main focus seems to be quietly filling the gap left by his late wife. And for this you don't even get great sex?"

"If the photos are to be believed, I'm significantly heavier than she was so I'd probably get stuck in the gap." Her attempt at a joke didn't even raise a smile. "This vacation is me pleasing myself. I want to spend time with them."

"Has he said he loves you?"

"No, and that's fine. I'm not sure I'm ready to hear those words." She gave a grunt of pain as she bent to cut some string. "I haven't said them, either."

"*Are* you in love with him?"

"Don't know. Trying not to think about it."

"You don't want to be in love?"

"Not if he isn't going to love me back. Loving someone who doesn't love you back is the ultimate confidence crusher." She thought of her aunt. "It's also exhausting and bad for the soul, because you keep thinking 'maybe if I do this or that, they'll love me,' so you keep trying but it doesn't make any difference and it's pretty hard not to take that personally. Before long you've twisted yourself into so many knots you don't even know how to get back to the person you were."

Julia stared at her. "How about just being yourself?"

"That never works for me. Or it never has in the past." She tied the bouquet, thinking about all the things she'd told Jack that she'd never told anyone else. Not even Julia. "With Jack, I *am* mostly myself. That's what makes it scarier. If he rejects me, he's rejecting the real me, not a manufactured version of me. Does that make sense?"

"Not really. When I met Geoff I loved him, he loved me. The real me. End of. It's pretty simple really."

"There is nothing simple about relationships. You two are lucky, that's all."

"Well, you obviously have strong feelings for Jack. And you love Molly, so Izzy is the only real obstacle. Do you even see how insane this is? If Izzy only likes you because you go running with her, then you'll have to run every day forever and that is going to kill you. Are you planning on being a fake person for the rest of your life?"

"Maybe I'll be a fitter person. I certainly ache more." She rubbed her spine and tried to ignore the pain in her legs.

"Have you tried stretching?"

"No. I can't move, let alone stretch. My objective is survival. I haven't had a heart attack yet, so that's got to be good, right? And if I'm spending the vacation with Jack, I need to look decent in a pair of shorts."

Julia gave her a dark look. "I think how your legs look in shorts is the least of your worries right now."

Was Julia right? Maybe.

One thing was sure—this holiday was going to be make-or-break. Flora hoped she wasn't the one who was going to break.

# 10

## *Clare*

"I've had an email from Jack." Clare spread butter onto toast, and added a spoonful of the orange marmalade she'd spent the whole of the day before making. Most of the jars would be stored and used for weekend treats over the coming summer, but she'd kept this one back. If she was going to toil over a boiling pan, the least she could do was savor the fruits of her labor.

"How's he doing?" Todd reached across and stole her toast.

She gave him a look. "Why do you always eat mine?"

"Yours always tastes better for some reason. And I love your marmalade. You should start a business."

They were sitting at the large kitchen table that had originally belonged to her grandmother and bore the scars of generations of family life. So many conversations had taken place here.

Clare ran her finger absently over one of the grooves, wondering who had carved it. "Just because you're good at something, doesn't mean you have to turn it into a business. Sometimes you can do something because you enjoy it."

"I've annoyed you." He leaned in and kissed her. "It was a compliment, not a real suggestion."

"No, I'm the one being sensitive. It sounded like—"

"—something Becca would say." He gave her shoulder a squeeze. "I know. The moment I said it, I knew you'd think that. Sorry. I didn't mean to make you think of her. So how is Jack?"

"He didn't email you? He was asking about the summer." Clare stood up and slid another slice of bread into the toaster, pondering on how different men and women were. Jack was Todd's friend, and yet he was asking her for an update. At one point during their friendship she and Becca had been in touch almost daily, exchanging small details of their lives, sharing feelings and revealing emotions. When Becca had injured her knee and been told she'd never dance again, it was Clare she'd emailed at three in the morning and it was Becca Clare had emailed when Aiden had been born prematurely and had breathing problems. From small irritations to major life heartaches, there had been virtually nothing about their lives that they hadn't shared.

If someone had asked her at any point how Becca was doing, Clare would have known and yet here was Todd asking her about Jack.

Was it that her relationship with Becca had been particularly close, or was it that male friendship was different? Male friendships tended to be anchored by activities rather than emotions. Todd, who had made several friends since they'd moved from London, contacted them to arrange sailing or hiking. They talked about wind direction or routes and bonded over an appreciation of the locally brewed beer.

Jack and Todd behaved like long-lost friends each summer, although their interaction bore no resemblance to the relationship Clare had with friends. They teased each other, exchanged good-natured insults, and generally kept everything light.

Maybe that type of friendship was less complicated.

Todd finished his toast. "You're the one who makes all the arrangements. Jack and I just come along and enjoy ourselves. What did the email say? Are they coming to see us?"

"Yes." And Clare didn't know what to make of it. She'd read the email with a sick feeling in her stomach and so many emotions she couldn't begin to untangle them. She started to type a reply and then stopped because her hands were shaking on the keys and she kept making mistakes. Feelings she'd worked hard to suppress had erupted past the barriers she'd put in place. She felt grief for Jack and pity for herself for having the bad fortune to find herself in this situation. She felt angry with Becca, and then guilty for feeling angry with someone who was dead.

Her fingers had finally stopped shaking but still she hadn't responded because she didn't know what to say. She loved Jack. She loved the children. But seeing them again would be hard. It would stoke all those feelings she'd worked hard to control. Grief. Anger. Guilt. Indecision. Oh yes, indecision. She'd burned the letter but the memory of its contents couldn't be so easily destroyed.

"That's great. The more the merrier. Jack and I can get some sailing and hiking in. The kids will love it." Todd glanced at his watch. "I have to get going. I have a site visit on the other side of the valley and you know what the traffic is like at the moment."

She did. It was another reason to be grateful she worked from home. Jack had converted one of the downstairs rooms into a study for her. The bay windows offered views across the gardens to the lake and often she found herself spending more time staring at the water than she did her computer screen.

Only as he was about to leave did she blurt out the information she'd been keeping to herself. "Jack's bringing someone with him."

Todd grabbed his coat from the back of the door. "I hope he's bringing Izzy and Molly."

"Yes, but this is someone as well as Izzy and Molly. Her name is Flora."

Todd lifted his eyebrows. "A friend of the girls?"

"I rather got the impression," Clare said slowly, "that she's a friend of Jack's." And she felt conflicted. Her feelings were already complicated. It seemed unfair of Jack to introduce yet another complication into the mix. Their two families meshed so well, and now he was bringing a stranger.

For all her faults, Becca had been her best friend. Clare had loved her. And now she was expected to welcome her replacement. She'd have to smile and make conversation. Laugh, even though her heart was breaking and all she really wanted was to see Becca living happily with Jack.

"That's great news." Todd picked up his car keys. "I'm happy for Jack."

He accepted the prospect of their visit with his usual enthusiasm. *The more the merrier.* He was an extrovert who was never happier than when he was in the middle of a social gathering. If Todd hadn't been so gregarious, Clare probably never would have met him. He was the one who'd struck up conversation and asked her on a date. He'd chiseled his way past her shyness to find the person inside. And she loved that he made that side of life easy for her. With Todd, there were never embarrassing silences or awkward moments. He could talk about anything with anyone. He and Jack had hit it off right from the start, and Todd was obviously looking forward to seeing him again.

There were no undercurrents. No complications.

Clare envied him. She and Becca had always told each other everything, which had felt good until "everything" had included details Clare wished she didn't know.

Her exasperation was tinged with envy. "Don't you think it's a bit soon? Is it a little insensitive, perhaps?"

"What is there to be sensitive about?"

*Me*, Clare thought. She and Becca had been the link that had brought the two families together. "Becca."

"Becca's no longer here, and I'm sure she would have wanted him to be happy, don't you?"

Clare wasn't sure of that. Becca had usually placed her own needs and happiness above everyone else's, including Jack's and the children's.

Whether at work or at play, Becca had been the center of attention, which was why Clare wasn't sure she would have approved of Jack moving on so fast. Most of the time Clare had made excuses for her friend. Becca's past had molded her into the person she was. But was that an explanation or an excuse? For how long was an adult permitted to use a difficult childhood as a free pass for all undesirable thoughts and actions? Deep down Clare wasn't sure if Becca's behavior was driven by a survival instinct or downright selfishness.

*It's every man for himself, Clare. How do you think I've got where I am?*

Clare finished her toast. "It's been almost a year."

"And? How long does a guy need to suffer before society stops judging him? I bet it was the longest year of his life. Grim. Or is there some time frame to grief that I don't know about?" His voice gentled. "I understand that it's hard for you but this wasn't just about Becca. Jack's our friend, too, Clare, and has been for more than two decades. He was best man at our wedding. It's never been just about Becca. We owe him our support."

"I know. And he has it, of course." She decided he was right. This was about Jack, now, it had to be.

"Then what's the problem?" A note of impatience. Todd, who found every social situation easy. Todd, the problem solver. *Lower the floor, add skylights*, whatever the challenge, he had a solution and he was always sure of it.

Clare had been drawn to him for many reasons, but the biggest had been his certainty. His confidence in his place in the world.

"It will feel strange to see him with someone else."

"He's still the same Jack. It's like remodeling an old house. The bones stay the same even if the outward features are different." He opened the door. "You don't even know it's serious."

"If it wasn't serious, he wouldn't be bringing her. Jack isn't the type to jump from one relationship to another."

"And it upsets you?" Todd paused, even though he was now almost certainly going to be late.

What should she say? She'd been on the verge of telling him so many times, but she'd always stopped herself. She'd never been a gossip, something that had frustrated and amused Becca in equal amounts.

*For once in your life can't you enjoy a good bitch about someone? Nice people are boring.*

Clare had laughed and tried not to be offended but of course she had been because all her life she'd tried to keep up with Becca. At school she'd been so shy she'd found it difficult to make friends. She'd been teased and excluded by the other children until the day Becca had arrived. Becca, the class rebel had, for some reason Clare never entirely understood, decided to give her best friend status. From that point on Clare had no problems with the other children. She and Becca were as close as sisters, and if some of the things Becca did made her uncomfortable, she accepted it as the price to be paid for friendship. No one was perfect, were they? No one did the right thing all the time.

Todd was watching her. "Is there something else going on, Clare?"

There had been so many times when she'd considered telling him the truth, but decided it wasn't fair to put him in the same position she was in, particularly as deep down she knew he hadn't liked Becca that much. What would he say if he knew the truth? What if he judged Becca or, worse, what if he judged Clare?

"It's been hard, that's all."

"It's coming up to the anniversary. It's a tough time for you."

It was, but it was also confusing. Part of her longed to talk about it, but how could she? It would mean admitting how angry she felt, and how confused. And it would feel disloyal. Clare was probably the only person in the world who knew everything about Becca. She knew all about Becca's childhood. She understood how Becca had become Becca.

But Becca was gone, and it wasn't going to help anyone if Clare kept dwelling on the past.

"It's tougher on Jack."

"Which is probably why he needs to get away. I know it must feel strange thinking of him with someone else, but life's tough enough without making it tougher."

"But it's three weeks, Todd. Not dinner, or an afternoon on the lake. Three whole weeks with a woman I've never met and don't know." And wasn't sure she wanted to meet.

"Look at it this way—after three weeks together, you'll know her."

How could you love someone and still want to kill them? "I'm not like you. I don't make friends in an instant."

"You're assuming you're not going to like her."

"It isn't that." Although it was partly that, of course. Could she really like Becca's replacement?

"Jack and I will be around, and you'll have the kids and the dog. In other words plenty of chaos. You'll make her welcome."

"Yes." When she'd worked in a busy London office she'd constantly had to talk to people she didn't know. But somehow it had felt different at work. Part of a persona she'd created. Clare, the magazine editor. "I just hope the girls are all right about it. It must be a big change for them." She felt a twinge of guilt that she hadn't been better at staying in touch. She remembered Izzy at the funeral, holding so tightly to Molly's hand it had been impossible to figure out who was supporting whom.

"Jack adores the girls. There is no way he'd get involved with someone they didn't like."

Clare imagined Flora emerging from the car with sinuous grace. She'd probably give a little wry smile when she saw the house and contemplated the prospect of three weeks of rural living. Another Becca. Men had a type, didn't they?

But she and Flora didn't share a history. What would they talk about? Clare had trained herself to make polite conversation for a short time, but three weeks?

"Do I put them in the same room? Separate rooms?"

Todd shrugged. "Ask him what he wants."

To him it was that simple, but she knew she wouldn't be able to do that. Her fingers would never be able to type out that email.

"I'll make up two rooms. If they want to share, that's their choice."

"Good decision. And I know you'll be kind to Flora. You are the perfect hostess. And Jack has good taste. Jack chose Becca, right?"

No, Clare thought. Becca had chosen Jack.

*I've met a man.*

"What time will you be home?"

"Not sure. Can I call you? I'll be driving past the farm shop. Want me to pick up some steaks?"

"Aiden is vegetarian."

"Still? I'd hoped he'd be over it by now."

"It's not a whim, Todd, it's a belief. A lifestyle choice."

"Right. Well I'll buy steaks for us and a large carrot for our son."

She laughed. "I'm making vegetarian lasagna. For all of us."

Todd shuddered. "What else are you doing today, apart from wrestling vegetables?"

"I have a feature to finish, and then I'm going over to the boathouse. The last guests left yesterday so I'm going to move some of our things back in and get it ready for the summer." They had an agreement that they never rented it during July and August, that way the family could enjoy their home without sharing it with strangers.

Clare loved the rental income, but she also loved the two months of the year she could take her coffee down to the lakeside in her yoga pants, without worrying that she could be seen by people she didn't know. She dreamed of the day

Todd's business took off and they were able to afford to keep it to themselves and not rent it out to strangers.

"Do you need help with that?"

"No, I'll enjoy it. I'm looking forward to having a day to myself." She felt like a child looking forward to Christmas. It was going to be a day entirely for her.

To her surprise Todd put his keys and his coat down and walked back to her.

"You're still okay with this life we chose?"

"Why would you even ask me that?"

"It's all the talk of Becca probably. She blamed me for making you throw in your glittering career and move out of London to follow my dream."

"We moved when my father died. We agreed it was the right thing. And anyway, this wasn't just your dream, it was my dream, too. We were both tired of working hard for other people. And my career wasn't that glittering."

"Free shoes and handbags?"

Clare laughed. "Crowded commutes and early morning meetings? And I don't have much of a need for expensive shoes and purses here. Wellington boots are the order of the day. And this wasn't an impulsive decision." They'd talked about it for years before they'd taken the plunge. Every Saturday over a bottle of wine, they'd plotted ways to move back here. "I was born here, remember? You'd never set foot in the Lakes until you met me."

"A lapse in judgment I will always regret." He brushed a toast crumb from her cheek with the tip of his finger. "So many missed years."

She knew that Todd loved the Lakes as much as she did. "Admit it, you married me for my family house."

"I did. Your mother's amazing chocolate fudge cake might also have played a part. I'd move across continents for that." He trailed his finger along her jaw. "You don't miss London and those days when you used to sit in your glass office with an assistant bringing you coffee?"

"I made my own coffee. And no, I don't miss it." She enjoyed making coffee here in her own kitchen. When she was leaning against the range cooker, warming herself in winter, she thought the kitchen might be her favorite room in the house. But then she curled up in the living room with its views across the garden to the lake and decided that was her favorite room. Or maybe her bedroom with its sloping roof and tiny balcony. "I love the life we've built here. It was a shared decision, Todd." Everything they did was shared. They were a partnership, and she loved that. Until last year, she'd been able to say she had no secrets from Todd. Thanks to Becca that was no longer true. It made her feel tainted.

She could almost hear Becca laughing.

*You tell your husband everything? Even your secrets? Oh, Clare! You should live a life full of delicious secrets and scandal.*

Clare couldn't think of anything more exhausting.

"Stop frowning." Todd rubbed his finger across her forehead. "If it's going to stress you having Jack and the kids, I'll call him and make an excuse."

"No! I don't want you to do that." But the fact that he would have done it made her feel warm and loved. "I want to see them, I really do."

"Then what?" He stroked her hair away from her face. "I know you and Becca had been friends forever, but I often thought you were growing apart. I hadn't realized that losing her would affect you this way."

"What makes you think we were growing apart?" And her own mother had said much the same thing.

"You two were very different people. How your friendship endured for so long I don't know. You seemed to have so little in common, but of course you and Becca were bonded virtually from birth so perhaps longevity was the glue." Todd kissed her and walked to the door, retrieving his coat and keys on the way. "Jack is moving on, and maybe when you see that you'll be able to move on, too."

Would it be that simple? She truly hoped so.

After he left, she grabbed her jacket and walked along the narrow path that led from the lodge to the boathouse. This section of the lake was densely wooded, the only sounds the soft lap of the lake against the shore, a chorus of birdsong and the insistent drumming of a woodpecker. Her jeans protected her from the sharp sting of nettles and the bite of insects and the sounds washed over her along with a sense of peace. Never, not once, had she considered it a mistake to move back here. She was in her element. She was aware that others might see it as a small life, but she saw it as a rich life. More importantly, it was the life she wanted.

They'd had an unusually dry spell, so all she had on her feet was running shoes. She breathed in air sweetened by the scents of summer and her heart lifted a little as the boathouse came into view. Splintered planks and spiders' webs had been replaced by Lakeland stone, cedar and acres of glass. Todd had worked on the conversion, using locally sourced materials and extending it to provide luxury accommodation while still retaining the charm of the original building. The project had attracted attention from first the local press and then a Sunday magazine, providing a publicity boost that Todd had needed.

When he'd left the large architecture practice he'd worked for in London to set up on his own in the Lake District, Clare had been nervous but apart from the nagging worry about income, it had been a positive move. Aiden settled easily into his new school, and Clare discovered that she loved the slower pace of life.

This was her favorite time of day, early in the morning. The air was fresh and clean, the only sounds the call of the birds and the occasional splash of water against the shore.

Boulders framed the edge of this section of the lake, some shiny and smooth, others rough and ragged, the surface roughened by wind and water. Clare had stood on those slabs as a child, shivering with excitement and fear as her father had urged her to jump into the clear water. She'd seen tiny fish darting and a tangle of weed and then she'd plunged and gasped as the ice-cold lake water closed over her skinny body.

The place held nothing but good memories and they seeped under her skin, diluting some of those nastier feelings.

Stepping inside the place gave her a holiday feeling. It was furnished for the top end of the rental market, a place where people could either continue their life of luxury or find it for a few weeks.

It was nothing like Todd and Clare's own house. Real life didn't happen in this place. There were no muddy hiking boots strewn in the entryway ready to trip up the unwary, no gouges on the table, weatherproof jackets, or school bags. No reminder of jobs to be done. Everything, from the art on the walls to the hand-carved wooden sculpture, had been carefully curated.

She opened the glass doors that led to the balcony, noticing that the previous occupants had moved the furniture. They'd been honeymooners and had barely emerged from the boathouse all week, captivated by the romance of the place.

Would Jack be expecting a romantic escape with his new friend? What would she think of the peace and calm of the lake?

Where would Clare take her if she needed a city fix?

The home of Beatrix Potter, or Wordsworth, wouldn't be enough.

She walked into the kitchen, telling herself that keeping his girlfriend entertained was Jack's responsibility not hers. And presumably he'd be thoughtful about it. He'd have the children with him and Jack was above everything else an excellent father.

She made herself a coffee and took it onto the balcony. As teenagers, she and Becca had brought their sleeping bags here and "camped" in the boathouse. At the time it had been exciting, but Clare had reached the age where she preferred luxury.

The irony was that she wouldn't have been able to afford what they charged to stay in this place. It always shocked her what people were prepared to pay, but as Todd always said their "normal" was another person's dream. And it was dreamy.

The reed beds provided a refuge for birds during the winter, and protection during the nesting season. It was usual to see cormorants and ospreys, as well as kingfishers. She watched as dragonflies danced together across the surface of the water, their iridescent bodies catching the light.

Maybe she'd put a bottle of wine in the fridge and persuade Todd to come over and watch the sunset. Or maybe they should spend a night here. They could sleep with the doors open, and breakfast on the balcony before the world was awake. It was her favorite time on the lake, when the surface had a glassy stillness.

It would be romantic.

She could almost hear Becca laughing. Romantic to Becca was Paris, or Rome, not a boathouse on a lake. She'd never understood Clare's contentment with the small things in life. She'd always wanted the big things.

Clare closed her eyes. She had to stop this. Becca was gone. That part of her life was gone. She should draw a line under it. Yes, there were times when she missed her friend, but the truth was it was their old friendship she missed, not the relationship they'd had in recent years. Todd was right that they'd grown further apart. It had been a shock and disappointment to discover that friendship could change over time. She still remembered Becca grabbing her hand on their first day at school and saying *Nothing is ever going to come between us.*

But it had. Time had come between them. Time, and all those small life choices that had gradually taken them in different directions.

This was a new chapter. Todd was right. If Jack could move on, then so could she. She'd welcome Jack's girlfriend into their home and try hard not to think about Becca.

# 11

*Izzy*

Izzy was silent as the car trundled along the leafy, winding driveway to Lake Lodge.

Molly had insisted on sitting next to Flora for the journey from the airport, and now she was asleep on her shoulder in the back of the car.

Pain ripped through Izzy. For a year, she'd been both sister and mother to Molly. She'd hugged her, comforted her, held her own feelings inside so that she could support her sister. And then Flora had appeared in their lives.

Why had she agreed to join them? She was either totally insensitive, or totally in love with Izzy's dad. Neither of those options were good.

Izzy felt betrayed, not only by her father but also by her little sister. She'd held Molly together, and now it seemed she was no longer needed. Like their father she had taken forward steps, moved on, so where did that leave Izzy?

She hadn't moved on. She was still stuck in the same confused, terrified place only now she wasn't sure what her purpose was. If she wasn't needed, what would happen?

Her dad threw her a questioning smile. "You're quiet. Everything okay?"

"Everything is fine." She'd become so adept at lying, it was a little unnerving. The slow buildup of emotion inside her was equally unnerving. She was terrified that at some point she was going to lose it. It had been a hideous, horrible journey.

What was wrong with her? She should be pleased that Molly liked Flora. She'd read enough books and talked to enough friends from blended families to know that stepmothers could be a nightmare. Flora wasn't a nightmare in that sense. She was kind. Fun, even. She was good with Molly. Izzy should be relieved, shouldn't she? Instead, she felt frightened. And a little angry. The nightmare for her wasn't that her father's new woman was a horrible person, it was that Flora was so likable.

Glancing behind her she saw Molly slide her hand into Flora's.

"I'm glad you're here."

Izzy wasn't glad. Right at that moment Izzy hated Flora.

They followed the curve of the drive and there, bathed in sunlight, was Lake Lodge. The front door was almost obscured by a profusion of climbing roses, and Izzy felt her heart beat a little faster because it was all so familiar and yet unfamiliar because this time her mother wasn't here with them.

She gripped her seat, trying to hold it together. Breathe. Breathe.

She saw the door open, and there was Aunt Clare, wearing a floral dress and a beaming smile, her fine blond hair cut short to frame her face. Behind her was Aiden, slouched against the door frame, his dark hair falling over his eyes.

Her heart beat a little harder.

*I love you, Izzy.*

Did he still feel that way? Probably not. She'd learned that feelings were strange, unpredictable things.

The moment the car stopped, Molly gave a whoop, unclipped her seat belt and raced across the gravel drive.

"Aunt Clare!"

Aunt Clare scooped her up and swung her round before giving her a massive hug and kiss.

Izzy felt her throat close. She felt vulnerable. Awkward. A thousand years older than the last time she'd been here. Life had seemed so simple then, but it hadn't been of course. It was just that she'd seen it as simple because she hadn't known the truth. Now she knew and knowing was like dragging a boulder along behind her.

"Izz?" Her dad was looking at her and she felt panic rising inside her like milk left too long on the heat.

Unless she wanted to handle questions, she needed to move.

She reached for the door but he leaned across and his hand covered hers.

"Are you doing okay? I know this isn't easy." He spoke softly. "You're thinking of Mom, and that's natural. I guess we all are."

She was thinking of her mother, but probably not in the way he assumed. The secret she'd been carrying formed a barrier between her and everyone else.

She'd never felt more isolated in her life. "I'm okay, Dad. Really. How are you doing?" It had to be hard on him, too.

"I'm good, and a lot of that is because of you." He squeezed her hand. "You've been a superhero, Izzy. I don't know what I would have done without you this past year. You're the best daughter a man could have."

His words made her eyes sting and her throat close. She knew she wasn't that, but she didn't say anything. She wouldn't have known what to say, particularly as Flora was still sitting in the back seat.

"Izzy, I promise you're going to have fun here. Flora and I are going to take care of Molly so you can do whatever you enjoy."

"I enjoy being with Molly, Dad. She's my sister."

Did she really have to say it? There wasn't a single person on the planet who understood her.

"But you should be spending time with kids your own age. I expect you'll be pleased to see Aiden again."

She was, although she was also nervous. What if his feelings toward her had changed? And she was so angry with everyone, what if she was angry with him? What if she hated him, too?

"We should say hi to Aunt Clare." With a quick smile, she fumbled for the door and exited the car hoping to leave her mini meltdown behind in the car.

She walked across to Clare a little hesitantly. Last time they'd seen each other was at the funeral, which Izzy barely remembered. The whole day had been a dark, heavy blur of horror.

Clare put Molly down and then Izzy felt herself wrapped in the same warm hug Molly had been given. She breathed in Clare's floral scent and closed her eyes for a moment, allowing herself the comfort even though it wasn't specific to her problem.

Aunt Clare had always been a hugger and a homemaker.

Izzy had often heard her mother say that she couldn't understand why anyone would give up a glamorous career working for a glossy, glamorous magazine to bury herself in the middle of nowhere and spend her day making beds after other people, wiping mud from boots and baking cakes.

Izzy didn't know anything about editing a glossy magazine. All she knew was that whenever you were with Aunt Clare you felt cared for and fussed over. She was never on her phone, distracted by which filters to use on a photograph she was about to post on social media, and she never cared about her hair or her makeup when she was hugging you. Even though she was busy, she was never in a rush. She seemed to live in the moment rather than pushing forward to the next goal, and nothing she did was for public consumption.

On the flight, Izzy had started to write a piece about the perils of presenting a fake version of yourself to the world, but then she'd realized she was guilty of doing exactly that. It wasn't the same, of course, not really. Keeping secrets and thoughts inside you wasn't the same as presenting a polished, happy image. She'd made that the point of the piece, the central question that she hoped would stimulate conversation. How much of your true self do you keep from the world?

"How's my Izzy?" The affection in Clare's voice made Izzy tempted to tell the truth.

*I'm completely messed-up. Help me.*

This wasn't the time, of course, but maybe—maybe later—

"I'm good, Aunt Clare." She softened her wooden tone with a wide smile. "How are you?"

"We're doing great, thanks." Clare eased away and stroked Izzy's hair back from her face. "But look at you. You look wonderful."

Molly tugged at Clare's arm. "You need to meet Flora."

Izzy saw an almost imperceptible change in Clare's expression and realized that this was probably awkward for her, too. Izzy's mom and Clare had been friends forever. Did she feel resentful that Jack was here with another woman?

Clare stepped forward, hand outstretched. "Good to meet you, Flora." Her tone was so cool and polite that Izzy was taken aback. Clare was normally warm and friendly.

"I so appreciate you inviting me—" Flora broke off, cheeks pink, as if she'd realized that Clare hadn't in fact invited her, and that she was really only here because of Jack.

"I hope you'll enjoy your stay." Clare sounded like a hotel owner greeting a guest who had trashed the room on their previous stay.

Izzy realized she was struggling and knew, right there and then, that she was never going to be able to confide in Aunt Clare. It would be too difficult. Clare had her own feelings to deal with.

No, Izzy was alone with this. She might as well have been shipwrecked on an island.

"You must be exhausted." Clare led them into the house and suddenly Izzy was standing in front of Aiden. Her heart gave a little kick and her breathing felt weird. She almost made that most annoying of adult observations, *you've grown*, but she stopped herself in time. But he *had* grown. Had his shoulders always been that wide? No, definitely not. She tried to work out why she felt awkward and realized it was because he seemed more man than boy, a stranger. And then he gave her that funny smile that tilted his mouth more to one side than the other and he was Aiden again.

"Hi." Deciding they were too old to hug without it seeming weird, she thrust her hands into the pockets of her jeans and grinned back.

He seemed a lot more comfortable with the situation than

she was, but he'd always been that way. He didn't much care what people thought of him. It was a trait she both admired and envied.

"Hey, Fizzy." He'd given her that name when she'd been going through a phase of wanting fizzy drinks and it had stuck. "Good to see you."

She wanted to say that it was good to see him, too, but her tongue stuck to the roof of her mouth and she found it hard to speak. It might have been awkward, but they were saved by the arrival of Chase, who barked loudly and smacked everyone's legs with his wagging tail.

"Chase." Molly bent down to hug him and he licked her face and jumped on her.

"Don't let him lick your face, sweetie. How many times have I told you not to jump!" Clare tugged at his collar. "Sit. Sit, you naughty dog."

Molly laughed in a way Izzy hadn't heard her laugh in a long time.

She made a fuss of the dog, too, all the time conscious of Aiden standing close by.

Thoroughly overexcited, Chase ripped himself away from Clare's restraining hand and leaped at Flora, jumping up and planting muddy paws on her bright orange top.

"Chase!" Clare was appalled and embarrassed. "What a greeting. I'm so very sorry."

"Oh don't be. He's adorable." Instead of backing off, Flora dropped to her knees and hugged the dog. She was laughing, her eyes closed as Chase took full advantage. "Are you excited to see us? You beautiful, beautiful dog." She stroked, tickled, made a fuss until Chase almost died of ecstasy.

Her orange top was spattered with muddy paw prints, but Flora didn't seem to care.

Clare was looking at her oddly. "You like dogs?"

"I love all animals," Flora said. "I always wanted a pet, but it wasn't possible."

Izzy stilled. She'd wanted a pet, too, but her mother had been horrified at the thought. *Dogs are fine if you live in the country, but they need walking, and they leave their hair everywhere—*

"Chase was a rescue dog." Clare gave his collar a little tug. "He was a year when we had him. Believe it or not we did a lot of training, but all that goes out of the window when he sees someone he likes."

"Can I take him for a walk, Aunt Clare?" Molly was on her knees next to Flora, fussing over the dog.

"He'd love that and frankly so would I, but why don't you wash your hands and have something to eat first? You've had a long journey and airplane food and the time change leaves you feeling strange. Come into the kitchen." Clare herded them inside. "Are you hungry? I made a stack of ham sandwiches, and the scones are freshly baked. We still have homemade strawberry jam from last summer. Flora, I'm so sorry about your shirt. You'll probably want to change and freshen up."

"That would be good, thank you." Flora grabbed her bag and paused, waiting to be directed.

Izzy saw Clare glance at her father and knew instinctively that she was wondering about sleeping arrangements. Izzy had been wondering that, too. Were Flora and her father sleeping together? She didn't know. If they were, then they'd been discreet about it. But here things would be different. There was no work, or rushing around. The whole idea was to spend time together.

Her stomach ached.

"I've put Molly and Izzy in the turret as usual." Clare

was brisk and matter-of-fact. "Flora has the lake room, and Jack you're next door. Hope that works."

"I know the lake room. I'll take you." Molly grabbed Flora's hand and they vanished from the room.

Izzy sat at the scrubbed kitchen table, looking at the stack of freshly baked golden scones and the thick, crusty sandwiches. The flight, the jet lag and the thought of this trip had left her stomach churning, but now she realized how hungry she was and also how tired. Not just from the journey but from life. The last year had been interminable. She was physically and mentally exhausted. She fought the impulse to put her head on the table and sob.

Her dad was asking about Todd, and Clare was answering.

Izzy was terrified she was going to break down. And then she felt a hand on her arm. It was Aiden.

"We bought a couple of paddleboards." He pushed the sandwiches toward her. "Do you want to try them out? It's fun."

The change of subject snapped her out of her panic. "Thanks. I'd like that."

"Turns out the lake is perfect for it." He talked, pretty much about nothing really, not expecting her to respond and she wondered if he'd noticed her moment of near panic.

Molly reemerged with Flora, who had changed into a clean T-shirt, this time in a pretty shade of blue. She wore a pair of yellow shorts and her wild hair was held back by a red scrunchie.

She reminded Izzy of a bunch of spring flowers.

Izzy watched as she hovered in the doorway, her gaze flickering nervously to the people in the room. It was the first time she'd realized that this must be difficult for Flora, too.

Her pang of sympathy lasted less than a second. Her situation was way more serious than Flora's.

She smiled at her sister and patted the chair next to her. "Come and eat something, Molly."

Molly grabbed Flora's hand. "I want to sit next to Flora."

Izzy gritted her teeth. "There are two chairs, so you're good. Flora can sit here, too."

Molly dragged Flora to the table, and helped herself to a sandwich. "Aunt Clare makes the best cakes, but we can't eat a cake until we've eaten the other stuff but that's fine because it all tastes good. Different from sandwiches at home. Try it." She passed the plate to Flora who gave a grateful smile and took one.

Izzy saw Clare glance curiously at Flora and then Molly.

Aiden grabbed a can of diet cola from the fridge and handed it to her, ignoring his mother's disapproving frown.

The gesture somehow made her feel better. It made her feel that someone, at least, knew a little about her.

She ate several sandwiches and then a scone. She wished she and Aiden weren't surrounded by people. The conversation between them was stilted, awkward, stuttering like a car that wouldn't start.

It was always like this when they met after a long break. A little tense, each of them was trying to find the familiar parts of the other so they could reconnect.

Was he thinking about last summer, too? Was he thinking about that conversation they'd had while lying on the grass by the lake?

Maybe he was, because he took another sandwich and glanced at her. "You have to stick to British time, even though you're tired, so the best thing is to be active. Do you want to take the kayaks out this afternoon?"

Did he mean all of them or just her?

Either way the answer was a yes. Doing something that required concentration might at least stop her thinking. Anything to get away from her life for five minutes.

"Sounds good. I brought a bathing suit and a wet suit."

"Cool. We can use the boathouse to change." He took a slug of his drink. "That okay with you, Mum?"

Clare handed Flora a mug of tea. "As long as you wear life jackets. You know the rules."

Izzy waited for Molly to beg to be allowed to tag along, but she didn't. Instead she was telling Flora about the birds and flowers that lived in the forest and suggesting they take Chase for a walk.

"Todd will be home soon," Clare told Jack. "As it's sunny, I thought we'd have a barbecue by the lake. I bought steaks and salmon, and we can barbecue veggies and halloumi for the veggies. What do you think?"

"Sounds great. We can help." He stood up. "I'll bring the rest of the luggage in from the car."

Without all Becca's cases, it had all fitted easily this time.

Aiden stood up, too, and gestured to Izzy to join him. "We'll see you later."

Izzy hesitated. "Will you be all right, Molly?"

Her sister nodded. "I'll stay with Flora."

Izzy was hurt at the dismissal, which made no sense because last year she'd been thrilled for every moment she'd been able to spend with Aiden without Molly tagging along.

Without bothering to unpack, she grabbed her bag with her swimming things and followed him across the lawn and down to the path that skirted the lake.

Aiden walked slightly ahead and she studied the soft fall of his T-shirt and the way his hair curled over the back of his neck.

They reached the stream with stepping-stones and he held out his hand.

"Don't slip. We've had a lot of rain and it's deeper than usual."

She hesitated and then took his hand, feeling his fingers close tightly around hers. It was the first time she'd felt safe in a long time.

"Are you all right?" His voice was rough and she nodded.

"Fine. Just jet-lagged, I guess. You know how it is."

"We don't have to take the kayaks out. I just said that to keep the adults happy. I've got the key to the boathouse. We can grab some drinks and chill on the deck if you prefer."

"Sure." She stepped carefully on the shiny, slippery rocks, determined not to lose her footing. By the end of the holiday they'd probably laugh about it together, but right now their relationship still had that slightly roughened edge. Neither was sure who the other was, or if they had changed.

As soon as she was safely on the path again, she pulled her hand from his.

They made it to the boathouse and she slid off her shoes and walked inside in her bare feet.

"This place is incredible. Do you ever get used to it?" She gazed up at the soaring ceiling, the acres of glass that somehow brought the lake into the room. "I mean, I'd live here."

Aiden headed for the kitchen area. "You'd go crazy, city girl."

"Just because I live in a city doesn't make me a city girl."

He reached into the fridge and pulled out a couple of cans. He seemed older somehow, as if an extra year in the world had added layers that weren't visible to the naked eye.

"The way I see it, we have a choice."

She took the drink from him. "What kind of choice?"

"Either we dive in and start where we left off, or we tiptoe around each other politely for a week or so and then finally click the way we always do and wish we hadn't wasted half our time together trying to find our way back to the place we always end up."

He had a way of finding clarity in situations that always seemed murky and complicated to her.

Flustered, she took a swallow of her drink. "What place is that?"

"The place where we feel comfortable to push each other into the water." He grinned and nudged her toward the jetty. Now he seemed young again. A boy about to push a girl off the dock.

"I haven't reached that point yet. I'm not ready to get wet." Her bathing suit was in her bag along with an oversize towel that Clare had thrust at them, but she wasn't in the mood. She sat down, watching sunlight dance over the surface. "I'd forgotten how perfect this place is. You're lucky living here."

"Yes, although I don't often have time to sit here. And we usually have strangers occupying this place."

"That must feel weird."

He shrugged. "It brings in money." He sat next to her, his arm brushing against hers as he lowered his feet into the lake. "But yeah, I'm possessive about this lake. I feel a sense of ownership."

She lowered her feet in too and gasped as the icy water closed around her ankles. "It's cold!"

"Wimp."

"Says the guy who has never lived through a winter in New York."

He laughed. "Last summer you were diving off here."

Last summer she'd done a lot of things she was no longer doing.

They sat with their feet dangling into the water as they had when they were children.

"So—" He leaned down and rolled the legs of his jeans up a little farther. "Do you want to talk about it?"

"About what? How cold the water is?"

He ran his foot along the surface, making ripples. "Does that mean you don't want to talk? You don't have to. Whatever works for you. I didn't want you to think I don't care, that's all. I remember you messaging me once telling me that none of your friends wanted to talk about it anymore. I don't want to be that friend."

A lump formed in her throat. "How do you know so much?"

"I don't know much." He set his drink down on the jetty. "But I know you."

She felt a slow warmth spread through her, a warmth that had nothing to do with the sun.

"It's complicated."

He said nothing, just waited quietly, offering companionship but nothing else. No judgment. No pressure.

"It's been a totally crap year. Horrible. I wanted to spend the whole time under the bedcovers, but lay there every morning knowing that if I didn't get out of bed our lives would fall apart. I felt needed. I *was* needed. I helped with Molly, with the laundry, I cooked—" The words slipped out slowly at first, wriggling past the barriers she'd held in place for so long. But he was such a good listener, and because he really did understand her, the barriers opened and the words started to flow.

And Aiden listened quietly, making the occasional murmur of understanding, asking a question or two, glancing at her just often enough to show that he was listening but not so often it made her feel uncomfortable.

"It's been tough. And it isn't getting better. It's just different. Weirdly, it might be even tougher lately."

He nodded. "Do you like her? Flora?"

How did he know that her biggest issue right now was Flora?

She glanced at him. His eyes were a warm shade of brown. Interested. Caring.

She liked the way he looked at her. It made her feel tingly and aware of every single part of herself. "I don't know her that well."

"That's what you say when you don't like someone, but you're not ready to admit it."

Izzy turned back to the water. "It's not her fault. I mean, she tries *so hard* to make us like her it's almost painful to watch. And Molly falls for it of course. For months I was the one who held her when she cried. I cooked her meals. I read to her. I even let her sleep with me. I've washed her sheets when she's wet the bed—" she glanced at him, her gaze fierce "—and if you as much as mention that—"

"I wouldn't."

She sighed. "It's all *Flora this, and Flora that*, like she's been bewitched or something." Embarrassed by her own indiscretion, she took another swig of her drink. The truth was thinking about Flora made her feel bad about herself. The nicer Flora was, the angrier Izzy became. She didn't know why. "Forget it. I don't even know what I'm trying to say." And now Aiden was going to think she was a total bitch. Maybe she was. A nice person would have embraced someone like Flora, wouldn't they? She hadn't fed them a poisoned apple or anything. It could have been a lot worse.

"Molly really likes her?"

"Oh yeah. It's a mutual lovefest." She knew she sounded bitter but she couldn't help it.

She waited for Aiden to say that it must be nice for Molly but for a few minutes he said nothing at all. He just stared at the water, thinking. Then finally he stirred.

"That must hurt your feelings. And the fact that she's nice—that kind of sucks, too."

"What do you mean?" It did suck, but she wasn't about to admit that when she already felt as if she had a "mean girl" neon sticker on her forehead.

"Well, it makes hating her an uncomfortable experience, because she isn't giving you good reason. Always assuming that you do hate her, which I probably would in your position."

Izzy swallowed. "You would?" No one understood how she was feeling. Not her family, not her friends.

But Aiden understood.

"Yeah. I mean, your world is all screwed up and in she steps, Miss Perfect. And she's not putting a foot wrong, from the sounds of it. If you want my opinion, I think it's kind of selfish that she isn't giving you a single reason to hate her."

Izzy choked on a laugh. "I can't believe you just said that. You're so bad."

"I'm not. And neither are you."

"I feel bad. Like I'm a truly horrible person."

"As you said—it's a crap situation, and none of it is in your control. You're not calling the shots. Flora has it much easier."

Izzy thought about Flora, red-faced and out of breath trying to keep up with her. Flora, trying not to look at all the photos of Becca that adorned the house. Flora, looking a little lost. "I don't think it's easy for her." She felt a flash of guilt. "I've made it pretty tough. The harder she tries, the more I withdraw. I can't help it. I just don't want her around and there is no real reason for that."

Aiden swatted a fly. "Your family changed shape, and you're not ready for it to change shape again. I'd say that's reason enough."

"How do you always know exactly what to say?"

"I don't. But in this case it's obvious."

"You don't think I'm terrible?"

"I think you're human. So what did you do to Flora? Put a frog in her bed?"

Izzy tried to smile. "Went out of my way to make her uncomfortable mostly. Baited her into doing stuff she doesn't normally do. But it hasn't worked. Nothing I do seems to shake her. I mean, it has to be hard but she just endures it, like she's willing to take the punishment. Or maybe she just loves my dad or wants his money or something and is willing to do whatever it takes."

"Why do you think she wants his money?"

"I don't know." She knew for a fact that Flora had insisted on paying for her own flight ticket because she'd been in the kitchen when she'd booked it. "Ignore me."

"Maybe she's a realist. If she's hanging out with a ready-made family, she has to take the good with the bad. And maybe she's just not used to being part of a family. It's like—" he thought about it "—like learning to play with an orchestra when you've only ever played solo."

"Why does she even care what I think of her? Why is she trying so hard? It's not like I'm the one she's dating." The journey and the jet leg suddenly caught up with her and suddenly Izzy felt exhausted and emotional.

"Because if she's going to be with your dad, she knows she has to get you to like her, too."

"And I can't do it. I don't know why. And it's not like I want my dad to be miserable. I want him to be happy. So why can't I just be happy for him?"

"Honest answer?"

"I don't know. Am I going to hate your honest answer?"

"You could never hate me. I'm way too cool and handsome. And my family owns a boathouse, so that's worth sticking around for." He looped his arm round her shoulders. "So this is what I think. You've been through hell. You're sad. Grieving. Surviving, day to day. And then suddenly your dad brings someone home and it all changes. He changes. Whether it's true or not, he seems to be moving on. And now Molly is smiling for the first time, and seems to be moving on, too. And now you have all this change to handle again, and you feel threatened."

"That sounds about right." Her throat was clogged. "I don't want to hate her, but I can't make myself be nice because she's—how did you describe it?—reshaping our lives and I have no say over it."

"And you had no say over losing your mother, either. It's okay to struggle with it, Izz. You don't have to pretend it's all okay and be this fake perfect person. You're allowed to be angry and sad. You can yell and cry."

"You'd totally freak out if I cried."

"I'd push you in the water."

She gave a snort. "Is that what you're going to do with your upset patients when you're a doctor?"

"Drown them? It's one solution, although probably not one the medical board would approve of."

She sniffed. "Normally I pretend I'm fine. People don't want to see you upset. They want you to be okay."

"I'm not 'people.' I want you to be you."

"I think what hurts most," she confessed, "is that Molly loves her so much, and that sounds crazy I know because nothing would be worse than Dad dating someone we both hate. And that's what I mean—the way I feel makes no sense. I should be pleased, shouldn't I?"

"Why?" He took another swallow of his drink. "Apart from all the other obvious issues, you lost someone you loved. And now it feels like you're losing someone else, too."

"That's it exactly."

"But you're not losing her, Izz. You do know that, right? You're not losing Molly. She adores you."

"Does she? I used to be the one she clung to. I was her life belt until Flora showed up." Izzy stared at the water. "The hardest, scariest thing is that I don't feel needed anymore. And if I'm not needed, then—"

"Then what are you? You're loved, Izzy, that's what you are." His arm was heavy and protective around her shoulders. "You don't have to earn your place in a family. You're born into it. Your dad doesn't love you because you help out with Molly, although I'm sure he's grateful for that—he loves you because you're you. Unless—" He paused, suddenly cautious. "Is this about—"

"No!" But it was, of course, at least partly. She felt her eyes fill and stood up quickly. This was the point where the conversation had to end. "I'm just being stupid."

"Does Flora know about that?"

"I don't think so." The thought that her dad might have talked about intimate things with Flora made her feel even more insecure.

Aiden stood up, too. "Then what's wrong?"

"Nothing."

"Don't do that." He gripped her shoulders. "We share how we feel. We don't dress sad in a smile, ever. We tell it how it is. We've always told each other everything."

Not quite everything.

She managed a smile. "It's fine. Honestly. Talking was

good, but I think I'm done with it now. My head is exploding. Best to just shove me off this dock and plunge my head in cold water."

He laughed. "I couldn't do that to a guest."

"No? Then I'll go first." She shoved him hard and he flew, his plunge into the water covering her in droplets of water.

She gasped and swept her soaked hair away from her face. She was laughing, and fortunately so was he.

"You—" He spluttered, coughed. "I can't believe you just did that."

"Me neither."

"So you have a choice, Isabella." His tone was deceptively pleasant. "Either you jump, or I'm coming up there to get you."

"I can move faster than you."

With his hair slicked back and water clinging to his eyelashes he looked like the lead from a teen movie. "I may not be a track champion, but I can run fast when there's something worth running for."

Was she that something?

To cover up what felt like an awkward moment she tugged off her T-shirt and her shorts and jumped without giving herself time to think about what she was doing.

She hit the water hard and sank under the surface. Sound was muffled, something soft brushed against her leg and she wanted to scream, except that then she'd drown and also screaming was for babies. She didn't want Aiden to think she was a baby.

She surfaced, gasping and he pulled her toward the dock.

"Refreshing, right?"

"That's not the word that almost came out of my mouth." She swiped her face with her palm, clearing her vision. "Something is stroking my leg."

"My hands are both visible."

"That's what's worrying me."

"Quit worrying. The wildlife here is friendly." He tugged her toward him. She could feel his thigh brush against hers. Solid. Strong. "I'm glad you're here, Izz." The look in his eyes made her heart thump a little harder.

"You mean here in this water?" She knew he didn't mean that, but she needed to hear him say it. It embarrassed her that she'd become so needy.

"I mean here in my home. With me." He lifted his hand to her face, rubbing away droplets of water with his thumb. It made her shiver, but not because she was cold. She clutched his arms, feeling the swell of his biceps under her fingers. His skin was cold from the water, but all she felt was heat. Searing heat.

For the first time in months she was thinking of nothing but him. Aiden. All the rest of it faded. The anxiety and the anger. The misery and the confusion. All that was left was excitement. That delicious feeling in the pit of her stomach and low in her pelvis. She didn't care whether this was love or not, because she wasn't even sure what love was anyway. All she knew was that being this close to him was electrifying. Had it felt this way last time? No, she didn't think so. Maybe her dad and Molly weren't the only ones changing.

She pressed her lips to his damp skin. "I'm glad I'm here, too."

# 12

## *Flora*

What was she supposed to wear?

She was a child again, confused and alone, desperate to make a good impression.

It wasn't that Clare hadn't been polite—she had been perfectly civil—but civil wasn't warm, was it? Civil wasn't enthusiastic. It was a mark of good manners. There was little worse than being tolerated, and she knew that right now she was being tolerated for Jack's sake.

All the power she'd felt when she'd confronted Celia had drained away. This was different. This *mattered*.

She heard Jack's laughter through the open window as he chatted easily with his friends and she stepped closer, staying out of sight as she watched him. He was entirely comfortable with these people, and it hadn't occurred to him that she might not be.

He was standing, beer in his hand, laughing and talking to a man who had his back to her. Todd, presumably. Todd, who had no doubt adored Becca.

And there, shimmering in the sunlight at the end of a long sweep of grass, was the lake.

Flora felt the stirrings of panic lodge in her throat.

Should she say something? Should she tell them? No. It would mean talking about something she didn't want to talk about.

There were plenty of other activities on offer here. There was no need for her to go on, or even near, the lake.

Molly was playing with Chase, their antics producing a symphony of barks and girlish giggles. Flora found herself smiling as she watched them. They were having so much *fun*.

It was such a contrast to the cold, sterile life she'd had with her aunt that for a moment Flora struggled to breathe. This was the type of home most people dreamed of having. It wasn't about the surroundings, although the place was idyllic, it was the feeling of love. She watched as Clare wiped Molly's hands before giving her an ice cream. She was an attentive, engaged mother and she reminded Flora of her own mother.

To distract herself, she glanced across the garden.

There was no sign of either Izzy or Aiden, but no one seemed concerned about that.

Flora was concerned. She was worried about Izzy and had tried raising it with Jack a couple of times, but he hadn't seemed worried at all. Their relationship was going so well, she didn't want to threaten it by overstepping. She wasn't his wife. She wasn't the girls' mother. There was nothing formal about their relationship. She didn't have a role, and yet she felt responsibility.

As she stood there, still wearing the robe Clare had

thoughtfully left out for her, Jack saw her and smiled and raised a hand. Todd turned, glanced up at the window where Flora had thought she'd managed to hide, and waved, too. She had no choice but to wave back.

Great.

Now they all knew that she'd been skulking, watching them, too cowardly to go downstairs and join them.

What would Becca have worn for their first evening together in the garden? Probably something flowing and white, with casual loops of silver round her neck and in her ears, and her hair scooped up into a messy bun that would have looked effortlessly elegant. She would have sipped champagne from a tall flute, rather than grabbing a beer bottle. She would never, ever, have doubted her welcome.

Flora laid two dresses side by side on the bed. A blue sundress with thin straps that was her favorite, and a white one she'd bought on impulse from a boutique in Greenwich Village.

Which would make her feel most comfortable? Dressing like herself, or dressing like Becca? As an experiment she scooped her hair up and fastened it at the back of her head. It fought her attempts to contain it, twisting and curling around her face until she looked like a Jane Austen heroine after a mad dash on horseback.

On impulse she texted Julia.

Having clothing crisis. White or blue?

The reply came back moments later.

White? You? Are you kidding me? Unless you're getting married, wear color! Be yourself!

Be herself.

She lifted her chin, trying to look confident and then she heard the thunder of feet on the stairs and Molly appeared in the doorway, breathless and pink cheeked.

"Why are you pulling faces in the mirror? Why aren't you dressed? You need to come and play."

Flora scooped her up and swung her round, flooded with gratitude. The child was almost too big to be lifted, but she felt Molly's arms creep around her neck and hitched her more securely. She breathed in the fresh, clean smell of strawberry shampoo and sun-warmed child. She closed her eyes, allowing herself to savor that uncomplicated moment of unreserved affection. She still hadn't dared examine her feelings for Jack too closely, but she was almost entirely sure that she loved his younger daughter. She'd always wanted children of her own, and spending time with Molly had simply increased that yearning. "Have you been having fun?"

"Yes, but I want you to come outside. Everyone is there."

"I need to change."

Molly frowned at the choice on the bed. "Don't wear white. If you wear white you won't be able to play in case you get dirty. And Chase will get you muddy and then you'll be mad."

"I would never be mad with Chase." Flora lowered her to the ground. "I'll wear the blue."

She dressed quickly, but left her hair up. "Is Izzy there?"

"No. I think she's with Aiden. She loves Aiden." Molly dragged her downstairs, chatting the whole way, mostly about Chase.

Flora crossed the lawn, warmed by the evening sun and everyone's glances.

"Hi." She smiled awkwardly, and Jack reached out and tugged her toward him.

"Love the dress."

"Me too, although I always think leopard print is more dog-paw-friendly." Todd was cheerful. "Welcome. Good to meet you, Flora." Instead of holding out his hand he embraced her and she hugged him back, relieved that he was so welcoming.

His greeting seemed genuine. Either he was an excellent actor, or he was pleased to see Jack with someone else.

It was a shame Clare didn't feel the same way.

Becca's friend was adding dishes to a long table that was already groaning with food. Sliced tomatoes and fresh basil glistened with olive oil. There was a large bowl of mixed salad leaves, a potato salad, sweet corn, its edges darkened from the grill, and fresh, warm bread scented with herbs and garlic.

Flora hoped she hadn't poisoned any of it.

Clare handed her a plate. "You should eat. I know your brain probably doesn't know what time of day it is, but I always used to find that eating a meal and having a good night's sleep helps you settle into the new time zone."

Flora welcomed the attempt at conversation. "Do you travel often?"

"Not so much now." Clare helped herself to salad. "I used to. Before I turned freelance, I worked for a fashion magazine in London." She saw Flora looking at her casual shorts and loose linen shirt. "You wouldn't think it, would you?"

Flora felt herself turn scarlet. "I wasn't—"

"I wouldn't blame you if you were. The truth is I don't have much use for designer labels here. What use are heels and glitter when I'm trying to tame the garden? Becca used to say—" She froze halfway through the sentence. "Sorry."

"Why are you sorry?" Jack joined them, and Flora tried to hide her discomfort. It was so obvious to her that Clare didn't want her here. That she was simply being a good hostess. Couldn't Jack see that?

"Nothing." Clare thrust a plate into Jack's hand. "Can you give that to Todd? You know how he always chars everything if we don't keep an eye on him. I don't want him to burn the food."

"You were talking about Becca, weren't you? It's allowed," Jack said evenly. "She isn't a banned subject."

Was that true? In some ways it was. What with the photographs, the stories and the way they were still living the life they'd lived with Becca she couldn't have been more present if she'd actually walked through the door to the garden. But in another way, she *was* a banned subject. Jack never talked about her unless the children did. He'd made it clear he didn't *want* to talk about her. Flora had assumed it was because he wanted to move on. That he found it hard. But what if there was another reason?

Clare had turned her attention back to the food.

"Rescue those burgers, Jack, for all our sakes." As Jack walked away, there was an uncomfortable silence and Clare poked at her salad.

Flora decided to address the elephant in the room. Things couldn't get much more awkward, could they? "I appreciate that this is difficult. You must have been shocked when Jack said he was bringing me."

"Not at all." Clare's response was a little too quick, and a little too smooth. "We always love to see Jack and the girls. I can't believe how much Molly has grown. Children hate it when you tell them that of course." She continued to talk about neutral subjects, avoiding the really sensitive issue—Flora.

"Molly is adorable. She loves drawing and painting and she has a really good eye."

"Yes." Clare speared a tomato. "And Izzy is such a smart, warm, funny individual. How are the two of you getting on?"

Smart, yes. Warm and funny? Not with Flora, although she'd seen her that way with her father and sister. But there was something about Izzy that worried her. Something she didn't feel was personal.

If she and Clare had been friends, she might have asked for her opinion and shared her concerns but didn't want to admit that she was finding Izzy a nightmare. It was something she tried not to admit even to herself. She made constant excuses. *She's grieving, it's hard for her to see her dad with someone else—*

In the end she dodged the question. "I haven't had a chance to get to know her as well as Molly, but she's been amazing. She's held everything together."

"It must have been hideous for her. Izzy was very close to Becca. She worshiped her mother."

Jack returned with a plate of meat, saving Flora the trouble of trying to find a suitable response. He placed it on the table next to the salads.

"I think I rescued it moments before we needed the fire service." He slid his arm round Flora and pulled her close.

Had he heard that comment about Becca? Maybe he had, because he was both protective and affectionate. Unfortunately, he chose to kiss her at the exact moment Izzy appeared at the bottom of the garden.

The timing couldn't have been worse. Izzy stopped so suddenly Aiden cannoned into her.

"Oops—" He caught her by the shoulders to steady her.

Flora instinctively tried to move away from Jack, but he had his arm firmly round her shoulders and tugged her back.

"Izzy! Food."

"Jack—" Flora spoke in an undertone "—I'm worried we'll upset her."

"And I'm worried you'll be upset by all this talk of Becca." He kept his arm firmly round her. "It's fine."

Was it fine?

Finally, Izzy approached, Aiden a few steps behind her. Flora had never been so tense.

"You two are soaking!" Clare put her plate down and made a clucking noise of disapproval. "What happened?"

"No point in having a lake if you don't use it. We swam off the dock." Aiden strolled to the table and scanned the food.

"In your clothes?"

Izzy was glaring at Flora. She decided eye contact was making it worse, so she looked away. Should she say something? Or was it better if Jack did?

His arm was still looped round her shoulders, protective. Possessive.

"It was an impulse thing." Aiden tore off a piece of bread and ate it without bothering with a plate. "It's a warm evening. Clothes dry. Don't fuss."

Clare turned to Izzy. "Do you want to take a hot shower before you eat? Change?"

"I'm fine, Aunt Clare." There was an instant change in Izzy's manner once her attention wasn't focused on Flora.

She wondered what she'd been doing with Aiden other than swimming. Were they together? A couple? Or just friends.

Using the food as an excuse, she managed to ease away from Jack's arm just as Molly sprinted up to her.

"Flora! Come and watch Chase run after the stick. He's so funny."

"Don't you want to eat?" Flora put a leg of chicken on her plate and added salad.

"Soon."

"I'll come," Izzy said, but Molly took Flora's free hand and tugged.

"Flora needs to see. She's never seen the way he does those spins."

Flora allowed herself to be tugged away. It was a relief, to be honest, because Izzy was scowling again and you didn't have to be a genius to know why. Jack shouldn't have been affectionate in public. On the other hand what sort of relationship would this be if they couldn't touch each other? Molly seemed to have accepted that they were together. How long would it take Izzy to do the same? Maybe it was never going to happen.

She watched as Chase raced after the stick, tumbling over himself each time he did an emergency stop. When Molly picked up the stick to throw it again, he trembled with anticipation, leaping on the spot and making her giggle. It was a delicious sound. Happiness in the moment, all dark clouds forgotten. Girl and dog.

Flora had always wanted a dog. She'd begged her aunt, but her aunt had considered dogs a rung below children on the ladder of inconveniences. She'd pointed out that a dog would bark, make a mess and need walking and Flora had wanted to say *But it will love me, and I will love it back.*

Now, listening to Molly's infectious laughter, she wondered what her childhood would have been like if it had been messier and filled with dogs.

By the time they returned to the group, Molly was grubby from stick-throwing and out of breath.

"Daddy, can we have a dog?"

"I'm having enough trouble caring for two-legged creatures. Not sure I can cope with four." Jack loaded a plate with food and handed it to her.

Izzy snatched it from him before Molly could take it. "She has to wash her hands first."

"Good point." Clare gestured to the house. "Go and wash them, sweetie. Use soap."

Chase whined and followed Molly toward the house. Flora followed her, and when they returned the conversation was still focused on pets.

"Maybe I should get a dog," Jack said, and Todd rolled his eyes and handed him a beer.

"Only if you're prepared for chaos. And to ditch those white sofas of yours. Crazy decision."

"Not my crazy decision."

Flora agreed with Todd. She thought white sofas were a crazy choice when you had children. *Don't go in that room, don't touch*—her aunt's most used word had been *don't*.

Had Jack protested at the choice of white?

"Bring me up-to-date on your news. Have you started applying for colleges, Izzy?" Clare handed a plate to Todd and he lifted the rest of the burgers from the grill. "Which place is at the top of your list?"

"I'm not going to college." Izzy spoke in a high voice, her announcement emphatic and clearly shocking to those who knew her.

Everyone stopped what they were doing. Clare glanced across at Jack, who stood with his empty plate held midair.

Even Aiden frowned.

Flora stood without moving. She'd sensed right from the first moment that Izzy was wound tight. She'd witnessed the emotion building inside her and wondered when and where they'd eventually be released.

Was this it?

Molly was the first to react. Delighted, she flung her arms round her sister. "Yay! You're not leaving."

In the few seconds before Izzy closed her eyes and hugged her back, Flora caught a glimpse of desperate vulnerability.

"You're not getting rid of me that easily, bunny. I'm going to be hanging around for a while, taking care of you and Dad."

Was that what this was about? Did Izzy feel she needed to stay at home and take care of the family?

"Wait a moment—" Jack's voice was even, measured, as he tried hard not to overreact. "What do you mean you're not going to college? Of course you're going to college. You've been planning it forever."

"Plans change, don't they? Life changes. Nothing stays the same."

There were so many undercurrents in her little speech that Flora wanted to throw her a life belt. Izzy was struggling. She'd been right about that.

"Some things have changed that's true, but not everything." Jack was gripping his plate. "Your home, me, your sister, your friends—being here with Aunt Clare and the gang. That hasn't changed. Your future doesn't have to change either."

"Yes, it does." The toss of her head challenged her father to argue. "I'm going to stay home, and then maybe I'll travel for a couple of years. The Far East. Vietnam. Cambodia. Spend some time in Thailand."

Jack struggled to find his voice. "Vietnam? Cambodia? What are you going to do there?"

"I don't know." She lifted a shoulder. "Get a job in a bar or a restaurant? Hang out on the beach?"

Flora wondered if she really wanted to travel, or if she was trying to push her father into a reaction.

She got one.

"You are not traveling alone through the Far East. And you're not hanging out on a beach."

He was always so patient with the girls, but Izzy's words seemed to flip a switch. Flora had never seen this side of him.

"Why not?" They were locked eye to eye, father and daughter, everyone around them forgotten.

"Where do you want me to start? First, because it isn't safe. You can't travel the world on your own."

"Because you'd worry?"

"Because it is an outrageous idea. Also, because you're going to college."

*She wants him to worry,* Flora thought. *She wants him to show that he cares.*

"I'm not going to college. I've decided." Izzy was all attitude, her expression mutinous. "That's not what my life is anymore."

"I want the very best for you, that's all." Jack took a deep breath and sent an apologetic look toward his friends. "Drop the subject."

Flora leaned closer. "Talk about it now. Take a walk together."

Jack shook his head. "It's our first evening with our friends. Clare has been cooking all day. We're going to enjoy ourselves and talk about this another time." He gave Izzy a loaded look that she returned. It was hard to figure out which of them was more wound up.

"I'm not the one who needs to talk. I've made up my mind." Izzy leaned down to hug Molly again, who this time wriggled and squirmed.

"Ow. You're squeezing me."

Jack put his plate down on the table, rattling cutlery. "But you've talked about college for ages." Despite his suggestion that they drop the subject, he seemed unable to. "How you're going to be a journalist and change the world."

"The best way to write about the world is to experience everything it has to offer. I can't do that if I'm trapped in a dorm room. I'm going to write about travel. Backpacking. Meeting new people."

"Izzy—sweetheart—I don't know what to say." There was something endearing about Jack's desperate honesty. "Your mother would have wanted you to go to college."

That was totally the wrong thing to say, Flora thought, and Izzy's reaction confirmed her suspicions.

"My mother isn't here." Izzy's voice shook. "I'm on my own now. We've all had to make changes. We've all had to make new choices, and maybe those choices don't work for all of us. I'm forced to accept yours—" her gaze flickered briefly to Flora "—so you should accept mine. This is my life. My decision. I'm not going to college."

Flora shifted uncomfortably. Was she the reason Izzy had changed her mind about college?

And why would Izzy feel she was alone, when she was standing here with her father, sister and close family friends?

Still, despite the personal gibe, Flora admired Izzy for having the strength to fight for what she believed was right for her. To carve her own path, even if it went against the wishes of others.

"Why don't you sleep on it?" Clare tried to reduce the tension but Izzy and her father were locked in battle. Izzy had a stubborn, miserable look on her face and Flora willed Jack to give her a big hug and take her off for a proper talk.

But when she looked at him all she saw was a deep frown of parental frustration. He was trying to work out what to say to make Izzy change her mind.

Was that why Izzy felt she was on her own? Because she believed she had no supporters?

"I don't want to sleep on it." Izzy's voice rose. "I know what I want. Why doesn't anyone at least try to understand? Why doesn't anyone listen? Sometimes I feel like I'm an alien, alone on a planet." Her pain was so obvious it was painful to witness. It sucked Flora back in time. She was a child again.

No one had listened to her. No one had been interested in what she wanted. It was expected that she'd somehow blend into the background of her aunt's life. She'd been expected to fit the mold someone else had shaped for her.

Flora stepped forward, even though it felt a bit like throwing herself in front of a speeding car.

"I understand, Izzy. And I'm listening." No one had supported her, or even cared what she truly wanted. That wasn't going to happen to Izzy. Not while she was around. She was here, and she was going to help. "I think you're right to stand up for what you want. It's your life. Your decision. And if you want to talk about it, I'm here."

Jack put his hand on her arm. "Flora—"

"Izzy is right. Sometimes when life changes, our decisions change, too." She ignored his effort to interrupt her. "And what is right for one person isn't right for another. Dreams are personal and everyone has a right to do what feels right for them."

Izzy looked stunned. She stared at Flora without speaking. Her fists unclenched slightly. The rise and fall of her chest slowed.

Flora felt a flicker of connection, and then it was gone and Izzy's face contorted.

"You think you understand? You have *no idea* how I'm feeling. None." She turned her fury and frustration on Flora, snarling like a rescue dog who hadn't yet learned to trust. "And you pretend that you care, but you don't. You're just desperate for me to like you because you're crazy about my dad and you need my approval if you're going to stay together. And you'll do anything for that, won't you? You'll even do stuff you totally hate, including running, which half killed you. I mean, how far are you prepared to go to fit in? I don't even know what you really like! But whatever you do, you're never going to be my mom and sleeping with my dad doesn't make you a member of this family, and—"

"Isabella!" Jack's voice cut through her tumbled speech and he pulled Flora close, providing a physical barrier between her and the weaponized words. "That's enough. Apologize, right now."

"No way!"

"Then go to your room."

"Go to my *room*? I'm seventeen, not six! Mom would *never* have said that to me." Izzy's voice was high and she was physically shaking.

Flora was shaking, too. Shaking and embarrassed. Izzy had made her sound so manipulative and cold. The implication was that she really didn't care at all, and it wasn't true. She cared a great deal. She'd been genuinely trying to get to know Jack's children by sharing their interests. Did Izzy even know how much she admired her? Not just the way she'd handled the past year, but the way she knew what she wanted and wasn't afraid to fight for it. She wished she'd been more like her as a teenager.

She tried to rationalize her own behavior but Izzy's words were stuck in her flesh like a thorn. *How far are you prepared to go to fit in?*

It was a fair and uncomfortable question.

*I don't even know what you really like.*

And why would she? Flora hadn't really shared what she liked. Once again, she'd been so desperate to be loved and accepted that she'd buried her own needs and thought only of other people. She hadn't even told them how afraid she was of water. How ridiculous was that? What if they invited her sailing? Was she prepared to risk a panic attack just to fit in and be part of the family?

"I don't understand." Molly spoke in a small voice. "Flora sleeps in her own bed, not with Daddy. And if she didn't care about us, she wouldn't spend so much time playing with us?"

Izzy dumped her plate on the table, stalked away from them across the lawn and disappeared into the forest.

Aiden ran his hand over the back of his neck. "Maybe I should—"

"Give her space. She needs time alone," Clare said and Jack nodded.

"It's my fault. I didn't handle it well." He sounded exhausted. "But when she started talking about not going to college I just—"

"It was totally my fault. I raised the subject, and I'm sorry I did. I thought it was a safe topic, but obviously not. You reacted as most parents would." Clare put her hand on his arm. "Don't beat yourself up. It's a tough situation. This was never going to be easy. She'll be okay, Jack."

"Not if she doesn't go to college."

"I'm sure she didn't mean it. Izzy is so smart, I'm sure she'll eventually make the right decision."

Everyone was delicately ignoring Izzy's almost hysterical reaction to Flora.

*You're never going to be my mom.*

Molly pulled Chase onto her lap. "Where is Cambodia? Is it in Arizona?"

Underneath her own layers of hurt feelings and self-contempt, Flora felt genuine concern for Izzy. She'd been so wildly upset. Where had she gone? What if she got lost in the forest? Or went into the lake? Someone needed to look for her, talk to her.

She touched his arm. "Jack—"

"I know. You're upset, and I don't blame you. She was rude."

"That's not—"

"It's been a tough year for her." He pulled her close and sent his friends a look of rueful apology. "I guess coming back here was harder on her than I thought it would be. I should have anticipated it."

Clare waved a hand dismissively. "Don't worry about us. We've known each other forever. It wouldn't be a holiday without a crisis of some sort. Remember the year Aiden had chicken pox and we gave it to your two? Nightmare."

"And then there was the smoking and alcohol year. And the exam year. Let's not even think about that one." Todd thrust another beer into Jack's hand. "Hang in there. You're doing great. Can't be easy raising girls when you're a man." He turned back to the barbecue, prodding the food, flipping a burger or two.

"It's not like her to lose it like that, though. I just want the best for her. I want her to be happy. I hope she knows that." Jack took a mouthful of beer. "Usually she is so controlled."

And that sounded worrying to Flora. She didn't pretend to be an expert on teenage behavior and development, but was it normal to be that controlled? What had Izzy been like before Flora had shown up on the scene? Had she grieved? Who did she talk to? She obviously wasn't talking to Jack and she didn't seem to see much of her friends outside school.

"Blame jet lag," Todd said. "It turns the best of us into savages. And, Flora, can I say you were the epitome of patience and understanding so don't blame yourself."

"Yes," Clare said. "You were kind to her."

For a fleeting moment she felt like part of the group. Accepted. She could have stayed like that, stayed silent, enjoying the moment, but Izzy's outburst had unlocked something inside her.

She stepped away from the protective circle of Jack's arm, feeling a little sick and a little shaky.

"Go after her, Jack. She needs you. Listen to her. Let her talk."

"No. I agree with Clare. What she needs most right now is space. I've learned that it's important not to overreact. Feelings come and go. Sometimes it's best just to wait until they wash away." He must have seen something in her face because he frowned. "If she's not back in an hour, I'll go and look for her."

An hour could feel like a lifetime when you were alone and miserable.

She was going to have to go herself, even though she was probably the last person in the world Izzy would talk to.

She put her plate down and then noticed Aiden heaping a plate with food. Either he had an extraordinary appetite, or he was intending to share it with someone. She was the only one who had noticed what he was doing. Everyone else was still dissecting Izzy's behavior.

*Teenager.*

*Under a great deal of stress.*

*Completely understandable.*

*Hideous year.*

*So many memories in this place.*

Aiden saw her watching him and froze. They stared at each other for a moment, and then she turned back to the group and drew the conversation and attention toward herself.

Over Clare's shoulder she saw Aiden slip away from the group, following the same path Izzy had taken.

Flora relaxed a little, relieved that someone was going after Izzy. It was going to be dark soon. She just hoped he'd be able to help. Maybe it would be easier for Izzy to talk to someone her own age.

They'd moved on to dessert by the time Clare noticed he was missing.

"Where's Aiden?"

Todd glanced around. "He was here a moment ago."

"These strawberries are delicious," Flora said. "The sweetest I've tasted."

"I grow them—" Clare launched into a detailed account of how she netted the berries to keep away the birds, how they'd ended up with a glut the previous year and she now had jars and jars of jam.

Flora was thinking about Izzy, but she was also thinking about herself. Thinking of all the times she'd buried her own needs and behaved in ways contrary to her nature in an attempt to be accepted. But it wasn't really acceptance, was it? It wasn't acceptance if you had to change who you were, or suppress your own needs. It wasn't acceptance if you were afraid to be yourself and live the life you wanted to live.

The sun gradually sank low on the horizon, sending sparks of golden light across the surface of the lake.

Clare took Molly to bed. The adults stayed on the sunloungers, enjoying the peace of the evening.

Flames from the firepit darted upward, warming the air around them and tiny solar lights picked out the path to the water and led all the way to the boathouse. On the far side of the lake Flora could just about make out the silhouette of two people sitting on the dock.

She hoped Izzy was talking and Aiden was listening.

Todd appeared with a tray of coffee.

Jack sat down on the sunlounger next to Flora. He was obviously still agonizing about Izzy. "She said 'I'm going to stay at home and look after you and Dad.' Did you hear her?" He took the coffee mug Todd offered with a nod of thanks. "Is that what this is about? Is it because she feels she has to look after us?"

Clare stretched out next to Todd. "Is that what she's been doing?"

"I suppose she has in a way." Jack stared at the flames flickering in the firepit. "She does a lot around the house. I'm not the world's best cook. And I miss things. I forget to send Molly with a drink. I make her sandwiches she doesn't eat because I can't for the life of me remember all the small details in the way Izzy does. Molly hates ham. I need to remember she hates ham. Anyway, Izzy took over, and I was grateful for it."

"It's probably been good for her, Jack." Clare was holding Todd's hand. "It's good to be busy and feeling she is contributing is important for her self-esteem."

"But she seems to think I'm inept and incapable." He gave a self-deprecating smile. "She could be right. I obviously need to get my act together and do more domestic stuff."

If that was the problem, why hadn't Izzy just yelled at her dad and told him he should be doing more?

Flora didn't ask the question aloud. She'd already said enough, and was relieved that her intervention and honesty didn't seem to have harmed her relationship with Jack.

She leaned against him, nursing her coffee in her lap.

"You're quiet." He trailed his fingers down her arm. "Still thinking about Izzy?"

She was, but not in the way he thought.

She could see now that she'd made a mistake working

so hard to get Izzy to accept her. Julia had been right about that. She needed to take a different approach.

Maybe she and Izzy would never be friends but hopefully, by being herself, she could earn her respect.

# 13

## Clare

"She's nothing like I expected." Clare flung open the windows of the bedroom. The cool morning air held the scent of rain and the promise of sunshine. It had rained in the night but now the sky was blue and it promised to be a hot day. Her favorite type of weather. "You?" She glanced through the open door of the bathroom where Todd was shaving.

"I'm a man. I don't have expectations." His chest was bare and he had a towel knotted around his hips. He put the razor down and met her gaze in the mirror. "All right, I'm going to ask the question you want me to ask. What did you expect?"

"I don't know. Someone like Becca, I suppose." She'd been astonished when Flora had stepped out of the car in her flowing skirt, brightly colored bangles and tumbling, Pre-Raphaelite hair. She hadn't matched the image in Clare's head.

"Thank goodness. She's a lot more easygoing for a start."

Todd finished shaving and reached for the hand towel. "Sorry, probably shouldn't have said that but you know it's true. I know Becca was your oldest friend, but she wasn't the easiest person and she did have a way of making everything about her. Also it was a pain constantly having to hang on to Chase's collar in case he wagged his tail against her pristine clothing."

"I wasn't blind to Becca's faults." She ignored Todd's raised eyebrow that suggested differently. "What do you think it says, that Flora is so different?"

Todd looked blank. "It says something?"

"Most people have a type, don't they? If I died, would you pick someone like me?"

Todd wiped his face on the towel. "This isn't a very cheerful conversation."

"But if you pick someone entirely different, does it mean you didn't like the person you were with? I mean, second time around would you pick someone without my flaws?"

"Flaws?" He stared at her in exaggerated shock. "You have flaws?"

"I'm shy. I enjoy my own company. I don't like walking into crowded rooms where I don't know people. I hate public speaking. The mere idea of team games brings me out in a rash because I was never the one picked at school." Why was she spelling all this out? "Maybe next time you'll choose someone who likes to be the life and soul of the party."

Todd paused, the towel in his hands. "First, there isn't going to be a next time. Second, I would never do that because then *I* wouldn't be the life and soul of the party. There's only room for one party animal in a relationship, and I nabbed that spot." He winked at her and she rolled her eyes to hide the fact that he charmed her, just as he'd charmed her a thousand times before.

"Does the party animal have a headache after last night?"

"I do not. Jack drank more than I did. Did you see the way he was with her?"

"With Izzy?"

"No, with Flora."

"I can't keep up with your thought process. He was protective of her. Possibly because Izzy was rude." Todd dropped the damp towel over the side of the bath but for once Clare didn't say anything. She was too busy thinking about Jack.

"Not just that. He couldn't stop touching her. He and Becca never did that."

"Well they'd been married a long time."

"We've been married a long time. We still touch."

"Yes, but I'm a sex god and you're temptation on legs so we're different."

No matter what the conversation, he always made her laugh.

"Do you think they've had sex yet?"

"I have no idea. I take an active interest in my own sex life, less so other people's. And talking of which—" He prowled toward her and she gave a gasp and a giggle as he powered her back onto the bed.

"Todd! The windows are open."

"Better not make a noise then." He flashed her a wicked smile and then kissed her as if he hadn't spent the past twenty years doing exactly this. He was as hungry for her now as she was for him. Those two decades hadn't dulled the edge of desire. She'd never stopped wanting him, or he her. Every touch they exchanged was tinged with a delicious familiarity, an intimacy that only came with deep knowledge of a person.

She gasped as he fastened his mouth over her breast. "Todd! What are you doing?"

"I'm searching for your flaws. So far I haven't found any but I'm going to keep looking." He kissed his way to her other breast and then paused, his breathing uneven. "God, you're beautiful."

Flattered, charmed, she slid her hands over his shoulders, her fingers lingering on his muscles. "You're not so bad yourself. I love your body."

"Me? I'm a puny architect. Can't lift more than a pen." But he quickly disproved that by flipping her easily, so that he was on his back and she was on top. "Except when it's my wife. For her, I'll move a mountain."

She stroked her hands over his chest and lower to the towel. "Did you lock the door?"

"No, but it's early. No one is awake. Aiden is a teenager so no chance of seeing him until lunchtime, and as for the Americans—with the time change I calculate that it's three in the morning for them. They'll be dead to the world for a while."

"Molly will be awake soon."

"If she appears in the doorway I'll tell her I couldn't undo the knot on the towel and you were helping me. No one is going to come in, Clare." He slid his hand behind her head and drew her face to his. His kiss was hungry and demanding and she melted into it, wondering how it was possible to love him more each day. They had their moments of course. Those minor irritations that were inevitable when you shared living space with another human being, even one you adored. But the foundations of their relationship were strong and solid. She wouldn't tempt fate by saying that nothing could shake them, but she was confident they could withstand most anything.

"I love you, sweetheart." He murmured the words against her mouth. "I love that you're shy and that you listen more than you talk. That's not a flaw, it's who you are, and when you say something it's always worth hearing. I'm not surprised you enjoy your own company—I enjoy your company, too. There's no one else I'd rather spend time with. I don't give a damn that you hate public speaking, and I promise that whenever I can I'll be by your side when you have to walk into crowded rooms full of strangers. Did I miss anything out?"

"Team sports?" She was reminded of all the reasons she loved Todd, not that she needed much reminding.

He put his hands on her hips and held her firmly. "When there are balls involved, I've always been more of a one-on-one kind of guy."

She gasped. "Todd Dickinson! What would your mother think?"

"I'm not having this conversation with my mother. I'm having it with my wife. And if we're having a conversation about flaws, I have more. And they're bigger."

She raised an eyebrow. "Are you being competitive about *flaws*?"

"I don't need to be, because I win. And I win big. I'm stubborn and never see obstacles—"

"—which is why we're together, because you ignored every obstacle I put in your path."

"It's also why I'm currently handling a nightmare project with an engineer who is desperately trying to make my design work."

"It will happen. You always make it happen."

"I talk too much. I dominate a room."

"Not true. You entertain people." She kissed his jaw, smooth now against her lips. "You're the perfect host. Maybe we're a perfect pair."

"Maybe?" He slid his hand down her back and pulled

her closer. She could feel him, hard and ready through the flimsy towel and she pulled it away.

He tipped her onto her back so that he was back in control. With hands, mouth, the whole of his body he used the knowledge he had of her to drive her wild and she did the same. Here, in this bed, with Todd, she'd never felt shy. She felt powerful and beautiful and sure of herself, and she was sure of herself now as she wrapped her legs around him and rose up to meet and match his passion.

Afterward they lay together, slick skin and tangled limbs bathed by the morning breeze and birdsong. Warmed and softened by love, she nestled in the curve of his arm. "I'm so lucky to have you."

"True." His eyes were closed and he grunted as she poked him in the ribs.

"You're lucky to have me, too."

"You won't hear me arguing with that."

She pressed her lips to his chest. "I suppose if I'm honest, losing Becca made me appreciate what we have even more. Not that I ever took it for granted—"

"You don't have to explain. I know what you mean." For once the teasing note in his voice was absent. "I know it's been tough for you, Clare. Losing your friend."

"Yes, but not as tough as it has been for Jack and the children. It can't be easy for Izzy, seeing her dad with someone else." Clare jumped out of bed and headed for the shower. She didn't protest when Todd followed. He'd designed the bathroom, adding skylights and widening the room. He'd then proceeded to install a walk-in shower with more than enough space for both of them.

Clare started to wash her hair, and then let him take over. "Did you see Izzy's face when she came back last night?" His hands were gentle and soothing and she closed her eyes.

The sex was good, but so was this. "I think she'd been crying. I feel bad for her."

"I feel bad for Flora." Todd turned off the water and handed her a towel. "You didn't say much to her, Clare."

She felt a twinge of guilt. "You know I'm shy."

"Are you sure that's what it was?"

His question forced her to face an uncomfortable possibility. Had she been using shyness as an excuse?

With anyone else she would have made excuses. "No." She forced herself to admit it. "It was probably more than that. It felt difficult, Todd. My tongue was in a knot. I kept thinking about Becca. You know I'm not good with strangers at the best of times, and Flora—"

"It's awkward, I get it, but sweetheart it's pretty damn awkward for her, too."

"Yes." And now she felt bad that she'd been focusing on herself and not Flora. "I'll try harder." She rubbed her hair with the towel and then styled it roughly with her fingers.

"It must be hard seeing Jack with someone else. All I'm saying is that I don't think it's easy for her, either."

Guilt slid through her. "I promise I'll try to be more chatty." She smoothed sunscreen onto her bare arms, thinking about the night before. "I didn't expect her to jump to Izzy's defense like that. I think Flora was genuinely concerned for her, don't you?"

"Yes, but I can see why it's hard on Izzy." Todd moved round their bedroom with swift efficiency, dressing quickly and retrieving his keys and phone from the jacket he'd worn the day before.

"I've never known her to have a meltdown like that. What would you do if Aiden suddenly announced he didn't want to go to medical school?"

"I'd think about all the money we'd save on fees. I'd book

a round the world cruise." His sense of humor sometimes drove her insane.

"You would not."

"All right, maybe I wouldn't. Cruising isn't for me. I'd sit him down and have a father and son talk. There'd be lots of frowning and serious expressions. I might pound my fist on the table."

"You've never pounded your fist in your life."

"There's always a first time. I'd want to know why he'd changed his mind." His hair was still spiky and damp from his second shower and she thought to herself that he looked almost the same as when she'd met him twenty years before.

"Exactly."

"Are you making some point here? Because I need it underlined."

"I'm trying to work out why Izzy has changed her mind."

Todd slid his phone into the pocket of his shorts. "I'm no psychologist, but if you want my opinion, Flora had it just right. She's had a traumatic year. That kind of thing is bound to shake you up."

What if it was more than that?

Flora had thought it was more than that. Clare had seen it in her face.

She stared out of the window. Should she try talking to Izzy? "Is anyone downstairs yet? I'm wondering what the atmosphere will be like at breakfast."

"There's food involved. Atmospheres are always improved by food. And then there's the fact that dogs and small children are no respecter of atmospheres." Todd kissed her briefly. "Stop worrying. They're not casual acquaintances. They're like family."

But family didn't always hold back, did they? If their relationship hadn't been so close, all the tensions might have stayed beneath the surface.

"I hope you're right."

"Put the coffee on. I'll be down in a minute."

But it wasn't Todd who joined her first in the kitchen, it was Flora. Judging from the dark smudges under her eyes she hadn't had any more sleep than Clare.

She paused in the doorway, saw that only Clare was downstairs and seemed to consider whether she should turn and leave again.

Clare felt terrible. She'd been thinking about herself, and Becca, and all the previous holidays they'd spent here. She'd felt as if she was betraying her friend by having Flora in the house, which made no sense at all now she thought about it. What was she going to do? Bar Jack and the girls from visiting again? Hardly.

She, who had always been so shy as a child and had frequently felt like an outsider, had made Flora feel like an outsider.

She felt ashamed of herself. Her mother would have welcomed a guest into her home regardless of the history or her personal feelings.

"Good morning! Did you sleep? Can I interest you in coffee?" Compensating like mad, Clare filled a mug to the brim and handed it to her. It was all very well deciding to be warm and friendly, but she didn't know Flora at all. What was she supposed to talk about? She'd never been that good at small talk. Where was Todd? He was never far from the coffeepot in the mornings, but he seemed to have vanished.

She just had to hope that Jack would join them soon. Presumably he and Flora hadn't shared a room.

Flora took the coffee gratefully. "Thank you. And I'm definitely a coffee drinker. When I start my day at the flower market coffee is the only thing that keeps me going. That and picking up roses by their thorns."

Flowers! Of course! That was something they had in common.

"Jack says you're a florist. How wonderful. I can't think of anything better than working with flowers all day." She winced as she heard her unnaturally cheerful voice.

To try to find some degree of normality, she busied herself in the kitchen. Whatever mood people were in today after the alcohol and tension of the night before, a good breakfast would surely help, and her kitchen always calmed and soothed her. "You have your own business?" She threw baby tomatoes into a baking tray, tossed them in olive oil and slid them into the oven to roast while she whipped up a bowl of frothy eggs ready for omelets.

"No, nothing so grand. I work for someone else, which means that they can worry about the income and the market." Flora slid her hands round the mug, warming her hands even though the room wasn't cold. "That probably sounds sadly unambitious to you."

"No. I totally get it." Clare sliced mushrooms until they formed a small heap on the chopping board. "You're looking at the woman who walked away from what some people thought was one of the most glamorous jobs there is, to live in a forest and focus on my family. Becca never understood it." The moment she said it she wanted to suck the words back. "I'm so sorry." *Becca, Becca, Becca.* What was *wrong* with her? She seemed to think and talk about her friend more now that she was gone than she had when she was alive.

"Don't apologize. She was your best friend. I understand that you need to talk about her."

Flora was a great deal more patient than she would have been in the same position.

"I suppose that with Jack being here—well, it slips out sometimes."

"I understand. When you lose someone you love, talking about them is a way of keeping them alive. Of remembering them."

Was that what it was? Was she keeping Becca alive? "It's just that every summer we—I mean...we've never had—"

"—a summer without Becca. I know." Flora took a sip of coffee and put the mug down carefully.

Clare fumbled for something to say. She was the one who was supposed to make Flora feel better, but so far it had been the other way round. "This must be hard for you, too."

"Not as hard as it is for all of you. I'm sorry if I've made this awkward. I tried to tell Jack it would be difficult, but he wouldn't listen and if I'm honest I couldn't stand the idea of not seeing him and the girls for three weeks."

She cared. Clare could see she cared. And Jack cared, too. He'd been smiling the day before. Happy.

At the funeral there had been a gray tinge to his face that had worried her. Now it had gone.

That tense knot inside her loosened.

"I'm glad you came. I'm glad you're here." As she said the words she realized that she meant them. "It's good to see Jack smiling again."

"He was in a pretty awful state when we first met." Flora took a breath. "I'm not trying to replace Becca. I hope you don't think that. I know I couldn't. She was as close to perfect as a person could get. I'm far from that."

Clare gaped at her. Was that what she thought? That Becca was perfect? If she hadn't been so astonished she might have laughed out loud.

"No one is perfect."

"Becca obviously came close." Flora gripped the mug.

"She ran marathons for charity, built a successful business, and did all that while running a home and being a wife and mother. And friend. Jack says you and Becca were friends from kindergarten. That's a special relationship. When you know someone for most of your life, you know the real person. Everything about them. You know what they've been through, and you understand them. There are very few secrets. You see them the way they really are."

"True." But sometimes, Clare wondered, that wasn't always a good thing.

"Really knowing a person—" Flora blew on her coffee "—that's a gift, isn't it? How many of us have a friend we can show our whole selves to and know we'll still be loved? Usually we feel we have to cover up the bad bits. It's like wearing makeup. We feel we have to present the very best version of ourselves all the time to be accepted. A real friend doesn't expect you to be perfect. They forgive your flaws and love you anyway." Something about her wistful tone made Clare think she'd never had that.

She felt a stab of guilt. She hadn't forgiven Becca her flaws. Not this time.

*A real friend doesn't expect you to be perfect.*

Had she been expecting Becca to be perfect instead of accepting her decisions and choices as part of who she was?

*I know you wouldn't do it, but you're not me*, Becca had said on numerous occasions and Clare had been forced to admit that she was often guilty of making judgments based on her own life experiences. Becca's experience was vastly different to hers. Clare had been a much loved only child, given whatever she wanted within reason. Becca had never been given anything. She'd worked, and earned, and fought for everything she had.

"You have quite an idealistic view of friendship." She

kept her tone chatty. "What if a friend did something you thought was awful?"

"I suppose it depends on how awful, and how much it conflicts with your values. Hopefully I'd accept it as part of them. And I suppose it depends on the friendship. I've never had a friendship like the one you had with Becca. Losing someone who you'd grown up with, and really knew you—that is a terrible loss. Something you can't replace."

That was it. That was exactly it.

Flora, who didn't know her, had instinctively identified the biggest issue for Clare—that she would never find another friend like Becca. Some people went through life picking up friends like dust on a flat surface. Clare wasn't like that. She had a few friends in the village of course, but nothing like the depth of friendship she'd shared with Becca.

It was true that Becca had really known her. She'd seen, understood and accepted all Clare's insecurities and been exasperated by many of them. But she'd done the talking in group situations, meaning Clare didn't have to.

Becca had been a loyal friend from the first day when a group of girls had stolen Clare's lunch and Becca had launched herself at them and then shared hers.

The memory made her smile. How could she have forgotten that?

It was the first time in a while she'd smiled when she thought of her friend.

The longing to see her again became a physical ache.

Clare tipped mushrooms into the pan and let them sizzle in the oil. "I can't ever remember a time when Becca wasn't in my life. Even when she was infuriating, she was still there. I don't think I've quite adjusted. But she wasn't perfect. Far from it. I don't want you to think that. She was human, like the rest of us. But she's gone, and we are learning to live with that. And the important thing is that Jack is happy. How did the two of you meet?"

She listened as Flora told her the story, first out of politeness and then from interest, easily able to imagine Jack looking lost as he tried to choose the perfect gift for his daughter. "Flowers. That's thoughtful, but Jack always was thoughtful. I'm sure Izzy loved them." Clare poked at the mushrooms, watching the edges darken and curl. "Do you have family in Manhattan?"

"I was raised by my aunt. My mother died when I was eight. I was just a little older than Molly."

"I'm sorry." Clare couldn't imagine a world without her mother in it, and didn't want to. Even now, after two decades of marriage and a child of her own, her mother still watched over her and fussed. And even though Clare protested that she was old enough to make her own decisions and her own mistakes, she secretly basked in the knowledge that someone cared so much about her well-being. "You were so young. Were your mother and your aunt close?"

Flora didn't answer for a moment. "No. They had nothing in common. My aunt was a career woman. She didn't want marriage or children. Then I came along. She considered it her duty to take me in."

"Oh Flora—" Clare pictured Aiden or Molly, orphaned, going to live with someone who didn't want them. It made her feel cold. "That must have been so hard."

"It was. I knew she didn't really want me there. I think it made me uncertain about my place in the world generally. I was never very confident. At school, I was never part of the cool crowd. I worked hard at being accepted both at home and at school. I was afraid to be myself." Flora paused. "Izzy was right about that. Sometimes I do try too hard. And I can't believe I just told you all that."

"Well as we're both being honest here I can tell you that I wasn't part of the cool crowd either. I was impossibly shy and socially awkward." She met Flora's surprised gaze and felt an unexpected connection.

"You?"

"Oh yes." Clare laughed. "School was pretty much a nightmare for me until the day Becca arrived. My parents weren't wealthy. I didn't have the right clothes. I didn't speak the right way. I didn't have a pony. But then along came Becca, and after about two days she was the coolest girl in the school."

"She had wealthy parents and a pony?"

Clare looked at her curiously. Didn't she know? Had Jack not talked about her at all? "Becca was raised in the foster system. She didn't know anything about the right clothes or the right way to speak, but she didn't care. She was so wild, she was cool. The coolest girl in school. She didn't care about pleasing people." She scraped the mushrooms into a dish and slid them into the oven to keep warm. "But she had one exceptional talent. She could dance. Other girls did ballet because their parents had signed them up, but Becca did it because she loved to dance. I think she found it to be the purest way of expressing herself. But when she wasn't dancing, she was disruptive, daring and—"

"—exciting to be around."

"Yes, I suppose she was sometimes. And sometimes it was stressful being around her." Clare topped up Flora's coffee mug, and then did the same with her own. The atmosphere had shifted from stilted to companionable. "She pushed me out of my comfort zone and in turn I think I gave her some of the stability she'd never had. She saw what a family could be." She'd never talked about Becca like this, not with her mother, not even with Todd. She'd said more to Flora about Becca in the last five minutes than she had to her own family in the past year. To Flora! Who probably couldn't bear to hear Becca's name. "I can't believe I just talked nonstop about the one subject you probably don't want to talk about."

"Actually, it was helpful. I need to hear about her. It might help me understand the children a little more. They were obviously a perfect family."

"I'm burning the tomatoes!" Clare stood up abruptly, knowing that she needed to end this conversation right now. She whipped the tomatoes out of the oven, and fried bacon until the edges turned crispy.

"Thank you for telling me a little about her."

"Jack hasn't done that?"

"No. I think he finds it difficult. If he wanted to talk about her, he'd talk about her."

*Not necessarily*, Clare thought. Sometimes men thought that the best way to handle a difficult topic was to ignore it. But who was she to think that was wrong? She knew she tended to chew on things until they were pulp. "Is your aunt still alive?"

"No. She developed dementia a few years ago. She managed to stay at home until the last year."

"Who cared for her?"

"I did. It was the least I could do. She gave me everything."

*Except love*, Clare thought. And now she saw it so clearly. Flora yearned for family. To belong. "And now? You live in the same house?"

"No. Her house was sold to pay for her care. I moved into an apartment. But last month the roof leaked and I had to move out. Jack invited me to stay with him."

"You're living with him?" Interesting. Why hadn't Jack mentioned that?

"Not living with him exactly. It's a temporary thing until I can find somewhere else. And I'm in the spare room."

Thinking of her morning with Todd, Clare sent her a womanly smile. "That must be frustrating."

Flora blushed. "I don't want to unsettle the girls, or hurt them in any way. Their needs have to take priority."

Did they?

Clare wondered if she would have been so restrained in the circumstances. "What about you and what you need?"

Flora had inadvertently given her a gift by stripping away all the anger Clare had felt toward Becca. Maybe she could repay the favor.

She carried on talking. "As women we often feel we have to put our needs bottom of the pile. But why are we less important than others? I love my son, and that love isn't diminished when Todd and I prioritize our relationship." She thought about the tangle of sheets upstairs in her bedroom. Had she left her underwear on the floor?

"You two are lucky."

"Maybe. But we also know it's important for us to have time together. We make that time. What I'm saying is that your relationship with Jack isn't all about the children. You matter, too." She could have said more, but she knew when to stop. She picked up the coffeepot. "I hope you have a good time while you're here. If there's anything I can do to make you feel more at home, let me know." Todd had asked her to be friendly and it turned out not to be hard at all. What she hadn't expected was that it might feel genuine. That she might in fact have found a friend in Flora.

Flora opened her mouth to speak, but at that moment the rest of the family piled into the room.

Aiden looked half-asleep, Todd was telling Jack about the barn conversion he was working on and Molly was playing with Chase who had managed to find mud in the garden despite the dry spell.

*Chaos*, Clare thought as she grabbed him by the collar and made Molly take him to the back door to wash his paws. The truth was that family life was a juggling act. She hoped Flora was ready for that.

Jack yawned and immediately took responsibility for Molly's breakfast.

"There's granola. You like granola, don't you?" He paused, bowl in one hand and packet in the other and looked relieved when she nodded.

"But not too much milk."

"Granola, go easy on the milk. Got it." He put together Molly's breakfast with the care of a surgeon doing a life and death operation, which Clare found both amusing and adorable.

Izzy was last to enter. Her hair was scraped back in a messy bun and she was wearing shorts and a strap top. She eyed the empty chair furthest away from Flora, and then with a resigned sigh chose the one next to her instead.

Clare wondered if she was the only person holding her breath.

"Berries, Izzy?" Flora pushed the bowl across the table. "They're delicious."

Clare's admiration for her grew.

She joined in. "There's homemade granola, fresh juice, bacon, mushroom and any type of eggs you like. If we're having an active day, it's important to eat."

Izzy checked Molly's bowl, nodded her approval and spooned granola into her own bowl. Then she added yogurt and berries. She picked up her spoon and put it down again.

She breathed deeply and then turned to Flora.

"I'm sorry I was rude. I shouldn't have spoken to you the way I did." Her voice was clear and steady, and Clare felt pride and pity in equal amounts. Pride that Izzy could do the right thing even when she was suffering, and pity because no child should have to go through what Izzy and Molly had gone through.

Todd put fresh, hot toast on the table. "Nicely said, Izzy."

"I'm sorry, too." Flora was generous and genuine. Instinctively she reached out to touch Izzy's hand, and then snatched her hand back, presumably afraid of another rejection.

"So today Aiden and I are going to take kayaks out onto the lake. And also maybe paddleboards." Izzy took a spoonful of granola. "You can come if you like, Flora. We have life jackets, and I can teach you."

Clare felt a rush of love for her goddaughter. It was a perfect gesture. She needn't have worried. The summer was going to be great.

But instead of looking relieved and accepting with the appropriate degree of enthusiasm, Flora sat in silence.

Clare willed her to speak. *Come on*, she thought. *Say yes.*

"That's a kind offer, but I can't."

Izzy clutched her spoon. Color shot into her cheeks. "You're still mad with me."

"It's not that."

"What then?"

The food on Flora's plate was untouched. "I don't like water. I'm not good with water."

"Oh that's right. You said you couldn't swim." Izzy shrugged. "I can teach you if you like." It was awkward and uncomfortable to watch, but at least she was trying. "It's not deep where we kayak. You can pretty much see the bottom as long as you stay along the shore."

"I can't."

Izzy put her spoon down with a clatter. "Because you can't think of anything worse than spending a day with me." Her voice soared upward along with her stress levels. "Right. I get it. It's all my fault for saying those things."

"No. If anything I'm grateful to you for making me take a good look at myself." Flora's breakfast was untouched. "You asked me last night how far I was prepared to go to fit in and it was a fair question. The answer is I'm not prepared to go this far. I won't do this. I can't. I hate water. I'm scared of water."

"Because you can't swim?"

"Because it's how my mother died." The words surged from Flora's mouth. "She drowned. And I was with her. I haven't been in the water since."

*Shit*, Clare thought, deciding that the occasion allowed for a little silent cursing.

Maybe the summer wasn't going to be perfect after all.

# 14

*Izzy*

"How was I to know? Am I some sort of mind reader now?" Izzy used anger to cover up the fact that she felt dreadful, but Aiden knew anyway.

"You're not a mind reader. Stop beating yourself up. It's fine."

"It's not fine, though, is it? I was rude last night—yeah, I admit it—I lost it and I'm not proud of that." And Flora had been the one person, the *only* person, to stand up in her corner. Izzy had been shocked. She was pretty sure Flora herself had been shocked, too. She wasn't the type to voice strong opinions and contradict people and she'd never seen Flora and her dad disagree on anything until last night. But she'd stood up for Izzy. "Now she probably thinks I asked her kayaking on purpose to make her feel uncomfortable."

"She doesn't think that. If anything she seemed a bit

grateful to you. Like she'd had an epiphany or something." Aiden steadied the kayak and Izzy slid into it, feeling it wobble and bob on the water.

"Yeah, right. Her epiphany was probably that I'm a total bitch. Do you think I'm a total bitch?"

"No. Izzy, we talked about this last night. You're allowed to blow up occasionally. Keeping all that emotion inside all the time isn't good. Why are you beating yourself up?"

Because she felt bad, all of the time. Bad about losing her mother. Bad about upsetting her dad, and now she felt bad about Flora, too.

When she was little she'd had a comfort blanket, until her mother had decided she was too old for such things and thrown it away. Izzy had suffered sleepless nights for months afterward. Flora's kindness the night before had reminded her of being wrapped in that warm, comforting blanket. She'd provided insulation from a cold, hard world.

The fact that Izzy had almost flung herself on her and hugged her was her secret. Thinking about how she'd almost blown it brought on a sweaty panic. She'd been so freaked out by how much she wanted to hug Flora that she'd ended up yelling. And by doing so she'd made sure that Flora would never want to hug or defend her again.

That thought upset her more than it should have done. She didn't care about Flora, did she? She wanted her gone.

She stared at the lake, wondering what it felt like to drown. And Flora had said she'd been with her mother. Izzy couldn't begin to imagine that. She thought constantly about what she could have done to save her own mother even though she knew there was nothing. The doctor had said she'd had a time bomb in her brain. But Flora—did Flora feel guilty for not being able to save her mother from drowning?

"Drowning wouldn't be a good way to die."

Aiden frowned. "Izz—"

"I'm not talking about myself. Just thinking, that's all. I mean, it wouldn't be that quick, would it? Do you think you know it's going to happen? Or do you keep fighting, and trying to swim until it's too late and then you just give up."

Had Flora asked herself those questions? Been tormented by detail?

She couldn't stop thinking that Flora had been on her own. No one protecting her.

Aiden rubbed her back gently. "What I think," he said, "is that you should think about something else."

"I bet Flora is thinking of nothing else, thanks to me."

"She seemed fine."

"That's because she's too polite to say what she was really thinking. She should have yelled at me, don't you think? What do I have to do to make her yell and lose her temper?"

"She doesn't strike me as the yelling type."

Which made Izzy feel even worse. "Do you think my dad knows? Would you invite someone to spend three weeks on a lake if you knew they were terrified of water?"

"I don't know. It depends on whether the person wants to stay away from water or not. Sometimes you choose to face the stuff that freaks you out."

"Er—did you see her face when I invited her kayaking? She looked the way I did when you made me watch that horror movie when I was nine."

"I remember. You turned green and threw up." Aiden levered himself into his kayak, his weight and the movement making the boat rock. "Are you sure you want to do this? We can go back if you like. You can spend the day hanging out with Flora and beating yourself with sticks."

"No. She deserves a break from me." And she needed a break from Flora, too. Being around her made her feel bad about herself. "If I go back, my dad will tactfully find a way to talk about college and I have too much of a headache to handle that right now." She immediately felt calmer being in her kayak. There was something about being this close to the water that soothed her. The lake stretched ahead in all directions. A pair of mallards scooted across the surface, ignoring Izzy, accepting her as part of life on the lake.

Aiden nudged her kayak with his. "Are you ready?"

She adjusted her grip on the paddle. "It's been a year since we did this together. Can we go to the island?"

"Let's stay close to shore today where it's sheltered. The wind is picking up and the island isn't an easy paddle."

"Are you calling me a wimp again?"

"No. This time it's me. I don't think my muscles can take it." He pushed off, paddling smoothly, his kayak gliding through the water.

She knew that wasn't true. He was more than capable of rowing to the island. He probably thought she wouldn't make it and he didn't want her to get any madder with herself. She probably should have been annoyed, but in fact she was touched. Nothing in life felt secure or smooth at the moment. There were moments when she was beginning to doubt her ability to cope, so it was true that not making it to the island wouldn't do anything for her mood or confidence.

She followed, watching his shoulders flex as he paddled. She wished she could keep paddling, just like this, with only the birds and the water to keep them company and the rest of her horrible, messed-up life back on the shore behind her. Everything seemed simpler, somehow, when she was out on the water.

They paddled until the sun started to burn their skin and then Aiden gestured and they maneuvered into a small creek. There, hidden by tall reeds and bulrushes, was a small dock.

"Dad built it last summer." Aiden clambered out of the kayak and tied it up. Then he leaned down to help her. "We'll leave the kayaks here and walk. I know a great place. And I have chocolate and some of Mum's shortbread." He patted the pocket in his jacket and she laughed.

"Are you ever without food?"

"Not if I can help it." He held out his hand and she took it, not because she needed his help but because she liked the feel of his skin against hers, and the way he held her so tightly. She was pretty sure that everyone else in her life would give her a big hard push given half a chance. It felt good to have someone so determined to keep her safe and keep her close. She knew she'd never forget how kind he'd been to her the night before. She'd rushed away from everyone and he'd followed her. They'd sat together on the dock until the sky turned from blue to black, until the sun was replaced by stars.

He'd made her feel less alone, and he was making her feel that way now.

"Watch your legs on the nettles." Still holding her hand, he led the way along a path and after five minutes of walking they left the trees behind and reached the edge of a meadow. It was a sea of color, wildflowers swaying in the breeze.

"This is very cool." She was about to sit down on the soft grass when Aiden stopped her.

"Wait." He threw down his coat. "You don't want to be bitten by insects."

"No one likes me enough to pay me that much attention." She meant it as a joke, but saw him looking at her. "What?"

"I don't understand why you're being so hard on yourself."

"Really? I was super rude, and then when I try to make

amends I end up traumatizing my father's girlfriend—I think I have reason to beat myself up, don't you?"

"No. I think it's a difficult situation and you're not being kind enough to yourself."

It made her feel better that he thought it was a difficult situation, especially as he didn't even know the worst part.

She sat on his coat, feeling the long grass tickle her skin.

"Do you believe in love?" She picked two daisies and threaded one through the other as she'd done as a child.

"Yes." Aiden lay back and closed his eyes. "Don't you?"

"I don't know. I don't understand it. People say they're in love, and then they get married and divorced. People die and move on."

Aiden raised himself up on his elbows. "Is this about your dad?"

"I'm just saying, that's all."

"But you're saying it because of your dad." He took the daisies from her before she could shred them. "Are you asking me if I think your dad loved your mum? Because I'm sure he did."

"So how can he fall in love again so easily?"

Aiden shrugged. "I said I believed in love, not that you can only love one person."

"You're going to have six wives, like King Henry VIII?"

Aiden brushed a daisy across her cheek. "You think that would be allowed? If I had one for every day of the week, that would be seven wives."

She flipped a daisy at him. It landed on his chest, on the open neck of his shirt where a hint of skin peeped through the V of the fabric. She looked hard at that skin, remembering when they'd swum in the lake in their underwear without thinking twice about it.

Izzy hadn't felt anything then, but she was feeling something now. Did she love Aiden? Or was it just that he knew her better than anyone? Or was it that she was flattered that he seemed to want her around when no one else did?

He made her feel wanted. Needed. There was a connection between them that she didn't feel with anyone else.

"Do you think either of your parents have ever had an affair?"

Aiden lay on his back and stared up at the sky. "No. Of course not."

"Why 'of course'? People have secret lives, you know." She lay down next to him on her side, so that she could see him.

"I know, but my parents don't."

"How do you know?"

He turned his head to look at her. "Well for a start because they're always hugging and kissing. Frankly I wish they'd stop. There comes a point where you just don't want to think about the word *sex* in the same brain wave as *parent*, you know?"

"But you don't really know, do you? What do we ever know about someone else's relationship?"

"I live with them." Aiden was ever logical. "If one of them was away all the time, or late home, or covered in lipstick I'd notice."

"Men never notice things like that."

"I would. I'm observant."

"What was I wearing yesterday?"

"Blue top. Jeans. Tight. Nice butt, by the way."

She took a friendly swipe at him, but still she was impressed. "If you ever witness a crime, you'll be able to draw one of those photofit pictures."

"I wouldn't. My drawing is crap. The police would take one look at the page and say 'you were assaulted by an alien dressed in a Halloween costume.'" He shifted on his side so that they were facing each other. "And your underwear was white and lacy. Except when you jumped into the water. Then it was transparent."

She gasped. "It was not."

"Believe me, it was." He flashed her a smile and she felt her face turn scarlet.

"Why didn't you say something?"

"Why would I say something? You looked great."

Warmed by his approval and flattered by the look in his eyes, Izzy leaned closer to him. She saw that he had tiny flecks of green in his eyes and that his lashes were thick and dark.

She wanted to kiss him, but she was afraid of doing or saying the wrong thing. Right now Aiden felt like her only friend on the planet. He was certainly the only person who came close to understanding her. She didn't want to screw it up.

She hovered, undecided, and he raised an eyebrow.

"Are you going to kiss me?"

She felt a rush of mortification that he could read her so easily.

"What if it ruins everything?"

"What is 'everything'?"

"I don't know." She gave what she hoped was a casual shrug and lay on her back next to him. The sun was warm on her face. "Us. Our friendship. Our relationship." Whatever that was, for however long it was going to last. She wanted it to at least last until the end of this vacation.

"What if it doesn't ruin everything?" He shifted so that he was half on top of her. "What if it makes everything better?"

"You don't know—"

"Instead of arguing, I have a better idea. Let's try it."

She knew a moment of exquisite excitement as his head blocked the sun and then his mouth was on hers and he was kissing her and she was kissing him back and it was definitely the best thing that had happened to her in the past year, possibly in her whole life ever.

*Aiden, Aiden.*

She slid her hands over his shoulders, feeling the warmth of his skin and the urgency of his mouth on hers. She could have kissed him all day. She could have kissed him for the rest of her days. If it felt this good why didn't people spend all their time kissing?

His kiss grew bolder, and when he slid his mouth across her jaw, down her neck to her breast she didn't push him away. She'd never actually had sex, even though most of her friends had. She'd come close, but then her mother had died and Izzy had found it impossible to connect with anyone. She'd felt isolated and alone. But she didn't feel alone now. Not with Aiden kissing her, and telling her how beautiful she was and how much he cared for her.

*I love you, Izzy, I love you.*

And she squeezed her eyes shut because she wanted to believe him so badly, and because she wanted this to last forever.

She stroked him, explored him, feeling like a sex goddess as he moaned against her lips.

And just when she thought they might do it, right here and now in a field of daisies, he pulled away and drew in a ragged breath.

"We should—" He broke off, swore under his breath and raked his hand through his hair even though all that happened was that it flopped back exactly where it had been in the first place.

She grinned. "I love that your hair does that." Her comment relieved some of the tension and he grinned back.

"Does what?"

"Falls into your eyes."

He dropped his gaze to her mouth and then gave a groan and sprang to his feet. "I'm going swimming." He sprinted away and she gave a choked laugh and sat up.

"Aiden! Wait."

"I'll see you in the water."

"But it's freezing."

"I'm counting on it." His words drifted back to her on the wind and she smiled and followed more slowly, dodging butterflies and bees as she headed back from the meadow to the shoreline.

He was already in the water when she joined him and they fooled around, splashed each other and then lay stretched out on the dock and let the droplets of water evaporate under the hot sun.

They laughed and talked, and at one point the thought crept into her head *I wonder if this is how Flora makes my dad feel*, and then she decided she didn't want to think about that. She didn't want to think that Flora might be a permanent fixture in their lives. For today she just wanted to think about herself and Aiden.

# 15

## *Flora*

"Why didn't you tell me?" Jack held her hand as they followed the trail that led through the forest. He'd refused to take the path that led alongside the lake. "I knew your mother died, but I didn't know how."

Sunlight filtered through the canopy of leaves. Apart from the occasional crack of a twig underfoot, their steps were silent, muffled by moss and vegetation.

Flora, used to the blare of car horns and sirens, found the peace calming.

"It's not something I usually talk about." But she'd just announced it in grand style at breakfast. She'd been almost as shocked as they were. Even Julia didn't know the details of her mother's death. So what had changed? How had she reached this point when a few weeks before she would have been so desperate to fit in and earn their approval she probably would have accepted Izzy's invitation and climbed into the damn boat?

And it was Izzy herself who was indirectly responsible for the change. Her sharp words had slid into Flora like a knife, all the more lethal because there was an element of truth behind what was said. She *did* have trouble speaking up.

Her words had stayed with Flora through the rest of the evening and through a long and sleepless night. And it wasn't only the words. In those few tense seconds before the teenager had yelled, Flora had seen vulnerability and gratitude. By stepping in and stepping up, Flora had made her feel a little less isolated and alone. And although the whole thing had blown up afterward, she'd still been left feeling a little closer to Izzy. She could see now that what their relationship needed wasn't for her to make more effort, but for her to be more honest. No relationship was ever going to have depth unless you were honest.

And while it was true that the timing and delivery could have been better because the *last* thing she wanted was for Izzy to think she was sulking, the most important thing was that they now knew she hated water. There would be no more invitations to go kayaking or swimming. That was a relief, but it also felt good that they knew her a little better.

And she'd been touched when Clare had pulled her aside earlier and checked that she was okay, not in that stilted polite tone that she usually used but with genuine warmth and concern. It felt to Flora that Clare had seen her as an individual for the first time, and not just Becca's replacement.

And now she wanted to forget about it and enjoy the silence, the fresh air and the feeling of Jack's fingers tangled with hers.

Jack, however, wasn't keen to be deflected. "Why wouldn't you talk about it? Flora, this is huge. I want you to feel you can tell me anything and I'm worried you didn't feel able to tell me this."

She stopped walking. Depth. Honesty. That was what she wanted.

On impulse she fumbled in her bag and pulled out the photograph she carried with her everywhere. "This is my mother."

He took the photograph from her, studying it closely. "You look like her. You have the same smile."

"We were similar in many ways."

"You've never shown me this before."

"I've never shown anyone. You're the first."

"I—" His voice was roughened. "I'm glad you shared it with me." He handed the photo back. "Do you want to share the rest? What happened?"

She never had before, but with Jack she wanted to share. She wanted him to really know her and how could he do that if she wasn't honest? "We were at the beach. My mother loved to swim." She wasn't sure how to tell the story because it wasn't one she'd told before. "She liked the feeling of weightlessness and freedom. She left me on the sand with a book. There was a family close by who said they'd watch me. *I'll be five minutes*, she said, *just five minutes*." The words started to come more easily. "She went into the water and swam out. She paused once to give me a wave, and then carried on swimming. That was the last time I saw her alive. They found her body the next day washed up on the next beach. They think she must have been caught in a riptide. That's it really. For the time she was missing, I stayed with her friend and then the friend called my aunt and she came to get me."

Jack rubbed his fingers across his forehead, opened his mouth to speak and then shook his head and pulled her into his arms. "Flora—" He held her tightly, pressing her against him in an effort to provide all the security she'd lost that day. "I'm sorry. So sorry."

Her cheek was pressed against his shirt. She loved the way it felt, being held like this. "It was a long time ago. I don't usually talk about. I never talk about it."

"I'm glad you talked about it with me. I want to know. I want to know all of it."

She could have stayed like this forever, but there were things she knew she had to say. "You don't talk about Becca."

"I talk about her all the time."

"Only in relation to the girls." She lifted her head and looked at him, trying to see the things he wasn't saying. "You don't tell me how you're feeling."

"I don't need to." He was tense. "I'm dealing with it."

Alone.

"Jack—"

"I don't want to talk about Becca. I want to talk about you. I wish you'd told me earlier that you were afraid of water." He cupped her face and his hands were warm and firm. "If I'd known, I wouldn't have brought you here."

Could she really blame him if he preferred to carry the weight instead of sharing? Hadn't she done the same herself? Sharing took practice. Time. She was going to give him time.

"I'm glad you brought me here. I like it." She squinted as the sun beamed into her eyes, and he reached out and pulled her under the shadow of a tree.

"I brought you to a lake, Flora. *A lake.* You're terrified of water, and you didn't say anything until today. I don't know what that says about you. I don't understand why you'd come—"

"I came because—" *I'm in love*, she thought. She'd come because she was in love. And it was an emotion stronger, and bigger, than fear. She was in love with Jack, with Molly, maybe even a little with Izzy. Not the snarling, angry Izzy, but the Izzy she sensed lurked beneath. "I came because I like being with all of you. If we'd been staying on a house-boat, that might have been a little different." She tried to make a joke, but he wasn't smiling.

"Do you want to go home? I'll take you home." He leaned closer, watchful, monitoring her every mood. She'd never had anyone pay attention to her the way Jack did. It was a heady, dizzying feeling to know someone cared.

"Home to Lake Lodge?"

"Manhattan. Back to the city."

"You'd do that?" She was touched, but even as she asked the question a part of her was thinking how much she'd miss the birds, the plants, the forest. As well as falling in love with Jack, she was falling in love with this place. She loved the mountains, or fells as they were called here. And although she didn't intend to get her toes wet, she liked the way the lake looked when it sparkled under the morning sunshine, or turned red under the evening sunset. She enjoyed watching birds skim the surface, and was fascinated by the shift-ing colors and its changing moods.

"We can go back right now and pack. We'll be on a flight tonight. Back in New York tomorrow if that's what you want."

"It isn't what I want." She was sure about that. "But thank you for thinking of it."

He was offering to put her needs above everyone else's. No one had done that since her mother died. Even *she* didn't do it, although she was determined to change.

"It was a serious offer. You matter to me, Flora. You—" He broke off, changing the words he'd been about to speak. "I'm so bad at this. There's so much I want to say."

"Just say it Jack. Say it."

"It isn't just the words, it's the timing."

"Timing?"

He hesitated, nervous, and she discovered that hesitation could be sexier than blistering confidence or masculine swagger. To be this nervous meant it mattered to him.

"This whole vacation must have been so hard for you. There's Izzy, and Clare—and more water than you probably ever wanted to see in one lifetime. If I'd known about your mother, I wouldn't have pushed you to come."

She had a feeling those weren't the words he'd been on the edge of speaking.

"That would have been a shame, because I like it here. And I chose to come, Jack." She'd come because she was excited by the possibilities opening up ahead of her. Tempted by a life that was different from the one she'd been living.

"You wouldn't have said no."

"Are you calling me a coward?"

"You?" He gave a faint smile. "You were like a lioness last night. When you went and stood next to Izzy I thought you were getting ready to savage me."

She'd temporarily forgotten about the night before. "Are you angry about that?" She'd wondered. After the flash heat of it had cooled a little, she'd stood there slightly startled at the words that had emerged from her mouth and wondered if maybe she should take them back. Izzy was his daughter, not hers. His problem, not hers.

"How could I be angry?" He stroked his fingers over her cheek. "You told me what you thought. You spoke the truth. That's the sort of relationship I want. I don't want you to feel you need to walk on eggshells. Intimacy means trusting each other. Sharing."

"I know you're worried about Izzy."

"I am, and last night I handled it badly. I should have been more relaxed about the whole thing."

"You don't want her to go to college?"

His smile twisted. "I'm not *that* relaxed. Let's just say I'm willing to back off and hope she comes to that conclusion herself. I honestly just want what's best for her, even if right now she doesn't believe that. But enough of Izzy. I want to talk about us. You. Coming here must have been so hard. Why did you agree to it?"

"I came because—" The words jammed in her mouth. Honesty. Intimacy. "I came because I have feelings for you. Strong feelings. And I know you have the children to think of, and that you probably—"

"How strong?" He leaned closer, caging her, his body pressing hers back against the rough bark of the tree. "How strong are those feelings? I want to know."

That confession had been scary enough, and he wanted more? He was asking her to reveal the depth of her feelings, to remove all the protection she'd layered around herself and make herself vulnerable. "They're strong. And I know you probably don't—"

"I'm in love with you, Flora. I've been in love with you for months."

Something happened to her knees because suddenly they felt shaky. She felt a little dizzy.

The air was still, the only sound the flutter of a bird's wing against leaves as it made a bid for freedom through the canopy of trees.

He had to be able to hear her heart hammering, surely?

"You—love me?" Those were the words he'd been nervous to say? She hadn't thought it. She hadn't dared think it. But she saw it in his eyes as he smiled down at her. The nervousness was still there, but now it was diluted by something else. Something that warmed every remaining frozen part of her.

"Are you asking for confirmation? How can you not know that?"

The list of reasons flew through her head.

*Too soon. Too complicated. Becca. Izzy—*

"You never—" Did he mean it? She didn't trust it, but maybe that was because she wasn't used to being handed something she wanted so badly. She wanted to gasp, and shriek and swing through the trees. "If that's true, then why haven't you said anything before now? Because of the children?"

"I wasn't sure you were ready to hear it. You already told me that in every other relationship you end up not being yourself just to please the person you're with. I didn't want that. I wanted you to be yourself. To be *you*. And I know you, Flora. I know who you are. So be sure that when I say I love you, I mean it. I'm not in love with some fabricated version of yourself you decided would work well for us. I'm rambling." He was deliciously flustered. "It might be nerves. Is this making any sense?"

"Yes." She liked the fact that his words weren't slick and practiced. It made it all the more believable, and she badly wanted to believe.

"I wanted you to feel comfortable being yourself with me. And wanted you to feel secure that you'd be loved no matter what."

"You think you know me?"

"I do know you." There was no sign of the nerves now, only confidence. "I love how creative you are, whether it's with a pencil or a paintbrush, or the clothes you wear."

"You like my clothes?"

"You dress as if every day is a party, and I love that."

Flora thought about the white dress lying unworn in her suitcase.

She wasn't Becca, but he wasn't expecting her to be like Becca. He didn't want that. He liked who she was. The white dress was going back.

He knew her. He loved her.

The rush of happiness was so intense it made her dizzy. And he was still talking.

"I love that you care so much about making people happy and yes, some of that comes from wanting to please people, and that isn't always a good thing, but some of it is simply because you're so damned caring and thoughtful. I've never met anyone like you before. You're beautiful, inside and out."

"Beautiful? Which part of me do you find beautiful?"

"All of you. Your smile, your great legs—did I mention your legs?—but most of all your heart. You have the kindest heart of anyone I've ever met." He lowered his head and kissed her. It was gentle, but she could feel the passion simmering beneath the surface. And she kissed him back, eyes closed, head dreaming.

He finally lifted his head, but just enough to allow him to speak. "I know this is complicated—that's what I meant when I mentioned timing—I know it hasn't been easy, particularly with Izzy. But we'll figure it out. We'll work through it. In time she will see this is the right thing, I'm sure of it."

Flora thought about the flicker of connection she'd felt the night before. "I haven't handled it well, either. She was right that I've been trying too hard. I need to be more myself." No more games, she thought. Just honesty.

"Well at least then you'll be less likely to rupture an Achilles tendon running in Brooklyn." He brushed his fingers over her cheek. "I think you might be the bravest person I know. Not just because I invited you to stay near a lake, but because it meant spending time with my friends even though you don't know them and in your mind you're an outsider, which is your worst nightmare."

"Jack—"

"Last night I should have stayed closer to you. I was so busy catching up with Todd, I didn't think. You must have been so stressed."

"I don't need a minder, Jack."

"How about someone who loves you? Do you need that?"

Yes, she needed that. She needed that more than anything. Her heart was full. Racing, and her mind along with it. No one had ever said these things to her, and the words were as seductive as the skilled brush of his mouth against hers and the knowing stroke of his hands.

This time neither of them pulled back. They'd waited so long. Too long.

She wrapped her arms round his neck and pulled his head to hers. She paused, her mouth a breath away from his, wanting to drag every least drop of pleasure from the delicious moment. She'd always been the same, thoughtful, patient, careful. She savored food. She savored flowers. Good things were never to be rushed in her opinion, and Jack was definitely a good thing.

But Jack approached things differently, and he crushed his mouth to hers, making the decision for them. She moaned, kissing him back, her mouth as urgent as his. They'd been patient, held back, kept their needs in check but now desire was like a wild beast released and it clawed at them, ripping through restraint and control.

His hands were impatient as they sought skin concealed by clothing, and then she felt the roughness of his palms against bare flesh and gasped as he stroked and explored. And she explored, too, her fingers lingering on the swell and flex of muscle, savoring their differences. Usually she was controlled and careful, but now she felt reckless.

*He loved her, he loved her.*

She tugged at his shirt, then moved lower, fumbling with buttons—*who invented buttons?*—and then, yes, a rush of delicious anticipation as she felt him hard and heavy against her fingers. He yanked her dress, hauling it up, lifting her. Mouths locked as they kissed, barely coming up for air as they fed on the desire that roared through them. She was deaf to everything except the sounds they made together, the rasp of breathing, the rustle of clothing. And then she felt the smooth, silken length of him against her. Everything was edged in desperation. She wanted to give, but she also wanted to take something for herself. He surged into her and she felt her body yield, slick and ready for him, welcoming the thickness and heat and drawing him in. With every skilled thrust the pleasure grew, building in intensity until she was consumed by sensation. Dizzy with it, she held on and rode out the storm, matching his demands with her own.

In that moment her whole world was him, and his was her. There was nothing but the passion. And finally the throbbing of her body eased, her head cleared a little, allowing the outside world in. She heard the distant sound of a woodpecker. The rustle of leaves. The harshness of his breathing, rapid and unsteady.

He lowered her to the ground. "Flora—"

She covered his lips with her fingers, not wanting him to talk. She didn't want anything to end this perfect moment. Real life would eventually intrude as it always did and she couldn't stop that, but she would keep it at a distance for as long as possible.

She leaned her head against his shoulder, flesh against heated flesh, prolonging the moment as long as possible, and then she felt his hand on her head, cradling her, possessive and protective.

"It should have been a five-star hotel." His mouth was on her hair, his voice was rough and low. "You should have had champagne and silk sheets."

She smiled against his skin. "I didn't need that. I needed you. This. Us."

"I love you. I love you so much." His hold on her tightened, and hers on him. She couldn't bring herself to let him go. Her heart, bruised for so long, felt healed and whole. Strong, for the first time. That hollow emptiness had gone. Intimacy, she thought. The cure for that loneliness hadn't been more friends or more activities, a busier day, a busier life. It had been intimacy. Trust.

Their breathing slowed, but still he held her.

"I should have taken more time."

It made her laugh that he'd thought he was the one in control of it. "I didn't give you that choice."

"True." He eased away so he could look at her. "I thought I knew you, but I didn't know you could be so demanding."

"I have a ruthless, killer streak didn't you know?"

"I didn't know, but I do now. I just saw a new side of you. You ravished me in the forest."

"Am I expected to apologize for that?" It wasn't clear who had ravished who, but she was enjoying the conversation too much to end it.

"Definitely not. Just as I'm not going to apologize for what happens next."

"What—" She didn't get to ask her question because he swept her up and carried her through the trees. "Jack! You can't—"

"I can. I am. Hold on."

"You're going to drop me in a patch of poison ivy." She

was breathless. Laughing. "Someone will see us. Someone will—"

"Losing your nerve now? What happened to the assertive woman who just had tree sex?"

"That was spontaneous." Although it hadn't been, not really. It had been building for weeks, months. The sexual tension between them had reached incendiary levels.

"This is spontaneous, too, only I want the version that doesn't include clothes and gymnastics against a tree."

She was about to ask where they were going when she saw the sleek lines of the boathouse. "How did we end up here?"

"I took the shortest possible route. I may have to explain away a rip in my trousers."

Before she could answer they were inside. He nudged the door closed behind them, swore as he struggled to turn the key without putting her down, and then carried her to the bedroom.

"I had no idea you were so good at multitasking."

"I'm about to show you how good." He set her down but he didn't let her go.

Dimly she wondered what would happen if someone else decided to use the boathouse, but then he touched her, kissed her, and she stopped thinking about anything but him.

This time they took it slower, savoring, drawing out the pleasure until she rose over him, taking him deep, making him hers in every way.

Finally, after a long shower that was made longer by his determination to explore every part of her, they collapsed on the bed.

He'd opened the doors to the balcony and she could hear birdsong and the soft lap of water against the dock. She wished she could freeze this moment, stay like this wrapped in his arms and warmed by the sunshine pouring through the glass.

The intimacy, the closeness, was something she hadn't experienced before.

She'd never shared herself with anyone the way she had with Jack. Their relationship was deeper than anything she'd experienced before.

She felt exhilarated, content, lucky, *loved*.

And Jack had shared, too. She ignored the tiny voice in her head that reminded her he still hadn't really talked about Becca.

# 16

*Izzy*

The pony trundled along the track and Izzy shifted in the saddle, trying to get comfortable. Her neck was burning from the sun, her whole body was sweaty. It was a long way to the ground. When Flora had brightly suggested pony trekking as an activity she should have made an excuse, but she was still feeling guilty about the scene at breakfast the day before and Flora's anguished confession.

She'd felt so bad about it that she'd been ready to agree to pretty much anything to make amends. She was tired of feeling bad about herself and tired of feeling guilty the whole time. Also, she didn't want to be left out of an activity that Molly was doing. Her almost childish desperation to cling to the ragged remains of her family was almost as embarrassing as her riding skills.

So here she was on a horse. She'd never been that into horses. She was a city girl. A city girl who was terrified.

Who was the people pleaser now?

If she hadn't been so afraid of falling off, she might have laughed.

They were riding in a line, with a delighted Molly bouncing in the saddle directly in front of her and then Aiden.

It was kind of annoying that he looked *great* on the horse, relaxed and in control, like he was a cowboy or something. Izzy scowled at his back, while at the same time admiring his shoulders and his athletic ability.

Maybe he sensed her scrutiny because he glanced over his shoulder and grinned at her and she pulled a face, partly because she was horribly embarrassed to look so red and sweaty in front of him, and partly because she had no idea how to ride. It was an uncomfortable, sticky nightmare and something she would have rather he hadn't witnessed. By the time she slid off this animal her ego would have shriveled to the size of a peanut.

"This is brilliant," Flora sang out from behind her and Izzy rolled her eyes to heaven. Brilliant? She was pretty sure she wouldn't be able to walk in the morning. If she hadn't known better, she'd have said this was Flora's revenge for those times she'd made her run to the Brooklyn Bridge. But Flora wasn't the type to take revenge. No, this was just her idea of fun. Trying something none of them had tried before, except Aiden.

"Look, Molly!" Flora was obviously enjoying herself. "See the rabbits in the field? They're so cute."

Clare rose up in her stirrups and laughed. "I see them! Well spotted, Flora."

Izzy had noticed a shift in the relationship between Clare and Flora. It seemed that despite the frosty beginning, they genuinely liked each other. And although it felt slightly weird to admit it, Izzy suspected that Clare had more in common with Flora than she'd had with Becca.

Izzy looked over the hedge, and saw wild rabbits bounding across the grass. Flora was always pointing things out. *Look at the colors on that butterfly. Taste this wild raspberry.* She noticed small things and Izzy was starting to notice them, too. She'd discovered that if you focused hard enough on the present, the future seemed to shrink a little.

She was still staring at the rabbits when her pony put his head down to snatch grass from the track. Izzy almost flew over his head. "Mine keeps eating!" She tugged ineffectually at the reins. "Why does he keep eating? Don't they feed him back at the yard?"

"He's taking advantage of you. Keep using your legs," the girl in charge yelled back at her. "Show him who is boss."

Izzy was in no doubt about who was the boss, and it wasn't her.

She gave another tug of the reins and pressed her legs against the pony's fat sides. He tore off another chunk of grass and ambled forward, munching.

"Grazing is bad for you, didn't you hear?" Izzy tried conciliation rather than coercion, patting his neck, and stroking her hand over the wiry fur. "I guess not. As you're a horse." It had to be hot, she thought, having fur and a mane and tail. And all those flies just buzzing around wanting to munch on you.

This was probably all her fault for accusing Flora of only doing what she wanted to do.

At breakfast Molly had been talking about how much she wanted to try horseback riding. Flora had suddenly said *"let's do it"* with so much enthusiasm that before Izzy could produce a suitable excuse Clare was on the phone booking for all of them, apart from her dad and Todd who had suddenly found a pressing need to take the boat out onto the lake.

Izzy would have exchanged her current situation for a day sailing. She'd do anything to feel the wind in her hair and the spray on her face.

Flies buzzed around the pony and he shook his head, irritated. Izzy clutched the front of the saddle, terrified of falling. There was probably symbolism here if she looked for it. Trying something new. Stepping out of your comfort zone. Letting go of the predictable.

Maybe she'd write a blog about it. How far should you go to please another person? Where did you draw the line between being easygoing and a total pushover? Right now she felt like a pushover, although it was true that the views were pretty good from the back of a horse. She looked over walls and hedges to mountain slopes dappled by heather and rocks. She looked down into fast-flowing rivers and was eye level with the lower branches of trees.

She realized that for the first time in months she didn't feel exhausted. She was sleeping better, waking to birdsong and cool lake air rather than nightmares or Molly crying.

They arrived back at Lake Lodge, tired and overheated.

Flora and Clare vanished indoors to shower and change.

Izzy rubbed her fingers in her damp, matted hair and eyed the lake. Wearing the hard hat had given her a headache. "Straight into the lake for a swim and cooldown, I think." She held out her hand to Molly. "Last one in is a big baboon."

"No!" Molly shrank from her and Izzy felt that rejection like a blow to the gut. She'd just been on a horse for goodness sake. She was starting to think her walk would never be normal again. The least her sister could do was join her for a dip.

"But you love swimming."

"I don't want to." Molly burst into noisy sobs while Izzy stood, stunned.

What was wrong? Her sister loved everything to do with the water.

Confused, Izzy dropped to her knees and hugged her. "There," she said soothingly. "It's fine. You don't have to swim if you don't want to." But why wouldn't she want to? Was this a tantrum? Was she tired after the horse-riding? Izzy's whole body ached from holding on and trying not to fall on her head and die, so that was possible.

Molly's sobs intensified until she was gulping in air in between each heartrending howl.

Izzy started to panic. This was her sister. She knew her sister. But she had no idea what was going on here. "What's the matter? Did something happen? Have you hurt yourself? Was it the horse? Did it bite you or something?"

Molly shook her head, her face crumpled. "I miss Mommy."

"I know, I know." Izzy hugged her, totally out of her depth. There had been the nightmares of course, and the bed-wetting, but those had been easier to deal with. This? She had no idea what had brought it on. It couldn't have been the horses. There were no memories there. Her mother wouldn't have gone within a million miles of a horse.

She rocked her sister as she howled and glanced desperately at the Lodge. Her dad was still sailing. Where was Aunt Clare? Probably in the shower at the back of the house. Aiden, too.

"It's okay, honey." She stroked Molly's hair. "It's okay." *Please be okay. Please stop crying.*

"Don't—want—" Molly hiccupped, her breath jerking as she tried to get the words out "—go in—water."

"You don't want to go in the water. I get it. You don't have to. You can sit on the edge and watch me, and—agh—" She gasped as Molly almost broke her ribs.

"Don't want you—to swim—" jerk, hiccup "—either."

Her sister's arms were crushing her. "Right. Okay." But it wasn't okay of course. It was bemusing and a little scary. She used to have confidence dealing with Molly, but right now she felt clueless.

Desperate, she glanced at the Lodge and saw Flora appear by the window.

Izzy hesitated, trying to breathe even though her sister's arms weren't giving her lungs the space to expand. She didn't want to ask for help. She wanted to handle this herself. She wanted to be indispensable. On the other hand Molly's sobs were killing her. She couldn't bear to see her sister this upset.

"Tell me what's happened, Molly."

But Molly just clung and cried and Izzy started to feel like crying, too.

She usually knew exactly how to comfort her sister, but not today.

With a huge effort, she forced herself to call out. "Flora!"

In an ideal world Flora was the last person she'd turn to for help, but this wasn't an ideal world, was it? In fact most of the time right now it felt like a pretty crap world.

Flora's head turned and she gave a little wave and then stopped, her hand suspended in midair as she took in the scene beneath her. "I'm coming—" She vanished and moments later was sprinting across the lawn toward Izzy and Molly.

*Thank goodness*, was all Izzy could think. Later, she was sure her insecurities would bubble over, but right now she was just relieved not to have to handle this on her own.

"What happened?" Flora knelt down beside her. "Hey, Molly, what's wrong, sweetie? Has she been stung or something? Is she in pain?"

Molly clung to Izzy, her fingernails digging in Izzy's flesh.

Izzy didn't know about her sister, but she was in plenty of pain.

She gritted her teeth and tried not to yell "ow." Her sister seemed determined to damage the few parts of her that weren't already aching after the horse-riding.

Flora was rubbing Molly's arms. "Did she fall? Hurt herself?"

"No. She just doesn't want to go swimming. Although why she couldn't just say that, I have no idea. It was only a suggestion. Molly, *please* stop crying." Her head had been throbbing from the heat and the riding helmet. Now it was threatening to explode. She'd always assumed she'd get married and have kids at some point in her life, but she was starting to question that

"She's probably tired." Flora sat down on the grass next to Molly. "You don't have to swim if you don't want to, Molly. You can swim tomorrow."

"Don't-want-to-swim-tomorrow." Each word was punctuated with a jerky breath. *"I don't ever want to swim again!"*

Izzy winced. Since when did her sister have such a loud and piercing voice? She was pretty sure their neighbors in Manhattan would have heard every word.

"Why don't you want to swim, Moll? And why don't you want me to swim?"

"Because you might drown and I don't want you to die like Flora's mommy." She flung herself down on the grass and Izzy met Flora's gaze above her sister's sodden, heaving body.

She saw horror and guilt. Izzy was just relieved it wasn't something she'd done.

"Oh Molly—" Flora rubbed the little girl's shoulders. "I'm sorry I scared you." She tugged Molly onto her lap, rocking her gently. "What happened to my mother wouldn't happen to you."

Molly sniffed and clung. "Why?"

Flora's face was a whitish gray. She looked almost as upset as Molly. She looked at Izzy and her quick, reassuring smile was strained.

*She doesn't want to talk about it,* Izzy thought, but then Flora settled herself more comfortably on the grass and did talk about it.

"My mother went swimming in deep water in the sea. And she didn't have a life belt, or anyone with her. That isn't what happens when you swim. You're always with Izzy, or your daddy. You're in your depth, and you have your floats."

Molly scrubbed her face with her palm and peered at Flora. "But you don't go swimming."

"That's not because it's unsafe. It's because—well, I'm scared of water." Flora tightened her grip on Molly. "I probably should have done something about it long before now, but I never have. There isn't much need or opportunity to swim where I live so I never had to push myself."

Molly sniffed. "Daddy says it's okay to be scared, but if you're scared of something you should just do it."

"And he's right. I should have just done it. I wish I had, because then you and I would be able to swim in that lake together."

"No, because now I'm scared, too." She started to cry again, heartrending sobs that made Izzy's stomach hurt.

She felt so out of her depth she might as well have been

in the middle of the lake, but Flora didn't seem to be floundering.

"You are brilliant in the water," she said. "I looked out of my window yesterday and I thought to myself *There's a dolphin in the lake. How did a dolphin get into the lake?* And then I looked a little closer and realized it was you."

Molly's sob turned to a little gurgle of laughter. "Dolphins don't live in the lake."

"You know that because you're smart. And being smart, you also know how to be safe in the water. I've seen you. You always have someone with you, you never go too far from the shore—you do all the right things. And then there's the fact that you're a great swimmer."

Molly sucked in a juddery breath. "Aunt Clare taught me."

"Right. So we know you're not scared of water, not really. Is there something else that scares you?"

Izzy thought about the question even though it hadn't been aimed at her. Lately it felt she was permanently scared. She was scared of living a life without her mother. Scared about that conversation she'd overheard. Scared of knowing things she wished she didn't know. Scared of Flora's presence in their lives. Scared of not being needed, and of losing her place in the family. She was pretty sure she could now add "scared of horses" to the list.

It was a good job Flora hadn't asked her the question. It would take Izzy at least two weeks to answer it.

Molly, however, only said one thing. "I'm scared Daddy and Izzy will die, too."

Izzy expected Flora to say *Of course they won't die*, but she didn't.

"When my mother died, I was scared, too. I think it's because as well as losing someone you love, you lose that sense of security. A good mother—and your mommy was obviously a very good mommy—makes you feel safe, and losing that feeling of being safe is a very scary thing. And you're scared it might happen to other people you love. But it's very rare for people to die the way your mommy did, and my mommy did. We have to remember that."

Molly seemed to think about it. "I miss her."

"Of course you do."

"Some days I can't remember what she looked like. What if one day I wake up and I don't remember at all?"

"I worried about that, too," Flora said. "So I took my favorite photo of my mother, and I had copies made and I carry that photo everywhere with me. So in a way, she is always with me. I like knowing I have her there. There's one in my purse, one in a frame I keep by my bed, one on my wall in my apartment. So if you have a favorite photo, we could do the same for you."

"I don't know which one is my favorite."

"Maybe you and Izzy can go through all the photos together and choose the one you like best. The one that reminds you most of your mommy. Maybe when she's dancing or laughing. Does that sound like a good idea? What do you think, Izzy?"

Izzy's throat was thick. How could she say that she worried about the same thing? Worried that one day she'd forget what her mother looked like. She kept her mother's perfume in her bedroom and on bad days when the images in her head were blurred, she breathed in the scent and remembered.

She cleared her throat. "Yeah, we can do that."

"And now about this swimming." Flora tipped Molly onto the grass and scrambled to her feet. "How about you and Izzy go swimming together and I'll make us some drinks."

"Will you watch me?"

Flora hesitated. "Of course I'm going to watch. Try stopping me."

"Will you sit right on the edge?"

"Absolutely." Flora's skin color took on a faint greenish tinge that reminded Izzy of algae.

"Not right by the edge." Izzy stripped off her T-shirt down to her bathing suit beneath. "We don't want to splash her."

When Flora gave her a quiet smile of gratitude, she couldn't help returning it. She might want Molly to herself, but she was willing to admit that there were times when reinforcements were a good thing.

Molly was wriggling out of her clothes, apparently forgetting her sudden horror of the water.

She grabbed one of the floats Clare kept in the box close to the water and sped down the grass.

"Whoa! Wait up! You're not allowed in without me," Izzy yelled after her, and then glanced at Flora, knowing she had to say something. "Thanks. Sorry you had to handle that."

"Well I seem to have caused it, so you're not the one who should be apologizing. And you were great. You are *so* great with her. No one can handle Molly the way you do."

Izzy felt like a parched plant that had suddenly been watered. She sucked up the life-giving praise through her roots and it spread to every part of her, reviving her wilting confidence.

She *was* good with Molly, she knew she was.

Just because she'd had to ask for help on this occasion, didn't mean she wasn't good with her sister, and it didn't mean she wasn't needed.

She gave a tentative smile. "Thanks." Why had she built Flora up into a monster? She was just another person doing her best to handle what life threw at her. And life seemed to have thrown plenty. She'd lost her mother, too, and she'd had no dad and no big sister. "You were brilliant."

"You're welcome. As I was the one who caused the meltdown, it was the least I could do." Flora paused. "Are you aching after the riding?"

Izzy pulled a face. "Like I've been kicked down the road by a pair of heavy boots. Or even a horse."

Flora grinned back and for a moment they were just two bruised and aching people who had shared a similar experience.

"Better move. I'm on lifeguard duty." Flora waved a hand and headed toward the water.

"No need to come any closer than that." Izzy dragged one of the garden chairs a safe distance from the water. "And don't worry. I've got a lifesaving certificate. You're just there for show."

"I hope so, because there is no way I could help anyone in trouble in the water. Thanks, Izzy."

Feeling confident and a little more sure of her place in the world, Izzy slid into the lake and joined her sister.

# 17

## *Flora*

The days passed in a blur of fresh air and sweaty, breathless fun. They hiked to the tops of fells, scrambling up twisty trails and over rocky outcrops, gasping as they finally collapsed at the top, lungs heaving and skin stinging from the heat. They gorged on Clare's delicious picnics and the incredible views, devouring chunks of fresh bread and local cheese while drinking in the valleys and mountain ridges spread before them.

"That's Windermere," Clare would say, pointing to the long ribbon of silvery water stretching into the distance, or she'd point at a rocky ridge, "That's Crinkle Crags and next to it Bowfell." She was able to recognize every mountain from its shape and Flora was impressed by her local knowledge.

"You've climbed all of them?"

"Yes. My father and I used to go every weekend."

She and Clare had slid into an easy friendship, and Flora was surprised by how easy it was to be with her. Any traces of awkwardness were long gone. It had taken only a few conversations for Flora to work out that Clare's occasional reserve masked shyness. She wasn't good with strangers and the more time she and Flora spent together, the more she opened up, particularly when it came to sharing this corner of the world she loved so much.

The sheer scope and variety of the scenery was breathtaking, from towering rock faces and craggy ridges, to moatlike lakes that snaked along the valley floor. As they clambered up steep sided gullies and cooled down next to frothing waterfalls, they saw buzzards, ospreys and red kites. They tramped through ancient woodland, the trees knotted and gnarled.

They left Molly with Clare's mother for a day and climbed Helvellyn, a test of physical fitness that made Flora finally give thanks for the running she'd done with Izzy. As she tackled the notoriously vertiginous ridge of Striding Edge she discovered two things. First, that she wasn't afraid of heights, and second, that she was in love with the Lakes, even though that affection didn't extend to actually dipping her toes in water. Her normally pale skin became lightly tanned, and a few freckles appeared on her nose. Her body felt stronger than it had in years. *She* felt stronger.

And whatever she did, Jack was there. They tried to be discreet, but she wasn't sure they succeeded. She discovered it was possible to communicate a great deal without touching. A look. A smile. That was all it took. And on the occasions when they managed more she wasn't sure which of them was more desperate. It was more a collision of need than a blending. Sometimes she looked at him and thought *he's gorgeous*, and other times she thought *he's mine*. Either way she couldn't stop looking, and the more she looked the better she knew him. She knew that look he wore when he listened to Molly, the way he smiled when he swung his daughter onto his shoulders and heard her belly laugh. And then there were the more intimate expressions. The look in his eyes when he and Flora were naked together, when her bare leg slid over his and when she arched into him, inviting.

Fortunately their deepening connection didn't appear to have a negative impact on the rest of the group.

Since the incident with Molly, Izzy was noticeably more relaxed with her. Flora was no longer nervous and on edge when they were together, and occasionally they even shared a laugh. They weren't friendly exactly, but the tension was a little less than it had been.

When it rained—*inevitable*, Clare had said—Flora made a pirate camp in the living room for Molly, draping sheets over the sofas and constructing a "ship" complete with mast. She soaked paper in cold tea and made a treasure map, even going so far as to burn the edges to add authenticity. Clare joined in and they played hide-and-seek, making full use of secret doors and cupboards in the lodge and hidden corners of the tangled, overgrown garden. Flora remembered doing the same thing with her mother, hiding under a bed, holding her breath, waiting in a state of delighted terror to be discovered. She told Molly about it and answered a dozen more questions about the things she'd enjoyed doing with her mother.

Aiden and Izzy were often absent, sometimes kayaking together on the lake, more often walking along the lake trail, heads close together as they talked.

Izzy seemed happier than she'd been in a while and the sensitive topic of college hadn't been mentioned again. Jack had confided in Flora that he thought it was best left for now, and she'd agreed with him. Time could soften things, she knew that. And time could provide clarity. She had a feeling Izzy needed both.

Although Flora had fallen in love with the mountains, she was equally happy spending time in the gardens of Lake Lodge. She spent hours deadheading, trimming, tending. Clare often joined her and they stood together, planning the garden together.

"Is it too late to prune the lupins?" Clare asked her one morning as she nursed a brimming mug of tea.

"Lupins? Oh, you mean lupines. It's fascinating how many differences there are between British English and American English. The answer is, definitely not too late. It will encourage new growth. Let's do it now." Flora put her mug down and was stuck into the gardening even as Clare protested that she was a guest and shouldn't be cutting back plants.

But Flora no longer felt like a guest. At some point she'd stopped feeling like an outsider and started feeling like part of the group. Welcomed. Accepted.

When she finished with the lupines, she removed side shoots from the wisteria and divided the clumps of bearded iris so that they'd form roots and buds the following year.

Occasionally, Clare would mention Becca, and gradually Flora formed a better picture of the woman who had been Clare's lifelong friend. Yes, she'd had ferocious ambition and talent, but she seemed to have been driven by deep-seated insecurities that she'd never been able to shift.

The realization that even the perfect Becca had her imperfections gave another boost to Flora's determination to be herself. Imperfections were part of being human. Trying to please her aunt had been her way of surviving a terrible time in her life and yes, it had escalated to ridiculous proportions, but she was more aware of herself now.

She should have known that such blissful calm couldn't last. It came to an end during their second week at Lake Lodge and it started with a fight about Chase.

It was the first time Flora had heard Molly and Izzy argue.

Izzy was sitting on the kitchen floor, rubbing the tummy of an ecstatic Chase. "Aiden isn't around today because he's sailing with a group of friends—birthday celebration—so I'm spending the day with Chase. I've made a picnic and I'm taking him for a long walk, is that okay, Aunt Clare?"

"No!" Molly's face crumbled. "He's ours! He's coming sailing. Daddy promised."

"He's not *yours*. And anyway, you've had him all week. It's my turn," Izzy's voice was level. "You can play with him later, when you're back from sailing."

"I want to play with him in the boat. He loves swimming."

Izzy stopped rubbing and Chase gave a whine of protest. "I'll take him swimming."

"You can't swim on your own. It's not allowed."

Flora felt a hard knot in her stomach. The sudden tension stressed her.

*Family life*, she told herself. This was just family life. It was simply that she wasn't used to it. What could she do? Say? She almost offered to go with Izzy, but then stopped herself. What use was she as a lifeguard? And anyway, she shouldn't take a side.

The day would work out, one way or another.

Jack and Todd were taking Molly sailing and Flora and Clare had planned to spend another relaxed morning in the garden. The day before they'd been to the garden center and Flora was looking forward to a day of planting and fresh air. She and Jack had sneaked into the same room for the past few nights and the result was a dizzying combination of ecstasy and exhaustion.

A day in the garden was just what she needed. An easy friendship was developing between her and Clare and she'd pictured a few delicious hours of gardening, chat and maybe a short nap in the sun.

She enjoyed the calm of it, basked in the easy friendship that was developing between her and Clare, but she could already see from the spark in Izzy's eye and the pout on Molly's lips that calm and conversation were unlikely to be coming her way today.

Izzy looked at her father. "Do you want me to come sailing with you?"

Jack was sorting through waterproofs. "Aren't you hanging out with Aiden today?"

"He had plans he couldn't change. So I could easily help out."

"That's a kind offer, but we'll be fine." He stuffed Molly's wet suit into a bag. "You have a great day doing your own thing for once. We can manage without you."

Izzy's face lost some color. "But I can help with the sails, and make sure Molly's okay. She's a little nervous around water right now—"

"She'll be great." He added sailing gloves and wet suit boots, zipped the bag and dropped it by the door. "We're going to have one of our special Dad and Molly days, aren't we, honey?" He gave Molly a quick hug and she hugged him back.

"Yay! A Dad and Molly day. Just the two of us and Chase." She danced a little on the spot and Flora was willing to bet that each time those feet thumped the floor Izzy felt they'd landed on her chest.

She knew for sure Jack thought he was being generous

to Izzy, but she could also see he was saying and doing the wrong thing.

"Okay. Sounds fun." Izzy's smile was almost painfully bright. "I'll make the picnic for you."

"No need." Jack picked up a bag from the counter and waved it proudly. "I've got it."

"Did you make ham sandwiches?"

"No, because Molly hates ham. You taught me that, and I paid attention. I made her cheese."

Izzy swallowed. "How about her drink? You always forget to pack a drink."

"Not today. I have learned from my mistakes and I have juice *and* water." Jack produced it from the backpack with a flourish. There was a hint of the triumphant in his smile. "Are you impressed? I think I've officially passed the dad test. We no longer need you to run the household, Izzy."

Izzy's hand stilled on Chase's belly. "Right. So—I'm not needed." Something in her voice made Flora wish Jack would stop talking, but he didn't.

"That's right. You can go to college without worrying that we're going to starve or be buried under a mountain of laundry."

Was that what this was? Was he trying to prove that he could survive without Izzy?

Flora wondered if the mention of college would trigger an explosion, but Izzy said nothing.

She watched as Jack bundled the picnic into the bag along with all the sailing gear.

Flora had a bad feeling and couldn't quite pinpoint why. There was no tantrum and no fiery words. Just a stillness and a sense of quiet misery that worried Flora more.

Was Izzy feeling left out? Was that what was happening?

She glanced at Jack but he was arguing with Molly over whether to pack apples or pears and didn't seem concerned.

Maybe this was family dynamics. Something Flora knew little about.

Izzy stood up. "Have fun today." She paused, but Jack was trying to persuade Molly to let him rub sunscreen on her neck and didn't seem to hear.

Izzy grabbed her backpack and left the room, closing the door quietly behind her.

Chase stood at the door she'd just shut in his face, wagged his tail in a bemused fashion and whined slightly.

Flora was as confused as the dog.

"Don't worry!" Having submitted to sunscreen, Molly sprinted across the room to him, wrapped her arms round his neck and kissed his head. "You're coming with us. You're going to be pirate dog. Say 'aye aye, Cap'n.'"

Chase barked and Molly collapsed with laughter.

Flora glanced at Jack, wondering if he was going to go after Izzy. "Jack?"

"Mmm." He grabbed sun hats and sunglasses. Flora could almost see him ticking things off on a mental list.

"When are we going, Daddy?" Molly was tugging on his arm and fidgeting.

Flora tried again. "Jack!"

He looked at her. "What?"

"Daddy?"

"Soon. In a minute." He hushed Molly and focused on Flora. "What's wrong?"

"Izzy." She gestured with her head. "Are you going to talk to her?"

He glanced out of the window. "What about? Why?"

"Because—" Hadn't he seen it? Was she the only one? "I thought she seemed subdued."

"Probably shock that I remembered to put cheese in Molly's sandwiches and not ham." His grin was engaging and Flora couldn't help but smile back, but it didn't shift the feeling of anxiety toward Izzy. She wanted to say more, but Molly was virtually dancing toward the door with Chase bouncing next to her.

"Dad*dy*!"

"Coming." He looked from Izzy to Flora. "She's fine. Probably my fault for mentioning college again. From now on I'm keeping my mouth zipped. I'm trying to do the right thing, but I'm not sure I even know what that is."

He left with Molly, taking the chaos, the chatter and Chase with them.

Flora glanced through the window and saw Izzy sitting on one of the sunloungers, her shoulders slumped as she stared across the lake.

She turned, intending to mention it to Clare, but before the words were even on her lips Clare's phone rang.

"What? You're kidding. Mum!" Her face lost color as she listened. "Are you okay?—well, of course—that goes without saying. I'll be with you in three minutes." Clare ended the call and dropped the phone on the kitchen table.

"Problems?"

"My mother cut her finger chopping mushrooms." Clare grabbed her bag. "She said it isn't bad, but I know my mother. She wouldn't be calling if it wasn't almost hanging off. She's probably lost her hand. Maybe even her arm. Damn. And Todd is so much better with blood and injuries than I am. I panic. Where are my keys? I can't find my keys. I know I had them."

Flora joined the hunt and found them next to a stack of old magazines. "Do you want me to come?"

"No, no, I'm fine—" Clare dropped her keys "—totally fine—"

"Are you safe to drive?" Flora retrieved the keys and handed them to her.

"Why wouldn't I be safe?" Clare scanned the kitchen.

"You seem a little—distracted. What are you looking for?"

"Something in case she bleeds in the car. My mind is blank. You're right, I'm distracted." Clare pressed her fingers to her forehead and breathed. "This is called overreacting, isn't it?"

"I think it's called love. Are you sure you don't want me to come with you?"

"Thank you, but no. My mother hates a fuss, which is how I know it must be bad." Clare was hunting around the kitchen and Flora grabbed a fresh towel from the counter.

"Will this do?"

"Perfect. You're a lifesaver." Clare grabbed it and headed for the door, a slightly wild look in her eyes. "You'll be on your own. I'm sorry—"

"Don't worry about me. I'll finish off that planting we started yesterday."

Clare was halfway to the car when Flora spotted her phone on the table.

She sprinted after her.

"You're going to need this." She dropped the phone into Clare's pocket. "Call if I can do anything. Drive carefully."

The door slammed. The engine revved and small stones flew as Clare accelerated along the drive to the Gatehouse where her mother lived.

Flora stared after her for a moment, and then walked back into the house.

Silence enveloped her.

The day, or at least the next few hours, stretched ahead but for the first time in as long as she could remember she was alone without feeling lonely. It seemed that the house retained the warmth even after the people had left. Or maybe it was Jack. Even when she wasn't with him, she thought of him.

She cleared the kitchen, loaded the dishwasher, swept the surfaces and floor until they gleamed. She allowed herself a brief moment to luxuriate in the pretense that this place was hers. Deciding that she'd earned herself another coffee, she made herself a cappuccino from Todd's terrifyingly sophisticated machine and took it into the garden.

The lawn still wore the evidence of the day before. Water pistols lay abandoned next to Chase's favorite ball and a half-inflated kayak.

Izzy was still on the sunlounger.

Flora approached cautiously. "Izzy?"

Those shoulders stiffened, but she didn't turn. "What? What do you want?" Both words and tone crossed the line into rude but Flora ignored that because as well as anger and resentment, she heard a distinct wobble in that voice.

Izzy was crying. And she was trying to hide it.

Flora had done the same many times. She'd cried into a pillow, cried in the shower, locked herself in the bathroom.

She reached out to touch the girl's shoulder and then pulled her hand back.

"Izzy—"

"Fuck off!" Izzy flew to her feet, her hair whipping round her face. Her eyes were red from crying, her cheeks soaked and streaked with the evidence. "Can't you get it into your thick head that I don't want you around? Just *fuck off* and leave me alone." She shoved Flora, then grabbed her backpack and ran across the lawn. She stumbled twice, righted herself, arms flailing.

*Can't see where she's going,* Flora thought, pulling her soaked T-shirt away from her body. Most of her foamy cappuccino was now on her body or on the lawn.

She put the empty cup down and sat down hard on the sunlounger Izzy had just vacated.

*Family life, family life.*

But her heart ached for Izzy.

She wanted to go after her but that would be stupid, wouldn't it? Izzy had made it clear she hadn't wanted to talk to her and the fact that Flora had witnessed the tears she'd been trying to hide wasn't going to endear her to the girl anytime soon.

She sat, with no idea what to do next. A butterfly danced across her field of vision, a swirl of color against the deep blue of the lake.

There was no sign of Izzy.

Flora stood up. Shielding her eyes from the sun, she squinted along the trail, and then moved closer to the water so that she had a better view of the boathouse.

Nothing.

Anxiety gnawed at her. She felt a rush of frustration toward Jack. She'd *known* something was wrong. He should have checked on Izzy before he left.

Jack hadn't seemed worried, but Flora was sure that he was missing something big.

Slowly she scanned the path that led along the side of the lake. Had she gone into the forest?

What if she swam on her own and got into trouble?

Flora would never be able to forgive herself. She was willing to endure more abuse just to be sure Izzy was all right.

She had to check. She *had* to.

She probably wouldn't even announce herself. As soon as she found Izzy and reassured herself that she was okay, she'd come back to the house and focus on the garden.

She returned to the kitchen, and stuffed a few provisions into a bag. Should she change her T-shirt? Deciding there was no time, she locked the back door and headed through the forest to the boathouse. As she drew closer, she could see no one had been near it. It was locked up and quiet. There was no sign of Izzy.

But she'd definitely walked in this direction, so where else could she be?

Flora skirted the side of the boathouse and stepped onto the dock, trying not to look down at the water shimmering beneath the planks.

In the time it had taken her to walk from the house the sky had grown darker. The only sounds were the call of a bird and the slow lazy flap of a heron's wings as it left the riverbank.

Flora scanned the lakeshore into the distance, and then turned to look at the island. It nestled in the center of the lake, an oasis of green and tall trees in the huge expanse of water.

Its only inhabitants were a few rare species of butterflies.

There was no way Izzy would be there.

She was about to resume her focus on the shoreline when she saw a flash of blue among the trees. Izzy's shirt. Izzy had gone to the island? No, surely not. How would she have got there?

And then she peered more closely and saw a little yellow boat hauled high away from the waterline.

Flora's heart almost stopped. Izzy had rowed there? Was she really that desperate? Poor Izzy. *Poor, poor Izzy.* She'd taken herself to a place where no one would look for her. A place away from everyone.

Now what?

Flora glanced over her shoulder, wishing she had reinforcements. Jack and the gang would be gone all day, and Clare was unlikely to be back for hours. What if Izzy didn't have hours? She'd been so upset.

Flora checked her phone, but as usual there was no signal, which was normally blissful but right now made her want to hurl the device into the lake.

No signal to call for help. There was just her.

Why hadn't she learned to swim? Or at least row a boat?

She glanced at the island again but the flash of blue had disappeared. She imagined Izzy, desperate and alone, staring into those waters.

Flora turned her head and looked at the remaining boat, tied to the dock.

No. No way.

But what if Izzy did something terrible? She'd never forgive herself. And even if she didn't do any of the things Flora's imagination was currently conjuring, there was still the fact that she was feeling alone.

Flora knew how awful that was and suddenly it was important to her, terribly important, that Izzy knew she wasn't alone.

She breathed deeply. How hard could it be to row a boat? You sat in it and paddled. You didn't even need to touch the water. If she kept her eyes up she wouldn't even need to *see* much of the water.

Without giving herself a chance to change her mind, she dropped her backpack into the boat that was moored on the other side of the dock.

Her fingers fumbled and slipped on the knot as she tried

to untie it, as if her body was trying to stop her doing something that was undeniably foolish.

Was she seriously going to climb into this boat and try to row herself to the island?

Yes, she was. She wasn't going to leave Izzy by herself, when she was desperate and upset. And yes, she knew she was probably going to be yelled at. Izzy would probably accuse her of all kinds of things and she wouldn't be able to beat a hasty retreat because there would be water between herself and freedom, but she was doing it anyway.

She stepped gingerly into the boat, felt it wobble and plopped down hard on the seat.

"Ooh—" She clutched the sides. *Breathe, breathe.* These things were designed to float. Why would it sink? If it was going to sink, it would have sunk already when it was tied to the dock.

Gingerly, confining herself to small movements, she retrieved the paddle from the floor and gripped it tightly. *Eyes straight ahead. Don't look down. Don't wonder how deep it is.*

The island wasn't that far. All she had to do was row steadily and not make any big movements.

She pushed the boat away from the dock and wasted several minutes moving aimlessly in no particular direction while she figured out how to paddle and steer. Finally, she was away, making slow progress. It was unsettling how close she was to the water. If she'd been given the choice of vessel she would have picked a cruise ship, or at least a large yacht.

The farther she traveled from the dock, the more vulnerable she felt. She glanced down and then wished she hadn't as panic gripped her by the throat. The water below her was deep and dark. She tried not to think about her mother, and how she'd been in deep water when she'd drowned. Too far out of her depth to save herself.

The sky had darkened and a few spots of rain hit her shoulders. Clare had warned her that the weather was changeable and she'd been here long enough to have witnessed it herself, but she wished it hadn't chosen this moment to change from sunshine to storm.

The surface of the lake grew rougher and the water slapped hard against the sides of the boat, testing her nerve.

If she was still alive at the end of this, she was going to kill Jack.

"It's fine, it's all fine, it's going to be fine." She talked to herself, soothed herself, kept her eyes fixed on the island.

It didn't seem to be getting any closer, but she hoped that was her imagination.

She kept paddling, wondering if she was doing something wrong. Was she going backward? No, the boathouse was far behind her now, which gave her hope but also a sense of panic. There was no turning back. No changing her mind and now she knew she couldn't, she badly wanted to. What was she doing? She couldn't swim, had never rowed a boat and Izzy didn't even like her.

A larger wave hit the side of the canoe and showered Flora with water.

She gave a yelp, froze and almost dropped the paddle in her panic, but realized instinctively how dire it would be to lose her means of rowing so she gripped it tightly. If she survived this, she was going to learn how to swim. She'd been rowing for so long her arms felt like lead. She'd had no idea it would be this far. The wind whipped up and the lake went from being glass smooth to bouncing waves.

Why had she thought this was a good idea?

Even though she was fairly sure Izzy would be glad to

see the end of her, drowning was taking people-pleasing to a whole new level.

She kept paddling, motivated by the fact that the island seemed much closer. She peered into the trees, looking for Izzy, but there were no signs of life.

What if she'd made a mistake? What if the flash of blue hadn't been Izzy? There was no way Flora would have the energy to paddle back to the shore. She'd be stuck on the island by herself.

It was so close now she could see the pebbles on the shore. Just a few more strokes of the paddle and she'd be there. She felt a lift of her spirits and then the waves smacked hard against the side, soaking her and rocking the boat violently.

She gave a scream and clutched the sides, dropping the paddle in the process. She made a grab for it but doing so unbalanced the boat and it capsized, plunging her headfirst into the lake.

First came the cold, then the shock. Sound was muffled. Water filled her ears. She thought *this is it. I'm going to drown.*

She swallowed a mouthful of water, thrashed and flailed and then she felt hands grab her and pull her to the surface. She gasped in air, thrashed around a bit more.

"Put your feet down!" Izzy's voice penetrated her water-clogged ears and Flora felt relief punctuate panic. Izzy was alive! She was fine. Flora had found her. She didn't even care that Izzy was yelling at her.

"Holy crap, Flora! Stand up!" Izzy half dragged her onto the stony beach, away from the snapping water and lay down panting next to Flora.

For a moment neither of them spoke.

Flora stared up at the sky checking that she really was

still alive and then Izzy's face appeared above her, contorted with anger, and she knew she was still in her usual world.

The world where Izzy couldn't stand the sight of her.

"What were you *thinking*?" Izzy exploded. "You hate water!"

It was a reasonable question, but Flora couldn't answer. She had water in her ears and panic in her heart. It was racing so hard she wondered if she was having a heart attack.

She could hear Izzy yelling, and feel her hands gripping her arms. She was yelling something about life jackets, and something else that Flora didn't understand. Her lack of response must have finally got through because Izzy drew breath.

"Are you okay? You look green. You're breathing really fast. I think you should try to slow down. Sorry I yelled but you frightened the *shit* out of me." She pulled Flora to sitting. "One of my friends gets panic attacks. Press the side of your nose. It will stop you taking in too much air. No, wait—" She scrambled to her feet and raced away, returning moments later with a paper bag. "Good job I made a picnic. Breathe into this." She put the bag over Flora's mouth and nose and encouraged her to breathe slowly.

After a few minutes the dizziness faded and Flora's heart stopped racing. At the same time she noticed that the wind had dropped and the sun had come out. The lake sparkled in the sunshine but looking at it made Flora shudder.

There was no way she was going near a body of water ever again.

"So you didn't answer my question." Izzy slung a towel round Flora's shoulders and squatted down next to her. "What were you doing in a boat on the lake?"

Flora coughed a few times. Had she swallowed the whole lake? "Looking for you."

"Me? Why?"

"Because you were upset. I was worried about you."

"I was fine. Totally fine. And I can't believe you followed me when I swore at you."

"You were crying. I wanted to check on you. I wasn't even going to tell you I was there, but then I noticed a flash of blue on the island and knew it was your coat. And then I panicked in case you—" She stopped, not wanting to voice what she'd thought.

"In case I what?"

"I don't know. I was probably being crazy, but it's so isolated here. Such a horrible place, surrounded by water, and I thought maybe you—"

"You thought I was going to harm myself?" Izzy's eyes widened and she rocked back on her heels.

"You were so upset this morning at breakfast. You looked so alone."

"So how come you saw that and my dad didn't?"

"Well I have a lot of experience in feeling alone." Flora rubbed her chest with her palm, trying to ease the burning. "And I can see why you might have thought your dad was being insensitive, but I think in his very clumsy way he was trying to show you how independent he is, and how he can manage. He feels guilty that he's put too much pressure on you this year. Also, he was focusing on making a cheese sandwich and remembering to pack a drink and men aren't always good multitaskers. Gross generalization, obviously. But I think he was so determined to get it right and not forget anything, he wasn't paying attention."

"But you were paying attention." Izzy gave up squatting and sat. She stared at the water.

"I wanted to help, Izzy. That's all."

"Er—correct me if I'm wrong, but I think I was the one who helped *you*. Rescued you."

Flora coughed again and nodded. "Turns out my rescuing skills aren't up to much."

"I was on the other side of the island, eating my picnic, and I heard you shriek."

Flora didn't know whether to be humiliated or relieved. "A wave hit me."

"I couldn't believe it when I saw you in a boat. I thought you were done with people-pleasing. Was this another attempt to make friends and impress me?"

The sun was out again but Flora couldn't stop shivering. "If I wanted to impress someone, I'd bake them a cake or arrange a bunch of flowers. I wouldn't do anything that involved water. And I hope we're already friends, at least a little bit. But even if we weren't, I'd still want to check you were okay. Feeling alone and isolated is terrifying—and yes I'm speaking from personal experience—so if I can help someone not feel that way then I will. And I know I'm probably the last person in the world you'd talk to, but if you do want to talk, then I'm here."

"Did my dad not try to stop you coming? Especially as he didn't even think anything was wrong."

"He doesn't know. He'd already left the house."

"Aunt Clare?"

"She's taken her mother to the hospital for stitches. Cut her finger chopping mushrooms," she added, seeing Izzy's face.

"Oh no! So no one knew you were doing this?" There was a tense silence. "Have you been in a boat or in the water since—you know?"

"No." Flora wiped water from her face with the corner of the towel. "And I've never been in a kayak before."

"That's not a kayak, Flora. It's a canoe."

"Oh. Is there a difference?"

"Yeah." Izzy squeezed water out of her hair. "Yeah, there is."

"Well no wonder I didn't know what to do with it. Are you going to kill me if I confess I dropped the paddle?" She saw that Izzy had a funny look on her face. "You are going to kill me. I'll buy you a new one, I promise."

"I don't care about the stupid paddle."

"What then?"

"You got in a boat and rowed yourself across here because you were worried about me?"

"Yes."

"That's it? No other reason. It wasn't because you wanted to try out the water, or rowing or anything."

"Nothing except extreme anxiety would have got me onto the water."

"Extreme anxiety—for me?"

"Yes."

Izzy jumped to her feet and exploded. "That is the most selfish thing I ever heard!" She jabbed her hands into her hair, paced a few steps and then paced back again while Flora sat frozen and confused.

"Selfish?" Stupid, maybe, but selfish? "Because I dropped your paddle?"

"No, because I've been trying to hate you, and you've made it *so hard* and now it's impossible because how can I hate someone who is prepared to do the one thing that terrifies her because she is worried about me?"

Flora unraveled that speech piece by piece. "You—were trying to hate me?"

"Yes." Izzy scowled. "But it turns out you're impossible to hate!"

Flora wasn't sure how she was supposed to respond. "Don't let my boat rescue affect you. You're still allowed to hate me." She tried to keep it light. "The rescue didn't come with any obligation."

Izzy gave her a look. "What rescue? Flora, *there was no rescue.* If anything, I rescued you. I thought we agreed on that."

"Exactly. So you definitely don't have to feel guilty about hating me. Go for it."

Izzy slumped down next to her. "I don't hate you. Maybe I did, for a little while, although it was never really about you. My life is a mess, but none of it is your fault. At least, not much of it. I kind of wish Molly didn't adore you so much. And that you weren't so good with her, and with everything in the house. But the truth is I'm not needed anymore—" her voice broke "—and that's not all your fault."

"Not needed?" Flora was horrified. "What do you mean?"

"You said it yourself. My dad doesn't need me anymore. For the first time ever he remembered to put cheese in Molly's sandwiches and he even packed a drink. He never remembers a drink." She rubbed her face with her fingers, leaving behind a muddy streak. "He's always been pretty hopeless at the domestic stuff— I mean, he tries, but he'll put laundry on and forget to put it in the dryer so it comes out smelling of wet dog, even though we don't have a dog. He has no idea that Molly wets the bed still—" She flushed and glanced at Flora. "I promised her I wouldn't tell anyone."

"I won't say anything, I promise." But it broke her heart to think of it. "I used to wet the bed, too."

"You did?"

"Yes. After my mom died. But I knew my aunt would be mad so I tried washing them myself. But that was a disaster, so for a few months I slept on the bathroom floor because it was easier to clean."

"Seriously? That's bad."

"It wasn't the best time, but you do what you have to do."

"Yeah, you do."

They sat close, shoulder to shoulder.

"I don't blame my aunt. It was really tough on her having me. She was a single woman with a job she loved and she ended up with a child she never asked for."

"But that wasn't your fault. It's not like you asked for it to happen."

"No. Lots of the tough things that happen in life aren't anyone's fault. In the end you just have to handle it best you can. You know all about that. Molly's lucky that she has you to change her sheets and hug her. She's so happy and well-adjusted, and that's down to you."

"She yelled at me this morning."

"And she has the confidence to yell because she knows how much you love her. The fact that you love her makes her feel secure. And it's because she knows you love her that she is happy to be around me. If she didn't feel secure, she'd be clinging to you."

"Do you think so?"

"I know it."

Izzy looped her arms round her legs. "Maybe. She clung at the beginning. I actually liked it. Is that pathetic?"

That honest admission brought an ache to Flora's chest. "No. It's human to want to be loved, but you *are* loved."

Izzy scrambled to her feet and paced to the edge of the water.

Flora wondered if there was something else going on here. "Izzy?"

Izzy rubbed her hands over her arms. "He's pushing me to go to college. He wants me to leave."

"Because he wants the best for you, and sees college as the best. He doesn't want to hold you back. But I can see how the things he said could be misinterpreted."

"Can you?" Izzy turned her head. "Really?"

"Yes." If Jack had been there at that moment, Flora would have pushed him in the lake. "Believe it or not he *is* thinking of you. He is so aware of everything you've sacrificed this year to keep things going at home. You hardly see your friends. You've cooked and cleaned and cared for your sister. He wants you to have a life of your own."

"I just thought—" Izzy shifted her gaze back to the lake and stared into the distance "—that he'd had enough of me. He was basically saying that the family would manage just fine without me in it."

Flora scrambled to her feet, too. "How can you think that, or say that? You're his daughter. He loves you so much. Nothing that happens is ever going to change that." She reached out but was shrugged away.

"Are you hungry? I've got food in my backpack. I'll fetch it."

She sprinted off so fast, Flora was left wondering if she'd said the wrong thing.

She seemed to constantly say the wrong thing. Family life should come with a manual, in the meantime she did what she could to figure it out.

Jack wasn't that great at communicating with Izzy that was true, and he could definitely be accused of being clumsy, but she'd never seen anything that might lead Izzy to think he didn't love her.

How had that thought formed in Izzy's head? She was sure Jack didn't have the first clue.

Izzy was back a moment later with a bulging backpack. "I raided Aunt Clare's fridge at breakfast. I've got cheese. Bread. Tomatoes. Apples."

Flora was so full of lake water she didn't think there was room for food, but eating was a bonding experience so she was determined to force something down. "I thought you'd come here on impulse."

"No. I came because I love it. It's peaceful. But my dad, Aiden—they usually try to stop me coming because it can be rough when the weather turns."

Flora had been trying not to look at the water. "I'd noticed."

"When I'm here, I pretend this is my island. No one can land without my permission."

"Except people who have no idea how to row a boat."

"Technically you're now shipwrecked." Izzy spread the picnic out on her coat and Flora discovered that maybe she was hungry after all.

"I love picnics. There's something about eating outdoors that makes the food taste better."

"Yeah?" Izzy bit into a hunk of bread. "Mom hated picnics."

"She did?" It was the first time Izzy had said anything about Becca that wasn't effusive praise. It made the conversation more real somehow. "Which part did she hate most?"

"Wasps, flies, picnic food. You name it." Izzy helped herself to cheese. "She preferred dining in smart restaurants. Champagne. Sparkling glass. Sorry. I know you don't want to hear about my mom."

"I don't mind."

"You're doing it again." Izzy scowled at her. "Doing stuff you don't want to do just to please me."

"Not true. I've given up trying to please you. But I do think you should talk about your mother whenever you want to."

"Did you?"

Flora picked at her bread. "No, because it upset my aunt and I hated upsetting her. But I carried a photo and looked at it often. That helped."

Izzy cut herself a slice of cheese. "I'm sorry I swore at you. And shoved you. I don't normally—"

"It's okay. I understand. You were upset. We all do and say things we don't mean when we're upset."

Izzy glanced at her. "So do you have it with you?"

"What?"

"The photo. Do you have it?"

"I—yes. I always carry it."

"Can I see it?" Izzy looked at Flora's face and stopped chewing. "Forget it. You don't have to show me if you don't want to."

"I do want to." Flora grabbed her backpack and pulled out her coat. "I don't normally show it to people, that's all."

"Why not?"

"Because then I end up having conversations I don't want to have."

"Makes sense. Sometimes people are so clumsy. My friends at home—" Izzy selected a tomato "—they drive me insane with their trivia."

"Yes. When you're hurting it seems unbelievable that the world is still going on without you. You feel like the whole thing should have stopped moving." While they bonded over the tactlessness of people, Flora dug around until she found her purse and then the photograph of her mother. Looking at it always made her emotional. "This was taken a month before she died, in the flower shop where she worked and where I still work."

Izzy took it and studied the picture. "She's pretty. She has kind eyes. And you look just like her."

"A lot of people who knew her say that."

"Has my dad seen this?"

"Yes. But only recently. I don't talk much about my mother." Those memories were the most intimate thing she could share, and she held them close. But she'd shared them with Jack, and now she'd shared them with his daughter.

Izzy nodded. "If you ever want to, you can talk to me. I won't ever repeat anything."

It was more than progress. It felt like a lottery win and Flora felt the sudden rise of emotion.

"Thanks." The words emerged thickened and unsteady. "Thanks, Izzy. And the same goes for you."

"What about your dad?"

"He left us before I was born. Not big on responsibility. You're lucky with your dad."

Izzy handed the photo back. "Remembering is okay, but sometimes it hurts. Grief is so weird. No one tells you how weird. One minute you're sobbing, then you feel kind of detached. And then there's the guilt—horrible guilt. And the anger."

Anger?

"Grief is like being strapped to a bad fairground ride you never paid to go on." Flora kept her tone casual. "Do you feel angry a lot?"

Izzy helped herself to an apple. "Yeah."

"Angry that she died?"

"That, and other stuff, too. Stuff she did. Sometimes I wish I could yell at her and shake her and ask her what the hell she thought she was doing. I mean she was my mom and I loved her but some of the things she did were real stupid, you know?"

Flora didn't know, but she wished she did. It was hard to say the right thing when you didn't know what the problem was. She was stumbling around in the dark. "Have you talked to your dad about it?"

"No." Izzy took a bite of apple. "He's the last person I could tell."

"If there's something upsetting you, I'm sure he'd want to know."

"He wouldn't want to know this." Izzy chewed slowly. "Did you ever feel mad at your mom? Like really angry for some of the things she did?"

Flora didn't want to lie. "I don't remember feeling that way, but I was a lot younger than you. Do you feel mad?"

"Sometimes."

"Is there something specific you're mad about?" Something in the way Izzy was staring across the lake made her think there was definitely something specific, but Izzy shook her head.

"No. Forget it."

"It's good that you have memories of your mother. I don't have that many, and the ones I have seem to have faded with time." Flora helped herself to food. "You'll have more memories than Molly. She'll probably want you to share them when she's older."

Izzy finished the apple and tore off a chunk of bread. "You think so?"

"Yes. My aunt didn't like to talk about my mother, but when she did it was like being given something precious. I used to rush to my room and scribble it all down, in case I forgot it."

Izzy dug her hand into her bag and handed Flora a bottle of water. "I like writing. I write a lot. I have a blog. I mean, no one knows that. It's kind of a secret."

"Well it's a secret that's safe with me. I'm glad you're writing. I bet you're good at it."

"I really do want to be a journalist, regardless of the whole college thing. Maybe I should write something down about Mom in case Molly wants to read it later."

"I think that would be great. If it didn't upset you. Not just your mom's achievements, like running a company or a marathon, but stories that say something about who she was. How she hated picnics because of the wasps. That's a good one."

Izzy twisted the cap off the bottle and drank. "She once wore a long dress to a school picnic. That was embarrassing. Everyone else's mother was in jeans, and mine shows up like she's going to the opera. I wanted to hide."

"She sounds incredibly glamorous." Flora waited to feel insecure or envious, but nothing happened. At some point Becca had stopped being this mythical, impossibly perfect creature and turned into a real person with flaws.

"She was glamorous. I think she felt she had to be. That she had this image to keep up. She wanted to stand out. Be the best."

*Insecurity*, Flora thought. It fitted with some of the things Clare had said when they'd been gardening together. "See *that's* why you'll be a good journalist." She slotted a slice of cheese into her bread. "You're finding the story beneath the facts. You're asking the question *why*. *Why* did your mother feel she had to wear a long dress to a picnic? Do you have pictures? You could write it up and add pictures. Then if Molly wants to see it when she's older, she can."

Izzy wiped her fingers on her shorts. "Tell me a story about your mom. Not a what story, but a why story."

Flora thought about it. "One day when I came home from

SARAH MORGAN

school she blindfolded me and made me identify flowers just by the scent."

"You're kidding."

"I'm not kidding. I smelled what felt like a hundred flowers."

Izzy grinned. "You sneezed and ended up in the emergency department?"

"Almost. And she was so creative. She decorated our apartment with things she found lying around on the beach. Shells. Pieces of driftwood. Our table was made from crates, but she sanded them and painted them and it looked like a work of art." Flora finished her food and licked her fingers. "That was delicious."

"Yeah, it was. I wish I'd stolen some cake."

"I can help with that." Flora reached into her backpack again and Izzy stared at her.

"You brought cake?"

"You probably don't want it, because bringing you my lemon cupcakes definitely falls under the heading of people-pleasing."

"If you've brought cake, I'll forgive you." Izzy almost drooled as Flora pulled the packet out of her drenched backpack.

"They might not be entirely dry."

"I don't care what state they're in. I'm eating them. Your lemon cupcakes are the best things I've ever tasted."

While she digested the cake, Flora digested the fact that Izzy had just paid her a compliment. And made a joke about people-pleasing.

"I think you should talk to your dad. Tell him how you feel."

"About what?" Izzy ate a second lemon cupcake, and a third.

"About leaving home. About not feeling loved or needed. He'd probably want to know what's going on in your head."

"He definitely wouldn't."

"Why not? Why can't you talk to your dad?"

"Loads of reasons, but mostly because I don't want to worry him or be a burden."

Flora felt a crushing weight on her chest. "Izzy, you're his daughter."

The atmosphere changed in an instant.

"See that's the thing—" Izzy scrunched up the remains of the picnic and stuffed it into her bag. "I'm not actually his daughter. Not his biological daughter. You already knew that, right?"

Flora forced the words out of her numb brain. "No. I didn't know that."

"He didn't tell you?"

"No." She could see Izzy wondering why. Flora was asking herself that, too. She'd thought their relationship had reached a whole new level. She'd shared secrets with him she'd never shared with another person. She'd felt close to him, intimate in a way that wasn't just about the physical. She'd assumed he was the same. Apparently not. And this wasn't just about her feelings. How was she supposed to understand and support his family if he failed to pass on crucial pieces of information? "He probably didn't want to invade your privacy."

Flora knew this had big implications for her, but she also knew that right now her priority had to be Izzy. She was obviously feeling terrible and the reasons for her insecurity were now becoming clear.

Izzy shrugged. "It's not a big secret. I've always known. Mom was pregnant with me when she met him. He married her anyway. He took me on. And we were a family, yes, but then my mom—" She broke off and stared out across the lake. "Well my mom isn't here anymore. And he's probably wondering when I'm going to leave and get out of his hair. You heard him. He wants me in college. And I don't blame him. I'm not really his responsibility. I suppose in a way I never was. And now he wants me to make my own life. So I guess that's what I'm going to do."

Flora felt slightly sick. Sick for Izzy that she would feel that way, and also sick for herself.

She'd been starting to feel part of the family. Included. But he hadn't shared this with her.

*Why not?*

"You need to talk to him about how you're feeling, Izzy. About feeling angry—all of it."

"No way!" Izzy jumped to her feet, panicked. "I can't— you have *no* idea—there's stuff—other stuff—"

"Okay, okay—" Flora lifted a hand "—but it might help to talk to someone." And Flora knew for sure she wasn't the right person. "How about Aunt Clare?"

Izzy stared at her, chest rising and falling as she breathed. "Aunt Clare?"

"Yes. She's known you forever and she loves you. You could tell her everything that is on your mind. All of it. Get it off your chest. Even if she can't help, I'm sure she'd be a good listener."

Izzy didn't answer for a minute. "I don't know. Maybe."

"Think about it." Flora zipped up her backpack. "If nothing else, it might make you feel better to have shared it. Less alone."

And what was she going to do?

Izzy wasn't the only one who needed to talk.

She did, too.

# 18

## Clare

Clare was up in the attic, braving dust and spiders when she heard her mother call up to her.

"What are you doing up there?"

"I'm looking for old photo albums. I know they're up here somewhere." Why was she so disorganized? She and Todd shoved everything that needed storing up here and there was no system. She'd come across baby clothes, toys and a pair of curtains she was fairly sure would never be hung by anyone anywhere. She badly needed to clear out but she was hopeless at throwing things away. Everything came attached to a memory. She'd just spent five minutes sighing over a scrapbook Aiden had made when he was four years old.

Todd had even talked about converting the loft into another habitable room but Clare couldn't begin to get her head round the work involved.

Her mother's head appeared at the top of the ladder. "Good Lord, Clare. This place is a fire risk. I've never understood your inability to part with things. If you like, I'll lend you my book on decluttering."

"One person's clutter is another person's hidden treasure. I don't like throwing things out in case I need them."

"You don't *need* any of this stuff, Clare. The fact that you can't even find anything up here tells me you don't need it." Her mother brushed dust from her sleeve. "What photos are you searching for?"

"The ones of Becca and me when we were young. You shouldn't be up here, Mum! We just spent four hours in the emergency department." The laceration had been deep and required suturing. "You're not supposed to get the dressing on your finger dirty."

Her mother made a dismissive sound. "If you wanted to see photos, you should have asked me. I have most of them over at the Gatehouse."

"Oh. That explains why I couldn't find them up here." Clare looked at the mess she'd created in her search. Maybe her mother was right. Maybe she should think about having a clear out. Next to her hand was a box of baby clothes, neatly folded. Why did she feel the need to keep everything? "I didn't know you had photos. Why do you have them?"

"Because I didn't want them vanishing in this space of yours. Photos are to be looked at and enjoyed, cried over and laughed over. They're not supposed to add weight to someone's ceiling. You boxed up all the photos ready to go into the loft, so I decided to take them with me when I moved."

Clare sat down in the dust and stared at her mother. "Which photos?"

"Most of them are of our family, and your dad of course, but there are lots of you and Becca, too, over the years."

"You've been looking at photos of Dad all alone and you didn't tell me? Mum!"

"What? Life goes on, dear. We all have to find our own way. One of my ways is to look at the photos. It reminds me of all the good times we had. So many good times, probably more than I deserved. The photos help me."

"I can't bear to think of you looking at photos and feeling sad."

"Who said anything about feeling sad? Occasionally, maybe, but far more often I find myself laughing. When I see photos of your dad wearing his slippers in the garden for example, the silly man. Did you know he called them his 'outdoor slippers'? Ridiculous, but endearing, too. And there's a wonderful one of him sailing. His hair is all over the place and his nose is scarlet because you know how forgetful he was about sunscreen. I've put that one in a frame. He would have been furious that I chose that one to be on display. We probably would have argued, but I would have won. It's the one I like."

"Where is it? I haven't seen it." Clare racked her brains, picturing her mother's living room.

"It's next to my bed. His lovely sunburned face is the last thing I look at every night before I go to sleep and the first thing I see in the mornings, just as I did when he was alive."

"Oh, Mum."

"Don't 'oh, Mum' me. I'm happy. Do I miss him? Of course. Every minute of every day. But it's a little easier now than it was in the beginning. Not the pain—that's the same—but I've learned to breathe round it. I've learned that the pain doesn't stop me doing things, it just comes along with me like a very annoying companion. And having the photograph right there makes him feel closer. If I confess that I talk to him, are you going to have me locked up?"

"Of course not. But why didn't you tell me all this sooner? Todd and I moved here so that we could be closer to you. So that Aiden could have you in his life."

"And I will forever feel lucky and grateful that you moved here. But it doesn't mean I need you on my doorstep every minute of the day. That would be irritating for both of us."

"But you miss him terribly."

"I do. I miss his smile, the way he always put his head on one side when he listened. I miss the way he always found the good in the bad. And of course I miss the sex—"

"Mum!"

"What? I'm only seventy. Seventy is the new seventeen, did you know?"

Clare didn't know. Her face was hot, and it had nothing to do with the stuffiness of the attic.

"Oh, Clare." Her mother looked both exasperated and amused by her discomfort. "You think sex ends when you're forty? Or fifty? Your father and I had a very active sex life right until the week before he died."

Clare felt light-headed. She couldn't believe they were having this conversation. Her mother never failed to surprise her. "I— Have you thought of dating again?" Was that the wrong thing to say? Apparently not because her mother had a thoughtful look on her face.

"I have thought about it. I've even gone online and had a look—"

"How?"

"Aiden helped me. I made him promise not to tell you. Judging from the look on your face, I assume he didn't."

"No." Clare felt faint. "No, he didn't." She thought about her boy, her baby, sitting next to his grandmother helping her log on to a dating site. Even while a part of her was handling the shock, another part was saying *good for him*.

"That boy is growing into a fine young man. He dropped by one day to see if I needed him to empty the bins because he knew his grandad always did it, but I have no issues with my recycling. It's other things I need help with. Anyway, in the end I didn't have the energy for it. Good sex isn't just about having the right parts. It's about intimacy and knowledge. For me, it's about caring. You can't buy that online. You can buy sex toys, of course. I bought a vibrator."

Clare swallowed. "Did Aiden help you with that?"

"I'm quite capable of making a purchase from the internet, Clare. I don't need teenage assistance with something as basic as that."

"Right." Was she about to have a conversation about vibrators with her mother? Because she was fairly sure she'd die. Todd, of course, would think it was hilarious.

"The vibrator is better than nothing, but not as good as your father. I imagine him smiling smugly from wherever he is."

Clare, who was imagining something quite different, decided that the conversation had to end right now. Yes, she was the one who had encouraged her mother to talk more about her feelings, but there were limits and Clare had reached that limit.

"I'd love to see the photos of Dad. And of Becca."

"I'll fetch them. I was looking at them just last night so I know exactly where they are."

Now that the topic of conversation was no longer her mother's lack of sex life, the guilt returned. "I wish you'd told me you were looking at those photos."

"Why? You'd only cluck over me and neither of us needs that. You have your own life, and I have mine. I love that our lives intersect regularly, but I don't need you checking on me. If I need you, I'll ask. I proved that this morning when I called you for a lift to the hospital."

"I'm glad you called."

"Well I couldn't figure out a way to keep pressure on the wound and drive. I would have ended up with blood on the upholstery, which would have been hard to explain if I was stopped for speeding."

Clare started to laugh. "You're the best, Mum. I don't tell you that enough."

"Good, because that embarrasses me as much as tales of my sex life embarrass you." Her mother sneezed. "Now could we go down and continue this conversation somewhere that has been vacuumed this century?"

"Sorry." Clare stood up and brushed thick layers of dust from her jeans. "And you're right. I really ought to have a clear out. I don't know why I find it so hard to let go of things."

"You were always the same. Didn't matter whether it was toys or friends, you were never able to part with anything."

Clare frowned. "Friends? What do you mean, friends?"

But her mother had already disappeared down the ladder.

Clare followed and closed the loft. "What did you mean about friends?"

"Wash your hands, dear, or you'll leave dusty prints everywhere."

There were times when her mother still made her feel about six years old.

"I'll wash my hands and then put the kettle on."

"And I'll fetch the photos while you do that. I'll drive back because there are quite a few boxes."

"Give me five minutes and I'll drive you."

"I drive along the Wrynose, the Hardknott and the Kirk-

stone passes on a regular basis. I think I can manage to negotiate my own driveway. But thank you."

"You're supposed to be resting your hand!"

"The doctor said that normal movement was perfectly
fine. Now stop fussing." Her mother disappeared, leaving
Clare anxious. But she was also proud.

Her parents had done everything together, but after
Clare's father had died her mother had continued to do things
alone. To begin with it had been a way to honor his memory,
but now it was a way of life. She'd forced herself to be independent, and in doing so had made a new life.

Clare had nothing but respect for her.

She couldn't imagine she'd do as well if she lost Todd.
She wasn't proud of how she'd handled losing Becca.

She scrubbed the dust and smears of dirt from her hands
and went downstairs to the kitchen.

Todd, Jack and Molly still weren't back and neither was
Aiden. She had no idea where Izzy or Flora were, although
she knew they were unlikely to be together.

Clare decided it was the perfect time to enjoy a cup of
tea and a chat with her mother, although certain topics were
going to be off-limits.

She had the tea brewing and the table laid when her
mother staggered through the door carrying three large
boxes.

Clare was on her feet in a moment. "For goodness sake,
Mum—" She grabbed the boxes and her mother flexed her
wrists.

"Turns out memories weigh a lot. There are three more of
these in the car. The boxes are labeled by year, and a rough
list of contents."

Clare hauled the rest of the boxes from the car and trans-
ferred them to the house.

"You sorted them?"

"Someone needed to, and it wasn't going to be you. The ones of your father naked are in the bottom box."

Clare froze and then saw the glint in her mother's eye. "You're terrible."

"And you're gullible. And also fun to tease."

Clare dumped the boxes on the floor with the others. "I knew you were joking. You wouldn't really have naked photos of Dad."

"I have several naked photos, but they're in the drawer by my bed, not in the boxes. Now sit down and let's enjoy the tea while it's hot. I'm parched. And I wouldn't say no to a chocolate-chip cookie."

Clare poured the tea, and made a mental note never ever to go in her mother's drawers. "When did you find time to sort through all those photos?"

"Last winter, when we were snowed in. It was very cosy. Just me, a large whiskey and all those memories." Her mother selected the box on top and put it on the table next to Clare. "These are early photos of you and Becca. There are some of that year the two of you camped in the garden. Do you remember?"

She remembered. "Becca hated the insects. She crept into the house in the middle of the night and slept in the living room."

"She was a girl who always knew what she wanted and wasn't afraid to go after it."

"That's true. She always said that no one was going to give her anything so she had to just take it." Clare forced herself to open the box. Nerves fluttered in her stomach. Was this going to make her feel worse or better?

"She had a difficult start in life. No child should grow up feeling unwanted."

Clare wasn't going to argue with that. She flipped open the first album and smiled. There was Becca, aged seven, a fierce look in her eyes as she'd urged a donkey on to greater speed.

"Look at her face. She was competitive even when she was riding a donkey. I always felt so inadequate. There were times when I wondered if she hung out with me because she knew she could beat me at most things."

Her mother put her cup down. "Clare—"

"It's true."

"I know she made you feel that way, and because we're being honest I'm going to tell you that I found it so frustrating. She made you feel bad about yourself. And you let her."

"I—"

"You let her, Clare. You didn't stand up for yourself. You didn't say what you wanted from the friendship. It was all about keeping Becca happy. You were so shy when you were little, and having Becca in your life brought you out of yourself so for a while I was pleased, but then I saw that she didn't really bring you out of your shell, she kept you there. And you were so anxious to be her friend, so afraid she'd reject you, that you allowed her to behave however she pleased with no rules or boundaries. You let her dominate you. Honestly? I think you were a little afraid of her. It was a very unbalanced friendship. Your father and I often talked about it."

"You—you did?"

"Yes. If Becca had been a boy we would have been talking to you about toxic relationships, but for some reason I didn't do that in this case so I bear the blame, too."

"Blame?"

"You and Becca outgrew each other a long time ago. Your friendship was glued together by history, her insecurities and your inability to accept that sometimes it's okay to let things go."

Clare stared at her. "You think we outgrew each other?"

"Don't you? It's not a crime, Clare. People change. Friendships change. You met when you were four years old. No one is the same person at forty as they are at four. Even saying that aloud sounds faintly ridiculous." Her mother topped up her tea. "It has always fascinated me that we're prepared to end a romantic relationship that is no longer working but are generally reluctant to do the same with friendships. Not all friendships are meant to last for life. People evolve, and friendships evolve with them."

It would never have occurred to her, even in the worst moments, to end her friendship with Becca.

But why not? Was it because she genuinely loved her friend? Was it because she couldn't imagine not having Becca in her life? Or was it, as her mother had suggested, because she'd been afraid?

She stared into her tea, trying to remember the last interaction with Becca that had made her feel good. Not the last month of her life, that was sure. Becca had demanded too much of her and put Clare in an impossible position.

But that wasn't all Becca's fault, was it? It was hers, for allowing it. Her mother was right about that. Clare could have refused. She could have stood her ground and said that she wasn't prepared to support her this time. She could have ended the friendship.

Even the thought of it made her heart race.

"Did you ever end a friendship?"

"Several times." Her mother was calm. "And I'm not pretending it was easy, but nor did I ever regret it. Life is too short to fill it with friends who don't care about you or bring you joy. Moaners, the people who drain you or use you, flaky friends who never show up when they say they will—unless those flaky friends make you happy of course, in which case keep them. But bad friends are like the old clothes in your closet. They're the stained shirt, the sweater with the hole in it, the dress that no longer fits. They have no place and should be cleared out."

Clare gave a wobbly smile. "I had no idea you were so ruthless."

"It's not ruthless to have respect for oneself. And being selective about who you spend your time with is part of self-care. Maybe it's to do with getting older. Time is precious. Time is always precious of course, but when we're young we squander it dreadfully."

Clare had a feeling she wasn't doing it right. "So you not only decluttered your house, you decluttered your social calendar."

"I did. And I can honestly say that I enjoy all my current friends immensely." She leaned forward. "Did you enjoy Becca? Really? Did you have fun together? Did you laugh? Did you know that she had your back and would always fight for you? I don't think so. Friendship has much in common with romantic love—caring about someone, loving them, should make you generous. You should want the best for them. You don't try to use them for your own ends."

Clare blew on her tea to cool it. Did her mother somehow know what she was carrying? Had she guessed?

"Becca was complicated."

"You won't find me arguing with that. I don't know what she did to upset you so, and perhaps it's best if you don't tell me because it might not be good for my blood pressure, but it's time to do what you couldn't do when she was alive and let her go. And you can do that without guilt. You have my permission. Don't let her control your life any longer.

And remember it's never too late to make new friends." Her mother helped herself to another cookie. "Talking of which, how have you been getting on with Flora?"

Clare felt herself blush, knowing her mother wouldn't have been proud of her if she'd witnessed the first day of Flora's visit. "I've never been good with strangers, as you know, and it felt a little strange having her in the house. I had this ridiculous feeling that I was being disloyal to Becca."

"And now?"

Clare sat up a little straighter. "Flora is a special person. She's very relaxing to be with. She lacks Becca's competitive instinct. I'd never realized how exhausting that side of her was."

"Poor Becca. She felt she had to prove herself continually. It must have been exhausting for her, too."

Clare turned back to the photos. There was Becca in a swimsuit, her arm looped around Clare. "I remember that day. She challenged me to a race. I won, and she sulked for two days so I made sure I never beat her again. It wasn't worth paying the price." And in that way she'd been a people pleaser, too. Just like Flora, she'd taken the easy route to keep someone happy.

It was ironic to admit that she and Flora probably had more in common than she and Becca ever had.

She placed her hand on the photo, touching Becca's face. "I miss her. Even though I'm angry with her, I still miss her. And maybe you're right that I should have ended the friendship, but that would have meant losing touch with Jack, Izzy and Molly."

"Well fortunately you no longer have to make that decision. You were a good friend to Becca, Clare." Her mother stood up and took her cup to the dishwasher. "Now let her go."

Clare knew she was right. Everything that had seemed

murky and difficult now seemed clear. She wished she'd talked to her mother sooner. On impulse she walked across the kitchen and hugged her. "Thank you."

"For what? Saving you from spiders in the loft? Introducing you to the idea that your sex life will still be good in your seventies?"

Clare laughed. "For always being wise. And for keeping the photo albums and labeling everything. I aspire to your level of organization."

"It's easy. You just have to be prepared to throw things out."

And she was going to do that, she really was.

Her mother was about to say something when there was a sound behind them.

They both turned.

Izzy stood in the doorway, with Flora directly behind her. Flora's hand was on Izzy's shoulder in a comforting manner.

Clare waited for Izzy to shrug her off, but she didn't. Did that signal a truce? "Hello you two! Sorry we took so long. There was a long queue of people before us." She noticed that Flora's clothes were wrinkled.

"I wondered—" Izzy broke off and glanced at Flora who gave her shoulder a squeeze. "I wanted to talk to you." Her hair lay damp across one shoulder and her face was pale. "I didn't know you were busy—"

"She's not busy, sweetheart! I'm the one who is busy and I shouldn't be sitting around here chatting." Clare's mother walked to the door, hugging Izzy on the way. Then she smiled at Flora. "Would you be kind enough to walk me to the Gatehouse? It will give us a chance to chat, and I'm feeling a little woozy after my accident."

Clare doubted her mother was feeling in the slightest bit woozy, but she was grateful for her tact. She just hoped she wasn't going to scandalize Flora with naked photographs and talk of vibrators.

As the kitchen door closed, Izzy shifted awkwardly. "Sorry. I hope she didn't leave because of me—"

"She didn't. I'm so pleased it's just you and me. We seem to have been surrounded by people since you arrived and haven't had a chance to catch up properly." In truth they'd had plenty of chances to catch up, but Izzy had ignored all of them.

But not this time.

She sat down at the kitchen table. "This is—honestly, it's awkward." She nibbled at the corner of her fingernail. "I don't know where to start."

"Just plunge right in." Clare poured her a mug of tea. "And there is no awkward between us, Izzy. I've known you since you were born."

"I know. And you knew my mom. You were her closest friend."

Was that what this was about? Becca?

"I was."

"And that's why it's awkward. Because it isn't about me. It's about her." Izzy started on a different nail. "I need to talk about my mother. About something that happened the night before she died."

# 19

## *Flora*

Flora walked Clare's mother back to the Gatehouse. She felt weighed down. She knew she should be thinking about poor Izzy and she was, but right now she couldn't stop wondering why Jack hadn't confided in her. This was *huge*. Knowing, might have helped her understand Izzy a little better. Why had he kept it to himself? What else was he keeping to himself? She'd thought their relationship was honest and open but it seemed that the only person who had been honest and open was her.

What was she going to do? In her previous relationships she might have ignored it and kept up the pretense that everything was fine until the whole thing crumbled, but she couldn't do that this time. How could she ever hope to be part of a family if she didn't really *know* them?

She struggled to focus as Carolyn chatted away.

"Poor Izzy must have had a very tough time." She paused at the entrance of the Gatehouse to tug out some weeds.

"Yes." The best she could manage was a monosyllabic answer.

She forced herself to stop thinking about her relationship with Jack, and focus on Izzy's relationship with him. It seemed that Izzy had somehow taken the fact that she wasn't his biological daughter and spun that into a scenario where now that her mother was gone, he wouldn't want her.

To Flora, who had no additional knowledge or information, it made a twisted sort of sense.

But how could Jack not have known Izzy might be feeling that way? She had more questions than answers and felt helpless and frustrated that she couldn't help Izzy.

Carolyn patted her arm, calm and steady. "Don't look so worried. She'll stumble through it, as we all do. Life is like a garden, don't you think? Sometimes glorious, and sometimes a disaster. It's messy, but always real. And sometimes all we can do is forge ahead, and if that means flattening a few daisies on the way, then so be it."

She'd craved real. She'd thought she had real and honest, but it turned out she'd been wrong about that. She was still being shut out. Once again, she was on the outside.

She'd been close to euphoric when Jack had left this morning, but after spending several hours with Izzy she no longer felt that way. She felt like an addict coming down after a high.

She made her excuses to Carolyn and returned to the Lodge, bypassed the kitchen and went straight to her room where she took a shower, scrubbed the last remnants of the lake from her skin and her hair, and looked critically at the clothes she'd packed for the trip.

Try to learn more about Becca, yes. Try to understand

her, yes to that, too. But dress like her? Act like her? No way. And that was something else that she could no longer ignore. Jack rarely talked about Becca. He dodged the subject, changed the subject, looked uncomfortable. She'd assumed it was his way of handling grief, that he'd share when he was ready, but what if she'd been wrong about that? What if there was something else he hadn't told her? Knowing what she now knew, it was hard not to wonder if there were other secrets he hadn't shared.

This time she didn't need guidance on what to wear. She grabbed a dress in a cheerful flowery print and pulled it over her head.

Hearing voices in the garden, she looked out of the window and saw Jack. He and Molly had just returned from sailing and he was deep in conversation with Todd, while Molly ran around the garden after Chase.

Flora pondered the best way to handle this. She hated confrontation. All her life she'd been afraid of it, believing that it would ultimately lead to rejection, but she saw now that fearing rejection had stopped her having honest relationships. Ironically that approach had led her to feel more lonely, not less. It had stopped her connecting with people. It had made her reluctant to make herself vulnerable. She'd tiptoed through her life instead of striding confidently forward. Clare's mother was right that sometimes you needed to trample a few daisies.

She had to decide if this relationship had a future, and the only way to do that was to confront Jack.

She was going to talk to him calmly and honestly about her feelings, but first she was going to make him talk about Izzy. She was the priority.

She walked out onto the lawn, her dress brushing softly against her legs. It fell to midcalf, but was nowhere near as modest as a first glance might have suggested. She saw

Jack's eyes darken as he caught a flash of leg. At another time she might have been flattered by the look he gave her, but this wasn't that time. Right now she only had one thing on her mind and it wasn't getting Jack Parker naked. Unless you counted stripping him down to bare thoughts and emotions. That, she intended to do.

He caught her round the waist and pulled her in, allowing himself a quick kiss even though Molly was within range.

"How was your day?"

Flora thought about the overload of emotion. Izzy yelling at her. Izzy crying. Her crazy boat ride. Almost drowning. The revelations. "It was interesting. Can we take a walk, Jack? Somewhere private?"

He must have detected something in her tone because he gave her a curious look. "Sounds good to me." Still with his arm round her waist, he flashed a smile at Molly. "Stay close to Todd. Don't go in the water. Flora and I will be back soon."

Todd winked at them and Flora thought that they wouldn't be exchanging such smug man smiles if they knew why she was extracting Jack from the group.

She took the trail to the boathouse, knowing there would be no one there. The dark clouds were back, hovering above like a threat. There was going to be a thunderstorm. The air was close and crackled with tension. She wondered if some of that was generated by her own stress.

When they were well away from the Lodge, Jack stopped and would have tugged her against him but she stepped back.

"We need to talk." She wasn't going to be deflected. She wasn't going to let fear push her onto another path. She was going to flatten as many daisies as she needed to. "We agreed to be honest. To share. You said that was what you wanted." She felt her voice rise and took a deep breath. This conversation had to be calm.

"It is what I want."

"Then why didn't you tell me about Izzy?" She'd expected him to look shocked, even a little guilty. She hadn't expected him to look bemused.

"What about Izzy?"

Did she really have to spell it out? "I know you're not her real father."

The shock came then. It flashed across his features as he stood without moving. "Who told you that?" There was a harshness to his voice that she hadn't heard before.

"She did."

"She shouldn't have—"

"Yes, she should, Jack, because it was important information. I'm trying to build a relationship with your girls, and how can I do that if there are major things I don't know? I've been stumbling around in the dark trying to understand Izzy, and now I discover that she isn't your child! Why didn't you tell me?"

"I honestly didn't think of it."

*"Seriously?"*

"Yes, seriously, because she *is* my child, Flora." There was a fire in his eyes that made her wonder if she'd misunderstood.

"Jack—"

"In every sense that matters, she's my daughter."

It started to rain, just a few drops at first and then a steady patter that slid from leaves onto her shoulder. "In every sense that matters?"

He tugged her under the shelter of a tree. "It's true that Becca was pregnant when I married her. Biologically Izzy isn't my child. I knew that. It was never a secret, and we were straight with Izzy from the moment she was old enough to learn about parents and families. She was fine with it. I was fine with it. And I've loved Izzy as my own from the first moment I saw her. You ask why I didn't share it—the answer is because I don't think about it. It wouldn't have occurred to me to mention it. I'm struggling to hold everything together here—I'm trying to remember not to put ham in the sandwiches, to make sure both girls get where they're supposed to be going, wearing what they're supposed to wear, and I lie awake most nights counting the ways I'm screwing this up and wondering what impact that will have on them. My head is so full it feels as if it's going to burst. And I can understand why you're upset, I really can. I can see how this might look from the outside and if I'd thought of it, I probably would have told you, but I didn't think of it because in my head and my heart, she's mine."

*I can see how this might look from the outside.*

She was the one on the outside, but she couldn't think about that now.

Her cheeks were damp. Rain and tears mingled. She wished Izzy could have heard that speech. She *needed* to hear that speech. "You're not screwing up, Jack. And when it comes to families, I'm a total beginner but I don't think it's about being perfect. It's not about always getting it right. It's about trying your hardest, and caring—" her voice broke "—and you do all that. You do that. The most important thing is that the kids know you love them."

"I don't know why Izzy would raise it with you now, but it isn't an issue."

"It is a huge issue to her." The rain was falling harder now, sliding through the thick canopy of leaves. "She's feeling desperately vulnerable and insecure."

"She lost her mother."

"And that has made her insecure about her place in the family. She's scared." She didn't want to add to the pressure he was already feeling, but how could she not speak up about this? "I believe that you don't think about it. And maybe it doesn't matter to you, but it matters to Izzy. And it matters to me! If I'd known sooner, it might have helped me understand her."

"There's nothing to understand. She's mine. That's the end of it. There was no reason for her to ever tell you."

The words were a slap. "So you're saying that you would *never* have told me? If Izzy hadn't mentioned it, I would never have found out? Oh Jack—" Her whole chest ached. Her throat ached with the emotion she was holding back. How could they ever be a family? She'd been kidding herself. She wanted to curl up in a ball and sob, but she couldn't do that because there was Izzy to think of, and Jack still wasn't hearing her. "Forget it. Right now you need to focus on Izzy. She needs to be able to talk to you, Jack."

"She knows she can talk to me!" He was bruised, insulted by the suggestion that he'd been a less than perfect father and she felt him withdraw even though neither of them had moved physically. And all her instincts made her want to reach out, and say something that would bring the warmth back into their relationship.

She hated confrontation. It made her palms sweat and her heart race. She was eight years old again and standing in front of her aunt. She wanted to say whatever needed to be said to diffuse the tension and keep things the way they were, but that wasn't going to happen this time. She pictured Izzy's face and stood up a little straighter.

"She doesn't know that, Jack. You can't talk to someone who doesn't want to listen, and you don't want to listen. You're so sure that she doesn't have a problem, but I can tell you she has a *big* problem. There is a lot worrying her. And maybe she'll be mad with me for telling you this and never forgive me but I'll take my chances on that because this is more important than anything."

"Becca was five months pregnant when we met. I was there when Izzy was born, when she took her first steps, started school. I've been there for her whole life. She *knows* I think of her as my daughter."

"But she also knows she's not your daughter. And she's feeling lost and terrified." Why couldn't he see it?

"She isn't lost and terrified. I have kept a really careful eye on both girls since Becca died. I made sure they both saw a therapist, although both of them chose to stop pretty quickly. Izzy said she didn't need it. She has held it together better than any of us." His voice wasn't quite steady and he seemed so upset she almost didn't tell him the rest of it.

It had been hard on him, too. And she hated to say what needed to be said because it was kicking him when he was down, but she knew she had to say it.

"Yes, she's held it together, not because she was doing great but because she was desperate for you to still need her around."

"What?" He dragged his hand through his hair, impatient. "Of course I need her around."

"She is anxious that now her mother has gone, you no longer have a reason to give her a home."

The only sounds were the relentless patter of rain and the rustle of leaves.

His hand dropped to his side. He looked stunned. "That's not— I have never—"

"You told her you could manage fine without her and that she should leave and start living her life." She saw him mentally rewind everything he'd ever said to Izzy and saw the exact moment he recalled those words.

"I didn't mean it that way. You know that."

"I do know that, but those words fed the fear Izzy is already feeling. I think it might have been the timing rather than the words. When we first met you told me Izzy had really stepped up. You said she was your little star. That she was coping better than any of you."

"She was."

Flora felt water slide off her hair and down her neck. She was almost as wet as she'd been when she'd fallen in the lake, but she wasn't going to end this conversation until she had the outcome she wanted. With this new information, the whole thing was falling into place in her head. "I don't think she was coping. I think she was trying to make herself indispensable."

"But—"

"Did she ever complain? Did she have moods or tantrums? Was she ever difficult?"

He shook his head. "Barely ever." He ran his hand over his face, clearing droplets of rain. "That's not normal, is it? I missed that. Damn, I missed that." He went from defensive to humble in the blink of an eye and if she hadn't been so upset with him she would have been impressed that he could admit his mistakes so willingly and openly.

"I'm no expert but I'd guess no, it's not normal. She thinks she's a burden, so she has been trying to make herself useful to you. It was desperately important to her to feel loved and needed. I threatened her feeling of security by bonding with Molly, because it seemed to her that Molly no longer needed her, either." It was difficult to imagine how hard it must have been for Izzy to see Molly crawling all over Flora. And she could see it clearly now. As her relationship with Molly had deepened, so her relationship with Izzy had become more fraught. "Her behavior makes so much more sense now." And while part of her was relieved that her relationship with Izzy had taken a giant step forward, another part of her was aware that her relationship with Jack wasn't what she'd thought it was. Maybe her aunt had been right. Maybe she expected too much of relationships.

Jack was still processing. "It still doesn't make sense to me. I've been her dad for seventeen years. Why would she think she doesn't have a place here?"

"I don't know." That part didn't make sense to her, either. "It seems to have something to do with Becca. She thought that with Becca gone, you wouldn't want her."

"So all that stuff about not going to college—"

"I'm guessing it's all linked."

"I had no idea all this was going on in her head. You're right, I should have talked to her more about her mother." He gave a groan. "I guess I don't find it easy to talk about and so when she didn't seem to want to talk either I was relieved rather than worried. I tried so hard to give the girls the support they needed, and I've totally messed it up. It's no excuse, but it's tough doing it on your own."

She wanted to point out that he didn't have to do it on his own, that she was here and willing to be part of it and that if he'd involved her maybe, just maybe, she might have been able to help. But was she deluding herself? Perhaps he didn't want that. Perhaps she was always going to be on the edge of his family and never fully a part of it.

*An outsider.*

She felt numb. Empty. The pain would come later, but for now she just needed to keep the focus on Izzy.

"I think you've done a great job, Jack, but you do need to talk to her."

He stared across the lake and she could almost feel his mind working. "When did she tell you all this? Why did she confide in you all of a sudden?"

"It doesn't matter." This wasn't the time to talk about

her trip across the lake. "And I don't understand it either, to be honest. Unless—" She hesitated, torn between the need for confidentiality and her anxiety for Izzy. "Did Izzy and Becca fight a lot?"

"Fight?"

"Was Izzy often mad at her mom?"

He gave a brief shake of his head. "No more than the average teenage girl is with her mother. Why?"

"Did she—" She hated asking because it felt intrusive. "I remember once overhearing my aunt on the phone to someone just after I went to live with her. She was talking about how this wasn't what she wanted but she was making the best of it. She said she'd been left her sister's baggage." She stepped back when he reached out to pull her into his arms. She couldn't let him hug her. Not right now. If she couldn't be fully part of his family, she wasn't sure what the future held for them.

He looked shattered. "Flora—"

"Did you and Becca have a fight? Something Izzy might have overheard that would have worried her?"

"No." He seemed shaken by her rejection. "No fight."

"Then I don't know why Izzy would feel so insecure. Perhaps there was no reason."

"There could have been a reason." Jack's voice was hoarse, and his skin had turned ghastly pale. "We didn't fight, but there were other things."

She wanted to yell *What things?* She'd wondered, of course, if it was something more than grief that had kept him silent on the subject of Becca, but she hadn't wanted to think it. And yet now she had the confirmation. Here was something else he hadn't shared.

Her heart plummeted. Fractured.

"Go and talk to her, Jack." Her lips were stiff and her legs felt shaky.

"Flora—"

"Go, Jack!"

He looked torn. "You and I need to talk. There are things I need to tell you, but you're right I need to see Izzy." He glanced at her face and then back toward the house, weighing his options. "Just tell me we're not over. I can't let that happen."

Couldn't he see that their relationship couldn't be separated from his family? She'd started to feel like part of that family, but it was obvious she wasn't.

Where did that leave their relationship?

Unable to answer his question, she walked back along the trail to the garden. Her shirt clung to her skin and her hair curled wildly. She knew she probably looked a total mess.

As they emerged from the trees she noticed that the rain had stopped and sun was peeping through a gap in the clouds.

Someone emerged from the house but it wasn't Izzy, it was Clare.

Her face was devoid of color. Either she'd received a terrible shock or was about to deliver one. "Jack. Where have you been? Goodness, the pair of you are soaked! I'd suggest you go and dry off, but we need to talk."

"Later." Jack was already striding past her toward the Lodge. "I need to find Izzy."

Clare reached out and caught his arm, her grip so tight her fingers whitened. "It's important, Jack."

"If it's about Izzy then I already—"

"It's about Becca."

The air left Flora's lungs in a rush. Clare wanted to talk about Becca?

*Now what?*

# 20

*Clare*

This was the conversation she'd been dreading. The conversation she'd decided not to have. But it seemed she was having it anyway. The last hour with Izzy had convinced her of that, although deep down she'd known for a while that this moment would come.

They went to the boathouse, scene of so many intimate and private conversations.

She grabbed a towel from the bathroom and threw it at Jack, wondering what he and Flora had been talking about that was too important for them to seek shelter.

He rubbed his hair, draped the towel around his shoulders to absorb some of the water in his shirt and then surprised her by pulling two glasses out of the cupboard along with a bottle of malt whiskey.

He sct it on the table outside on the deck and for a moment she wondered if he'd misunderstood. Did he think this was social? Two old friends catching up?

"I had no idea we had whiskey here. Where did that come from?" She sat down, hands in her lap to hide her nerves, wishing she'd taken the time to change and apply some makeup. She didn't feel together and for a conversation as important as this one she needed to feel together.

"It was left by your previous occupants. Todd and I discovered it a few days ago."

"James and Alysson McGuivan." They'd booked a few days on their way from Scotland to London. They'd paid the going rate without a whimper of protest and left the place as pristine as it had been when they'd first moved in. She wished all the people who rented it were as thoughtful.

"Well the McGuivans had excellent taste in malt whiskey and were generous enough to share the love. Perfect for emergencies."

"What makes you think this is an emergency?"

"The look on your face." He sloshed whiskey into both glasses. "Drink, Clare."

Without even bothering to sit down, he knocked it back.

She didn't touch hers. She knew the courage she was seeking had to come from within, and she needed her head straight for what would undoubtedly be the most difficult conversation of her life. She pressed her hand to her stomach, feeling physically sick. How should she put it? Would the order of the words make a difference to the impact? How did you soften something so harsh?

Jack put his glass down on the table. "It's not fair that you should do this, so I'm going to do it. You're trying to find a way to tell me Becca was having an affair."

She looked up at him. "Jack—"

"And after you've told me that, you're going to tell me she was leaving me."

A heron swooped, skimming the water close to them but neither of them noticed.

At that moment her whole world was him. "You knew?"

"Yeah, I knew." His shrug was all pain. Hurt. Raw. "I knew." He stood up, and she pushed her chair back and stood up, too.

"Oh Jack—" It hadn't occurred to her, not for a minute, that he might already know. But why not? She was fairly sure she'd know if things weren't right with Todd.

She couldn't find the right words so instead of speaking she went to him, wrapped her arms round him. She'd never punched or done physical harm to anyone, but if Becca had walked onto the deck at that moment she would have knocked her out cold.

She felt his arm close around her shoulders, comforting.

"I'm sorry, Clare." He held her. "So sorry."

She pulled away. "*You're* sorry? Why would you be sorry?"

"Because you were caught in the middle of this. You're a kind, decent person. If I'd had the slightest idea that you knew, I would have said something a long time ago."

"She told me during that last vacation, on the last night. We were barely speaking when you all left. And then she wrote me a letter—" She clung to him, this man who had married her friend and then become her friend. Yet again she was questioning all the decisions she made. "I didn't know what to do. She was dead, Jack. I didn't see the point of hurting you and the girls by telling you. It didn't occur to me that you knew." But perhaps it should have done, because Jack had always known who Becca was. Right from the beginning.

"I'd known for a while."

"A while? How long had it been going on?"

"Not sure. At least six months. You didn't know that part?"

"No. Not until the end. And you stayed together?"

"I'm not one to give up on things, you know that. It's a flaw."

"Loyalty—and sticking with something—isn't a flaw, Jack. It's a quality. One of your many qualities."

"Maybe if it had been just me—" He shrugged. "Who knows? But it wasn't me. I had the girls."

The girls. Those two beautiful girls. Clare thought about Aiden, about Todd and their happy, settled family life.

"I'm so mad at her right now." She stepped away from him and closed her hands over the rail. A family of ducks skittered away, perhaps sensing danger. "She made some crazy decisions in her life, but this—"

"You know Becca. She needed to win, whether that was in business or in love. She needed more, bigger, better."

"They don't come better than you, Jack."

"But she already had me. That was probably why it collapsed. I should have kept her uncertain, unsure, but that isn't who I am. I admired her strength and her focus. I loved the wildness and the restlessness. I understood it. But all qualities have a dark side, don't they? In the end, that wildness and restlessness drove her to leave."

"Did you—" Was she going to make it worse by talking about it? "Did you try to stop her? Did you see someone? Get therapy?"

"No." He pulled off the towel and draped it over the rail. "I wanted her to go, Clare. The children weren't aware, but I knew that probably wouldn't last. I didn't want them growing up with that. I wanted them to have stability. They deserved that. And I made a rule for myself after the first time. That was it for me. I set boundaries, and she knew what they were."

"The first time?"

"She left me before." He turned to look at her. "The first time was when Izzy was three months old."

"That can't be true. She would have told me."

"She told no one. She came back. I don't know why. There was Izzy, of course, but I like to think it was because she loved me."

"She did. Oh God, Jack, she did love you." *I met a man.* "I know she did."

"I think she did, too, in her own way. But it wasn't enough. The other part of her, that damaged insecure part, was stronger. Always pulling at her, pushing her away from the safe and secure. Maybe she didn't know how to be if she didn't have to fight and strive. It was easier when she was dancing because she threw everything into that, but after the injury things went downhill. We had a brief time when things seemed stable— Molly was a result of that time."

"I always wondered why you didn't have children right away."

"I wanted that, but she didn't. It scared her, the sense of responsibility. She didn't feel she was a good mother. She talked about you constantly, *Clare would know how to do this, I wish I was more like Clare, you should have married someone like Clare.*"

Tears stung her eyes. Never once had Becca said those things to her. "There is no one version of a good mother."

"I told her that. But after she came back I think she was a little shocked herself that she'd left her child. No one even knew, but she couldn't forget that she'd done it. She didn't trust herself. And it was tough on me, too. I wondered if it was possible for her to settle with one man and a home, but she assured me she could. And for a while it worked. Then she started seeing a man she'd met through her work." He turned away again, so that all she could see was dark hair and strong shoulders.

"And she was going to leave again."

"I told her to leave. I didn't want to draw it out, and have the kids suffer. I wasn't going to chase after her again. No more trying to glue something that just couldn't be stuck back together. We were going to tell the children together, but then she—well, it was all taken out of our hands and in the end I was telling the children their mother was dead. They didn't need to know the rest. I decided it was better to leave them with the memories they had."

Clare felt the sun on her face and a faint breath of wind lift her hair. He thought the conversation was over, but she knew the hardest part was yet to come.

She wished she didn't have to say it, but she had no choice. "Izzy knew, Jack."

"What?" His voice was harsh. "What are you saying?"

"Not all the stuff you just told me. But she knew Becca was leaving you. She knew about the affair. She didn't know you knew. It's the reason she's been feeling so insecure I think. Her mother was leaving you, and the only home she'd ever known. Izzy couldn't figure out what that meant for her. She didn't know what her future was. Was Becca going alone or taking her and Molly? Just Izzy? She was going crazy with it, and then Becca died and she couldn't ask her."

"She could have asked me. I'm her father."

"She didn't want to be the one to tell you her mother was having an affair and about to leave you. I sympathize with that. I made the same decision. Believe me, it wasn't easy, only in my case it was just my ethics and principles that suffered. For Izzy it was far more personal. She was embarrassed by her mother, mortified, shocked, angry—you name it, she felt it. Mostly she felt insecure. She believed she had no right to be living in your home." Clare couldn't remember hearing Jack swear before, but she heard it now.

"How do you know all this? I didn't know she was talking to you, although obviously I'm glad she was talking to someone."

"I only found out today. I've tried to talk to her a few times, but she shut me down. Said she was fine."

"Fine." There was frustration in his voice. "I hear that word a lot. I'm starting to think that what it really means is 'not fine at all, but I don't want to talk about it.' So why today? How did you suddenly persuade her to start talking?"

"I didn't. She came to me and said she wanted to talk about Becca. I suspect you have Flora to thank for that."

"Flora?"

"Funny isn't it, that the one person Izzy held at a distance was in the end the person who got through to her. I don't know what she said to Izzy. I don't know what they talked about. I do know that something she said persuaded Izzy to open up."

Jack walked the length of the deck and back again. "Flora kept telling me I needed to talk to Izzy, but I thought I knew better. I thought the best way to handle it was to give her space. I assumed it was all part of adjusting. Being a teenager."

"Don't beat yourself up. It was an impossible situation. You had no way of knowing she already knew. You didn't want to upset her by telling her something she didn't need to know. She didn't want to upset you by telling you something you didn't need to know. I think the time for rethinking that is past, Jack. All you can do now is move forward.

I think if you tell her the truth, and yes I probably do mean the whole truth, in the end it will be easier. If Izzy knew that Becca had left once before, but that you had kept her, been there for her, maybe she'd feel more secure."

"She has a home with me forever if she wants it. She can live with me until she's wrinkled and her teeth fall out." There was no doubting his sincerity and Clare smiled and put her hand on his arm.

"I hope she leaves home and has wild times and adventures. I hope she lives her life to the full, and then comes home and tells you all about it. I hope that sometimes she'll show up here for our summer vacation, or at least for part of it. Sometimes all you need to give you a feeling of security is the knowledge that home is there for you. That the people you love are there for you. You don't need to be with them all the time." She could virtually see his brain working as he thought about it.

"I understand now why me bringing Flora home might have seemed like the final straw." He was making all the connections, seeing the pattern. "Still more evidence that she was losing her place in my life."

"It's frustrating what the brain can imagine, and how our thinking and judgment can be distorted by our own fears. I think she feels guilty about Becca. She's taking responsibility for it."

"I'll talk to her about that, along with all the other things." He seemed to make a decision. "We might have to postpone dinner."

"Mealtimes are somewhat fluid in this house as you've probably noticed." Because she knew he was anxious to get back and talk to his daughter, she walked across the deck and took the steps to the path. "I like Flora by the way. I'm glad you brought her here."

Jack smiled for the first time since the conversation began. "She's the best thing that has happened to me in a long while."

"She might be the best thing that has happened to my garden in a long while, too." Clare stepped along the path, her heart and mood lighter, freed from the burden she'd carried for the last year. She felt very strongly that she'd found a friend. That she and Flora would be more than two people brought together because of family tradition.

The path opened up onto the garden and they walked across the lawn to hear raised voices.

Jack glanced at her. "Any idea what's going on?"

"No. But that's Aiden." And he rarely, if ever, raised his voice. Maternal intuition made her walk faster, and she reached the terrace to see Aiden gesturing to Todd. He had the car keys in his hand and they seemed to be arguing about something. "What's wrong?" There was always something, she thought. Life was less a roller coaster and more a series of hurdles, with no breathing room in between them.

Aiden looked stressed. "I was on my way back and I passed Izzy going in the other direction."

"I don't understand."

"In a cab! She was in a cab. She turned her head away when she saw me but I'm pretty sure she was crying. Did something happen?"

Jack looked at Clare. She knew what he was thinking because she was thinking the same thing. Izzy was leaving because she believed she no longer had a place in the family.

The emotional side of Clare wanted to sob for the girl, but fortunately her practical side took over.

She pulled out her phone. "There is only one cab firm in the village. I'll find out where they've taken her."

"They won't give you that information."

"Of course they will. Todd gave the owner a friendly rate when he extended his house and I do yoga with his wife. Hello?" She was swift with her request and the response came back equally quickly. "They've taken her to the station."

Aiden nodded. "I'm going after her." He started up the garden but Jack stopped him.

"Wait, Aiden. I know you care for her, but—there's more to this. It has to be me."

"I'm the one she's going to talk to." Her son's reaction convinced Clare that Izzy had confided in him, too.

She decided a compromise was in order. "Aiden should drive you, Jack. It will be faster. He knows the way. He can wait in the car while you talk to Izzy."

She just hoped they'd make it in time to have that conversation before Izzy boarded the train.

# 21

*Izzy*

Izzy sat miserable and alone on the edge of the seat on the station platform, wondering where the train was. She'd never actually traveled alone in England before. She wasn't sure if she felt sophisticated or scared.

The station was unlike any she'd seen before. She was used to Manhattan and the roar, shriek and rumble of the subway line, the chaos and grandeur of Grand Central Station, the press of people breathing the same air and pushing, always pushing, to get on or get off. Here the air was clean and fresh. No one was pushing. She saw a bird with a pinkish breast settle on the wall nearby and opened her mouth to point it out, but then realized there was no one to tell.

There were only three other people on the platform and they hadn't even glanced toward Izzy, which was just as well because she knew she looked a mess. She'd cried all the way in the cab, and then almost died of horror when she'd seen Aiden driving the other way.

She was fairly sure he'd seen her, which was why she needed the train to arrive quickly.

Luck wasn't on her side. She checked the time on her phone and when she looked up Jack was standing there.

She was trying to train herself not to think of him as "Dad."

Her first instinct was to rush at him and hug him, the way she'd done when she was a little girl and she heard his key in the front door at the end of the day. She craved that same feeling of security she'd had then when his arms had wrapped round her.

But she wasn't that little girl anymore.

She assumed her most nonchalant expression. "What?"

"What? You took a cab to the station without leaving so much as a note, and you're seriously asking me *what*?"

"I just—I have to go. You wouldn't understand."

He sat down next to her. "Try me."

"I don't want to talk about this."

"I can see that, but it's weird because the Izzy I know, my daughter, never runs from a problem. She looks it in the eye and handles it. Or she asks me to handle it, because that's what dads do. What she doesn't do is climb in a cab without telling anyone and get a train to a city she doesn't know."

"It's time I started being more independent."

"Maybe. We'll talk about that at another time, but for now we're focusing on why you ran away."

"I've told you—I don't want to talk about it."

"Well I do, and I'm your father so you have to listen to me."

"We both know you're not." She glanced at him and her heart lurched as she saw the hurt in his eyes.

"When did I ever give you the impression that I don't think of you as a daughter? Because if I messed up as a father I deserve to know so that I don't make the same mistake in the future."

"You didn't mess up."

"Did I love you less than I should have done? Tell me, because something has made you think you don't belong with this family and I need to know what it is."

Crap, did they really have to have this conversation? "I'm not yours."

"Oh honey—" His voice was rough. "You were mine from the moment you were born. Screaming your lungs out, by the way. If I'd wanted to give you away or back out, that would have been the time to do it but I didn't because I loved you. I never believed in love at first sight until you came along. And maybe I should have told you how I felt more often, but I'm a guy and we don't always get it right. If you're going to be a journalist, and I know you'll be a great one, you need to learn to examine the facts. And there is a ton of evidence if you look for it."

"I don't—"

"Maybe I didn't yell 'I love you' every time I walked through the door, but I showed you, Izzy. I showed you all the time. Let's do some fact-checking. Remember when you were nine years old and were crazy about dinosaurs?"

"You took me to the American Museum of Natural History."

"And then we came home and I spent two days making you Jurassic scenery, complete with a papier-mâché volcano."

Remembering it made her smile. "It was cool. Until you got red paint on a chair. Mom was furious."

"She was, and I didn't care. Do you know why I didn't

care? Because you had the best time. The smile on your face stretched all the way from Brooklyn to Connecticut. You played with your dinosaur world for two months."

"Until Molly crawled on top of it and it collapsed."

"That's right. The perils of having a baby sister." He looped his arm round her shoulders. "I didn't spend hours building it because I thought it would be a fun project, although it was a fun project. I did it because I loved you. Then there was the time you decided you wanted to do a trip to the top of the Empire State Building for your eleventh birthday. I took you. Remember that?"

"Yeah. You almost crushed my hand."

"That's because I'm not good with heights and I was scared out of my mind."

She snorted. "You were not."

"Terrified. I was jelly. But I did it because it was what you wanted. Love got me up there and love got me down again. Do you believe I love you yet, or do I need to keep going?"

"I guess I believe you."

"You guess?"

"I—I believe you. But—"

"No 'buts.' I love you. You're my girl and I'll always love you. Nothing is ever going to change that. Nothing you do. Nothing your mom did. And now it's time to talk about that." He glanced along the platform to where the three people were still waiting. "I was going to suggest going somewhere private, but this is pretty private. It will do. Clare tells me you know your mom was having an affair. That she was leaving."

Panic threatened to strangle her.

Izzy stared down the track, willing the train to come right now but there was nothing but trees, and fresh air, and this conversation she didn't want to have.

"I know this is difficult and you don't have to say any-thing, sweetheart." Jack's voice was gentle. "I'll do the talk-ing."

Where was the train?

"I can't imagine what this past year must have been like for you and I'm gutted that you didn't feel able to talk to me about it, but I understand why you didn't. You didn't want to hurt me. You love me. And I didn't mention it to you because I didn't want to hurt you. I loved you too much. More evi-dence right there. If she hadn't died then I guess we would have had that difficult conversation back then, but she did and so there didn't seem any value in raising it. Except of course I didn't know that you knew. Which either makes us both caring, or a pair of idiots. Not sure which."

*He knew? All this time she'd been protecting him and he knew?*

"I heard her on the phone. We had a terrible, terrible fight before she went out that night. I thought there'd be time to talk about it again—" She felt the tears rush to her eyes and fought to hold them back, but this time her body refused to cooperate. They fell, poured, and with the tears came the sobs and she couldn't stop any of it. It was all too much. Something inside her had burst.

She felt him pull her against him, was dimly aware of being held, of his voice soothing and calming her, telling her everything was going to be okay, that she had no need to feel guilty and still she cried, soaking his shirt. She cried until she was empty, and even when her sobs eventually stopped she stayed where she was, utterly drained and exhausted.

"There." He stroked her hair. "This is my fault, sweet-heart, not yours. After she died, it was chaos. And we were all dealing with it, and maybe if we hadn't been I would have noticed something was worrying you. But every time

I saw you behave differently, I assumed it was grief. Bad judgment on my part."

"No!" Why had they never talked like this before? She didn't want the train to come, not quite yet. She wanted to have this conversation. "I'm sorry she cheated on you."

"Oh honey—" He kept his arms wrapped around her. "You don't have to be sorry. Her decisions weren't yours. My love for you wasn't, and isn't, tied up with my feelings for her."

She sniffed. "You're so forgiving."

"I'm not forgiving." He paused. "I'm mad with her, if you must know. And that's been difficult. Grieving someone, and being mad with them—it's a weird feeling."

"I know." She lifted her head to look at him. "I feel the same way."

"Yeah? We should have shared that. We could have gone to the gym together and thrown a few punches."

She managed a small smile. "We could still do that." And because he was so generous and understanding the emotion flowed over her again, swamping her like the incoming tide. "She didn't think about me at all. It's like I didn't matter." The words burst out of her and she felt his arm tighten.

"It wasn't that she didn't think of you, although I can see why it might seem that way. She was pretty troubled. Your mom didn't have an easy life."

"She was married to you. That was like winning the lottery and she, like— I don't know." Izzy clung to the front of his shirt, his soaked shirt. "She tossed it away."

"Some people find it hard to move on from the past. I know you keep a diary. And write a blog. Did you write all this down?"

"Some of it. Some of it felt too personal."

"Writing is good. Someday you'll use the experience.

Maybe it will make you understand someone a bit better, or perhaps you'll use it as inspiration when you write your blockbuster."

"You think I'm going to write a blockbuster?"

"I think if anyone stands a chance, it's you. Did you know I bought you your first pen?"

"I didn't know that."

"You drew on the wall."

She laughed. "I bet Mom loved that."

"She was away touring with the ballet company. I painted over it before she came home and told her I thought it was time we redecorated the kitchen."

"I guess that was love, too."

"It was." He pulled her closer. "And also self-preservation."

"She was going to walk out and leave Molly and me." And she couldn't get that out of her head.

"I'm not going to lie, because if I lie you'll never trust me again and I want you to trust me. Yes, she was going to leave us."

"So she didn't love me. There's the evidence right there."

"She did love you. Sometimes evidence can create a false trail. Only the best journalists would take the time to dig deeper. It's the 'why' that really tells the story, Izzy. Remember that." He sighed. "She thought I'd be a better parent to you than she ever could be. It was the reason she married me."

Izzy was appalled. "She loved you."

"She did, in her own way, as far as she could."

She should have felt agonized that her mother had been prepared to walk out and leave her, but instead all she felt was relief that she would have carried on living with Jack.

"Can I say something to you?"

"Anything. Anything at all."

"I loved my mom but honestly I think she was batshit crazy."

He gave a tired laugh. "The best response I have to that is that sometimes people we love do things we don't understand or even necessarily agree with."

"Talking about people we love, Flora rowed a boat to the island. Did she tell you?"

"No. She didn't tell me that. She got in a boat? That must have been— I mean why would—"

"She was worried about me."

"Oh right. Well that would explain it."

"She fell in the water and totally freaked."

"No kidding. I don't suppose she'll ever go near the water again."

"I couldn't believe she'd do that for me."

"I can believe it. It's how she is. She doesn't make a fuss. She's warmhearted and generous, and she genuinely cares about you. She had a tough time too when she was growing up."

"I know. She told me a few things. And she showed me a picture of her mom." Izzy fiddled with the hem of her shirt. "I saved her, kind of." Did that sound boastful? She didn't mean it to. It was her way of letting her dad know she didn't want Flora to drown.

He stirred. "I'm glad about that, because I really like her."

"You more than *like* her, Dad."

"Right. Good point." He cleared his throat. "I love her. Does that upset you?"

Izzy discovered that it didn't, perhaps because of her own deepening feelings for Aiden. Love was incredible actually, although she was finding it almost impossible to write about. It didn't make logical sense when you thought about it. But one thing she knew was that you didn't have a choice who you fell in love with.

Thinking of that made her feel a little better about her mother. What had Aunt Clare said? She wasn't a bad person. She just made bad choices. For some reason that made sense to Izzy. But the best thing was how easy it had been to talk to Clare—and she'd insisted Izzy had called her Clare. *I'm not your aunt, but I'd very much like to be your friend.*

Izzy no longer felt as if she was living on an island.

"It doesn't upset me. I like Flora, although I've probably driven her crazy."

"I've probably driven her crazy, too. And she may want nothing to do with me after this because I've messed up in a big way."

"With Flora? How?"

"Because I haven't told her any of this stuff about your mom, and I should have done. I should have shared it. And I tried to handle too much without involving her, and I've made her feel as if she's on the outside."

Izzy thought about what she knew. "That's a biggie for Flora."

"Yes. I should have shared more. I should have drawn her into the family more."

Izzy felt a stab of guilt. "I pushed her away, so that's partly my fault."

"No, honey, it's mine. It doesn't matter what you said or did—I should have shared my worries with her, instead of trying to protect her and handle everything. I have to figure out a way to convince her she's part of this family. And that I love her."

She could hardly believe her dad was saying all this stuff to her. It made her feel ridiculously grown-up. And she didn't want to blow it by saying the wrong thing. She wanted to say something wise and helpful, not totally lame. "I guess you should just talk to her. And listen."

"I'm definitely going to start doing more listening. Always assuming Flora is still willing to talk to me."

Izzy tried to imagine Flora not talking to someone. No matter how hard her mind worked, she couldn't picture it. "Flora is very patient and kind. She's not the sort to stomp out of the room and not listen. Just tell her the truth. Also, she's nuts about flowers. She'd probably appreciate a bunch of those."

He nodded. "That's a good thought."

Izzy sat there feeling like a proper adult for the first time in her life.

"You know, I've been thinking, maybe I will think about college. I mean, you haven't given Molly ham in a while, so maybe she wouldn't die if I left."

Laughing, he pulled her closer. "I hope my parenting isn't so bad that I'd accidentally kill your sister, but there's no need to rush into a decision. Think about it. Take your time. If you need a listening ear then I'm here and I promise not to try to influence you in any way."

"How are you going to manage that? You want me to go to college, I know you do."

"Only because I want the very best for you, and I think it's an experience you'd enjoy. But how will I not influence you?" He stretched out his legs. "I will pretend to be very calm and neutral about the whole thing, and work hard to keep all my parental panic on the inside. Parenting involves a lot of internal panic."

"So basically you'll be freaking out and I won't know it?"

"Sounds about right."

"You're not that good an actor. I'm going to know if you're freaking out."

"I'll work on it, but you should also know that the reason I'm freaking out is because I love you, and I want nothing but good things for you. But whatever you decide, and whatever happens with Flora, I'll be right here backing you up. I want you to fly, sweetheart, but know that you can always come back home. And you will always have a home wherever I am, I hope you know that."

She discovered that she did know that, and knowing it brought tears to her eyes even though she was sure that physiologically her body had to be as dry as the desert by now.

She blinked several times. Adults didn't sob like a baby. "Thanks for coming to find me."

"Anytime, although next time I hope you'll call me before you call a cab."

"Did you remember to drive on the left side of the road?"

"Aiden drove."

"Aiden?" She lifted her head. "He's here?"

"In the car. Waiting to drive one, or both of us, back. I'm hoping it's both of us." His voice wasn't steady. "Can I give you an embarrassingly big kiss or would that make you leap on the train?"

She grinned. "Well I've already embarrassed myself without your help so I'm beyond caring." She leaned against him again, her head on his shoulder as she'd done so often as a child. She felt his lips on her hair, but most of all she felt his love and it was so powerful she wondered how she could ever have doubted it. "Are there snakes in Vietnam?"

"Thousands of them. They're everywhere. You probably won't be able to put your feet on the ground without treading on at least six of them. Not that I'm trying to put you off or anything. It's totally your decision. And there are spiders, too. Massive hairy spiders who never shave their legs."

She didn't know whether to giggle or shudder. "Maybe I'll go to college after all."

"Wherever you go, whatever you decide, I'm here for you. Until you meet a hot guy of course, and forget about your old dad."

She'd already met her hot guy, but she wasn't ready to tell him that. Maybe soon.

And then Aiden appeared on the platform, out of breath and noticeably lacking in his customary cool. "I saw the train coming—I was afraid you might get on it without giving me a chance to talk to you. I love you, Izzy."

Izzy squirmed. Not now. Not in front of her dad.

The thought came to her naturally and she realized that she'd always thought of Jack that way so there was really no reason why he shouldn't think of her as a daughter, too.

Jack stood up. "I may not have won many awards for parenting lately, but I know when it's time for me to leave."

"No." Izzy grabbed his hand. "I don't want you to go."

Finally, the train rattled into the station, grinding to a halt. The three passengers boarded the train. Doors slammed.

Jack glanced from her to the train. "We can stay here and chat on this train platform, which is charming as train platforms go, or we could go home and have this conversation somewhere more comfortable. And I can talk to Flora."

Izzy held tightly to his hand but she was looking at Aiden.

"Let's go home."

# 22

## *Flora*

The lake lapped relentlessly at her ankles, drawing her deeper into the water.

Flora forced herself to keep walking, even though her limbs shook with every step. The water was up to her calves now, the shock of the cold water making her gasp. It was summer. How could the water be so cold in summer?

She tried not to think about Jack, or her dream of being part of his family. She forced it all out of her mind, so she could focus on this one thing.

She was going to do this, alone and quietly, with no one around to talk her out of it.

She was up to her waist now. The water closed around her. She wanted to scream but fear gripped her throat so tightly she couldn't make a sound.

*Just do it*, she told herself and tried to summon up the courage.

She was concentrating so hard on taking the plunge that at first she didn't hear the sound of voices behind her.

They grew louder and finally she heard Molly yelling. *Flora, Flora.*

A chorus of panicked voices reached her ears and she closed her eyes, frustrated.

She'd intentionally picked a time when no one was around. She hadn't wanted anyone to witness this. She'd wanted to step into the water alone and sort this out once and for all without any fuss or bother but that wasn't going to happen. Families, she was discovering, came with plenty of drama. Also, very little opportunity for personal time. It was what Julia always complained about and what Flora had always wanted.

She turned to see Izzy, Molly and Jack charging into the water fully clothed.

What on earth had happened to make them so desperate?

It took a moment to realize she was the source of their panic.

"Flora! Stop. *Stop!* Don't do it."

There was splashing and more shrieking and then Izzy appeared next to her, followed by Molly who thrashed forward in a wild dog paddle like Chase, and then finally Jack.

Flora gasped as she was showered by water.

"You can't go in the water." Molly's arms flailed like an octopus. "You can't swim."

Flora wiped her face and then caught the child, worried that she might drown both of them. "I never said I couldn't swim. I said I hated water. I haven't swum since that awful day and I wanted to try it. It's way beyond time."

Izzy reached her, her wet T-shirt clinging to her body. "You were going swimming? You weren't—"

"I wasn't what?"

Izzy swallowed. "Trying to drown yourself."

"*Drown* myself?" And suddenly she realized why they'd all raced into the water. "That was never my intention, although given that I haven't been near deep water for more than two decades I suppose it was always a possible outcome. You may not have noticed but I'm wearing a bathing suit. And I borrowed a pair of wet suit boots because I didn't like the idea of being barefoot in the lake."

Izzy gave a little sob and flung her arms round her. "I thought maybe I upset you again. Or my dad made you want to drown yourself."

Flora didn't know whether to laugh or cry. She actually felt like crying but that was probably because Izzy was hugging her for the first time. Tightly. Holding on. Clinging.

Flora clung back. "You didn't upset me. And I'm not big on giving life advice, but I would suggest that no woman should ever drown themselves over a man."

"Are you mad with Daddy?" Molly was clinging, too, her fingers wet and slippery. "I get mad sometimes when he gives me ham. But he does good things, too, and Aunt Clare always says that no one gets it right all the time."

"That's true enough." Flora glanced at Jack who was standing fully clothed and dripping wet behind the children. The look on his face was one she'd remember for a long time. He loved her, she could see that. Whatever he hadn't said, whatever mistakes he'd made, he loved her. "You forgot to take your clothes off."

His gaze held hers. He didn't smile. "I had other things on my mind. I can't believe you went into the water on your own. Are you crazy?"

"I needed to do it this way."

"He *totally* freaked out when he saw you in the water. He

wanted to save you," Molly said sagely. "We all wanted to save you, but you didn't need saving, so that's good."

"Why didn't you wait?" Izzy pulled away from Flora and tugged at her soaking T-shirt. "If you wanted to swim, I would have come with you."

"I didn't know how I'd react. I thought I might flip out and not be able to do it at all. That would have been embarrassing."

"I wouldn't have cared if you'd flipped," Izzy said. "I wouldn't have judged you. But I could have rescued you."

"Not being able to do something you just have to try harder," Molly told her. "That's what Aunt Clare says."

"And Aunt Clare is right."

Molly clung to her hand. "If you want to try it again, I'm here and I'll save you if you drown."

She was surrounded by arms, legs and love.

And she realized that becoming a family wasn't something that happened overnight. It took baby steps, patience, understanding and a willingness to forgive when things went wrong.

"If you cling to her like that she *will* drown." Izzy gently prized her sister's fingers away from Flora's arm. "You're a deadweight. But Molly's right. If you're going to do something that scary, you should have people who love you close by. So we'll stay right here and you can pretend you're on your own if you like."

Flora looked at the three of them and then at the water.

"You're here now," Molly said, "so you might as well do it. Kick hard and use your arms. I try to copy Chase."

"Which is why you're never going to win any style points," Izzy murmured.

With all of them watching her she felt self-conscious. "I really don't think—"

"Just do it," Jack said. "Do it, honey."

"I know, we'll swim, too." Molly plunged into the water with joyous abandon, showering everyone with water.

With a whoop, Izzy did the same thing.

"And now you're trying to swim in churning water." Jack looked exasperated but Flora didn't mind. If she was doing this then she needed to do it, and not care if she was splashed. She could still put her feet down. Jack and Izzy were capable of helping her if she got into trouble. There really was no risk, apart from in her head.

She leaned forward and slowly lowered her body into the water, feeling it close over her chest and then her shoulders as she kicked forward. Panic loomed in the background, and then she was swimming. Really swimming. Her body felt weightless. Panic was replaced by euphoria as she moved through the water, everything else in her world temporarily forgotten. She'd never felt this close to nature, or to her fears. Fear fluttered in her belly but she ignored it and carried on moving her arms and legs in a steady rhythm, feeling herself grow stronger with each stroke.

She didn't know how long she swam, but it was long enough for fear to turn to exhilaration. Long enough for her to trust her body not to let her down. Long enough to know that the past wasn't going to drag her down like a stone. Long enough to know that her belief that she'd never swim again had been wrong.

Life wasn't static. Just because you were scared of something, didn't mean you had to stay scared of it. She'd let fear hold her back, and she saw clearly now that it was fear that was behind her instinct to end things with Jack. Yes she was in love, but she was also scared. Scared that she'd made herself vulnerable. Scared that she'd fallen in love with his family, when he still saw her as an outsider. Scared that she'd trusted him with her secrets, when he hadn't trusted her with his. But maybe he was afraid to do that. He was human, as she was. He had his own fears. Instead of walking away, she should talk to him. Tell him how it made her feel when he kept secrets from her. Use this rocky moment to understand him better, and help him understand her. Just as life wasn't static, a relationship wasn't static either. There were bound to be bumps along the way and they had to learn to negotiate those bumps together. It was a process. A discovery. An adventure.

She swam until her arms were tired and when she finally stood up she was laughing and so was Izzy.

"Well wow." Izzy's hair clung to her shoulders, wet and sleek. "So that's swimming sorted. Next we need to give you kayaking lessons. Lesson one is not to drop the paddle."

Molly was shivering, her skin blotchy and tinged blue from the cold. "I'm c-cold. Can I have hot chocolate?"

"Good plan. You and I will go indoors." Izzy scooped her up and rubbed her back to warm her. "Flora and Dad need to talk."

"Can I talk, too?"

Izzy glanced at Flora and then at her dad. "You're not invited to this talk."

"You should listen to him, Flora," Molly said, her arms round her sister's shoulders as she waded to the shore. "I think he wants you to marry us. We'd like that, too. And if we could have a dog, that would be good. I don't mind if it's a small one."

"Oh my goodness, you don't marry a whole family, you marry a person!" Izzy hugged her and scolded her at the same time. "Whatever you plan on being when you're older, don't pick anything that involves diplomacy."

"I don't know what that is."

"That," Izzy said with the superiority of the older sister, "is pretty obvious." She reached dry land and set Molly down. Then she draped a towel round her shoulders. "You and I are going to make hot chocolate."

Molly glanced over her shoulder to Flora and Jack who had also emerged from the water. "But—"

"With whipped cream."

Molly paused, tempted. "Okay, but maybe we should—"

"—and marshmallows, with a chocolate flake."

That did it. Molly sped up the lawn toward the house and Izzy followed.

Flora watched them go, part of her wishing she could join them. Her skin was stinging from the cold water and her heart was racing. She felt bedraggled but euphoric.

She'd swum. She'd done it. It was amazing what it had done to her confidence and belief in herself. Right now she felt invincible.

"I couldn't believe it when I saw you in the lake." Jack wrapped a towel round her and rubbed her arms. "I can't remember when I last panicked like that."

"It was a few hours ago, when you discovered Izzy had gone to the station."

He gave a laugh. "It's been a day of drama, that's for sure."

"I'm assuming your conversation went well, as you all arrived together."

"Yes. We talked about a lot of things. Things we should have talked about a long time ago. And I did the same thing with Clare." He took her hand and tugged her down onto one of the sunloungers. "The only person I haven't been honest with is you. I don't mean about the whole Izzy thing—I was being truthful when I told you it's something I simply don't think about. But Becca—I didn't tell you about her, and I owe you an explanation for that. You deserve to know it all."

"Jack—"

"All I ask is that you listen to what I have to say before you speak, and if at the end of it you decide this isn't for you then that's fine. Well, it's not fine, but I'll try hard to accept your decision and not pester you to change your mind." He tugged the towel more firmly around her. "I met Becca in an airport. We were both waiting to board the same flight. We dated for a month before she told me she was pregnant."

"She pretended it was yours?" No matter what he said, she wasn't going to be shocked or overreact.

"No." He shook his head. "Becca was always straight. I think she expected me to walk out. Almost everyone she'd encountered in her life up until that point had walked out at some point or another. She didn't know consistency or security. She hadn't known love."

Flora felt a flash of sympathy. Her childhood had been different, of course. In many ways she'd been lucky, certainly luckier than Becca. But that didn't change the fact that she understood how it felt to know you were on your own, with no one in your corner.

"She had you."

"Yes, and I had no intention of walking out. But I'm not sure she ever felt entirely sure of me. She never found it easy living as part of a family. She kept expecting it to fall apart, and when it didn't she was ready to sabotage it herself."

Flora listened as he talked, and hiding her shock became more of a challenge when he told her that Becca had left him when Izzy was only three months old. It was hard not to judge, even though she tried not to.

Maybe Becca hadn't been loved as a child, but she'd been

loved as an adult. You could have a bad childhood and still make a good life. Choice came into it.

And that was true for her, too, of course. She could walk away from this, or she could choose to stay.

She carried on listening as Jack told her about the most recent affair.

It was the last thing she would have imagined of the perfect Becca. Except that she hadn't been perfect, had she? She'd been human, as flawed and individual as every other person.

"She was going to leave me. Us. All of us."

Flora put her hand on his. "Oh, Jack—" No wonder he'd struggled to talk about it. Who would want to?

But he was talking about it now, and he told her everything, outlined every painful detail of those last months and days, and she listened without interrupting, knowing that there would be time to ask questions later, time to tell him her thoughts and hear his.

"The kids didn't know— at least I didn't think they knew, but it turned out that Izzy had overheard her talking on the phone. I had no idea. She didn't say anything and it didn't occur to me. She planned to confront her mother about it, but Becca went out that night and never came back. Izzy was left in a horrible position. She assumed I didn't know and she didn't want to be the one to tell me. There seemed no point, as Becca was gone anyway."

"So she's been carrying this huge secret." Flora's heart ached for her.

"Yes."

The final pieces of the puzzle slotted into place. "She knew her mother was leaving you, and she thought that would have been the end of your relationship, too."

"Her thinking wasn't as clear as that initially. She was

in shock, devastated by the loss but angry with her mother. And it ate away at her feelings of security. She started to feel guilty, as if she was somehow responsible for her mother's actions. She thought that I would no longer want her."

"She probably felt she didn't deserve to be with you. She was punishing herself for Becca." Flora's cheeks were wet. "Poor Izzy. I wish she'd told you."

"I'm just relieved she said something to you or goodness knows how long this might have gone on, or how it would have ended."

"She didn't tell me any of that. I just picked up that she was angry with Becca."

"I should have seen that. Particularly as I had plenty of anger of my own. I focused all my energy into being there for the girls. And then I met you." He paused. "You were the brightest, most hopeful thing that had happened to me in a long time and I was terrified."

"Terrified?"

"Yes, because it was too soon, the wrong time, the girls had to be my priority—you name it, I felt it. I didn't intend to ask you for a coffee that first day, and I didn't intend to ask you to meet me for lunch every day after that. But being with you felt so good I couldn't end it. It would have felt like denying yourself water when you're thirsty. But I knew it was too much."

"Too much—for me?"

"It was never going to be a simple relationship. It could never be just about you and me."

"I knew you had the girls, Jack. I knew it from that first day."

"I was afraid to get too close, and afraid to let the girls get close after Becca."

"Grief makes you fearful of losing the other people in

your lives. It's something we don't generally think about. We mostly go through life feeling we're immortal, but death forces us to accept that we're not."

"I still need to decide how much to tell Molly, but that can wait for now." He glanced at her and shook his head. "I can't believe you swam."

"I wanted to swim because—" Should she tell him? Was this the right time? "I hope we'll carry on coming back here every year and I want to be able to join in."

"Really? You want to come back?"

"Yes. I love it." She stared out at the water, seeing only the beauty and not the menace. "It felt like a real step forward. I'm guessing you and Izzy have taken a step forward, too."

"We have." His fingers tightened on hers. "What about you? Us? You didn't sign up for this crazy, complicated family life. I know you hate conflict."

She smiled. "What I hate even more than conflict is being shut out. Being on the outside. But now I'm on the inside. When the girls ran into the water I realized I am part of your family, your crazy, complicated family, even if we're all still figuring out what that means and how it looks. And I've never been happier."

Relief spread across his face. "Really? I thought I'd blown it."

"I thought I'd blown it with Izzy. None of us is perfect, Jack. I don't expect that. I don't want it. I know how hard it is to be open and honest with someone. It's scary. I'm not used to talking about my feelings. I used to think it was because I just didn't know how to do it, but I think it's because I was afraid of sharing anything truly personal. It was a way of shielding myself from rejection. The more someone knows about you, the more they can hurt you. We're both learning. Maybe we can do it together. We just need to keep talking.

Keep sharing. We can handle anything life throws at us if we do it together."

"I feel guilty that you are constantly having to handle my family issues. You don't have to be part of this. You can still decide to walk away."

His words made her realize that he had his insecurities, too. Everyone did, didn't they? And how could Becca's rejection not have left a scar?

She turned to him and she took his face in her hands, felt the roughness of his jaw under her palms and saw the concern in his eyes. "You have no idea how much I want to be part of exactly this. A family, with all its complexities and ups and downs. I don't want to walk away. I will *never* walk away." She said it firmly, so there could be no mistake, but the fact that he'd been protecting her, thinking of her, warmed her in a way she'd never been warmed before. "You were really protecting me?"

"Yes. And I might have been protecting myself a little, too. I was worried that if you realized just how full-on and emotionally exhausting family life is, you might change your mind about me. I don't want that to happen. I love you too much."

"And I love you." The words felt strange. Unfamiliar. She hadn't said them to anyone in so long. Not since she'd stood in the drafty kitchen in her aunt's apartment and tried to form a relationship.

*We don't have to love each other, we just have to learn to live together.*

Flora had wanted so much more, and now she had more.

She was about to say the words again but he grabbed her and kissed her until her head spun and she couldn't remember her own name let alone anything else.

Finally, reluctantly, he lifted his head. "You have no idea how long I've waited to hear you say that. You love me?"

"Yes. And it feels amazing."

A smile tugged at the corner of his mouth. "You love me, even though I come with responsibilities."

"If you're talking about Izzy and Molly, I love them, too."

"You're willing to put up with the hormonal explosions, and the silences, and the constant nagging feeling that you've said the wrong thing again? You really want this?"

"I am. I do." It sounded as if she was saying her vows and she shifted away from him, suddenly awkward. "Well that was—"

He pulled her close and kissed her hard. "Molly already proposed to you, I think. If you're expecting tact and finesse forget it. You don't get that with a seven-year-old around the house. You get whatever comes out of their mouths."

She laughed, realizing that if she could find enough courage to swim in the lake, then she could find the courage to tackle awkward situations. "I'm not waiting for you to propose, Jack. All I need is to be with you. Nothing more or less than that." And if she ever felt she needed marriage, she'd tell him. Maybe she'd be the one to propose. Why not?

For now, all she needed was his love, and she had that. She understood why he hadn't told her everything, and she knew it had made him think hard about their relationship, too. In the end it was a reminder for both of them that healthy relationships needed love, thought and care, but they also needed trust.

She shifted in his arms and noticed, for the first time, a large bunch of flowers abandoned on the lawn. "What's that?" She sat up, wondering how she hadn't noticed it before.

"Those were for you."

"You bought me flowers?" No one had ever bought her flowers. She'd always had to buy them herself. She stood up and retrieved them, burying her face in their soft petals and inhaling their scent. "They're beautiful. I can't believe you bought me flowers."

"In the spirit of honesty I have to confess it was Izzy's idea."

"Izzy?" She lifted her nose out of the blooms.

"I was all ready to present them to you in the most romantic way possible, but then I saw you in the water and I—well, I'm not sure what happened. I might have flung them."

"Flung them." She looked from him to the petals on the ground. "You flung them."

"What can I say? I panicked when I saw you. Next time I buy you flowers, I'll make sure the mode of delivery is better. But knowing your love of flowers, I hope you'll love them anyway."

"Oh, Jack—" She clutched them, knowing that even missing a few petals this would be the most precious bunch of flowers anyone had ever given her.

He knew her so well. He knew she loved flowers. He knew she struggled with confrontation. He knew she was as afraid of rejection as she was of water. He knew she sometimes did things just to please other people. And he knew about the deep loneliness that had felt like a huge hollow space inside her. He knew all that. He knew the important stuff.

Still holding the flowers, she leaned her head against his chest. "I'm going to miss this place."

"Me, too. But I'm also looking forward to going home. I have some ideas."

She lifted her head and looked at him. "Care to share them?"

"In time. Let's just say that you can stop looking for

apartments. You're moving in with us while I put plan A into action."

She was about to ask about his plan, but decided it didn't matter. She didn't need to know. All she needed to know was that whatever it was, they'd be doing it together as a family. That he loved her as much as she loved him.

And as he lowered his head and kissed her again, there was no doubt in her heart.

# epilogue

"This is my bedroom!" Molly's voice echoed through the empty house. "I want this top one. It has a view of the river."

"I should have that one, because I'm the oldest." Izzy could be heard arguing with her sister, their feet thumping on bare floorboards as they chased each other from room to room.

"But you're going to college."

"Not forever. And I'll be back often to make sure you're behaving."

Jack slid his arms round Flora and kissed her. "How about you? Have you picked your bedroom? Fancy misbehaving?"

The house was a beautifully renovated nineteenth-century Greek Revival in the heart of New York's historic Hudson River Valley. It had been a mutual decision to move out of the city and this had been the second property they'd viewed. They'd fallen in love with it right away, and on their second visit, less than twenty-four hours later, they'd brought the girls and now here they were in their new home.

They'd first seen it in the spring and Flora had fallen in love with the orchard, the fruit trees heavy with blossom. Jack had immediately seen its potential and earmarked the old barn as office space. He'd spent long hours on the phone with Todd, discussing how they could turn it into a modern space while protecting the original features and character.

Even with all the technology he planned to install, Jack would still have to spend some time in the city, and his skills were increasingly in demand in places farther afield but he intended to pick and choose the jobs so that he could be at home as much as possible.

The Brooklyn house had sold quickly and the new owners had opted to buy most of the furniture.

Jack had insisted that this was a fresh start and that they should furnish it together. They'd picked out sofas although they weren't arriving for another week and Flora had started painting canvases to hang on the walls.

Molly had already decided she wanted a horse-themed bedroom, complete with a stable door. Together with Flora, she and Izzy had gone through all the photographs of their mother and picked out their favorites to have in their rooms.

Remembering how much her photographs of her mother had meant to her, Flora was pleased to see it. Becca was just part of their story now, not their whole story, and so much of their story lay ahead.

She stepped through the open French doors onto the wide porch. Jack had insisted she take the keys and she held them tightly, until they left an imprint in her palm.

*Home.*

She could hear the girls laughing and bickering through the open windows, caught the words *I'm going to tell Flora,* and smiled because it all felt so normal and she'd never thought that this would ever be her life.

She stood, absorbing the moment and details of their new home.

There was a rocking chair on the porch and a two-hundred-year-old maple shaded the garden nearest to the house.

Jack was already talking about putting in a swimming pool, and Flora had plans for an organic herb garden and flower beds. Outside the breakfast room was a section of land that she planned to turn into the vegetable garden.

Jack stepped up behind her and put his hands on her shoulders. "We can go and test the master suite if you like. At least we have beds, even if we do have to sit on floorboards for another week."

She smiled, anticipating their first night there. The huge windows looked out across the river toward the Catskill Mountains. The previous owner had described the sunsets as sublime.

She turned. "I don't care where I sleep, as long as you're there, too."

"Daddy?" Molly hollered from upstairs. "There's a paddock. Can I have a horse?"

"Say no," Izzy yelled. "No one is ever getting me near a horse again. I don't want to feed it, or groom it, but most of all I don't want to ride it."

Jack glanced at Flora. "Still want to be part of a family? You haven't changed your mind?"

Why would she change her mind? "Everything I ever wanted is right here."

"Hey—" He frowned and took her face in his hands. "What's wrong? Are you upset?" He brushed her cheeks with his thumb. "I can take just about anything life throws at me, but not you crying."

"They're happy tears." She sniffed. "I was just thinking, that's all."

"About what?" He always listened to her. Always paid attention. Tried to make her happy in a thousand tiny ways.

"About all those days and nights when I felt lonely. I'm wondering if maybe feeling that way is making me appreciate this even more."

He wrapped her in his arms, holding her tightly. "Honey, I predict there will come a time when you'd *kill* for a lonely moment."

She laughed, knowing he was probably right, but also knowing that there would never come a time when she took this for granted. "I can't believe this is my life."

"You'll believe it when the girls are fighting." But he lowered his mouth to hers, unable to help himself, his kiss urgent and impatient. She kissed him back, her arms wrapped tightly round his neck even though he didn't seem likely to stop anytime soon. His mouth devoured hers, the erotic slide of his tongue driving all thought from her head. When he finally lifted his head it was so that he could murmur words that made her blush. She loved the time they spent as a family, but she also looked forward to the time they spent alone.

"We may not be in the bedroom—" he kissed his way along her jaw "—but how would you feel about a kitchen counter? I'm reliably informed that it's soapstone, which probably makes it a vastly superior option to the bed anyway if not quite as comfortable."

She was so desperate for him she might even have gone along with his suggestion, but fortunately part of her was still functioning and she heard the thunder of footsteps on the stairs.

"Kitchen sex will have to wait." She pulled away and straightened her clothes a few seconds before Molly charged into the room.

Her cheeks were flushed with excitement. "I've checked, and there is enough room for four horses at least."

"Four?" Izzy sauntered into the room after her and rolled her eyes. "If you're going to have even one horse, I am *definitely* going to college."

Molly grabbed Flora's hands and danced with her round the kitchen, twirling and spinning.

In a snatched moment between breathless laughter Flora met Jack's gaze and shared a smile of satisfaction.

Molly was dancing again. Not just with her arms, legs and the rest of her body but with her whole heart.

And then Izzy joined them, grabbing Flora so that the three of them danced together.

At some point Jack was pulled into it, and Molly complained as he trod on her toes but then forgave him when he swung her high into the air. When he finally put her down, Molly slid across the kitchen floor, treating it like a skating rink. "What's for dinner?"

"Ham," Jack said, and ducked as Molly flung her soft toy at his head. "I thought we could all go out for pizza. There's a place a short walk from here."

That suggestion gained everyone's approval and while the girls hunted down their shoes, Flora stepped back, breathless and dizzy from dancing, and put one hand on the kitchen counter—*her kitchen counter*—to steady herself.

But she didn't have time to linger on the joys of finally having her own home because Molly and Izzy were arguing about what dog they should have, even though no one had officially agreed that they were having one.

Flora smiled, slid on her shoes and got ready to referee.

Molly got to her first. "I want a Labrador like Chase."

"We should get a rescue dog." Izzy grabbed a sweatshirt and opened the front door.

"Our neighbors have a dog," Jack said. "Also a daughter, same age as you, Izzy. You two should get together."

Izzy paused, hand on the door. "Maybe."

"I know you've mostly lost touch with your old friends and I think it would be good if you—"

"Dad." Izzy was firm. "I said I'll think about it."

"I don't want you to be lonely. Annie is off to college, too, and I thought the two of you could—"

"Jack!" Flora intervened. "Enough." She knew how much he worried about Izzy, but she also knew that Izzy had to be allowed to find her own way. There would be new friends, she was sure of it, but Izzy had to build her own life now. Their role was to support, not dictate.

"It's okay, Dad." Izzy smoothed her hair. "I'm not going to be lonely. And you and Flora are going to come visit."

He pulled the door shut behind them and Flora stared at the house, a strange feeling in her chest.

She'd never had her own front door before.

Her own home.

Her own family.

Jack and the girls had filled all the empty spaces in her heart.

"I want a Labrador!" Molly raised her voice because no one was listening. "Can we have one, please?"

"I want a spaniel." Izzy walked, talked and messaged at the same time.

Jack joined in. "How about a Great Dane?"

All three women turned to stare at him. Izzy was the first to speak.

"You want a Great Dane?"

"No." Jack pocketed the keys. "But I thought if fighting about dog breeds was going to be tonight's entertainment, I'd like to join in. And we can't just get a dog without fig- uring out if we can give it a good home. We have to think it through. For example, who is going to walk it when Izzy is at college and you're in school, Molly?"

"Flora will." Molly dumped the responsibility on Flora without a second's hesitation.

"What if Flora doesn't want to?"

"We all have to do things we don't want to do," Molly said. "I have to tidy my room. And clear the table. It's part of being a family."

"You're expecting her to pick up your dog's poo."

"It's not my dog, it's the family dog."

Never had Flora thought that being taken for granted could feel so good. As they argued their way down the drive she hung back, giving herself time to enjoy the moment.

The gardens reminded her a little of Lake Lodge, and she remembered that she'd promised Clare some new photos. They emailed almost every day and used video chat every week or so. Flora was already looking forward to spending those few precious summer weeks in Lake Lodge the following year.

Jack, Izzy and Molly were still arguing about dogs, none of them prepared to back down or compromise.

They'd have plenty of times like this, Flora thought as she watched the interplay between the three of them. Plenty of laughter, probably plenty of fights, too. But that was family life. You could speak up, say what you thought, and still know you were loved and accepted. It was something most people took for granted, but she didn't. She wasn't sure she ever would.

Jack turned to see where she was, pausing to give her time to catch up and she smiled, warmed by the fact that he'd noticed her absence.

She hurried across to him, eager for their new life to begin.

\* \* \* \* \*

# acknowledgments

I feel lucky not just to be a writer, but to be working with incredible and talented publishing teams who work hard to put my books into the hands of readers. There are so many people involved that it's impossible to thank all of them, but I appreciate the dedication that goes into each part of the process, from cover design to sales, marketing and publicity. Thank you to HQN in the US, in particular to Loriana Sacilotto, Dianne Moggy, Margaret Marbury and Susan Swinwood, also to Leo MacDonald, Cory Beatty and the rest of the fantastic team at HarperCollins Canada. In the UK, I'm grateful to the team at HQ Stories for their endless enthusiasm and hard work. I'm so lucky to get to work with you. Particular thanks to Lisa Milton and Manpreet Grewal. It's easy to write about strong, inspiring women when I'm surrounded by so many role models.

My editor Flo Nicoll is an endless source of encouragement and great ideas. Without her I wouldn't be able to write a thank you note, let alone a book.

My agent Susan Ginsburg is wise and calming, essential qualities to balance my overactive writerly imagination. I feel lucky and grateful to work with her.

My family displays endless patience when I focus obsessively on a book, offering love, support and food and never once suggesting a different career.

And to my readers, old and new, thank you from the bottom of my heart.

*Sarah*
x

*If you loved* The Christmas Escape, *Sarah Morgan's next book,* Beach House Summer, *will be essential reading!*

*Turn the page for a sneak peek...*

# 1

## *Ashley*

She slid into his car, hoping this wasn't a mistake. It hadn't been her first choice of plan, but the others had failed and she was desperate.

He smiled at her, and there was so much charm in that smile that she forgot everything around her. The way he looked at her made her feel as if she was the only woman in the world.

In case charm wasn't enough he had the car, a high-performance convertible, low, sleek and expensive. It shrieked *Look at me!*, in case the other trappings of wealth and power hadn't already drawn her attention.

Her mother would have warned her not to get in the car with him, but her mother was gone now, and Ashley was making the best decisions she could with no one close to offer her advice or caution. She remembered the first time she'd ridden a bike on her own, unsteady, unbalanced, hands sweating on the handlebars, her mother shouting *"Keep pedaling!"* She remembered her first swimming lesson, when she'd slid under the surface and gulped down so much water she'd thought she was going to empty the pool. She'd been sure she was going to drown. But then she'd felt her mother's hands lifting her to the surface and heard her voice through water-clogged ears, *"Keep kicking!"*

She was on her own now. There was no one to tug her to the surface if she was drowning. No one to steady the wheels of her bike when she wobbled. Her mother had been the safety net in her life, and if she fell now she'd hit the ground with nothing and no one to cushion her fall.

He turned onto Mulholland Drive and picked up speed. The engine gave a throaty roar. The wind tugged at her hair as they sped upwards through the Hollywood Hills. She'd never been in a car like this before. Never met a man like him.

They climbed higher and higher, passing luxury mansions and seeing flashes of a lifestyle beyond the reach of even her imagination. She felt a stab of envy. Did problems go away when you had so much? Did the people living there experience the same anxieties as normal people or did those high walls and security cameras insulate them from life? Could you buy happiness?

No, but money could make life easier—which was why she was here.

Spread beneath them were views of Downtown Hollywood and the San Fernando Valley.

*Stay focused.*

"I know the best place to see the sunset." His warm, deep voice had helped propel him from being yet another TV personality to a megastar. "You're never going to forget it."

She didn't disagree. This moment was significant for so many reasons.

He drove with one hand on the wheel, supremely confident.

What would happen to that confidence when she told him her news?

Nausea rolled in her stomach and she was relieved she'd been unable to eat breakfast or lunch.

"You're quiet." He threw her another smile.

One hand, no eyes. She didn't drive, but even she knew that wasn't the safest combination. She wanted to tell him to keep his attention on the road.

"I'm a little nervous."

"Are you intimidated? Don't be. I'm just a normal, regular guy."

*Yeah, right.*

He was driving fast now, enjoying the car, the moment, *his life*. She hoped they wouldn't be pulled over before she'd had a chance to say what she needed to say. She'd rehearsed a speech. Practised a hundred times in front of the mirror.

*I've got something to tell you...*

"Could you slow down?"

"Don't worry—I can go slow when I need to. What did you say your name was?"

He didn't recognise her. He didn't have a clue who she was. How could he not know?

She sat rigid in her seat.

Was she really that forgettable and unimportant?

In this part of town, where everyone was someone, she was no one.

She fought the disillusion and the humiliation.

"I'm Mandy. I'm from Connecticut."

Her name wasn't Mandy. She'd never been to Connecticut. Couldn't even point to it on a map.

He should know that. *She wanted him to know that.* She wanted him to say *I know you're not Mandy.* But he didn't, of course, because women came and went in his life and he was already moving on to the next one.

"And you're sure we've met before? I wouldn't have forgotten someone as pretty as you."

She'd had dreams about him. Fantasies. She'd thought about him day and night for the past couple of months, ever since she'd first laid eyes on him.

But he didn't know her. There was no recognition.

Her eyes stung. She told herself it was the wind in her face, because her mother had drummed into her that she shouldn't cry over a man. She wouldn't be here at all except that she'd felt alone and scared and had needed to do something to help herself. She was afraid she couldn't do this on her own—and he had to take some responsibility, surely? He shouldn't be allowed to just walk away. That wasn't right. Like it or not, they were bonded.

"We've met." She rested her hand on her abdomen. Blinked away the tears. The time to wish she'd been more careful was long gone. She had to look forward. Had to do the right thing, but it wasn't easy.

Her body told her she was an adult, but inside she still felt like the child who had wobbled on that bike with her ponytail flying.

He glanced at her again, curious. "Now I think about it, you do look familiar. Can't place you, though. Don't be offended." He gave her another flash of those perfect white teeth. "I meet a lot of women."

She knew that. She knew his reputation. And yet still she was here. What did that say about her? She should have more pride. But pride and desperation didn't fit comfortably together.

"I'm not offended." Under the fear she was furious. And fiercely determined.

They were climbing now. Climbing, climbing. The road wound upwards into the hills while the city lay beneath them like a glittering carpet. She felt like Peter Pan, flying over the rooftops.

*Should she tell him now? Was this a good moment?*

Her heart started to pound, heavy beats thudding a warning against her ribs. She hadn't thought he'd bring her somewhere this remote. She shouldn't have climbed into his car. Another bad decision to add to the ones she'd already made. The longer she waited to tell him, the further they would be from civilization and people. People who could help her.

But who would help? Who was there?

She had no one. Just herself. Which was why she was here now, doing what needed to be done regardless of the consequences.

Thinking of consequences made her palms grow damp. She should do it right now, while half his attention was on the road.

She waited as he waltzed the car round another bend and hit another straight stretch of road. She could already see the next bend up ahead.

"Mr. Whitman? Cliff? There's something I need to tell you."

# 2

## Joanna

Joanna Whitman learned of her ex-husband's death while she was eating breakfast. She was on her second cup of strong espresso when his face popped up on her TV screen. She grabbed the remote, intending to do what she always did these days when he appeared in her life—turn him off—when she realized that behind that standard head-and-shoulders shot wasn't a sea of adoring fans, or one of his exclusive restaurants, but the wreckage of a car in a ravine.

She saw the words *Breaking News* appear on the screen and turned up the sound in time to hear the newsreader telling the world that celebrity chef Cliff Whitman had been killed in an accident and that they would be giving more information as they had it. Currently all they knew was that his car had gone off the road. He'd been pronounced dead at the scene. His passenger, a young woman as yet unnamed, had been flown to hospital, her condition unknown.

A young woman.

Joanna tightened her fingers on the remote. Of course she'd be young. Cliff had a pattern, and that pattern hadn't changed as he'd aged. He was the most competitive person she'd ever met, driven by an insecurity that went bone-deep. He wanted the highest TV ratings, the biggest crowds for his public appearances, the longest waiting lists for his restaurants. When it came to women he wanted them younger and thinner, choosing them as carefully as he chose the ingredients he used in his kitchens.

*Fresh and seasonal.*

On most days Joanna felt like someone past her sell-by date. She was forty. Were you supposed to feel like this at forty?

She stared at the TV, her gaze fixed on the smoking wreckage. She'd always said his libido would be the death of him, and it seemed she'd been right.

Her phone rang. A friend offering support?

She checked the screen.

Not a friend—did she have any true friends? It was something she often wondered about... Rita. Cliff's personal assistant and his lover for the past six months.

Joanna didn't want to talk to Rita. She didn't want to talk to anyone. She knew from painful experience that anything she said would find its way into the media and be used to construct an image of her as a pathetic creature, worthy of the nation's pity. Whatever Cliff did, *she* somehow became the story. And no matter how much she told herself that it didn't matter, because the woman they wrote about wasn't really her, she still found it distressing. Not just the intrusion—and the stories *were* intrusive—but the inaccuracies.

She wanted to correct their mistakes. She wanted to stand up and yell *That's not me!* But she didn't because no one was interested in the truth. For years she'd been outraged by the injustice of it—which was surprising, because she'd always known the world was an unjust place. She'd grown up in a small town, the focus of gossip and scrutiny, but even that uncomfortable experience hadn't prepared her for life in the spotlight. Every time Cliff had an affair, people judged her. Unfair, but that was how it was.

She rejected the call, muted the sound on the TV, but continued to stare at the words scrolling along the bottom of the screen.

*Celebrity chef Cliff Whitman killed in car accident. Dead at the scene.*

Well, damn.

She'd spent the last few years wanting to kill him herself, and she didn't know whether to feel elated or cheated. After everything he'd done, everything he'd put her through, it seemed unfair of the universe to have deprived her of the chance to play at least a small part in his demise.

A hysterical laugh burst from her and she slapped her hand over her mouth, shocked. Had she really just thought that? What was *wrong* with her? She was a compassionate human being. She valued kindness above almost all other qualities—possibly because her encounters with it had been rare. And yet here she was, thinking that if she'd seen his car hovering on the edge of a ravine she might have given it a hard push.

What did that say about her?

Her legs were shaking. Why were her legs shaking?

She sat down hard on the kitchen stool.

Her journey with Cliff had been bumpy, but she'd known him for half her life. She should be sad, shouldn't she? She should feel something? Yes, Cliff Whitman had been a liar and a cheat who had almost broken her, but he had still been a person. And there had been a time when they'd loved each other, even if that love had been complicated. There had been good parts. At the beginning of their marriage he'd brought her breakfast in bed on Sunday mornings—flaky, buttery croissants that he'd baked himself and juice freshly squeezed from the citrus fruit that grew in their home orchard. He'd listened to her. He'd made her laugh. She'd organized his chaotic life, leaving him free to play the part he enjoyed most. Being Cliff. He'd said they were a perfect team.

She stood up abruptly and fetched a glass of iced water. She drank it quickly, trying to cool the hot burn of emotion.

Whatever had happened between them, death was always a tragedy.

*Was it? Was she being hypocritical?*

She should probably cry—if not for him then for the woman who'd made the bad decision to get into the car with him. Joanna sympathized. She was never one to judge the bad decisions of another. When it came to Cliff, she'd made so many bad decisions she could no longer count them.

She thought about Rita. Would she be shocked to discover she hadn't been the only woman in Cliff's life? Why was it that a woman so rarely believed that a serial cheater would cheat on *her*? They all thought they were different. That they were special. That they would be the one to tame him. When he'd said, *"You're the one,"* they'd believed him.

Once, a long time ago, Joanna had believed that, too.

She'd wanted so badly to be special to someone. To have someone whose love she could rely on.

Putting the empty glass down, she took a deep breath and forced herself to think. She and Cliff were no longer married, but they still shared the business. Cliff's was a brand, but now its figurehead was gone. What did that mean for the company they'd built together? She'd invested twenty years of her life into its growth and success, which was why she hadn't walked away from it at the same time as leaving her marriage. That, and the fact that she had no idea what else she would do. Cliff's was one of the few things she'd done right in her life—although the media didn't understand that, of course. They didn't understand how she could still work alongside a man who had humiliated her so completely.

She closed her eyes. *Forget that. Don't think about that.*

Right now the worst part was that there would be a funeral—and she hated funerals. No matter whose funeral it was, it was always her father's funeral. Again and again. Like some kind of cruel time travel trick. And she was always ten years old, shivering as the cool Californian rain blended with her tears. This was different, of course. She'd adored her father, and her father had adored her back. He was the only man whose love she'd been sure of. And then he'd left her…swept out to sea by a riptide, his body recovered a week later.

And now there would be Cliff's funeral. Did she have to go? Yes, of course she did. Everyone would expect it. Divorce or no divorce, it would be the respectful thing to do. People would be watching. Everyone would want to know how she felt.

*How did she feel?*

She heard sounds in the distance, and then the insistent buzz of her gate's intercom. Without thinking, she stepped to the window and looked down the curving sweep of the drive to the large iron gates that protected her from the outside world.

A camera flashed and she gasped and quickly closed the shutters.

*No!*

Unlike Cliff, she'd never sought fame or celebrity, but she'd been caught in his spotlight anyway. It was one of the reasons she'd moved to a different neighborhood after the divorce. She'd hoped to be able to slide away from the dazzling beam of attention that always landed on him. She'd chosen to live in a small discreet community, rather than up among the flashy mansions in Bel Air, where Cliff entertained lavishly on his verdant terrace overlooking the Pacific Ocean. They'd found her, of course, because the media could find anyone. But she'd hoped that by living a quiet, low-key, non-newsworthy, Cliff-free life she'd become less interesting to them.

She'd been wrong. It seemed she'd never be free of Cliff. She was anchored by the past, unable to sail away, her secrets played out in public for all to enjoy. They knew about her father's death. They knew she was estranged from her stepmother. They'd managed to track *her* down in the little house up the coast where she now lived. Predictably, she'd been only too happy to voice her opinion. *"She's no daughter of mine. Always was a difficult child."*

Her phone rang, dragging her back from a downward spiral into the past. This time it was her assistant, Nessa.

Joanna answered it. "Hi."

"Let me in! I'm outside the garden room. I came via the back entrance."

"I don't have a back entrance."

"I took a secret route. Could you just let me in, boss? We'll talk tactics later."

Joanna walked to the back of the house, mystified and a little alarmed.

She'd chosen the house precisely because it was so secure. When she'd first viewed it, instead of admiring the kitchen appliances and ceiling height, she'd been checking areas of vulnerability. The fact that the house backed onto dense woodland had been a plus. And this was an unfashionable area. There was no road, and no running trails. Her property was protected by a high wall and tall, mature trees that concealed the house from view.

It had been a carefully considered purchase, but when she walked through the door she never once thought *I love this house*, or even *I'm home*. She didn't think of it as home. Home was a place where you felt safe and able to relax. Neither of those things could happen when you were an object of public interest.

She walked through the garden room and saw Nessa standing on the deck, glancing furtively over her shoulder. Normally impeccably groomed, she had twigs stuck in her hair and her shoes were muddy and scuffed.

Shaken by the fact her home wasn't as secure as she'd thought, Joanna opened the door and Nessa virtually fell inside.

"What is *wrong* with people? I tried coming in the conventional way—actually through the front door, you know, like a normal person? But there are a million people with cameras and two TV vans—which, frankly, I don't get. Because why are *you* news? You're not the one who was trying to have sex in a moving vehicle. I mean, I'm all for multitasking, but it depends on the task, doesn't it? Sex and driving—call me boring, but those two things do *not* go together."

"Nessa, breathe."

"So, I've been thinking about this…" Nessa shrugged off her backpack and toed off her shoes. "I've ruined my shoes, by the way. I was thinking maybe we can charge them to Cliff as expenses, as this is all his fault. Do you have any antiseptic? I scratched myself coming through the woods.

I don't want to die of some vile disease, because you need me right now."

Joanna's head was spinning. "You—you came through the woods at the back of the house?"

"Yes. I remembered you telling me that's why you picked this place. They can't get to you from the back, only the front. That's what you said. You only have to watch one direction. So I thought, *Right, I'll get to her from the back.* But it's not pedestrian-friendly. Do I have mud on my cheek? I bet I do." She scrubbed randomly at her face. "I am not cut out for wilderness adventures. Give me California sunshine and beaches and I'm there. But a dark forest full of spiders, snakes, bears, coyotes and mass murderers… That's me out. Can you check me for spiders?"

She turned and showed her back to Joanna, who dutifully checked.

"You're spider-free. But even if you made it through the woods, how did you get over the wall?"

"I climbed. Don't ask for details." Nessa tugged at a twig that was tangled in her curls. "I grew up with two brothers. I have skills that would make your eyes pop. And don't worry—no one followed me. No one is that stupid. Also, there were no humans in that wood. At least no live ones. Willing to bet there are a few dead ones, though. Bodies undiscovered…" She shuddered. "That place is scary."

"Nessa." Joanna brushed a leaf from Nessa's shoulder. "What are you *doing* here?"

"I'm your assistant, and I figured you'd need assistance."

"I—I'm not really thinking about work right now."

"Of course you're not. I'm here for more than work. I'm your right-hand woman. The dragon at your gate." Nessa adjusted her glasses. "When you employed me, you said I had to be there for you in both calm and crisis—so here I am. I assume this is the crisis part? We're in this together. Bring it on."

*Together.*

Joanna felt pressure in her chest. Someone had thought of her. Someone wanted to help her. She wasn't going to think about the fact that Nessa worked for her. She still didn't have to be here.

"You don't want to be exposed to this circus."

Nessa tilted her head. "*You* are."

"I have no choice. You do."

"Well, I choose being here with you, so that's decided."

The strange feeling in Joanna's chest spread to her throat. People generally distanced themselves from her, afraid of being tainted by association. They didn't want to find themselves in that spotlight.

"Have you really thought this through?"

"What is there to think through? We're a team. In my interview, you said I'd need to be versatile. I hope you'll remember the whole climbing the wall thing when you give me a reference—not that I'm planning on leaving you anytime soon, because this is my dream job and you're my dream boss. Now, what can I do? We can make a statement. Or I can call the cops and get them to move on that mob with cameras at the end of your drive."

Joanna looked at her assistant's flushed, earnest face and suddenly didn't feel quite so alone.

She wasn't alone. She had Nessa.

Hiring Nessa as her assistant two years earlier had been one of the better decisions she'd made in her life. Her team had lined up a selection of experienced candidates for her to interview, but then Nessa had bounced into the room, fresh out of college, vibrating with energy and enthusiasm. Ignoring the disapproval of her colleagues, Joanna had given her the job and never regretted that decision. Nessa had proved herself to be discreet, reliable, and as sharp as the business end of a razor blade.

*Not all my decisions are bad*, Joanna thought as she locked the back door.

"I'm glad you're here, but I don't want you to do anything about the cameras. Leave them."

"Nothing?" Nessa gaped at her and then looked guilty. "I'm so thoughtless. Here am I, worrying about spiders and press statements, and you've just lost the man you were married to for two decades. I know you were divorced, and that he wasn't exactly…" Her voice trailed off as she studied Joanna's face. "I mean, twenty years is a long time, even if he was a—" She swallowed and gave a helpless shrug. "Give me some clues, here. I want to say the right thing, but I don't know what that is. How *do* you feel? Are you sad or mad? Do I get you tissues or a punch bag?"

Joanna's laugh was closer to hysteria than humor. "I don't know how I feel. I feel…strange."

"Yeah, well, 'strange' about covers it. Can I grab a glass of water? Turns out covert operations in dense woodland is thirsty work. Then I'll brush my hair, work magic with some makeup and get to work."

"Go through to the kitchen. Help yourself. I'll join you in a minute."

Joanna went through the whole of the ground floor at the front of the house, making sure all the blinds were closed before returning to the kitchen. They could all stay there with their cameras, but she'd give them nothing to photograph. And if someone was brazen enough to breach her gates they wouldn't be rewarded for it.

Nessa had settled herself at the kitchen island. She had a glass of water in one hand and her phone in the other.

She was scrolling through social media. "We're trending—no surprise there. Interesting hashtags… Lots of speculation about what they were doing when the car went off the road…" She sent Joanna a sideways glance. "Sorry. This is awkward."

"It's fine."

"Some people are saying it's a shame, because it was his recipe for lemon chicken that made them realize good food wasn't just for restaurants."

*He created that recipe for me*, Joanna thought. *He was trying to teach me to cook. I ruined the chicken. He laughed. We ended up in bed.*

"Others are saying he was a sleaze, and good riddance… yada yada…" Nessa continued scrolling. "They've managed to get a comment from two of the women he— *What?* No way…" She stared at the screen.

"Read it out."

"No. You don't want to know. If you want my advice, you'll delete all your personal social media accounts."

"I don't have any social media accounts."

"Good decision." Nessa carried on scrolling, her expression alternating between disgust and surprise.

Joanna sighed. "That bad?"

Nessa hesitated. "There are a few decent people out there. People saying a death is always sad. And some of the comments are pretty neutral, wondering who the woman was…" She sneaked a look at Joanna.

"I don't know."

"Of course you don't. Why would you? You're divorced from him. Whoever she is, I bet she's wishing now she'd got into a car with a different guy. I mean, we've all had bad dates, but *that*—" Nessa shrugged, took a gulp of water and continued scrolling. "Some people are wondering if this will mean the end of the business. Will it?" She glanced up. "The business is called Cliff's. And Chef Cliff is—" She stopped.

Joanna sat down opposite her. "Dead."

Chef Cliff was dead.

But Nessa was right. It would affect the business. The business they'd built together. She'd given up on their marriage, but she hadn't given up on that. It was their baby. She'd nurtured it and watched it grow.

She felt a pang, thinking of the actual baby she'd lost. Would her priorities have been different if she'd had a child? Her life? Her marriage? She used to think it might have been. She used to blame herself for everything that was wrong between them. But that was before.

Her phone rang again and Nessa glanced at her.

"Do you want me to answer that?"

"No."

"It might be a friend."

If she said *I don't have any real friends* Nessa would feel sorry for her, and Joanna didn't want anyone feeling sorry for her. She wanted to protect the last fragile strands of her pride.

"If it is, then I'll call them back."

"It's probably a reporter."

"Yes, and I'm not talking to them."

Her heart rate increased. Of all the bad things about being married to Cliff—and there had been many—the media attention had been the worst. Cliff himself had been emotionally bulletproof. Whatever the media had accused him of he'd laugh, wink, give them a *"No comment"* or a *"Let's focus on what happens in the kitchen, not the bedroom."* And for some reason Joanna had never understood, his bad behavior had increased his appeal. He'd been shocking, but supremely watchable. His TV ratings had risen. He'd been unapologetic about his colorful personal life, so sure that his charm would ultimately guarantee him forgiveness for all his misdeeds that it had been impossible to shame or embarrass him.

Joanna, however, had been continually shamed and embarrassed. It was an irony that she'd escaped life in a small town, where her every action had been scrutinized and criticized, only to find the situation magnified a thousand times here.

She'd always loathed being the subject of attention and gossip, whereas Cliff had hungered for the limelight—and not only because it had been essential to building his brand. If attention had been a large pie, he would have greedily devoured the whole thing without offering her a sliver.

*How did she feel about his latest affair?*

*Why didn't she leave?*

*Had she no self-respect?*

She'd become a fascinating case study in humiliation. She'd been photographed from every angle. They'd commented on the weight she'd lost, how haggard she looked. Their speculation had been cruel and deeply personal. They hadn't judged Cliff—they'd judged her.

*If he cheats, it must be her fault.*

They'd speculated on whether in marrying a man fourteen years her senior she'd somehow been trying to replace her father. That suggestion had offended her more than any of them. Cliff had been nothing like her father. Hearing the two of them mentioned in the same breath had made her want to lash out.

The buzzer rang again. She ignored it.

Nessa frowned. "They're like hyenas…ready to chomp down on a carcass. And you're the carcass."

Joanna gave a faint smile. "Yes."

"The stuff they say about you is all total crap. Aren't you ever tempted to give your side of things? I guess today they need to milk the story, and to do that they have to talk to someone. Cliff's dead, so he's not going to be saying anything, that girl is in the hospital—that just leaves you. They'll want your reaction."

What *was* her reaction? What *did* she feel?

"Dead." She said the word aloud again, trying to make it real. Testing herself. Pressing, to see if it hurt.

Nessa eyed her. "Can I pour you a drink? A real drink?"

"No, thank you."

Her thoughts were complicated enough without clouding them with alcohol. Untangling her emotions was complicated. Was she feeling humiliated? Cliff's behavior had continually embarrassed her, even after they were divorced. Was she prostrate with grief? Angry at the impact his actions might have on the business and the people they employed?

Joanna finished her coffee, ignoring the fact it was cold. She felt oddly detached. She felt grief, yes. But was it grief for Cliff or grief for the life she'd wanted that had never turned out the way she'd hoped?

She wasn't sure what she felt. It couldn't be relief, because that would make her hard-hearted.

*Would it? Or would it make her human?*

The buzzer sounded again. Annoying. Persistent.

Nessa slid off the stool and refilled her glass. "I'll tell people in the office you won't be in for a few days."

"I won't hide."

"You're not hiding—you're avoiding intrusive questions. Also, if we're being practical, you're trapped." Nessa added ice to the glass, splashing droplets of water onto the tiled floor. "Unless you're going to wear a disguise and shimmy over the wall like I did, your only way out of this place is through the front entrance. You can drive over the photographers, but then you'd be arrested, and I don't have enough money in my account to bail you out. You could ignore them, but they'll follow you. I suppose you could just make a statement and hope they'll go away."

"They won't go away."

She knew how this worked. There would be endless gossip. In the past she'd even been the subject of a women's daytime chat show: *Successful women who stay with men who cheat.*

Joanna had watched it, appalled, not recognizing the woman they were describing. Apparently she was a doormat, a coward, a disgrace to women. Where was her strength? Her dignity?

To them she wasn't a person, she was a story. She was ratings, sales, a commercial opportunity, a talking point. They weren't interested in the truth. They focused on one angle and one alone.

They didn't know anything about her relationship. They didn't know anything about her life before she'd met Cliff. They weren't interested in the fact that she'd had her own ambitions. They didn't know that although Cliff had been the face of the business, it had been her hard work that had made him famous. Now there was a popular TV show, a chain of expensive restaurants, branded cookware, cookery books... The franchise had grown like a monster.

*"Please, Joanna, I can't do this without you."*

He was the face of the company, but she was the engine. She kept everything going, and he knew it.

*Had known it*, she reminded herself. It was in the past tense now. There was no more Cliff.

*Why did you crash, Cliff? Were you driving too fast?*

Nessa put a glass of water in front of her. "It's a crappy situation, boss, no doubt about that. But, as my mom always says, no matter how bad things get there's always someone worse off than you. I hate it when she says that. Super-annoying, actually. But I have to admit that mostly she's right. And although it's true that right now I wouldn't want to be you—"

"Thank you, Nessa."

"Do you know who I *definitely* wouldn't want to be?" She tilted her head and gave Joanna a knowing look. "That girl in the car. Don't know who she is, or what she was doing, but I would *not* want her life."

The girl in the car.

Joanna didn't know who she was or what she'd been doing, either.

The one thing she *did* know was that, even though he was dead, Cliff Whitman had still managed to ruin her day.

# Get 4 FREE REWARDS!

**We'll send you 2 FREE Books plus 2 FREE Mystery Gifts.**

**FREE**
Value Over
**$20**

Both the **Romance** and **Suspense** collections feature compelling novels written by many of today's bestselling authors.

---

**YES!** Please send me 2 FREE novels from the Essential Romance or Essential Suspense Collection and my 2 FREE gifts (gifts are worth about $10 retail). After receiving them, if I don't wish to receive any more books, I can return the shipping statement marked "cancel." If I don't cancel, I will receive 4 brand-new novels every month and be billed just $7.24 each in the U.S. or $7.49 each in Canada. That's a savings of up to 28% off the cover price. It's quite a bargain! Shipping and handling is just 50¢ per book in the U.S. and $1.25 per book in Canada.* I understand that accepting the 2 free books and gifts places me under no obligation to buy anything. I can always return a shipment and cancel at any time. The free books and gifts are mine to keep no matter what I decide.

Choose one: ☐ **Essential Romance**
(194/394 MDN GQ6M)

☐ **Essential Suspense**
(191/391 MDN GQ6M)

Name (please print)

Address                                                                                              Apt. #

City                                    State/Province                              Zip/Postal Code

Email: Please check this box ☐ if you would like to receive newsletters and promotional emails from Harlequin Enterprises ULC and its affiliates. You can unsubscribe anytime.

> **Mail to the Harlequin Reader Service:**
> **IN U.S.A.:** P.O. Box 1341, Buffalo, NY 14240-8531
> **IN CANADA:** P.O. Box 603, Fort Erie, Ontario L2A 5X3

Want to try 2 free books from another series? Call 1-800-873-8635 or visit www.ReaderService.com.

---

STRS21MAXR2